CONJURE

A PARANORMAL EROTIC HORROR

HARLEIGH BECK

Editing: Nice Girl Naughty Edits
Proofreading: Traversingfiction & Amber (sinful.spines)
Cover: Crimsons Designs
Blurb: Nicole Kincaid

CONTENT INFORMATION

I'm an author of extremely **dark** and gritty stories, and this erotic horror is no exception.

It's worth noting that it's a *horror*, not a romance, so a HEA is not guaranteed.

This story is not intended for sensitive readers. Remember, it's fiction! This author doesn't condone the darker themes within these pages.

Please visit the link below for a full list of content warnings:
https://harleighbeckconjure.carrd.co/

ONE

CAMRYN

A SENSE of foreboding wraps around me as I exit the backseat of the car.

Up ahead, a Victorian-style mansion framed by dead, gnarly trees appears, menacing and imposing, with peeling blue paint, boarded-up windows, and wilted rose bushes. It has seen better days.

Mom shuts the car door and quickly wipes the look of weariness from her face. Not only has she lost her husband in the last year, but also the house. Now she's ladened with me and my stepbrother, Dominic, our golden retriever, and a derelict house that is, according to her, all we can afford.

As I stare at the property, I can understand why.

It's a shithole.

A warm breeze feathers through the overgrown grass as Dominic exits the vehicle, slams the door shut, then opens the trunk and hauls the suitcases outside. His gray T-shirt clings to his broad shoulders when he walks past me in a cloud of citrus and leather, dragging his suitcase behind him. I let my gaze wander over his muscled back and light blue jeans, which hug his ass.

The material of his T-shirt sticks to a streak of sweat between his shoulder blades, somehow making him even more attractive.

It doesn't matter that he's an asshole or that he hates me; I can't keep my eyes off him.

Our dog, Bruno, sniffs the dried lawn as he follows Dominic, his tail wagging.

The heat from the sun beats down on my head, and when I step forward, the smell of something rotten drifts to my nose.

I look down at the ground and pause at the sight of a decomposing rat surrounded by a swarm of flies.

Saliva fills my mouth as my stomach turns.

"That's a creepy tree," Mom mumbles, staring at a large oak tree outside the house. "Are you coming?" she asks me, grabbing hold of the handle of her suitcase.

Tearing my gaze away from the dead rat, I shake off the feeling of foreboding that refuses to let go, clinging to my skin like the sheen of sweat at my nape.

I follow her to the porch and haul my heavy suitcase up the steps. Dominic is already inside, no doubt picking his bedroom before I can get a chance at dibs.

As I enter the house, a shiver runs through me, and I fight the urge to tuck tail and run. There's something in the air. Something...*dark*. Don't ask me how I know. I just do. I can sense it.

I pause, waiting and listening.

"I know it's in a state of disrepair," Mom says, sweeping her eyes over the large hallway. "But as you can see, it still has its original Victorian detailing."

She flashes me a hopeful smile, and I smile back as I walk past her, not wanting to make this even harder. But I can't ignore my unease.

Overhead, a massive chandelier covered in dust and cobwebs gives me the creeps.

"It has one in every room."

Well, that's reassuring...

Swallowing thickly, I gaze away and enter the spacious living room. Standing in the middle of the space, I take in the dusty sheets on the furniture, peeling wallpaper, the chandelier over-head with broken strings of crystals, and ripped curtains.

Mom points out the positives. "Look at the handcrafted built-in bookshelves and millwork. I think it'll be perfect for us once we've cleaned this place up." She walks up to the large, antique-looking fireplace and runs her hand over the dusty top. "Every bedroom has one, too, which will be useful in winter."

The soft patter of claws on the wooden floor announces Bruno's arrival as he enters the room, wagging his tail and sniffing the floor.

Dominic sucks the air out of the room as he swamps the doorway with his towering build, his brown eyes sweeping over the gaps in the floorboards and old portraits on the walls.

"Couldn't have found us a nicer place, *Mom*," he sneers in that condescending tone of his that always puts me on edge.

"This was all we could afford, Dominic," she replies tiredly, pleading with her eyes for him not to make this harder than it already is.

She lost her husband.

He lost his father and twin brother.

With a disgusted snort, he spins around and then exits the room. Mom blows out a breath, eyes glassy with tears, and scratches Bruno behind the ear.

I don't like how rude Dominic is to Mom when all she's done is give him a home and stability after his father died. She didn't have to do that. Dominic isn't her son, but she refuses to drop him because he is the son of the man she loves and has no other family. Responsibility runs deeper than death.

As silence settles over the house for a moment, it dawns on me how cold it is—much colder than outside. I rub my arms to ward off the chill, suppressing another shiver when something shifts in my periphery.

A darting shadow.

There and gone.

A trick of the eye.

"Let's explore upstairs," Mom says as she moves past me.

It takes me a long time to haul my suitcase up the warped stairs. Dominic is nowhere around to help, but as I near the top, rock music blasts from one of the bedrooms.

"You okay?" Mom asks, out of breath, a small smile gracing her lips. "We know to pack lighter for next time."

Huffing a laugh, I head toward the sound of music.

"That's your bedroom, I think," Mom says, pointing out the one across from Dominic's.

She takes a right and walks down the opposite hallway, and I roll my eyes, seeing it for what it is. She wants me to stay close to Dominic, hoping we will finally learn to get along.

It won't happen any time soon.

Dominic has hated me from day one.

At first, because he didn't want our parents to marry, and now because he blames me for the car crash that took his dad.

My chest tightens, but I shake off the thoughts and push open the bedroom door.

The room is small and has a double bed covered in a white sheet to keep the dust off, a wooden desk, a chair, and a large mahogany wardrobe. Torn curtains in a shade of deep green frame the large, cloudy windows overlooking the forest at the back of the property. I step up to the window seat and inhale the scent of musty upholstery and stale air. Outside, thick clouds roll in to suffocate the natural sunlight as a subtle breeze moves through the naked trees.

I wonder what I look like to an outsider as I stare out from the bedroom window, like a haunted silhouette—

The floorboards creak behind me, and I whirl around to see Dominic leaning against the doorframe, ankles and arms crossed. His gaze falls down my body and then back up just as fast before he pushes off and leaves the room.

I try to swallow even as my dry throat constricts, hating how suffocated I feel around him. How he unnerves me with his heated looks of hatred and rage, as though he wants to peel the skin off my bones and feed me to the dog.

My gaze drifts back to the window and the thicket of trees outside. Something about the woods calls to me, urging me to explore, to disappear into its depths, to get lost.

Turning my back on the windows, I unpack my suitcase and put my clothes away. I don't own much, and the rest of our belongings are in storage for now, so it doesn't take long.

As long as I have the precious, tattered copy of *Wuthering Heights* that my grandma gifted me before she passed away, I'm fine.

Deciding to leave my room to help Mom clean up, I enter the hallway but stop short. Dominic's door is open.

I shouldn't invade his privacy. More importantly, I shouldn't be this curious about him.

Glancing left and right, I worry my bottom lip. Then I cross the hallway and enter his room, careful not to let the noisy floor-boards announce my presence.

His space is much larger than mine, with a four-poster king-size bed framed by heavy curtains, like something from medieval times.

Something for royalty.

I turn in a slow circle as I sweep my gaze over the chest of drawers, a mahogany desk—similar to the one in my room, stacked with a pile of his Vinyls—an armoire, and a large armchair by the window.

The stale air already smells of him—citrus, leather, and all things forbidden. It feels wrong to be in here without his knowledge and to inhale his scent deep into my lungs, but like an addict, I can't help myself.

Just one more breath—

"Camryn." Mom's voice drifts through the floorboards beneath my feet.

Torn from my thoughts, I leave Dominic's room and hurry

downstairs, cursing my own weakness where my stepbrother is concerned.

Mom exits the living room with a sweeping brush in her hand, cheeks flushed and covered in dust. She holds the brush out and smiles. "Let's clean this place up."

I wake with a start, trapped in the hazy remnants of a nightmare. Sweat clings to my forehead, and I swipe damp strands of hair from my brow before glancing at the window, where the shutters rattle on the outside.

The wind whistling through the old house adds to the creepy sensation slithering over my skin. It is still dark outside.

I look at the alarm clock and breathe in deeply. It has only just passed four in the morning.

After lying down and turning on my side, I pull the quilt to my chin. Dread twists my stomach and sweat beads on my neck. There's something in the corner of the room, beside the door. Something is watching me, something that chills me to the bone. Something evil.

Shadows thicken and swirl like mist on a forest floor, and my nostrils fill with the scent of sulfur as the taste of ash fills my mouth. Outside, the wind picks up, slamming the shutters against the window in time with the erratic beat of my heart.

As I lift my head off the pillow, I see what looks like a hooded man coated in shadows and cruel intent. But I can't make out his face—only the outline of him.

A gasp flees my lips before I shoot upright in bed, fumbling to switch on the lamp on my bedside table. Light floods the room, almost instantly chasing away the shadows and the scent of sulfur.

I clutch the quilt to my chest as I stare at the empty corner and the closed door.

My gown hangs from a hook.

A gown that looks like a man in the dark.

It was just my imagination.

Relieved, I flop back down and run my hand over my face, feeling stupid. I'm on edge and easily spooked. I turn back over on my side, snuggling deeper into my pillow as I glance back at the door. Now that my mind isn't playing tricks on me, I can see the gown clearly in the darkness.

My eyes drift shut and I inhale deeply, relaxing every muscle. If I fall back asleep now, I can get a few more hours of rest.

TWO

CAMRYN

DUST swirls along the streak of sunshine streaming through the open kitchen window. According to the app on my phone, it's an unusually hot summer's day, but the chill in the house remains.

As a warm breeze drifts over my skin, I bite into my jelly toast.

Freshly showered and dressed in a white T-shirt and black jean shorts, Dominic has his AirPods in his ears and studiously ignores us all while playing with his Zippo. The guy doesn't smoke, but he carries that damn thing everywhere because it used to belong to his dad.

Seated beside him, Mom glances his way before reaching for her coffee cup and bringing it to her lips. She takes a sip and clears her throat. "Dominic will drive you to school today."

I swallow down the piece of dry toast in my mouth. "Great."

When I look at him, those hard, dark eyes swing in my direction. Dominic clenches his jaw, then looks past me like I don't exist, as though I'm unworthy of his attention. He flicks the Zippo and strikes the wheel.

My chest tightens when a flame jumps to life, and I suck in a breath, hating how his dismissal hurts.

I finish my toast in silence, enjoying the breeze from the open window and the birdsong outside. Such a novelty.

8

Before we moved here, we lived in the city, amongst the misty sewers, pizza smells, and the sound of honking cars and angry taxi drivers. I'm not used to this peaceful silence.

Mom discusses installing the surveillance cameras we brought from the previous house. I'm only half-listening. "We're in the middle of nowhere. I doubt anyone will break in."

That's the understatement of the year.

"You can never be too careful," she replies. "Dominic, can you help me install them later?"

"Sure," he mutters.

"How do you guys feel about today?" Mom asks, sipping her coffee. "First day at your new school."

Another light breeze brings with it the scent of dry grass and pine.

Shrugging my shoulders, I glance at Dominic, who's now typing on his phone and ignoring the world around him. "I don't know yet."

"It's okay to be nervous," Mom replies in a soft tone. "It's a new start."

The move doesn't bother me.

Unlike Dominic, who had an on-and-off girlfriend back home, I had no friends. He made sure of that when my mom married his dad.

This can be a chance for me to change all that. Though I don't mind being alone, I would like to have a friend.

"Don't worry, Mom." I smile reassuringly. "Everything will be fine."

A loud scoff across the table steals my attention, and I fix my gaze on Dominic, whose dark eyes gleam with pure sadism as he stares at me for long minutes, though it could be mere seconds. I feel naked beneath that heated look. Dominic doesn't have to speak. No, the gleam in his gaze tells me everything I need to know. Nothing will be different now. He will still go out of his way to make my life hell.

Without another word, he stands up, pockets his phone and

Zippo, and walks out. Shortly after, the front door slams. Mom releases a tired sigh as she rubs her eyes to ward off a migraine.

"Don't worry about him, Mom."

I feel sorry for her.

She's lost everything, yet fought to stay strong for us, but I can see she's two seconds away from breaking down.

When that day finally arrives, she won't be able to get back up. That thought sobers me enough to stand. Dominic won't wait for me forever.

I put the dishes away while Mom stares out the window with a faraway look. Bruno sits beside her, thumping his tail against the threadbare carpet, his tongue hanging out.

After I pick up my backpack from the back of my chair, I stroke him behind the ear and kiss Mom on the cheek.

She pats my hand on her shoulder, smiling sadly. "Have a good day, sweetheart."

"You too. I hope your first shift at the hospital goes well."

On one hand, it's good news that she found a position with an immediate start. At least it's something after all the bad luck we've had as a family. But on the other hand, it's an hour and a half commute, and that's not in peak traffic. Our new home truly is in the middle of nowhere.

I exit the house, slamming into a wall of heat. Hot and sticky sweat beads on my forehead as I hurry down the front steps, backpack slung over my shoulder.

Dominic is already in the car, his hand hanging over the steering wheel as he tries to tune the radio.

When I open the door, a blast of heat escapes, and I thank the heavens for putting on frayed denim shorts and a light gray tank top. It's already difficult to breathe in this scorching summer weather.

I climb in and place the backpack between my feet, the leather seat burning my thighs and shoulders. Dominic twists the knob until a warped voice breaks through the static before it's gone again.

"Fuck this," he mutters.

Strapping myself in, I unzip my bag and dig through it for my water bottle, knowing I'll guzzle water in this heat like it's going out of fashion.

Droplets spill onto my chin, so I wipe them off and then offer him the bottle. Dominic disregards my presence, twisting the knob a few more times before giving up and revving the engine, leaving the static noise to fill the silence.

Though I'm used to his asshole behavior, the urge to toss my water bottle at him strikes me so hard, I have to clutch it in my grip.

It would be a waste of water on a hot day.

Dominic puts his arm behind my headrest and twists his body, spinning the wheel as he reverses out of the driveway, which is just a path of dirt road.

Surrounded by citrus, leather, and a hint of sweat, I hold my breath, trying my damnedest not to inhale his drugging scent.

While my heart thrashes hard against my ribcage, his breathing remains the same. Calm, steady, and unaffected.

He sits back, and I can finally inhale a breath into my oxygen-starved lungs, though his smell, his masculine, clit-tingling smell, still lingers in the air. As I roll down the window to let in some fresh air, his enticing scent mixes and mingles with the nearby crops and cow manure.

With nothing but the country road ahead and the heat shimmering in the distance like a mirage, my thoughts drift. There's something to be said about the novelty of driving down an open, sunbaked road without congested traffic, toxic car fumes, and honking horns. I could get used to the feel of the warm summer breeze in my hair and the sight of tall cornstalks and barn structures.

What I don't like as much is the roadkill we pass, and when we drive past another crushed armadillo with its innards spilling out, I swallow down the saliva in my mouth, wishing I could wipe the sight of dried blood on the cracked asphalt from my mind.

Tapping his thumb on the steering wheel, Dominic swings his eyes in my direction, then switches off the radio, fed up with the loud static.

The thick silence that follows only intensifies my unease. Dominic isn't easy to be around. He has this...aura that radiates hostility and nefarious desires. At the best of times, he's stand-offish and apathetic. In moments like these, when I'm trapped with him inside a confined space, it's claustrophobic.

His deep voice rumbles in the small space like an incoming storm rolling across the sky. "You'll have to find another way to get to school from now on."

My shoulders stiffen. "I don't have a car, and it's too far to walk."

"Not my problem."

I glare at his handsome side profile as we drive past a pasture of yellow canola flowers.

Dominic doesn't care if I have to walk an hour to get to school. No, he would drive by me with a taunting smile and a raised middle finger.

He confirms as much when he says, "You don't have to walk. There's a school bus."

Crossing my arms, I look out the window, ignoring his presence the way he ignores mine.

Neither of us speaks until we pull up in the parking lot outside a small college.

As one, we peer through the windshield at the gray building that resembles something out of the seventies.

"It looks like a prison," I mutter.

Beside me, Dominic scoffs as he opens the door and exits the vehicle. His head pops back inside and he pins me in place with his dark eyes. "Don't talk to me. Don't even so much as look in my direction."

Then he's gone, slamming the door shut behind him.

I watch him stride toward the building and ascend the front steps in that assured way he has of a cocky, full-of-himself man who has always fit in and never stood out against the grain. This won't be any different. It doesn't matter that he was born and raised in the city. People flock to him everywhere he goes.

When he passes, wide-eyed and flustered women stop to look at him. Yes, Dominic has that effect on women, and it sours something inside me.

I push open the door and reach for my bag in the footwell. Stepping out into the scorching heat, I shut the car door behind me and settle the bag on my shoulder.

The sun beats down on me as though I have personally offended it.

A bead of sweat trickles between my breasts as I gaze up at the imposing building in front of me.

Unlike my stepbrother, with his unshakable confidence, nerves twist my stomach, and my palms grow clammy. I'm not good at social settings. I'm even worse at making friends.

Before my anxiety gets the better of me, I set off toward the entrance, pretending I don't notice how the students observe me with their curious, assessing eyes.

"Hey, new girl," someone calls out as I near the entrance.

I turn my head to locate the voice, spotting a few guys near a large tree on the lawn—

Slamming into a big body, I stumble, dropping my backpack, which is still partly unzipped after I rooted through it for the bottle of water. The contents spill out on the ground.

With mumbled apologies, I kneel to pick it all up as a set of legs pass me, and a voice tells me to watch where I'm going. Tears prick my eyes as I shove the pencil case inside the bag. I zip it back up and rise to my feet, not trusting my shaky legs to carry me inside.

Laughter drifts on the wind—the same boys who called me out minutes earlier. Nausea overwhelms me and my cheeks burn, which has nothing to do with the unnaturally hot weather.

As I enter the building, I keep my head down and clutch the bag to my chest. If I thought it would be cooler in here, I was wrong. The heat feels stifling and almost panic-inducing.

Weaving through crowds of strangers, who all turn their heads as I pass, I locate reception and place my bag on the counter.

The lady behind the desk peers at me from behind her kitten glasses. "You must be the second Barker sibling?" She hands me a file and then types a few notes on a very old, outdated computer. "You'll find everything you need in there."

Behind me, a girl with curly, green-dyed hair and black lipstick clears her throat. "Camryn Barker?"

The lady behind the counter ignores us.

Apparently, I'm dismissed.

Shouldering my bag, I turn to the girl. "That's me."

"Nice to meet you. I'm Gwen." She has a toothy smile and cute freckles on her nose.

Freckles that I envy.

"I'm here to show you around." Gwen invades my space and forces me back. She swipes up the file on the desk, and then sets off walking, expecting me to follow.

I exchange a look with the receptionist, who lifts a shoulder in a careless shrug. "Better hurry. She waits for no one."

"You don't say."

I don't miss the receptionist's small smile as I make my way down the hallway, barely catching up to Gwen before she turns the corner in a whirlwind of cherry body spray and studded boots.

"So, new girl, is it true you moved into the Victorian estate behind Wilfred Miller's farm?"

Distracted, I tear my gaze away from Dominic, who has not only found his lecture hall but also surrounded himself with big-busted women who ask him a million questions in their southern accents.

"Yes," I reply, as his eyes clash with mine and darken. He looks away just as fast, and I face forward, clearing my throat.

"This is your lecture hall," Gwen says, stopping so abruptly that I nearly crash into her. She taps the door beside her and steps back.

I take the file, turning page after page until I find my schedule, wondering why they still use paper files.

While I skim the information, her curious emerald eyes lined with kohl bore into me, and she scuffs the ground. "How much do you know of the estate's history?"

"Not much," I reply. "Have you seen the place? It was cheap because of how much repair work it needs."

She takes my paperwork before I've had a chance to memorize my schedule, leaning closer. "It was cheap because no one wanted to buy it. The place is cursed."

A chuckle of disbelief bubbles up from my chest. "Cursed?"

"People died in that house. You should look it up."

She walks off before I can ask more questions. But I promptly follow, baffled and a little confused.

Gwen has an aura about her that I covet. She moves like she owns the place, and like other's opinions of her are irrelevant.

I find it refreshing.

She shows me around the college, talking animatedly about everything under the sun until my social battery is drained and I feel ready to hide in the bathroom for the foreseeable future.

"Your brother has been here for less than five minutes, and the girls are already flocking to him like flies to a pile of shit."

I nearly walk into a group of boys, nowhere near as familiar with these hallways as she is. "He's always been popular. Let me guess, you think he's hot, too?"

She pulls a face. "God, no. I'm into girls."

I love her a little bit at this moment.

The only girls who ever spoke to me back home were those who used me to get close to Dominic, but then, as soon as they realized he hated me, they dropped me faster than you could blink.

"I hope you're okay with that?"

Taken aback, I purse my mouth. "Why wouldn't I be?"

She flings her arm over my shoulder, prickling my nose with her cherry scent. "I knew I liked you. You're not like the other stuck-up girls from around here."

My throat closes, and my chest swells. I've never had a girl, or anyone, say they like me before.

By the time we finally enter the library, I've found out she has a little brother, Kai, who likes comic books but isn't a fan of fried eggs, her mother is a vet and insists on Gwen volunteering on weekends, and her father once won a cornhusking competition.

Gwen leads me toward the back to a table near the window, where a group of students have gathered.

They look up when she releases me and slams her hands on the surface with an almost manic smile. "Hey, fuckers," she says. "I want you to meet the new girl." She straightens up and shoves me forward with a hand on my back. "New girl, meet my friends Benny, Aron, Brittany, and Lily."

Four sets of eyes take me in, sweeping over my raven hair, makeup-free face, gray tank top, denim shorts, pale legs, and red Chucks.

Benny, a lanky guy with curly brown hair and full lips, waves first with an open-palm sweep of his hand and a kind smile.

Beside him, Brittany winks in greeting, which I find strange but sweet, then runs a hand through her pink tresses.

Lily speaks first. "You're the one who's moved into the haunted house behind Wilfred's farm."

It's impossible to miss how the energy shifts.

Aron kicks out a chair beside him in an invitation, and I drop my bag to the floor before lowering myself, feeling nervous and out of my element.

I have no experience with friends.

Gwen joins us, too, plopping down in the only other free seat beside mine.

She looks at me, with her elbows on the armrest. "It's said a demon haunts the grounds."

"What a way to drop her in it," chuckles Benny. "You'll scare her off."

"She needs to know—"

"A demon?" I ask, as my heart beats a little faster.

Aron leans forward, his black hair falling over his brow. "From the underworld."

"You're scaring her," Lily says, then smacks his arm, which causes him to laugh.

"It's the truth," he argues, still chuckling.

"What do you mean by a demon?" I ask, looking between them all.

Brittany considers me, arms crossed, then sits forward and places her elbows on the table. "It's said that a family used to live in that house a long time ago. They kept to themselves. Never really spoke to anyone. The father was into all that dark stuff. Apparently, he bargained with the souls of his family members for money and eternal life. They all went missing one day and were never found again, except for the dad, who'd committed suicide." She shrugs. "At least that's how the rumor goes."

"And ever since," Gwen says, looking at me sideways, "the house has stood empty, and anyone who ventures near it dies."

"Dies how?"

She shrugs once more and eases back in her chair. "Suicide, mostly, or some freak accident."

Aron chuckles with a shake of his head. "It happened once." Then he looks at me pointedly. "No one goes near it because the whole town thinks the place is cursed or some shit."

"Oh, shut it," Brittany says. "They both died a week later. What are the odds of that?"

Aron rolls his eyes, and Benny coughs into his closed fist to hide his snicker.

My eyes widen. "What happened?"

"Clarissa was a freshman at high school, and Harvey was on the football team. They'd been to a party. It was all part of some stupid dare. They were supposed to enter the property and film themselves making out in one of the rooms. Your typical high school shit."

"And then what?"

"A week later, Clarissa disappeared."

"Disappeared?"

"A witness in a passing tractor saw her enter the woods that back onto the property."

"She disappeared?" I press, biting the inside of my lip.

Gwen nods. "But it doesn't end there. The same day she disappeared, Harvey's parents found him in the bathtub. He had electrocuted himself with a hairdryer."

Goosebumps erupt over my arms as a chill slithers down my spine. "I don't believe in the supernatural. Whatever happened must have logical explanations."

They exchange amused glances before Brittany pops her gum and smiles brightly. "We should do a séance at your house one day to see if we can communicate with it."

Lily's lips part as she gasps. "Are you crazy? No!"

"Why not?" Brittany looks at me then. "She's up for it."

"Why not?" She opens and closes her mouth like a fish. "Because it's dangerous. People die who venture inside that house, or have you forgotten? I don't want to go anywhere near it."

Gwen smiles apologetically, sensing my discomfort, while they continue bickering. Aron plays on his phone, and Benny studies me, as though he finds me intriguing.

I suppose I am the city chick.

The outsider.

The new girl who has never seen cornstalks or scarecrows in real life until yesterday.

"Welcome to the unhinged gang," Gwen whispers in my ear, loud enough for the others to hear, and pulls me close with her arm around my neck.

I think I've officially made some friends.

THREE

CAMRYN

TAPPING the pen on my notebook, I stare out the window at the setting sun.

Dominic begrudgingly drove me home after school and didn't speak a single word the entire journey.

Now, as I watch the trees sway in the breeze, the sound of his electric guitar drifts through the walls. I can't focus on my homework. Not because of his strumming. Something about those trees calls to me.

My curtains dance as another gentle gust brings with it the scent of pine and rotting wood.

A headache blooms behind my eyes, and the words blur in and out of focus. Putting the pen down, I squeeze the bridge of my nose and rise to my feet, the chair scraping against the wooden floor. I walk up to the window, kneeling on the window seat and pressing my face against the glass. Beside me, the curtain billows, bringing the sound of…whispers?

My breath fogs the glass as I strain to listen. When Dominic strums his guitar again, my eyes fall shut with frustration. But then the music fades into silence, and the whispers come again, urging me to lean closer to the glass and peer beyond the trees.

"Camryn."

I tumble backward with a gasp, landing hard on the floor as my heart thumps. Inhaling shaky breaths, I feel my pounding headache intensify behind my temple.

Wincing, I press my palm to my forehead before rising to my feet and steadying myself on the desk. Fuck this. I need to get out of this house. I need fresh air.

After entering the hallway, I glance at Dominic's bedroom. His door is open, and I catch sight of his long legs on the bed, crossed at the ankles. Hurrying down the stairs, I put on my shoes and leave the house. It's late afternoon, but the heat still slams into me as I step outside, though it's not quite as stifling as earlier.

Rounding the side of the house, I let my hand drift over the rough bricks while the tall grass tickles my bare ankles. A bumble bee flies tirelessly from wildflower to wildflower, and crickets chirp somewhere in the thicket of the overgrown yard.

I turn the corner and make a beeline for the forest, called forward by something inside me. Something that responds to the whispers in the afternoon breeze.

Whispers that call my name.

My damp neck pricks with awareness as I draw to a halt, turning slowly to look up at the window.

Dominic, shirtless and with that dog tag hanging around his chest, gazes down at me with an intense, unreadable expression.

One that sees through me.

I clench my hands to hide the slight tremor and start to turn back around, but I pause when I see a different figure.

A figure that peers down from my bedroom window: a stern-looking older woman dressed in all black, with a severe bun and pale, gaunt cheeks.

Ice slithers through my veins even as a bead of sweat trails down my spine. I blink, and the woman is gone.

"What the…?" I stiffen.

Dominic is still watching me intently, his eyes never wavering as they strip me bare.

My own window remains empty.

Behind me, the trees rustle when their branches move in a vagrant breeze—

A sudden insect bite stings my bare arm, and I slap my hand over it, but it's already gone.

"Fuck," I whisper as I turn around to enter the woods. I scratch my skin, making the red welt worse by dragging my dirty nails over it. Let's face it—it feels fucking good.

Greeted by the mustiness of moss and the earthy scent of pine and rotten bark, I venture deeper, noting the temperature drop in the air.

A sudden chill causes me to shiver. Despite the summer heat, I shudder, dragging my hands over my arms to rub some warmth back into me.

It doesn't work.

Twigs break underfoot as the trees groan and sway in the wind, seeming to sing a haunting tune. I don't know what possesses me to keep walking, but a calling from deep within, an urge I can't place, pulls me forward.

"*Camryn,*" the whisper comes again, and I stumble to a halt, snapping my head from left to right to locate the voice. Silence settles over the forest once more like a swirling mist that suffocates everything in its path.

"*Camryn.*" Again, much louder. This time, from right behind me.

With my heart in my throat, I spin around so fast, my hair whips me in the face. Spindly trees reach up toward the sky, their twisted branches creating ominous shadows on the ground. Nearby, a thicket of blueberry bushes bristles with dark, glistening fruit, their sweet scent mingling with the damp earth and decaying pinecones.

A crow lets out a loud caw somewhere in the distance. My breath catches, but then something else snags my attention—a repetitive thud or a whack up ahead.

I set off toward the noise, frowning as I move branches out of the way while stepping over fallen logs. Once I reach a clearing, I take cover behind a tree.

A young man, not much older than me, places a piece of wood on a log. His red flannel shirt is unbuttoned to reveal his tanned chest, and his brown hair falls over his brow.

He's unaware of my presence as he wipes the glistening sweat off his forehead with the back of his hand. I can't look away from the bulging muscles in his arms or how he picks up the axe leaning against the trunk.

Brow furrowed with concentration, he raises it in the air and brings it down on the log to split it in half. A gasp leaves my lips, and he stills, as if the sound carried through the trees. His eyes fly up to mine, where I peer around the trunk, and he places the axe back down and takes a step toward me.

Panic floods my body.

Panic because I've been caught spying.

Without a second thought, I turn and run.

Branches scratch my skin and slap me in the face. I barely notice. All the while, the forest whispers all around me, whispers which soon turn into shouts and cackles.

Whispers that taunt and reach for me like limbs with claws, and gnarly, old fingers with torn, yellowed nails. They pull at my clothes and tangle in my hair.

It won't stop itching. I'm slowly going insane. I dig my nails into the angry, red bite on my arm, and then, scratching almost furiously, I wince. Fuck, it won't stop itching.

"Are you alright, sweetheart?" Mom asks as she places my plate full of steaming rice and butter chicken in front of me.

"I'm fine," I reply, looking across the table at Dominic, who pulls out his chair and sits down.

Mom plates his food next before joining us with her own. Pouring herself a glass of water, she smiles encouragingly. "Who wants to tell me about their day? Camryn? Dominic? Did you make any friends?"

Dominic shovels food into his mouth, and images of seeing him around the college on our first day, surrounded by curious women, leave a sour taste in my mouth.

He just has to exist to be popular. Everything comes easy.

I thought that maybe, just maybe, it would be different once we left the city. But no.

I glare at him while scratching my arm. He smirks, but then his gaze falls to my arm, and he pauses with the loaded fork halfway to his mouth. I look down and stiffen when I see the smeared blood under my nails and between my fingers.

Mom is oblivious, cutting her chicken. "Did you make any friends, Camryn?"

Ignoring Dominic's rage-filled gaze, I hide my arm beneath the table, wiping my bloodied nails on my jeans before reaching for my fork and stabbing a piece of chicken. "Gwen, who showed me around school, introduced me to her friends."

Mom's face lights up. "That's fantastic news."

I suppress the urge to wince, hating how defective her excitement makes me feel. I know she worried about me back home, hoping and wishing I'd make friends, and sometimes, that worry was worse than being alone.

I'm fine alone. I'm used to it. I've never felt like I belong.

The only times I struggle are when Dominic has his friends over, and I can hear them laughing through the walls, or when he throws a party, and I have to hide in my room. In those moments, I sometimes wish I felt a sense of belonging.

My arm stings, and my appetite is gone.

Oblivious to the tension in the room, Mom keeps talking, the sound of her cutlery scraping against the plate.

Dominic's glare intensifies until I can't take it anymore and meet his stare head-on, caught in those dark eyes that make my mouth go dry. I hate how my body responds to that glare. Hate how it makes me want to squirm beneath the heat in those voids. These feelings are wrong for so many reasons.

Sometimes, I can't decide if he wants to skin me alive or devour me whole. Possibly both.

No one looks at me like Dominic. No one makes me feel so invisible yet seen all at once.

"How was your day, Dominic?" Mom asks him, breaking our stare-off or, more accurately, mine. Dominic still doesn't look away, and my cheeks heat the longer he keeps his burning attention on me.

His response comes as an affirmative grunt, and Mom lets it go, offering us both a gentle smile.

After dinner, I help Mom wash up while listening to her talk about her day, but my thoughts are elsewhere as I stare out the window behind the sink.

The soapy water is too hot, turning my skin pink, and bubbles stick to my arm when I place another plate on the rack.

My hand plunges back into the scalding water, and I furiously scrub another plate. "Mom, have you met Wilfred Miller yet?"

"Wilfred, who owns the farm next door?" she replies, wiping the table behind me.

"Yes."

"No, not yet. Why do you ask?"

As I place the plate on the dish rack, soapy bubbles slide down the porcelain. I glance back out the window at the tall oak tree that sways gently. "I saw someone in the forest today. A young man."

"Oh?"

"He was chopping wood. I wondered if Wilfred had a son or a grandson, maybe?"

"Most likely." She hesitates. "We should say hi to the neighbors, right? It's the polite thing to do."

We are from the city, where no one speaks to their neighbors, but things are different here.

"Right?" she asks as she comes up beside me to shake bits of stray rice off the dishcloth. She rinses it clean, then places it over the faucet. "I'll knock on their door tomorrow."

"Don't forget the gift basket," I tease, making her laugh on her way out of the room.

I finish the dishes, wipe my hands on the towel, and look back at the woods. The sun has almost set, and the shadows grow longer as the branches tremble in the evening breeze. It could be a beautiful view—in fact, it is beautiful—but something about this place gives me the creeps.

A hand wraps around my elbow and spins me around. I gasp, caught in Dominic's stormy eyes.

"What the hell is this?" he all but growls as he yanks me closer to inspect the bite on my arm.

His thumb swipes over the dried, smeared blood and red skin in a deceptively tender touch that sets me on edge more than the hardened glint in his eyes.

Dominic doesn't have a kind bone in his body. Faced with a choice, he would pick violence every day, no questions asked. So, to see him glare at me with such intensity sends my heart sprinting down a hill to escape the fire in his eyes.

"It's just a bug bite," I reply, then yelp when he grabs me by the throat in a ruthless grip.

He leans in close and bares his teeth. "What were you doing out in the woods by yourself? You could get lost. We're not in the city anymore, Camryn."

I open my mouth to reply, but startle when the kitchen door slams shut so forcefully that a picture on the wall crashes to the floor. Dominic stiffens and looks behind him, his thumb stroking my throat. I don't even think he was aware of the action, but then the moment passes, and he levels those dark eyes on mine.

All oxygen seems to get sucked out of the room when he's this close.

Close enough that I can feel his heat through his clothes. Every ridge of his muscles.

I can't look away, my pulse thundering beneath his fingers. He has always disliked me, but the sheer force of his ire dampens my palms as I clutch his T-shirt. It's on the tip of my tongue to provoke him to see how far that darkness runs. My fear begs me to try, but I don't have a death wish, so I remain silent.

Door forgotten, he tightens his grip, and my heart takes off at a gallop. I tug on his T-shirt, creasing the soft fabric. His heart thunders beneath my hands. Just when I think he's going to kiss me or kill me, he steps away. "Don't go walking in the woods by yourself."

"Is that concern I hear?" I bite out as he turns to leave. "You never talk to me, so why start caring now?"

Instead of replying, he walks up to the door and crouches to pick up the broken frame, his T-shirt stretching tight across his shoulders as the muscles shift in his broad back. Not that I'm checking him out. Okay, so maybe I am. Sue me. He is attractive, even though he is an asshole.

As the seconds tick by, I frown.

What is he studying so intently?

Intrigued, I step closer. "Dominic? Everything okay?"

At the sound of my voice, his shoulders touch his ears, but then he relaxes and continues collecting the pieces of glass. I lower myself beside him, careful not to kneel on pieces of shards, and we clean up in silence.

Dominic cuts himself, hissing under his breath, a bead of red sliding down his finger before he sucks it clean. I try not to be too obvious when I gaze at his lips.

"Careful," he warns, but it's already too late.

A sudden sharp sting makes me suck in a breath, and I look down to see a jagged piece of glass embedded in my finger. "Fuck."

Dominic snatches my wrist, holding my hand steady as he removes the piece before wrapping his warm lips around my finger. A spark of liquid desire shoots to my core at the heated look in his eyes. I'm entrapped, held hostage by that possessive stare.

He trails his warm tongue over my finger, then drops my hand and rises to his full height. I peer up at him, still on my knees, at eye level with his crotch, and now it's all I can focus on. When he continues gazing down at me, I try hard not to peek at the bulge, but it's right there.

Tense seconds tick by.

I'm parched.

There's a pulsating sensation between my legs—a sensation that becomes more difficult to ignore the longer his eyes stay locked on mine.

Then, like he's pulled out of a daze, Dominic steps around me and walks away. I inhale a ragged breath, unsure if I'm relieved or not. His effect on me is terrifying. I shouldn't be this flustered.

My attention lands on the photograph on the floor, and I pick it up, then slowly rise to my feet.

The older woman in the photo is the same woman I saw in the window, but that can't be right.

Frowning, I take a seat on a kitchen chair, scanning the picture in the hopes of finding a date stamp in the corner, but there's nothing. The woman's dead eyes seem to see through me, and I fight a shiver as I place the picture back down.

I must have imagined the whole thing, right? This can't be the same woman I saw in the window. We've not had visitors yet.

Picking the card back up, I run a finger along the worn edge. The woman looks just as severe as that time when she gazed down at me, half hidden behind the curtains. Her cold eyes are just as cruel.

I turn the card over and pause.

Psalm 106:37

They sacrificed their sons and their daughters to the demons;

FOUR

CAMRYN

"*Camryn,*" a voice hisses, the sinister sound echoing around me as I shoot upright in bed, clutching the quilt to my chest. Sleep lingers at the fringes of my consciousness as I rub my face. The darkness is pierced by an ominous, vicious growl that sends a chill down my spine. My heart races, pounding in my throat as I take a shaky breath.

I slowly turn my head toward the door, every nerve in my body on high alert. Bruno bares his sharp canines, poised to attack, when another rumbling growl fills the silence.

"Bruno?" I glance at the door, seeing nothing but the outline of the gown hanging on the hook behind it. The hairs on the back of my neck stand up as I swallow hard. "There's nothing there, Bruno."

Instead of quieting, his low growl intensifies, and he inches backward closer to the bed. I turn on the bedside lamp with trembling fingers and look back at the door. As I thought, my peach gown hangs on a hook.

After removing the quilt, I sit at the edge of the bed and run my fingers through his coarse fur, feeling his tense muscles contracting beneath my touch.

Dread twists my gut as I whisper, "Bruno? What do you see, buddy?"

When he continues to snarl, I rise to my feet, walk past him to the door, and spin around. "There's no one here."

Even though my voice trembles, I offer him a reassuring smile. I know it's reckless to approach him while he's so distressed, but I can't help taking a step closer, my hand outstretched in a placating gesture. "Calm down, Bruno. It's okay."

A sudden chill at the back of my neck makes me still and hold my breath. Someone is behind me—someone or something evil. There has to be. I've never been more sure of anything.

With a wall of ice behind me and Bruno in front, snarling low in his throat, I'm truly trapped. There's nowhere to run, and the last thing I want to do is to turn around.

Within my next breath, the chill shifts and moves past me. Bruno yelps and scampers away, his claws pattering on the wooden floor. My heart hammers harder, and I gulp past the lump forming in my throat. Whatever that *thing* was, it's gone now, though I still feel as if I'm not alone, like it's watching me.

My gaze lands on the gaping gap in the armoire doors. A gap I can't stop staring at—it seems to suck me in.

Striding over, I tear the doors open, yanking the clothes apart, almost expecting something to jump out at me. Of course, there's nothing.

I'm alone.

Gwen swipes a paper napkin across her mouth before crumpling it up and tossing it on the coffee table. Meanwhile, my glazed doughnut remains untouched.

She suggested a trip to the local bakery after class, so here we are, seated on the saggy couches nestled next to a large bookshelf near the back. An unlit fireplace to our left has more stacked books on top, and if I were to describe the scent here, I'd say it smells of old books, coffee, and the fresh batch of chocolate chip cookies that were brought out when we arrived.

On the couch across from me, Benny inhales his third macaroon.

Lily bites down on ice and puts her glass of fizzy Coke on the table. "You'll get a sugar-induced coma soon."

Benny simply shrugs, unbothered.

Beside me, Gwen eases back and jerks her chin at me. "So what's the house like? Have you noticed anything supernatural yet?"

"Give her a chance to eat her doughnut before you start your interrogation," says Brittany on my other side, popping her pink bubblegum that matches her hair.

Aron lies half-slouched on the couch with one arm behind his head and a lazy smile on his lips. His other hand rests on his jeans-clad thigh as he taps his thumb to an imaginary beat. That is one thing I've noticed about him lately: outwardly, he's the sloth in the group. But if you look closely, you'll notice he's never still. He's always moving, whether he's tapping his foot or drumming a beat with his fingers.

"So?" Gwen pushes. "Have you seen ghosts yet?"

Benny stands up and walks to the counter at the front of the bakery.

"Don't let him buy any more macaroons," Lily calls out to the elderly woman behind the cash register, and Aron clamps a hand over her mouth.

"Well? Don't hold out on us?" Gwen nudges me with her elbow.

As I lift the doughnut from the crackling wax paper and take a bite, a soft moan escapes my lips.

"It beats the doughnuts in the city, doesn't it?" Brittany asks.

Nodding, I swallow it down.

The doughnuts back home are nice, don't get me wrong, but this is a taste of heaven.

Sugary glazing coats my lips, so I reach for a paper napkin and wipe my mouth clean. I shake my head, addressing Gwen. "No, I haven't seen any ghosts."

"Nothing out of the ordinary?"

"No," I lie.

At least, I don't think I have. The woman in the window—the same woman from the photograph that fell off the wall—was a figment of my imagination. Ghosts aren't real.

"Nothing at all?" She sounds disappointed.

"I still think we should do a séance," Brittany says, chewing her gum like her life depends on it while she twirls a strand of pink hair around her finger.

"Not this again," Lily complains, and Aron slams his hand over her mouth.

"I'm with Brittany. We should do it."

Lily shoves his hand away as Benny returns with more macaroons. "Why? What good could come from it?"

"Do you believe in demons?" he asks her.

"No, of course I don't."

"Then what's the problem?"

"Do you really think it's a good idea to dabble in the occult?"

Aron ruffles her blonde hair. "You say you don't believe in demons, so it can't do any harm."

"I don't believe in demons. I still think it's a bad idea."

"So you do believe in them."

"No—"

"You do, or you wouldn't be so against the idea of a séance. They either exist or they don't."

While they bicker, I eat the rest of the doughnut.

Aron levels his bright, blue eyes on me. "What do you say? Let's bring a spirit board and copious amounts of alcohol to your house over the weekend."

I freeze, fingers sticky with sugary glazing. Somewhere in the background, the slide of the cash register mixes with the bell over the door and the hum of conversation. For a small café, it's busy.

"We'll have so much fun." Gwen pulls my ponytail.

I look between them all, trying to think of an excuse to back out. "I'm busy this weekend."

Gwen pouts, tugging on my ponytail again. Aron pokes Lily in the cheek, and she bats him off. Brittany blows a big bubble that pops and covers her nose and chin.

"Have you ever been to the house?" I ask out of curiosity as I ease back, and they all shake their heads, but it's Gwen who answers. "No, never."

"But you still believe the rumors?"

"There's something not right about that property," Lily replies.

"Ha!" Aron points a finger at her with a wicked gleam in his eyes and a wide smile. "So you do believe in demons."

"No," she says, rolling her eyes, "but you can't deny the house's history. Weird stuff happens there. People go missing." A visible shiver runs through her, and she looks at me with a crease between her eyebrows. "People die."

I swallow down the unease as I suppress a shudder. "They could all be coincidences."

"They could be, but locals stay away from that property for a reason." She sweeps her gaze over our little group. "Everyone here seems to have forgotten that."

"Relax," chuckles Benny around a mouthful of macaroon. "No one is going to die or go missing."

This conversation makes me uncomfortable, so I stand up and make my way over to the counter. The middle-aged man in front of me orders a slice of berry pie and a black coffee. Once the register slides open and shut, the man leaves with his tray. A dash of black and red shifts in my periphery, and I whip my head around.

"Can I help you?" the lady behind the counter asks, but I can barely hear her.

Overhead, the bell dings as the man I spied in the forest leaves the café. It's him. It has to be.

"Excuse me, ma'am?"

"I'm sorry," I mumble, turning around and walking out.

It must be the same man.

The bell dings again as I hurry outside, coming to an abrupt halt. I scan the desolate sidewalk and the parking lot, but there's no sign of him.

Where did he go?

A warm, stifling breeze chases away the chills on my arms, and the insect bite itches, so I scratch it, ignoring the bite of pain.

"Camryn?"

I spin around to see Gwen in the doorway. She scans the empty street and looks back at me with a confused expression. "Are you leaving already?"

Peering left and right again, I shake off the odd feeling that clings to me like sweat on my neck. "I thought I saw someone," I say.

Gwen's frown deepens, and she steps back as I enter the café. "Are you okay? You look pale."

"I'm fine," I reassure her, joining the queue at the counter. "Do you want anything?"

"What the hell?" I whisper, scooting up into a sitting position in bed, scratching my arm almost furiously. Judging by the warm slickness beneath my fingers, I know I've drawn blood even before I switch on the bedside lamp.

Blinking under the bright light, I lean against the headboard as I look down at my arm, sucking in a sharp breath at the sight of smeared blood. The itching burrows so deep I want to scratch the bone itself.

Throwing off the quilt, I make my way to the ensuite bathroom and flick on the overhead light. My tired reflection stares back at me in the mirror, dark circles framing my eyes. Gwen was right; I'm paler than usual. I turn on the tap, adjusting the temperature until the water errs on the side of too hot. As the sound of running water fills the air, I catch a glimpse of myself in the mirror, which is slowly fogging up. I slide my hand across the glass to clear it, fighting the urge to claw my itchy skin open.

Scooping up a handful of water to wash off the blood, I pause. Something moves under the skin in search of a way out, and the sensation of crawling insects makes me stumble back a step and crash into the toilet behind me. I even knock down the toilet roll holder as I skirt the seat.

I'm clutching my arm, watching the skin bulge and strain, dizzy with panic.

Maggots erupt from the flesh, then crawl down my arm and fall to the floor.

I don't even know when I start screaming, but then Dominic is there, palming my face and jostling me.

"Camryn, fuck, look at me!" He shakes me again with enough force to make my head knock off the wall. Not hard, but enough to stun me back into reality.

When the sensation of his warm hands on my cheeks finally registers, I stare into his dark eyes while my heart races.

He jostles me again, weaker this time. "Look at me, dammit!"

Citrus and leather filter through the haze of adrenaline, and like a warm fire on a snowy winter's night, the rich notes of his cologne thaw the fear inside me. I breathe easier as I lose myself in his hard stare.

"What the hell is wrong?" he asks tersely, gripping me so hard it's almost painful.

Blinking him back into focus, I shove his hands away from my face. He doesn't fight me. Instead, he steps back and scans the room as if he's trying to figure out what spooked me.

He zeroes back in on me, and a divot forms between his brows. I'm shaking and staring down at my arm with tears hanging precariously from my lashes.

Where's the blood? The maggots? The scratch marks? Why is my skin healed?

"What's wrong?" he asks, though there's nothing gentle in his icy tone.

I meet his gaze, still clutching my arm. "There was... I have..."

"There was what?" he presses and moves closer.

Worrying my bottom lip, I look down, unsure. How do I even begin to tell him about what happened just now or all the other things? "Have you noticed anything weird since we moved here?"

With his hands on the wall on either side of my head, he peers at my face so intently that I fight the urge to shrink back.

"Anything weird?"

"Yes?"

"No," he states, flicking his eyes between mine. "Nothing. What happened just now to make you scream the place down?"

I try to look away, but he follows me.

"Eyes on me, Camryn, and answer the question."

"Nothing happened." I tip my chin, even as my bottom lip trembles.

I don't want to tell him about the maggots, Bruno's growling at the corner last night, or the whispering woods. I sound insane.

"You're a terrible fucking liar," he sneers, pushing off the wall and straightening up. I look away, but he grips my chin and jerks my eyes back to his cold ones. "Have you told your mom you're losing it?"

"I'm not losing it!" I wrench free.

"No? So tell me why you're screaming yourself hoarse in the bathroom in the dead of night?"

The itch is back with a vengeance, worms wriggling beneath my skin. I ignore it as I spit, "None of your fucking business."

"You have some backbone, after all," Dominic replies in a tone laced with amusement. "Not such a wallflower like you want the world to believe."

"Get out!" I point to the door, fed up with the knowing look in his eyes.

He thinks he is so smart, that he knows anything about me. He doesn't.

Chuckling, he leaves the bathroom, his broad shoulders disappearing through the doorway.

As soon as the door clicks shut, I find myself scratching my arm furiously until the soft welt bursts like a ripe pimple, releasing a swarm of slick, wriggling maggots. But when I look down, there's nothing there.

I'm losing it, just like Dominic said.

FIVE

CAMRYN

I STRUGGLE to concentrate during breakfast, in class, or when Benny holds court, telling us all about his progress with the operation, 'get the popular cheerleader to notice him.'

My brain is in a haze like I'm walking through a dense layer of fog. Everywhere I turn, I feel eyes on me. And to make everything worse, my arm won't stop itching.

I snap out of my thoughts when Lily, with her blonde hair tied up in a messy bun, says, "Give up, Benny. So what if Erica and the quarterback are on a break? You know that counts for nothing in the world of the rich and popular. If you lay a finger on her, the football team will come after you."

We're seated near the fountain, roasting beneath the unforgiving sun, with no shade in sight. However, it's better than hiding away inside the muggy hallways that stink of cheap perfume and sweat.

Aron's floppy raven hair moves in the summer breeze as he pretends to shudder. "I'd listen to him if I were you."

"Erica won't look at him twice," Gwen says with a shrug and gazes out over the students milling about. "He'll soon learn it the hard way."

"Why are you reaching above your station anyway?" Brittany asks as she ties back her hair.

Benny glances disbelievingly at her. "Well, jeez, thanks."

Brittany is unperturbed, letting her freckled shoulders rise and fall. A strand of her pink hair defies gravity and sticks to her damp forehead. "I don't mean any harm by it. People like us don't get along with people like them. There's a hierarchy, and we're at the bottom."

Benny narrows his brown eyes. "Who says we're at the bottom?"

Gwen and Aron chuckle—Gwen with a lollipop in her mouth and Aron with a paper plane he has spent the last couple of minutes perfecting. He sends it flying. "Why don't you just ask her out?"

Lily nods in agreement. "Yes, what are you waiting for?"

"These things require careful planning," Benny argues as I uncap my bottle and take a large sip of the lukewarm water.

"Sure, sure. We believe you." Gwen's voice drips with sarcasm.

"Laugh all you want," Benny grumbles. "I'll soon show you how it's done."

"When you speak of the devil, he appears, or, in this case, she." Brittany tips her chin toward the building's front doors, and we all look over in unison to see Erica and her posse exit in their too-short skirts and high heels that would break my ankle. I'll admit that she's stunning with her blonde, cascading hair, which always looks freshly brushed with soft curls, and long, tanned legs. No wonder the boys turn heads when she walks by. As her heels click on the pavement, and her feminine laughter rings like bells, I wonder what it'd be like to receive that kind of attention.

"Damn." Aron whistles. "I'd nut within seconds if I ever got close to her."

Gwen pulls a face, and he does a double take before throwing his arms wide and nearly knocking my water bottle out of my hand. "What's that look for? She's hot as sin and also fucking scary, okay? At least I admit it, unlike Casanova here"—he jerks his chin in Benny's direction—"who thinks he stands a chance."

"Hey, I could last long enough to satisfy a girl like her," he argues, and Aron snorts, shaking his head.

"Boys, let's not argue," Brittany says, biting back a laugh.

Just then, a shadow falls over me, and I look up to see Dominic glaring down at Aron with enough venom in his eyes to make the toughest of men cower. "Move."

With one fleeting glance in my direction, Aron scoots over as an awkward silence settles over the group. Dominic focuses his burning gaze on me, and my nape breaks out in a cold sweat. I steel my spine, unsettled. "What do you want?"

I'm not used to his full attention like this. Dominic has always avoided me at every turn for as long as I can remember. Now he invades my space as if he has any right to suck the oxygen out of the muggy air. His big build settles between me and Aron, and his arm against mine sets me on fire. "Is that any way to welcome your brother, Sis?"

There's a cold bite to his tone, a warning that makes my breath catch. The others exchange uncertain glances until he asks them questions to put them at ease. Dominic has always excelled at working the crowd and could fit in anywhere, like a chameleon. This is no different.

I crumple my empty bottle of water and glare at the side of his face until his amused, dark eyes slide in my direction. But I'm prepared for their full-scale invasion this time. Pulling some deep-rooted longing from the depths of me like an anchor from an ocean bed, I rise to my feet and walk away.

I refuse to let him steal this good thing from me. He can use his stupid charm on someone else, not my friends.

His masculine scent follows me as I enter through the front doors. I'm instantly assaulted by the faulty, rattling AC overhead, which should be blowing out cold air but blasting me with heat instead.

"Camryn," he shouts behind me.

I quicken my steps as I escape around the corner, but I'm not fast enough. He grabs hold of my arm and shoves me against the door behind me. Dark eyes lock onto mine, his grip tight enough to induce a pinch of pain that makes me come alive. I focus on my breath and the rise and fall of my chest.

"He has his eyes on you."

"Who?"

"The black-haired one."

"Aron?"

Grinding his molars, he clamps his hand over my mouth. "Shut up."

Confused, I stare at his rugged face as he slides his hand from my mouth to my neck, feeling my pulse thud heavily beneath his touch. "I don't want to hear his name on your lips."

I swallow roughly. "Why do you care all of a sudden?"

"I don't," he states, so matter-of-factly that fiery anger rises within me. Instead of cowering, I whisper, *"Aron,"* and draw out each vowel to provoke a reaction from him.

It works.

He clamps his hand over my mouth and whacks my head against the wall. Then he snarls in my ear, sounding more animal than human. He's just about to open his mouth when a voice interrupts our silent battle of wills.

Mr. Jones, the human sciences professor, puts his hand on Dominic's shoulder, and he stiffens against me.

"Don't you have somewhere to be, Mr. Barker?" The professor's firm tone leaves no room for arguing. Dominic's cold eyes pierce mine for a heartbeat too long. Finally, he steps back, shifting his intense glare to Mr. Jones. Without another glance in my direction, he turns and walks away, leaving a chill in the clammy air.

Mr. Jones watches him leave with a deep-set line across his forehead. Then he turns his attention on me, lingering long enough to make me grow cold despite the heat.

I shrink back against the wall as he removes his hand from his pocket and runs it down the length of his navy tie. He moves closer, his lips curving in a small smile. "Your brother is awfully interested in you."

"He's not my brother," I clarify, looking around, surprised to see the hallway deserted. An overhead light flickers intermittently, yellow and glaring. My head whips left again, trying to locate the sound of a dripping tap.

Mr. Jones hums, his sickly scent of sweat and tobacco mixing with something else. Something that draws my attention back to his pock-marked face and graying beard.

"What are you doing?" I ask, trapped against the wall with nowhere to escape.

Sulfur and ash prick my nose as he leans in to whisper in my ear, "His obsession with you is delicious. I can almost taste the jealousy on my tongue." He begins to chuckle, the eerie sound growing in volume until it seems to echo all around me. But then he grows still—so still that fear sinks its claws deep into my heart.

"Psalm 106:37," he drawls, twisting his meaty fingers in my hair. "They sacrificed their sons and their daughters to the demons."

I grow icy cold, but before I can ask him why he recited that Bible verse, the same one on the back of the photograph, he breathes me in and drags his nose over the curve of my neck. A second or two passes where I stare at the flickering light overhead while my heart flutters wildly. His nose lowers again, breathing me in obscenely loud. Grabbing my jaw, he bares his teeth and snaps them inches from my face before descending into crazed laughter. He leans in to sniff me again, then snarls like a creature straight out of a horror movie.

His breath is wet against my ear. "You're succulent."

The initial panic morphs into something else, something provoked, like I'm an animal locked in a cage too small. I try to shove him off, and when that doesn't work, I knee him in the balls.

Bent at the waist, his eyes swim with black as he spits in a foreign language—an ancient and shiver-inducing language.

My arm itches.

Fuck, how it itches.

Flies crawl and buzz over my skin.

I tear at it with my dirty nails, scratching and clawing.

Noticing, he cocks his head. Then, faster than I can react, his mouth gapes wide, and he attacks.

"Hey, hey, Camryn?" Gwen taps my cheek a little too hard to be considered gentle. "Earth to Camryn?"

Dazed, I blink.

"There you are. What happened just now?"

Mr. Jones looks uncomfortable as he puts his hand on my shoulder, causing me to jerk away. "I think she needs to see a nurse," he says.

I'm at a loss and struggling to make sense of the situation. When I look at Gwen, she explains, "You freaked out on Mr. Jones when he came to speak to you."

I glance around the once again crowded hallway before slumping back against the wall. My eyes sting, but not from tears.

Exhaustion.

What's happening to me?

"Did I…" I swallow, unable to look anyone in the eye. "Did I hurt you, Mr. Jones?"

"Hurt me? God, no. You were mumbling words under your breath that I couldn't make out. I'm impressed by your foreign language skills, Miss. Barker."

I frown. "I don't know any other languages."

I can tell he doesn't believe me and that my distress makes him uncomfortable. He turns to Gwen, patting her reassuringly on the shoulder. "Take her to the nurse. It's probably a heatstroke."

"I will." She puts her arm around my waist and leads me through the crowded hallways. "You're okay, Camryn. No one is looking."

I know they are. Rumors spread like wildfire in a small town like this, jumping from tongue to lip, reshaping and transforming by the second until the truth is buried beneath the rubble of white lies. I'm the new girl who threw a match to a field of dry wheat with my freak-out.

What's happening to me?

I keep my gaze on the floor until we enter a small room with a cot. Gwen sits me down, swipes my hair off my damp forehead, and flicks her eyes between mine. "It's the heat. It gets to the best of us. It's about time they get the AC fixed."

Swiping unbidden tears from my eyes, I smile weakly, grateful to have been offered this one simple excuse. It doesn't feel like a heatstroke, but she's right—it doesn't get this warm in the city.

The door creaks open, and a woman pops in with a wide smile and a fresh bottle of ice-cold water dripping with condensation. I gulp it down before handing the empty bottle back.

"My, my, you were thirsty," she says, touching my clammy forehead. "You'll be alright, sweetheart. Let's rest for a bit, alright."

Though we're blessed with a cloudy afternoon, the heat still remains, and a thin layer of sweat coats my skin at all times. It doesn't matter how many showers I take or how much water I guzzle. Short of keeping my head in the freezer, I can do nothing but slowly lose my sanity. Boob sweat is another constant, and as if that's not bad enough, my tank top sticks to my spine.

The heat was bearable at first, but not anymore.

I toss the bag in the trash can and shut the lid on the buzzing flies. The reek in the air is so foul that I press the back of my hand over my nose as I step away. I suppose that's what happens when food waste and old milk cartons bake in the sun for too long, but it doesn't change the fact that it's gross.

I turn on my heel, about to head back inside, when I grow still.

"Camryn…"

Spinning around, I search the tall oak and fir trees for the source of the whisper. Overhead, the branches sway in the mild breeze.

Another string of hushed whispers raises the hairs on my neck, their ancient notes seducing me as they wrap around my heart, pulling me closer.

When I near the tree line, the buzz of flies inside the trash can fades into the distance, and I'm pulled forward by disembodied, hushed voices in the breeze—voices that know my name and seem to grab at my clothes and hair.

A sudden silence swallows me whole as I disappear into the trees. Not even the breaking twigs beneath my rubber sole disturb it.

The air is still, too. Not a trembling leaf rustles. Not a bird tweets.

I turn to look behind me and gulp down a breath. I'm no longer near the yard's edge, and the looming estate is no longer visible through the branches. No, I'm deep in the woods, so far that I've lost track of where I am.

"Camryn!"

Panicked, I spin around and almost stumble over an exposed root. A squirrel darts up a tree branch beside me, and mushy leaves get crushed beneath my shoes as I take another step back. Something is wrong with these woods. Something has lured me here to feed on my fear, and not for the first time. I don't know how I know, but I do.

It feeds on every thudding heartbeat and spike of anxiety while watching me from behind thick trunks and beneath the carpet of pines and decomposing leaves. It's in the heavy air and all around, dancing over my exposed skin with the next vagrant breeze. Curious, it travels up my arms, searching, hunting, and testing me.

"Camryn."

I fall back against the soft moss with a startled cry, my heart pounding. Overhead, a raven breaks through the canopy of greens. Its eerily haunting caw cuts through the thick, heavy silence before the last note fades into nothingness.

I turn over on my front, but before I can climb to my feet, a strong hand encircles my arm and pulls me up. Surprised, I lock eyes with the man from the woods, the same man I spotted in the café the other day.

"Are you okay?"

It seems I've lost my ability to talk, because I say nothing. Just gawk at him.

When the silence stretches on, he lets go of my shoulders and rubs his neck, but then he seems to remember his unbuttoned shirt, and I watch his long fingers deftly do up the buttons.

"I'm sorry if I startled you?"

"It's okay," I reply shakily.

His fingers pause, but I still don't lift my gaze, unable to look away from his scarred knuckles and veiny hands. They're a working man's hands.

He finishes the last two buttons, hiding that firm chest from view, but not before I catch the silvery scars.

"These woods are dangerous," he says, as though he's tired or fed up. "If you get lost, you might never find your way back."

"What do you know of the woods?" I ask.

He studies me with his forest-green eyes. "I know people have got terribly lost in these woods, ma'am."

I blink.

"What made you venture this far out?" he asks, keeping a respectable distance. The low rumble of his voice reminds me of a summer storm.

"I didn't," I respond, then realize how stupid that sounds, considering that we're miles into the woods, but I can't tell him I have no recollection of walking this far.

His throat jumps when another mild breeze moves the branches overhead, and he jerks his head to the left and says, "Come on. Let's get you back."

We walk in silence. I'm dying to ask questions, but my tongue feels too thick for my mouth, and all I can focus on are his muscular legs in those denim jeans.

"Are you not warm?" I blurt.

He glances at me over his shoulder and shrugs. "I'm used to it."

"I saw you…" I say, surprised by my sudden eagerness to engage in conversation. "The other day, I mean… You were chopping wood. Do you live around here?"

"Do you make a habit of sneaking around in the woods?" he asks, dodging my question.

My eyebrows pull down low as I step over a fallen branch. "It's not private land, is it? You won't shoot me with a shotgun or anything?"

"If I tell you yes, will you stay out of the woods?"

"Unlikely," I reply as he holds a branch out of the way.

I like the way he follows me with his eyes. It's not sexual, but it's not void of interest, either. He is intrigued and trying to figure me out.

"I didn't have a choice… The whispers—" My mouth snaps shut. No, I refuse to sound insane when I've barely known him for less than five minutes.

He lets go of the branch and falls into step beside me. We continue in companionable silence, lost in our thoughts.

Sounds slowly filter back in—birds tweeting, twigs snapping underfoot, and a rolling of thunder overhead.

"Will you believe me if I tell you weird things happen in these woods and that you should stay out for your own good?"

I glance at him, taking in his dark hair, forest eyes, and the set line of his lips. He has an air of mystique about him, and I can't help but feel drawn in by it. I don't think I would want to fight the pull, given the choice.

"You walk these woods…" I leave the words hanging, hoping he'll offer me his name.

He inclines his head and says, in a humorous tone, "I know

these woods like the back of my hand." His voice lowers. "You don't."

We step through the tree line, and the large estate greets us as it rises into the clouds, thick ivy crawling across the bricks.

Looking back at the stranger, I hike a thumb over my shoulder. "Would you like to come inside for a glass of water?" When he fails to answer, I tuck my hair behind my ear. "We have iced tea, if you prefer—"

"Camryn!" a hard voice calls out behind me.

I turn to see Dominic striding toward us with a murderous expression and clenched hands. He stops beside me and narrows his eyes on the mysterious man at my side. "Who are you?"

"Dominic," I hiss, cheeks heating. "Don't be rude. I got lost in the woods, and he helped me find my way back."

Dominic's blazing eyes land on my face. "The woods?" Fury radiates off him with every sharp inhale. "The fucking woods? What have I said about you entering the woods?"

"I told her the same—"

"Walk away! You're not welcome here." Dominic pulls me behind him. "If I see you near my sister again, I'll make you regret it, understood?"

"Dominic!" I shove his unmoving back, the muscles rippling beneath his sweat-stained T-shirt as he holds me back with his arm. The infuriating man is a behemoth with anger issues. I fucking hate him.

"Walk!" His voice brokers no argument.

The stranger's footsteps retreat, but Dominic doesn't relax until he is out of sight; only then does he inhale a deep breath before spinning around and pinning me with his glare.

I flip him off and then stride toward the house, kicking up the dried grass. Fuck him for telling me what to do and for threatening the man who helped me find my way back.

I've barely made it two steps before Dominic spins me around. "I told you not to enter the woods."

47

"What I do is none of your business." I wrench free and level him with a glare that would set him on fire if this was a cartoon.

"You're my sister—"

"Don't!" I hiss, poking his chest. "We both know you're not. So don't go using the brother card whenever it suits you. I'm nothing to you, remember? Those were your words before we moved here."

Shoving my finger away, he steps into me. "Sis." He drawls the word with a sneer that borders on a toxic smirk. "I'm an asshole with no regard for secular morals, remember? Those were your words. So what makes you think I give a flying fuck about your opinion? Let's get one thing straight—"

When I glance around, distracted, he grabs my chin and pulls me back. I bat him off. "Listen."

Confused, he looks up and scans the yard and the tree line. Chills erupt over my skin as the wind moves my hair around my shoulders.

"The silence..."

"The silence?" His throat jumps and he slowly turns beside me.

"The crickets stopped chirping," I point out, inching closer to the house and glancing toward the trees as thunder sounds again in the distance.

When I look up at the darkening clouds, a sense of foreboding and an urgency to run grabs hold of me.

Something bad is about to happen.

I reach for Dominic's arm. "Please, can we go inside?"

Surprised, he looks down at my hand on his skin and nods. "Let's go back."

I turn to leave when a breeze sweeps over my shoulder, like a cold breath. My fingers fall away from Dominic's arm as a shudder runs through me. But I don't turn around to look at him, not now when the sky is almost black and the wind whips my hair around my face.

Every instinct warns me to run for safety.

Whatever is behind me—stroking my hair away from my shoulder—is evil, toying with me like a cat with a mouse.

Dominic's usually warm fingers feel cold to the touch.

"I do find his attraction to you delicious." He steps closer, his T-shirt grazing my back. My lashes flutter as I hold my breath. "The human doesn't want to feel this way about you." His low chuckle drifts closer to my ear. "He fights it."

His fingers drift down my arm in a slow path toward my wrist, and he smiles against my ear before whispering, "He knows…"

No…

Panic threatens to drag me under, and I run blindly toward the doors, stumbling up the porch steps. Once inside, I slam the door shut and lock it. I even pull the keychain into place.

What the hell happened out there? What was that…that *thing* I felt move past me? That took hold of Dominic? Is that what it did? Took hold of him? It certainly wasn't my stepbrother who whispered those things in my ear. Why would he taunt me like that?

I press my forehead to the wood and squeeze my eyes shut.

He doesn't know.

He doesn't know—

A loud bang startles me, and I scream as I jump back.

"Camryn?" Dominic shouts on the other side, rattling the handle. He bangs again, and I yelp. More bangs follow.

Mom enters the hallway and looks between me and the door, confused. "Is that your brother?"

"Let me in, Camryn!" He bangs again, then kicks it.

Mom shoulders past me to unlock the door, but I don't wait around to see Dominic's rage or the evil glee of whatever that *thing* is as I flee upstairs to my room.

SIX

CAMRYN

"YOU CHANGED YOUR MIND?" Gwen's eyes bug out.

I called this emergency meeting at the café after school, and now we're seated on the couches at the back while the summer rain spatters on the window to our left. You'd think the rain would bring with it cooler temperatures, but no. Even the rain is warm.

"You were right all along," I reply, sinking deeper into the couch, unable to meet anyone's gaze. "Weird things happen in that house."

Gwen stares at me for a beat, but Benny lights up on the armchair. "I knew it. Tell us everything."

"Just...things."

"Things?"

I slowly nod, as the lady behind the counter bags up a slice of blueberry pie for an elderly customer. "It's hard to explain."

Without sounding crazy.

"So why did you change your mind?" Gwen asks, holding up a finger when Benny opens his mouth to talk. "Why do you want to do a séance now?"

"I guess I want...to find out if it's real or all in my head."

Gwen's gaze softens. "We'll get to the bottom of it."

"I still think it's a bad idea," Lily says on Gwen's other side, shaking her head.

"Thought you said you don't believe in the paranormal," Aron teases as he stands up and digs his wallet out of his back pocket.

"I don't, Aron." Lily rolls her eyes and crosses her arms. "I can still disagree with it."

Aron pulls out cash, puts his wallet back in his pocket, and smirks. "Sounds to me like you believe in it."

As he moves to the counter, Lily sticks out her tongue at his back. Brittany returns from the bathroom and slides between Gwen and me, forcing us to shift to the side to make room. "What did I miss?"

"Séance at Camryn's house this weekend," Benny chirps, slouched on the couch with his ankles crossed and his brown hair sticking out from beneath his black cap that's halfway down his forehead. "Let's summon the demon."

Lily sits up straight with a worried look, her gray eyes bouncing between us. "Please tell me we're not summoning this… thing."

"I'm starting to believe Aron is right," Benny drawls in a bored tone. "You do believe in demons and ghosts."

Lily glares at him.

"You don't have to come," Gwen says reassuringly. "We don't want you to be uncomfortable."

They bicker while I let my distracted thoughts drift. Maybe Lily was right that we're better off leaving it alone.

Was there even an *it*?

For all I know, I've suffered a heatstroke or, worse, a mental breakdown and imagined things that weren't there, but it seemed so real.

Sulfur still lingers on my tongue when the memory of his voice caressing my ears invades my mind, and icy chills race down my spine. Yesterday, instinct told me to run and not look back, and I listened. Do I really want to try to communicate with it? Whatever "it" is.

"So?" Aron asks as he returns with a slice of blueberry pie in a paper napkin. "Are we doing the séance or not?"

Gwen's smile grows impossibly wide. "We're doing it."

"Sweet!" He collapses in the armchair. "Looks like we're summoning a demon."

My insides coil as I watch him unfold the paper napkin and take a bite. "Maybe it's not such a good idea—"

"Thank you!" Lily exclaims. "Finally, some common sense."

Across from us, Aron speaks around a mouthful. "Ignore Miss Uptight here. It's an excellent idea—probably the best idea anyone has had all year."

Benny holds out his hand for a fist bump, and they touch knuckles.

"I'm sure you've noticed that it's not exactly a big town. Nothing exciting ever happens here."

"I don't know—" I start, but something catches my eye by the entrance—an elderly man with scraggly, silver hair, weathered skin, and a long beard.

He's staring straight at me as the bell above the door jangles, and a couple enters, briefly hiding him from view.

"Who's that?" I ask.

Gwen follows my line of sight. "That's Wilfred Miller. Your neighbor."

"Why is he staring at me?"

It unnerves me that he won't look away, those beady, grey eyes boring into me from across the café.

Aron crumples up the paper napkin, and then tosses it onto the table. "Don't worry about him. He's weird but harmless."

"Weird, how?"

"Like I said, this is a small town. Everyone knows everyone. Wilfred, on the other hand, lives alone and never talks to anyone."

"Lives alone? I ask. "I thought he had a son."

Lily frowns, but before she can add to the conversation, Aron replies, "No, it's just him. No close family."

"I've never seen him in here before," Brittany murmurs with unease in her tone.

"He hardly ever leaves his farm." Aron shrugs. "You're lucky if you see him in town once a month."

"I wish he wouldn't stare." I break eye contact and look out the window at the heavy rain bouncing off the cracked pavement.

"You're new in town," Gwen says, as if that explains everything. "You stand out."

Aron finishes off his blueberry pie while the others fall into conversation. My attention soon drifts back to the door, but the man is gone.

———

The steps unfold in front of me to reveal the gaping hole in the ceiling. I stare up at the attic when a cold draft, which should be welcoming in this heat, raises the hairs on my arms.

According to Gwen, we need an item that used to belong to one of the missing victims for the séance.

While I know it's a bad idea to dabble with the occult, I want to learn more about this place and the family members who supposedly went missing.

With that thought in mind, I suppress a shiver and retrieve the flashlight from my back pocket. When it fails to work, I smack it on my palm. It flickers but stays on. I place it between my teeth and then take hold of the creaky steps as I start to climb. My head pops through the hole, and I scan the dark space before me.

Cobwebs hang like ghostly lace in the corners of the room, and a thick layer of dust blankets every surface, untouched and forgotten.

I grab the flashlight and sweep it around the attic to reveal piled crates, one with a creepy, broken porcelain doll perched against it.

Beside the crates, a circular window barely lets any light in through the grimy, weathered glass.

I place the flashlight down and heave myself up before gazing through the hole. From up here, it looks like a long fall.

My attention is diverted when something crashes to the floor, and I scramble for the flashlight. Why are attics always cold and creepy?

I raise the flashlight and gulp.

Bats. Lots and lots of bats hang from the ceiling, asleep.

"Just great," I mutter, focusing the flashlight on a group of boxes stacked in the corner. One of them, which is made of cardboard, sags, and its contents threaten to spill out.

I climb to my feet, careful to duck so I don't disturb the sleeping bats as I step closer. The doll seems to watch me out of the corner of my eye, and the floorboards creak beneath my weight as I pause near a book beside the boxes. Crouching down, I trail my fingers over the curled, water-damaged pages before closing the book to read the title. "Devil-Worship in France, or the Question of Lucifer," I read out loud before shining the flashlight across the room. The chilling sensation of beady eyes watching me from the shadows crawls over my skin, but a sweep of the light reveals nothing except an old coat rack in the corner.

I'm unable to shake the uneasy feeling, so I scan the room again. When nothing jumps out at me, I turn back to look through the boxes but pause as the beam catches on the doll, which is now directly in front of me, propped up against the crates.

I scream and fall back onto my ass, scrambling away as the soles of my shoes slip against the dusty floorboards. My heart races, threatening to escape my chest. I direct the flashlight to the space where the doll was when I first entered the attic, but it's gone. Cold sweat dampens my neck as the flashlight trembles violently in my grip.

Slowly, I let my gaze drift back to the doll, and the tremble worsens until the light flickers.

Behind me, another crash disturbs the silence, and a rat scurries across the floor, while I let out another terrified scream. Silence settles like a heavy blanket over the room, disturbed only by the whistle of the afternoon breeze outside. The flashlight flickers, so I smack it against the palm of my hand. "Work, dammit."

Now is not a good time to freak out. Not up here with the bats and the rats. Don't get me started on the porcelain doll.

I crawl forward again, never letting my eyes move from the doll. A mop of brown, matted hair that hasn't seen a comb in decades stands in all directions, and a crack runs through its pale cheek. Its dark eyes watch me approach.

Unease twists my insides the closer I get.

Ignoring the voice in my head that warns me this is a bad idea, I pick up the doll and catch a whiff of its musty blue dress. The lace trimming at the neckline has yellowed with time, and one of the shoulder-length sleeves is ripped.

"Creepy," I mumble, then nearly jump out of my skin when Mom's voice drifts through the gap from downstairs.

"Camryn, are you up there? I heard screaming."

"Shit…" I crawl over to the opening and poke my head through. Mom stands with her arms crossed and an alarmed look on her face.

"Hi, Mom."

The expression morphs into one that's far less impressed. "What were you doing up in the attic? This is an old house. It might not be safe."

"Sorry. I was curious." After sliding the flashlight into my back pocket, I climb back down. The moment my foot touches the ground, Mom points a finger at the doll in my hand. "What is that?"

I hold it up. "A doll."

"Looks like something straight out of a horror movie. Why would you bring it down here?"

Good question. I needed something for the séance, and since I didn't have time to root through the boxes, the doll would have to make do. Mom pulls a face, then turns on her heel.

"Wait," I call out, folding the steps back into place and shutting the hatch to the attic.

Mom turns around, and I catch up.

"Did you visit Wilfred yet?"

"No, not yet. I need a gift basket."

"I wouldn't bother." A shiver that has nothing to do with the doll in my hand or the ghoulish-looking attic raises the hairs on my arms.

Mom's eyebrows knit together. "Why not? It's the polite thing to do."

"My friends from school tell me he is a loner who doesn't like people."

"All the more reason to visit him."

"Just…be careful." I kiss Mom on the cheek and return to my room. Once the door is shut, I place the doll on the dresser, staring at it as if I expect it to do something, like move or talk. When it doesn't, I back up until my calves connect with the bed.

Plopping down, I blow out a long breath. The doll stares at me, and I stare at it. I've never known silence to be so thick or so… charged.

The door flies open, and my insufferable stepbrother barges in, barely sparing a glance at the doll. "Where did you go after classes finished?"

"I met up with my friends."

He snorts. "You don't have friends."

"Is it so difficult to believe things are different here?"

As always, he sucks out the oxygen in the air when he peruses my room. I try not to stare, but keeping my eyes off his broad back is impossible, especially when he looks out the window at the trees beyond before spinning around and pinning me with his dark, blazing eyes.

"I waited for you."

"You told me to take the bus."

His jaw clenches, and with his next step, the floorboards creak beneath the sheer force of his weight. I still don't know what he wants when he used to ignore my existence. Is he suffering the ill effects of the intense heat, too, or is he unnerved because I'm no longer a wallflower? The rules have changed, and he's unsure of where I fit on his board.

At least, with the contempt in his gaze, he seems himself, unlike yesterday when I locked him out. I still don't trust that he won't flip.

"What are you doing in here?" I ask as he approaches me, one slow step at a time.

His muscles ripple while his eyes dare me to challenge him. Instead of answering, he hovers over me, his hair falling over his brow. He slides his hands into his pockets, as if to hold himself back. And then he says in a low but threatening tone, "I'm driving you home tomorrow, so I expect you to wait for me after class."

"And what if I don't?" I ask, out of sheer curiosity. Some morbid and unwelcome part of me hopes to push him that little bit further.

"You don't want me to embarrass you in front of your new friends, right?" His lips tilt in a sinful smirk, the kind of smirk that makes my breath catch and my nipples harden. "I wouldn't mind taking your precious Aron down a notch or two."

I rise to my feet, my nails digging into my palms. "Stay away from my friends."

"Little sister," he drawls, sliding his hand out of his pocket to pull a strand of my hair. "Why so tense?" The humor in his voice is undeniable. I stand my ground, refusing to be the one to look away first. He won't win this time, and I refuse to let him intimidate me anymore.

"Why do you hate me so much?" I ask.

He visibly tenses as the humor dulls in his eyes, replaced by raw fury. For the first time, I'm scared of Dominic and the darkness in his eyes. It chills me to the bone.

"You know why," he sneers, his voice deadly calm. "You're the reason my dad is gone."

"I didn't have anything to do with it. The crash wasn't my fault—"

Dominic is in my face so fast I fall back onto the bed. He grabs me by my top and hauls me off the mattress until I feel his hot breath against my lips. "Save your lies for someone who believes you." His head cocks to the side, and he says, "Like your mom." Then he drops me and storms out, leaving me to tremble on the bed with my heart thundering and my thoughts whirling.

SEVEN

CAMRYN

"I CAN'T BELIEVE we're skipping school for this." Brittany sounds delighted as she enters my house, her ponytail swaying.

I caught a lift in Gwen's car, and we drove here as soon as our first class ended. It was the only time we could have the house to ourselves. Mom is at work, and Dominic is in class. I don't trust that asshole not to barge into my room to interrupt us. There's no chance he would stay away if I brought friends home for the first time. No, he'd insist on inserting himself and ruining the night with a look of satisfaction on his smug face. Because the fucker *would* enjoy every minute of watching me squirm like a fish on a hook.

"I can't believe we convinced Lily to come along," Aron teases, his arm wrapped around her shoulder as they walk up the drive.

"Someone has to keep an eye on you all," she replies with an eye roll.

Benny walks past me with a soft chuckle. Aron and Lily enter, and I walk in behind them and close the door.

Ahead of us, Gwen makes a beeline for the kitchen with the box in her arms, putting it on the table while I remove the vase of fresh flowers.

I'm more nervous than I should be, my clogged throat making

59

breathing difficult. There's no logical reason to be this anxious. Lily said it herself: ghosts don't exist.

Right?

After placing the vase of flowers on the counter, I slowly turn around. Gwen removes the spirit board from the box and puts it on the table. "Do you have any candles?"

It takes me a few moments to realize the question is directed at me, and I root through the drawers until I find two candlesticks and their holders. Once placed on the table, Benny fishes a lighter out of his pocket and lights them up.

Gwen flicks her attention to me. "Did you bring the item?"

"I'll get it now."

Walking upstairs, I force down the insistent feeling of stepping into unknown territory. Warning bells blare inside me, but I ignore them. What's the worst that could happen? Ghosts don't exist. And if they do, what can an entity possibly do to us? They don't hold any sway here in the physical realm. If something more dangerous is at play, why would it need to be called forward by a silly spirit board?

I return to the kitchen with the porcelain doll and place it next to the spirit board. Lily pales, and Gwen tilts her head as she studies it closer.

"It's...ugly."

"You mean creepy as fuck?" Brittany asks, pulling out a chair and sitting down. The others follow suit until we're seated around the table, swapping uncertain glances.

"Has anyone done this before?" I ask.

Gwen shakes her head. "I guess we link hands and invite it in?"

"Invite what in?" Lily looks alarmed, her eyes wide and jaw slack. "We're not encouraging it, are we?"

"Relax," Benny drawls, adjusting his cap so it sits backward, strands of brown hair sticking out behind his ears. "Ghosts don't exist, remember?"

"Yeah? You obviously believe they do, or we wouldn't be here, doing something this…this reckless."

Laughing under his breath, Benny shakes his head. "Take a deep breath so that you don't pop an artery or something from all the undue stress."

Gwen takes my hand and then holds hers out for Lily, who reluctantly accepts it with a glance in my direction.

When we're all holding hands, Gwen lowers her voice as a strand of green hair slides from behind her ear. "Let's close our eyes and empty our minds."

"Empty our minds?" Benny sounds stupefied.

"Just…think of nothing."

Brittany bursts out laughing, the sound sudden and piercing. "I'll be surprised if Benny ever has a single thought in his thick skull."

"Rude!" Benny scowls. "I think sometimes."

"Sure." Brittany winks.

Gwen demands their attention. "We're wasting time. Let's close our eyes and keep our minds quiet and receptive."

My eyes shut, and I tighten my grip on Gwen's and Aron's hands. Silence settles over the room as the seconds tick by. Someone coughs—a girl, by the sound of it—and my brow furrows. I try to clear my mind, but it races, jumping from thought to thought like clouds in the sky.

"Are we ready?" Gwen asks beside me, releasing my hand. "Let's each put a finger on the skull dial."

I blink my eyes open and place my finger on the cool surface, swallowing down the nerves churning my stomach. Lily looks almost green as she hesitantly follows suit.

"Okay," Gwen breathes, glancing at us all, back to business. "Keep your finger lightly on the dial. Don't try to manipulate it in any way. We take turns asking questions. No one cheats, understood?"

I stare at the letters on the board, wondering if I should stop this before it's too late. We can still back out.

Something—call it intuition, if you will—tells me I should. I'd regret it if I don't speak up now, but one glimpse at the doll with its empty eyes steels my resolve. We're doing this. I need to learn more about this place and the weird things that have happened to me in the few weeks I've been here.

"Who wants to go first?" Gwen asks.

When no one replies, she looks between us, sets her jaw, and scowls down at the dial in concentration. "We wish to communicate with the spirit that haunts this property."

We wait in tense anticipation, hoping—no, *expecting*—something to happen. The seconds tick by, accentuated by the thudding heartbeat in my ears. Seconds that seem to stretch into eternity. The tips of my ears burn. I feel foolish.

It was my idea to skip class to play a silly board game.

"We welcome you, spirit, to our circle."

"No," Lily hisses, but Gwen ignores her pleas.

"Is there anyone here with us?"

"This is stupid," Benny mutters under his breath, causing the burn in my ears to spread to my cheeks.

"We are your earthly vessel, and we welcome you—"

"Earthly vessel," chuckles Benny.

Clouds suffocate the sun outside, and the light in the room darkens significantly, but the sudden change in weather isn't why Aron's grip on my hand tightens or why Gwen trembles.

Eyes wide, I stare at the smoke swirling from the wick.

"Did that...blow out?" Benny asks in a voice thick with apprehension and an undercurrent of disbelief and...excitement.

"It did," Aron confirms.

"It could have been a coincidence."

"Probably," Aron responds, but his grip on my hand remains tight, his palm clammy.

"Please tell me someone blew it out," Lily says uncertainly while I watch the smoke swirl and disperse.

"Ask it another question," Brittany suggests, eyes alight with the thrill.

Gwen looks unsure for the first time, her throat jumping. "Okay…"

The flame flickers back to life, taking us all by surprise. Lily even releases a startled scream.

"What's happening?" I ask as the flame burns brighter and taller, jumping violently in a non-existent breeze.

"We're not alone," Gwen breathes.

Brittany's wide eyes glitter in the candlelight. "This is so cool."

My heart thunders behind my ribcage. Cool isn't the word I would use to describe this moment. Terrifying seems more fitting.

"Are you a spirit?" Gwen asks.

We fall silent, gazing intently at the dial.

Just like before, nothing happens. The seconds tick by while the flame continues to dance.

Just when my heart is about to sink from disappointment or relief—I'm yet to decide—the dial moves.

A gasp falls from my lips, and I glance around at the others, only to be met by equally bewildered expressions.

"Who's doing this?" Gwen asks in an accusatory tone, but Brittany shushes her and then reads out the letters.

"N…O"

"Can we stop?" Lily begs as a tear clings to her lid. "I want to leave."

"So…not a spirit." Gwen worries her lip, ignoring Lily's question. "An entity?"

The dial moves again.

Outside, thunder rumbles in the distance.

I hold my breath, whispering each letter. "S…O…M…E…T… H…I…N…G." The dial pauses, and I swallow down the saliva in my mouth. It moves again. "F…A…R—"

"Worse," Gwen finishes, her worried eyes clashing with mine. "Something far worse."

"What could be worse than an entity?" Lily asks, her voice high-pitched.

The candle flickers out, and the darkness presses in from all angles despite it being after lunch. Another rumble of thunder rolls across the stormy sky outside, and rain splatters against the window almost violently, as if the gods are punishing the house for standing after all this time.

"Are you a demon from the underworld?" Gwen asks.

Amused by the situation, Benny chuckles, but soon shuts up when the dial slides across the letters.

"Yes…" I exchange a look with Benny, whose jaw tightens. Beneath that 'Nothing Fazes Me' exterior is a guy with doubts.

"Why are you here?" Aron asks beside me, his voice a soft grumble.

As I glance at the doll with matted hair and dead eyes, the dial slides across the wood and stops on letters, as if to build anticipation.

A lightning flash illuminates the crack in the porcelain, and a roll of thunder follows, like a bowling ball heading straight for the pins.

I quickly look away, but I can't shake the feeling that it's watching me, which is ridiculous. It's a spooky doll—a forgotten toy. Nothing more.

"To feed on chaos." Benny frowns. "What chaos?"

The dial moves again, and Benny visibly stiffens. "I didn't mean that as a question."

"Well," Brittany whispers around a thick swallow, "it wants to respond."

"D…E…A…T…H." I meet Benny's eyes again. "Death."

The tension in the air thickens until it's hard to speak. I'm still locked in Benny's gaze when Aron blows out a breath that seems loud in the reigning silence. "What do we ask now?"

"Nothing," Lily answers. "We stop this now before we take it too far."

"It's too late." The next flash of lightning highlights Gwen's haunted face. "It only responded when we said we're its vessel."

"I never offered myself up as a vessel. Those were your words."

"You didn't object or stop me," Gwen points out, then freezes when the dial moves again.

"No one asked a question this time," Brittany murmurs, barely audible above the splattering rain against the window.

"It wants to communicate."

"Please make it stop," Lily whines.

It moves from letter to letter, sometimes slowly, sometimes so aggressively that we struggle to keep our finger on the dial as it shoots across the board. My heart hammers wildly. I can't think about anything except my growing dread.

"Camryn," Aron whispers, peering at me sideways. "It spelled your name."

A sudden lightning bolt right outside startles me. I rip my hand from his palm, but he grabs it and asks our mysterious guest, "What do you want with Camryn?"

I try to pull free, done with these games, but his grip remains iron-tight. Lily is crying now, and even Benny has paled.

When the dial fails to move, I yank free and shoot to my feet. "What the hell was that?"

Aron slumps and then picks up his head and stares at me over his shoulder with regret. "If the history of this place is anything to go by, you better convince your mom to pack up and leave."

"I can't do that. Where would we go? We don't have any money left." I huff a humorless laugh, looking between them all. "We can't just up and leave."

"Aron is right," Gwen says, placing her elbows on the table and dragging her hands over her face. "I thought it was all baseless rumors at first." She lifts a shoulder. "All small towns have an urban legend. I thought the demon was one. But after today…"

"We invited it," Brittany finishes for her.

"Exactly."

At a loss for words, I remain mute, looking at them all in turn. Anger and something else, something far more painful, something that pinches my chest, wells up inside me until I struggle to hold back tears. "This was your idea. You suggested a séance."

No one says a word.

Swiping at my wet cheeks, I ask, "So now what? It gets worse?"

"I don't know."

The dejection in Gwen's voice pisses me off. This was her idea. We wouldn't be in this mess if not for her careless suggestion. It was she who offered us up as vessels to an unseen deity.

I open my mouth to speak, but Lily beats me to it. "No one listened to me."

"Shut up," Benny growls, pinning his hard eyes on her. "You don't believe in the paranormal, remember? Why don't you go ahead and blame it on one of us manipulating the dial or something equally ridiculous."

Hope flares inside me, and I straighten up. No one looks at me.

"Aron," I plead, and he slowly lets his eyes drift to me. "Please tell me it's a prank. You moved the dial."

Instead of replying, he lowers his gaze, and I pin my attention on Benny next. "Was it you?"

Crossing his arms, he shakes his head.

My eyes swim with tears when I look at the others. "Anyone?"

They look anywhere but at me.

I spin around. Rivulets of rainwater race toward the bottom of the glass. It's hard to breathe, and with every inhale, my chest aches. I clench my jaw as the tears fall. "It could have been a trick of the imagination."

"Maybe," Aron replies, though I know he's only agreeing to placate me.

"We need to find out more about the previous inhabitants." I turn back around, desperation heightening my tone. "We need to find out what happened to the previous family. They can't just have disappeared without a trace."

Lily sniffs. "Nothing is going to happen, right? People play the spirit board all the time without anything happening." Her eyes light up, and she clasps Gwen's elbow. "You found this at the local toy shop. It's not like these games would be readily available if people died playing them. I bet we would discover reasonable explanations for why the dial moved if we googled the science behind it all. It must have been a subconscious thing."

I nod along. "You're right."

"Let's hope so," Gwen says, scooting her chair back and standing up. She reaches for her bag on the floor and offers me a small smile. "Emotions were running high, and we got carried away." Walking up to me, she wraps an arm around my shoulder. "Don't worry about it, Camryn—"

We both look up when the front door slams shut. My step-brother's voice echoes through the house. "Camryn!"

Heavy footsteps sound in the hallway. Then he's there, looming in the doorway and taking in the somber atmosphere. His gaze falls on the spirit board on the table, and he stiffens. "What the fuck have you done?"

EIGHT

CAMRYN

DOMINIC STALKS deeper into the room. "You skipped class for... this?"

Rocking back on her heels with an apologetic look on her face, Gwen clears her throat. "We better get going. See you tomorrow, Camryn."

Thunder rumbles in the distance as they leave in a somber line. Dominic keeps his eyes on me, deliberately unnerving me. The moment the front door shuts, he walks up to the table and grabs the doll. "What the hell is this?"

"It's nothing," I reply. "Why are you home early anyway?"

"I bought a beat-up truck."

"A truck? Why?"

He shakes his head. "Don't change the subject, and don't lie to me. What the hell is it?"

"I found it in the attic."

"You found a creepy doll in the attic?"

My throat jumps and I look past him to the kitchen entryway, unable to meet his gaze. "We needed something that belonged to one of the family members who lived in this house before us."

Dominic's eyes flick to the table as if he only just remembered the reason for his anger, and a look of confusion crosses his features. "Why were you doing this?"

"I told you…" I try to steady my voice, when another flash of lightning streaks across the sky through the window. "Weird things are happening in this house."

His jaw clenches once, then twice. He puts his hands on his hips and trains his eyes on me. The anger from earlier is gone, replaced by something softer, something I haven't seen before. I'm not sure how it makes me feel, and when he looks at me, my heart thuds hard against my ribs. I struggle to swallow.

It's a swift, visceral reaction that's not entirely welcome, yet, at the same time, intriguing. I move closer, pulled forward by some magnetic force, much like the storm clouds overhead.

"What weird things?" he asks.

"You wouldn't believe me if I told you."

"You're probably right."

"Then why ask?" I stop in front of him, staring at the broad expanse of his chest inside that T-shirt. His minty breath fans my nose as he stares down at me, but I don't look up.

"What happened the other day? Why did you lock me out?"

"I don't know what happened," I answer truthfully.

My eyes drift past his collarbones, tanned neck, and scruffy jaw. His lips thin and he works a muscle in his cheek, but it's his dark eyes that hook me.

"I'm seeing things," I finally admit on a breath.

"You're seeing things?" He grabs hold of my wrist and brings my arm up. It has healed with no sight of the insect bite. "This?"

I nod, keeping my gaze averted. "There's something in my room at night, too."

Outside, the storm clouds darken as if Dominic commands the weather. "What's in your room?"

"I don't know." I fall silent as thunder claps against the window. "Bruno sat by my bed and growled at the corner, almost as if trying to protect me against something…unseen."

Dominic watches me while the rain comes down heavier

outside. The earthy scent is rich in the air despite the closed window. When he shifts closer, it dawns on me that it's him. His damp clothes smell of the forest, with its secrets and whispers.

"So why the spirit board? What were you trying to do?"

"I wanted answers," I murmur.

"Answers," he repeats, sweeping his eyes over my face as if hunting for clues to an unsolved riddle.

"Yes..." I flinch at another clap of thunder. "Does this mean that you...believe me?"

Instead of answering, he hands me the doll. "Don't bring that Aron guy here again."

"Aron?" My eyebrows knit when he walks past me, his bicep brushing against my shoulder. "That's all you have to say? *Don't let Aron come around again?*"

He turns in the doorway, and I almost flinch when I see the hard look in his eyes. "Don't let me see him here again."

Why am I such a nosy person who can't leave things alone? One of these days, my own curiosity will get me into a lot of trouble.

While the afternoon sun beats down on me like we didn't have a storm mere hours earlier, and the tall, dry grass tickles my bare ankles, I walk the perimeter of the barbed-wire fence. Beyond it, nestled amongst tall fir trees, is a weathered ranch house with peeling white paint and a wide deck. A rusty tractor sits in the shade beside an old silver Volvo.

I glance back at the house as a bead of sweat trails down my temple. The heat in this godforsaken town shows no sign of easing up.

"Your brother looked angry," Gwen's disembodied voice sounds in my ear, and I stiffen.

I forgot she was on the phone.

"He's not my brother." I crouch down, white knuckling the phone when the door swings open.

"Why are you whispering?"

"I'm not," I whisper.

Dressed in mucky denim overalls over a plain T-shirt, Wilfred walks to his car with a shotgun in his hand.

"You're so whispering! Don't deny it. Wait… Don't tell me you're on some secret spy mission and failed to invite me?"

Wilfred opens the driver's door, tosses the shotgun onto the passenger seat, and gets behind the wheel.

A cloud of exhaust fumes fills the air, and I duck down as he reverses out before spinning the car around and driving down the dirt road, stopping to open the fenced gate.

"Is it normal to carry a shotgun around here?" I ask, waiting for the sputtering car to disappear from sight.

"What kind of a question is that? Wait a minute… Where are you?"

I rise back up, then continue skirting the property's perimeter until I come to a gap in the fence that's large enough for me to sneak through.

"Camryn," Gwen says with a hint of a warning in her tone. "Where are you?"

"Wilfred Miller's farm," I admit as my top catches in the fence.

"Wilfred's farm… Are you crazy?"

"He's harmless, remember?" I investigate the torn fabric just below my breasts, wiggling a finger inside the hole.

"Those were Aron's words. Not mine. Wilfred Miller is creepy as hell if you ask me."

"Well, he's gone anyway. Drove off in the car."

"So…I should expect the worst if I don't hear from you again?"

I dash across the overgrown yard, past a chicken coop, then slow to a halt as I approach the run-down porch. A buzzing bee collects nectar from a bright yellow sunflower swaying in front of a stack of tires, but that's the only spot of color in this eerie place.

Outside the door sits a tied-up trash bag, with flies buzzing all around. The windows are covered in heavy curtains, blocking out the daylight.

"Camryn?" Gwen's worried voice assaults my eardrum.

"I have to go." I hang up before she can say anything else, then pocket my phone. Stepping onto the decking, I try the door, but it's locked.

So, he's a safety-cautious man who takes precautions. Interesting—unless he's hiding something.

My gaze lands on the trash bag, and I pause. My palms are damp with sweat, so I rub them on my shorts as I scan the yard. The logical thing would be to turn around and walk back home, but my curiosity won't let this go until I've investigated.

I crouch down, carefully untying the bag, then wipe the sweat off my forehead with my arm. The foul smell hits me first, and my stomach turns at the stench.

When it finally opens, a swarm of flies exits, and I release a squeal as I fall back onto my ass. My heart pounds as I watch them disperse into the air until I'm once again left with the distant sound of clucking hens in the background. I crawl closer, shifting the plastic aside to reveal matted, bloodied fur. "What the fuck?" I breathe, the bag crinkling in the summer heat.

"Looks like a cat."

I startle and release a scream.

"Sorry, didn't mean to scare you," the mysterious man who walked me home from the forest—the axe-wielding man—says as he holds out his hand for me to take.

Propped on my elbows, I stare at his long fingers and open palm, then him. I swallow any concern and clasp his hand.

He hauls me up with no effort at all until I'm pressed against his chest. His scent is everywhere—mysterious, like the wilderness.

"Do you always go places you shouldn't?" he asks.

"I'm prone to putting myself in less than stellar situations."

"You don't say." He looks down at me, a slight frown creasing his brow. But then he seems to shake himself off and steps back. "You shouldn't be out here."

"Why not?" I ask, watching him closely.

"Besides the fact that it's private property? You could get lost."

"I won't get lost," I say as he steps off the decking.

"I told you." He gazes at me over his shoulder. "These woods aren't safe."

A slight breeze rustles through the trees, bringing with it the nauseating scent of decomposing flesh. My stomach rolls again, so I join him beside the stacked tires. "Why do you speak in riddles?"

His eyes glitter in the summer sun as he looks down at me, a smirk playing at the corner of his lips for the briefest second before he peers back out at the forest.

As much as it intrigues me, his silence grates on my nerves. I want to find out more about him. "What's your name?"

No answer.

"Do you live here?"

"Come on," he says, ignoring my questions. "Let's take you back."

His long legs eat up the overgrown grass as he stalks toward the fence. Once there, he holds it out of the way and jerks his chin in an unspoken demand to follow him.

I peer behind me at the tall house rising from the ground, with its heavy, moth-eaten curtains covering the large windows. Beside the door, the plastic bag crinkles in the breeze as a handful of flies hovers. The uneasy sensation of eyes on me crawls over my skin like ants, and my feet move before I realize it.

Crossing the lawn, I slip through the opening in the fence, careful not to brush up against him. My top goes unscathed this time.

"Thank you," I say as the fence squeaks behind me. "Now, are you going to tell me why you speak in riddles—" I turn around and pause.

He's gone.

I spin in a circle as I peer all around, but there's no sign of him. He was here one minute, helping me through, and then what? Did he disappear into thin air?

With a huff, I cross my arms. I'm not *that* bad to be around. He didn't have to run off the first chance he got.

Despite my brain telling me not to take it personally, my ego smarts. Why does he have to be so mysterious? Maybe I wouldn't be this intrigued by him if he would just tell me his name instead of warning me away from the forest. What is so bad about the woods?

Even as the fleeting thought enters my mind, I can't stop a full-body shiver from taking hold. I glance back at the house. The trash bag is barely visible from here, and the wind whistles through the leaves like a haunted melody while the grass at my ankles tickles my sensitive skin.

I cross my arms around my midriff and scan the area again. My gaze skips over the tractor, the stack of old tires, the chicken coop, and even the trees behind the house. But there's no sign of him.

My attention snags on one of the windows upstairs, where the curtain twitches. I swear someone is watching me through the thin gap, someone who wants to stay hidden.

Swallowing past a lump in my throat, I stare at the gap until my eyes burn, the unease twisting my insides. My feet move back, one small step at a time, until my internal warning bells become too loud to ignore, and I spin around, refusing to look back.

This place, this *town*, is all wrong. There's something dormant here that can't be ignored, something that can only be felt.

Rain comes down heavily on the windshield as we drive down the dark road. Keith, my stepdad, glances at his phone on the dashboard when it rings, but he makes no move to answer Dominic's phone call. Instead, he ignores it with a swipe of his finger and eases back in his seat.

"How did it go?"

"How did what go? The ballet exam?"

He nods, and I'm impressed he remembers it was today.

"I passed," I reply with a small shrug.

Dominic's twin brother, Lewis, ignores us in the backseat while typing on his phone.

"You don't sound happy about it."

Keith has always been perceptive about things. He knows I want to quit.

"It's complicated," I reply, hoping he'll drop it.

"You know…" he starts, staring out the windshield while the wipers struggle to keep up with the heavy rain. "We've had this conversation. It's okay if you don't want to do ballet. Your mom will understand."

I study the straight line of his nose and the day-old stubble on his sharp jaw. Keith looks at me and smiles softly.

"I'm not sure." I drop my gaze to my lap. "Mom was the best ballet performer in the state at my age. She would have made it into a career if she hadn't injured her ankle."

"You're not your mom. You don't have to follow in her footsteps."

"I know, but I don't want to disappoint—" My eyes widen as I look out the window.

There's a man in the middle of the road, soaked from head to toe, with an axe in his hand. A man in a flannel shirt and jeans. A man who's staring at the approaching headlights with dark-rimmed, dead eyes.

I grab hold of Keith's arm and shout, "Look out!"

He slams the brakes, but it's too late. Screeching tires follow, and I jerk forward, held in place by the seatbelt. Just as we're about to hit the man, he disperses like fine mist into thin air. Keith loses control of the car, and I scream as we careen into a murky river—

Startling awake with a cry, my heart hammers wildly. I gulp down breaths as I try to gain my bearings. It's been a long time since I had a nightmare about that night. I thought they were over, but I was wrong.

"It was just a dream," a deep, gravelly voice interrupts my

racing thoughts. I stiffen, only now noticing the large shadow that sits on the floor by my bed.

Dominic scratches Bruno behind the ears, his eyes locked on the closed door. "Go back to sleep."

Surprised, I blink, but he's still there, draped in shadows. "Dominic?" I ask, sitting up in bed and staring at the back of his head. "Why are you in my room?"

The seconds tick by while I wait for his response. Seconds that stretch into minutes before his deep tenor disturbs the silence. "You said someone comes into your room at night."

My heart stalls. I'm sure of it. "Not someone," I whisper. "Something."

He hums, petting Bruno, and then he drawls, "Go back to sleep."

"I can't just go back to sleep with you in here," I say as I switch on the lamp on my nightstand.

"Don't," Dominic orders, leaving no room for argument. "Leave it off."

"So what's this? Are you my knight in shining armor now?"

"Careful," he warns. "You don't want to test me."

"Or you'll do what? Spank me?" I don't know where this spark of attitude is coming from. I'm secretly relieved he's in my room, especially after my nightmare. My nerves are shot, but I'll never admit that to him.

"If that's what it takes," he says with a dark undertone that makes my stomach swoop.

I stare at the back of his head, unsure of my next move. Logically, I should tell him to leave and shove him out of my room, but I don't want to be alone. His presence makes me feel safe, even if he hates me.

"Why are you protecting me, Dominic?" I ask quietly while my heart thumps harder.

"Go to sleep."

NINE

DOMINIC

Sleep descends from the corners of the room, and my eyes droop. I quickly jerk my head up and rub my eyeballs with the heels of my palms.

I've spent four nights in Camryn's room while she slept. For four nights, I've sat here, guarding her like I'm some prince in a fairy tale. It's pathetic. *I'm* pathetic. Why am I here? Must be some twisted voodoo shit on her end, because I find myself back here every night, listening to her breathe. But fuck, it's getting difficult to stay awake.

"Good boy. Stay here," I tell Bruno, scratching him behind the ear before rising to my feet and stretching my arms overhead. I'm thirsty as hell.

I peer at Camryn, whose long, pale leg peeks out from beneath the quilt. She looks peaceful when she sleeps.

Drawn closer like a magnet, I brush a strand of hair away from her face, careful not to wake her. Her skin reminds me of fragile porcelain—so smooth it should be illegal.

I trail my finger lower, pausing at the corner of her mouth, my heart thudding in the ensuing silence.

Her soft lips part, and I know I should walk away. This temptation, this *urge,* is not welcome. But I trace her lips like a druggie that says, *Just one hit, and then I'll stop.*

"Fuck me," I breathe as her next warm exhale fans my skin. This is torture.

It's official: I'm a masochist. I don't even like Camryn. If it weren't for her, my father and brother would be alive. They weren't even supposed to collect her from the studio that day. Her mom was.

Slowly easing my middle finger inside, I slide it over her wet tongue, and my cock hardens as I fill her mouth with my ring finger, too.

"Have you ever sucked dick, little sister?" I whisper, fucking her sweet mouth with my fingers in time with the insistent throb in my cock. My balls ache with the need to dump my load inside one of her tight holes. I'm not picky.

Besides, I can go back to resenting her tomorrow and hating what my life has turned into because of that night. I wouldn't be stuck in this forsaken town in the middle of nowhere if it weren't for this little vixen with her seductive lips—

"Dominic!" a feminine voice whispers from behind me, and I spin around in time to see the door slide shut with a soft click.

Bruno growls, his body tense and quivering. With my heart now clear in my throat, I glance at Camryn, who whimpers softly in her sleep.

A peal of feminine, haunting laughter travels through the thin walls as I exit the room, ordering Bruno to stay.

Nothing happens when I try the light switch, which is fucking typical. Nothing ever works when I need it to.

A sense of dread has wormed its way beneath my skin, so I shake it off and set off down the hallway. It's a clammy night, and the intense heat lingers despite the thunderstorm earlier in the day. My T-shirt sticks to the sweat between my shoulder blades.

Up ahead, something dashes across the hallway in a flurry of long hair and a flowy skirt. I come to an abrupt halt, my heart pounding. What the hell was that? A child?

"Dominic!" Another peal of laughter disturbs the thick silence, this time from downstairs. I slowly step forward, straining to see in the darkness.

The hallway seems to stretch on for miles.

When I finally reach the stairs, I grab hold of the railing and begin my descent into the thick void below, which gapes like an open mouth.

The wood creaks beneath my weight, and the temperature drops with every step. I hold my breath as goosebumps raise the hairs on my arms. Why is it so cold down here? How is it even possible?

"Dominic," a woman's voice sing-songs like a twisted lullaby designed to lure me closer. "I'm in the kitchen."

As I step onto the landing, my shadow falls on the silvery strip of moonlight on the floor. "Who's down here?"

The entrance to the kitchen opens up like another hungry mouth, much like the stairs.

"Dominic…" The ethereal voice is everywhere: in the walls, the floor, and the roof. It's in the moonlight illuminating the floorboards and within the frantic beat of my heart.

I walk closer to the yawning doorway, closer to the chill in the air and the sense of foreboding.

My shoulder brushes up against the doorframe, and I pause before I can step over the threshold. A woman stands by the sink with her back to me, dressed in an obsidian dress with a high lace collar. Her dark hair is tied up in a severe bun, revealing her pale neck, and a white apron breaks up the inky black. She's beautiful in a regal way, breathtaking yet ghostly.

She slowly turns around to face me, the candle in her hand flickering and casting shadows across her features. "You came, Dominic." Her sharp eyes swim with blackness as I enter the room. "I've waited for you."

"Dominic," a child's voice taunts behind me.

I turn around to see the girl from upstairs hovering in the

doorway with a doll clutched in her arms and tattered ribbons in her raven hair. I remember that doll from somewhere.

I sway as I shake my head to clear the haze clinging to me like a foggy mist.

"Run along now," the woman tells the child, her voice washing over me like a warming drug.

Something is very fucking wrong.

Turning around, I frown when my stepsister drops to her knees in front of me, dressed in her little sleep shorts and tank top. "Camryn?" I ask, confused. "When did you wake up?"

Instead of answering, she lowers my joggers and strokes my hardening cock. I lose my train of thought when she peers up at me with those big eyes. Beside her on the floor, a candle dances wildly in its holder.

"What a big cock you have." She takes me in her enticing mouth and gives it a hard, long suck before releasing me with a pop and gazing up at me with a mischievous smile. "First, I tasted your daddy's, but it was too big. Then I tasted your brother's, but it was too small. And then I tasted yours, which was neither too big nor small." Her voice distorts, taking on a frightening quality as her grip on my dick tightens. "It's just right."

Nausea swirls in my stomach, but I can't move, frozen by morphing fear and pleasure.

The candle flares brighter and flickers over her sharp features, revealing her blown pupils. She drags her tongue up the hard length of my dick, tracing a blue, angry vein. "I like it so much, I'm going to eat it all up."

With a final flick, a small tease, she takes me into her mouth before my sluggish brain can register the sinister edge behind her words. She hums around my dick and sucks me deeper.

"Jesus fuck," I grunt as my fingers get lost in her locks. I have never once experienced anything like it. She deep-throats me like she was born to suck my dick, her tight throat strangling my length. But what makes me lose my damn mind, what finally pushes me over the edge, is the way she digs her nails into my balls.

Pain erupts, and I barely restrain a chest-deep groan as her head bobs in my hands with enough enthusiasm that I have to plant my feet to keep my balance.

She releases me and grips my balls in a tight, fierce grip that borders on a threat. "Give me your fucking cum, *brother*. I want it all over my face."

I can barely breathe, my fingers tangled in her locks, while she jacks my dick like she's on a mission to milk me dry. I'm convinced of it.

"This is what you've always dreamed of, isn't it? Me on my knees, at your mercy, like a good little whore? Yes, I can see your thoughts. Every deviant, delicious desire."

Another twist of my balls, and I jerk.

"That's it, *brother*. Come on my face. Paint me like a dirty slut."

I erupt.

Strings of cum rain over her face as I choke on my own saliva. She sticks her tongue out and tries to catch it before smiling wickedly. When she looks at me, cum is beading on her lashes and dripping down her face.

"Now," she whispers, still stroking my sensitive cock as she leans in, "it's time to die."

I stiffen at the sound of playful giggles behind me, just as a sharp pain erupts across my lower back. Glancing behind me, I see the little girl smiling up at me with a letter opener in her hand that's covered in blood.

She jabs me again, sinking the blade deep, this time in my side. I grunt as I stumble back, blood pouring from between my fingers like a river of crimson—so dark it almost looks black.

Losing my balance, I fall to the floor. She comes for me with her doll gripped in one hand and the letter opener in the other. Then she's on me, sinking the blade deep into my eyeball.

I jerk awake. Bruno lifts his head, whimpering, before licking the side of my face. Still groggy from the nightmare, I pat my waist to ensure I'm uninjured, then scan the dark bedroom. Camryn is asleep on her front with her arms beneath the pillow and the quilt pooled around her waist.

"Jesus," I breathe, rubbing my tired eyes. What the hell was that nightmare? I'm fucking losing it.

Bruno nudges my arm with his damp nuzzle. Rubbing his scruff, I gaze back at the door. Something catches my eye that wasn't there before. "What. The. Fuck?" I whisper, unfolding and rising to my feet.

There, propped up against the door, is the doll.

TEN

CAMRYN

His long legs stretch across the floor as sunlight pours over his slumped body. I shouldn't like the sight of him asleep against my bed, but I do. I like it so much it's starting to worry me. Bruno has his head on his lap, as if he, too, stayed up all night to guard me against some unseen force. My heart swells at the sight. I scoot up in bed, careful not to wake them. How many nights has this gone on for now? I've lost count. Dominic is an enigma—a puzzle I can't solve. He hates me, but he can't seem to leave me alone.

The quilt pools around my waist as I slowly crawl forward to kneel behind him. His hair looks soft. I've oftentimes wondered what it feels like.

I carefully sift my fingers through the raven strands and then lower until I brush up against his nape. His warm skin erupts in goose bumps as I slowly let my touch travel over each vertebra, gliding my finger across his black collar, mesmerized by the slow rise and fall of his shoulders.

A crow caws outside, and the sudden sound steals my attention. Distracted, I look away from Dominic's neck, then gasp when he strikes.

He curls his warm fingers around my wrist and climbs onto

the bed, forcing me to fall onto my back. The mattress dips beneath his weight as I gaze up at his severe face, noting the barely restrained anger bubbling beneath the surface and the subtle twitch of his jaw.

Dominic seizes my other arm, trapping both my wrists above my head with one hand, his grip pinching my skin and eliciting a sting of pain. This is the first time I've seen Dominic above me, and what a devastating sight it is to behold. My fragile heart will never recover from seeing the strands of his inky hair fall over his heated eyes and the glimpse I catch of his chest from inside his T-shirt's collar.

"What the hell are you doing touching me?" Each word slithers over my skin, delivered with enough venom to make me squirm.

My lips part on a whimper. His dark eyes flick down to my mouth and linger for a hauntingly long second before he grips my chin and digs his fingers into my cheeks. "Don't ever touch me without my permission, understood?"

My thighs clench, painfully aroused by the feel of his weight. I try to nod, but his ruthless grip prevents me from moving. I'm truly at his mercy, and he knows it.

As if to provoke me, he rolls his hips, a treacherous moan threatening to give me away when his hard length presses against me. Fuck. I like this untamed side of him.

"I always knew you were a whore," he sneers, eyes heated with putrid hatred and unbridled lust as toxic as the sparks of desire between my legs. "Look at you, squirming for my cock. You think I want to fuck your tight cunt?" A wicked chuckle raises the hairs on my arms. He flips me over, grabs the back of my neck, and shoves my head into the pillow until I can't breathe. Then he yanks down my sleep shorts and smacks my bare ass.

Surprised, I yelp at the sudden sting. But the sharp pain has nothing on the humiliation coursing through me when he drags two thick fingers through my arousal.

"Your pathetic cunt is the last one on earth I want to fuck."

A cry rips from my lips when he rams two fingers deep inside my back hole without warning.

"This tight ass, however." His smoky voice drifts over my ear. Shocked and turned on beyond rationale, I struggle to breathe as another cruel chuckle drowns out my gasps. He pulls his fingers out, only to thrust back in as the pillow slowly suffocates me. "I'll tear through it with my cock while you cry for me to stop."

The moan I barely held back earlier returns with a vengeance, ripping from my lips. There's nothing I can do to stop it. More embarrassing sounds follow. I have no shame. I'm a whore for the pain he's dishing out like cotton candy at a carnival.

"But we both know 'stop' really means 'more,' doesn't it? Your pussy weeps for me."

My ass is on fire. He moves on top of me, grinding his big cock against the back of my thigh in time with his fingers. My pussy clenches around nothing, creaming and making a mess of his jeans.

"Touch me again, Sis, and I'll stuff this ass with cum and make you suck my dick clean."

I gasp as he wrenches himself free, walks out, and slams the door so firmly that the picture frame rattles against the wall.

Oxygen rushes back into my lungs as I sit up and rub my sore neck. What the hell just happened, and why did I like it so much? Unmoving, I gulp down breaths. My sleep shorts are halfway down my sticky thighs.

Why did his punishing grip on my neck and his breathy growl turn me to putty? Sex isn't supposed to hurt. Even so, the more pain he forced on me, the higher I became, and the more I'm now craving his brand of pleasure, as twisted as it is. One thing is for sure, Dominic doesn't simply fuck—he devours. He's a deadly storm that tears through the soul like a twister and leaves nothing but rubble behind.

Reaching between my legs, I slide my fingers through my wetness. I'm soaked. Dominic wreaked havoc on my body with his expert touch.

I lie back down on my front, trying to recreate the scene from minutes earlier with my face buried in the pillow. My muffled moans ring out in the silence as I rub my clit and grind my hips. But I can't recreate his touch, no matter how deep I press my face into the damp fabric or how hard I push down on my sensitive clit. Even my best attempts lack the sensation of helplessness and the bite of pain his fingers evoked—

My thoughts come to a grinding halt when the mattress shifts behind me. I pause, barely daring to breathe. "Dominic?"

An icy chill in the air accompanies his punishing fingers. He digs them into my hips and yanks me up on my knees. Did he change his mind and return to finish what he started? My heart soars even as I fight the urge to beg him to fuck me. I need him inside me.

I try to look at him over my shoulder, but he shoves my head back into the pillow and rams his cock inside me in one go. I cry out as my pussy clamps down on his throbbing length. Fuck, he feels so damn good. Nothing could have prepared me for how big he is. I can barely fit him, but he allows me no time to adjust. He pulls back out to the tip, then thrusts back in, and delicious pain spreads like wildfire. He fucks like an animal, dirty and hard—so hard I'm unsure if he's trying to fuck me to death, but I love every second.

"Fuck, Dominic," I whimper, the sound muffled as I push back against him. My eyes roll back at the feel of his thick cock rubbing against my rippling inner walls while mindless moans and mewls escape my chest. I sound like I'm starring in a cheap porno. I'm not even embarrassed anymore. Not when he fucks me this good.

My tits bob wildly as my sensitive, pebbled nipples rub against the bed. The extra friction, combined with another hard slap on my ass, has me exploding around his dick with a scream.

I'm still floating in a sea of bliss when a distorted voice that isn't Dominic's snarls, "Such a good little whore."

I freeze and terror locks me in place as strings of cum rain over my ass and back. Spinning around, I swing my gaze around the empty room. There's no one here. Just me, my erratic heartbeat, and the fucking doll propped at the end of my bed.

As I blink at the beady eyes and the crack in the cheek, shivers slither over my skin. I skim my hand over my ass but find no semen. My skin is dry. With a gulp, I look at the doll. And then I scratch my arm, unable to shake the terror crawling under my skin. A burning, sharp pain anchors me as my jagged nails claw a path through my skin, over and over and fucking over.

I scramble forward and snatch the doll, only to realize that my shorts are halfway down my legs. With a quick tug, I pull them back up and storm out of my room, racing downstairs to toss the doll in the trash can. My heart pounds powerfully as I stare at the kitchen cupboard beneath the sink—

Something outside the window catches my eye—a mysterious man I've seen a lot recently. I watch him enter the woods with the axe on his shoulder and a determined look on his face.

Where is he going? Intrigue wins out.

I don't even think as I rush into the hallway to put on my shoes before dashing outside. The heat is pressing from all angles and my rubber soles thunder across the overgrown yard.

Silence sweeps in as I enter the trees, suffocating even the faintest sounds. It's a peaceful feeling, and I let my fingers graze the rough bark and the slimy mushrooms that grow on the trunks.

Venturing deeper into the woods, I cross a small stream of water when I hear his axe up ahead. Excitement curls my lips as I trudge forward, ducking beneath branches and moving others out of the way until I emerge into the clearing.

Where is he?

A frown mars my forehead. I scan the stacked pieces of chopped wood and the axe propped against the stump. Fragile sticks break underfoot and pinecones sink into the soft earth when I walk forward.

I stop in front of the waist-high stump and trail my fingers over the wood block on top, noting each ridge and groove. Curious, I pick up the axe, studying an interesting carved symbol on the handle as I feel its weight in my hand. It's much heavier than I thought, and I struggle to lift it over my head. When I swing it down, I miss the wood block. The blade gets lodged. It's proving even more difficult to yank it out. I try three times before it finally gives—

"I thought I told you not to wander into the woods." His heat at my back makes my breath catch. He places his big hand over mine on the handle and says, "Put one hand here and the other up here. It will improve your aim."

Barely able to breathe, feeling like I've been caught doing something I shouldn't, and loving the thrill, I let him show me how to chop correctly. I swallow down my nerves, acutely aware of how little effort he required to chop the piece in half.

"Now," he whispers in my ear, his breath teasing the curve of my neck, "what will it take for you to listen to my warning about these woods?"

I still haven't recovered from Dominic's treatment this morning. Something about this compromising position with a stranger has heat settling low in my core. I want him to bend me over the stump and fuck me with the axe's handle. Where are these thoughts coming from? I'm not this promiscuous.

"Dangers lurk in these woods, ma'am."

"That sounds like a threat," I state bravely.

He chuckles, replying, "Hear that?"

The wind moves through the canopy of shifting leaves overhead, like a haunted lullaby or a song of woes.

"Hear how it whispers?" His lips brush the shell of my ear, making me shiver. "That's when you need to run."

A whimper threatens to slip from my lips.

He wraps his hand around my throat. "When you hear its whispers travel through the rustling leaves, you run as fast as you can. You hear me? Don't look back."

My clit pulses almost painfully as my grip slips on the axe. He takes it from my hands and props it against the stump. "Good girl," he praises, straightening back up. His warm lips find my ear again, and his soft breath caresses my skin. "Now, run."

I don't hesitate. Every nerve ending in my body screams at me to flee.

So I do.

I run like my fucking life depends on it.

ELEVEN

CAMRYN

"I'm telling you, we shouldn't be here," Lily says, ever the worrier, as we look around the crowded living room. It was Brittany's idea to drag us all to a party, and now we're here, looking out of place in a stranger's home.

"They're all too drunk to pay us any attention," Gwen says, pointing at a girl in a short skirt who walks past.

Brittany sways her hips in time to the beat on her way to the kitchen. We follow behind, trying our best to go unnoticed.

Cluttered countertops greet us, with countless half-empty bottles littering the room. Plastic cups roll across the floor as we gather around the island. Benny—dressed in a black hoodie—adjusts his backward cap, then rubs his hands together in anticipation while Aron pours us each a shot. He hands them out, winking at me with a playful gleam in his eye, and downs his in one go.

I mirror him, swallowing the too-sweet liquid, which burns a path down my throat.

"That's disgusting," Lily mutters, screwing her face up.

"Really? I thought it tasted of strawberries." Brittany blows a strand of pink hair away from her lips and scans the room.

Outside, hollers ring out as the footballers take turns cannon-balling into the infinity pool.

"Why are we here again?" I ask.

Gwen rolls her eyes, then slides the bottle toward her and pours a second shot. "Our delusional friend, Benny, thinks he stands a shot with Erica, the cheer captain, remember?"

The man in question accepts her shot with a playful smile. "Now that we have survived the séance, which, let's face it, was freaky as fuck, and no crazy demon is coming after us, I have learned a thing or two about life."

"Let's hear it, then." Gwen hands me a shot, and I eye the pink liquid.

Benny tosses his back, then discards the shot glass over his shoulder. "Well, life is short. We need to seize opportunities as they come our way and go after what we want."

"Aren't you the philosophical man all of a sudden?" Brittany teases, sliding his backward cap around.

He fixes it and hands her a shot glass. "It's your turn. Don't bow out on us."

Aron's fingers ghost my lower back, and I pretend I don't notice as I lock eyes with none other than Dominic over by the staircase. A blonde girl hangs off his arm, pushing her tits against him while his eyes drill holes into my head.

Of course, he's here. Where else would he be on a Friday night?

"Give me that." I grab the bottle, pour my third shot, and swallow it down. I'll need all the liquid courage I can get to face him after he's glared daggers at me for days.

He still sleeps on my floor, though.

I level him with a glare of my own as I pour another shot.

Aron clears his throat, subtly taking the bottle from me and placing it back on the table. But he doesn't stop me from taking my fourth shot.

"Wow," Gwen says, her voice thick with amusement. "Our girl here is on a mission to get drunk."

Lily watches me warily, but I'm not in the mood for pity tonight. My feelings are all over the place. I want to kiss my stepbrother one minute, then slap him the next. Seeing him with *her*, the way she presses up against him, churns my stomach.

Soft fingers graze the exposed skin at my lower back where my tank top meets my shorts. Aron whispers in my ear, "Are you okay?"

I stare at my stepbrother in the eye. "I'm good."

I can see him tense from here, and fuck if it doesn't arouse me.

"So, about the séance," Gwen says, but Aron shakes his head.

"We agreed not to talk about it. Nothing has happened since."

Gwen looks at me, her eyes softening. "Are you sure everything is okay? That house—"

"I'm fine," I bite out, escaping Aron's featherlight touch. "I need the toilet."

Weaving through the crowds, I try to walk straight, but the room tilts on its axis. I've had too much to drink, and now everything is a blur.

I feel Dominic's hard eyes on me as I make my way up the stairs, surprised I don't trip and break my back in a spectacular fall.

When I reach the landing, a hiccup slips from my lips. I blink to clear the haze before looking left and right, the carpeted hallway stretching out on either side.

I'm screwed.

I laugh under my breath, amused by my own predicament. And then I take a left, bumping into the wall and almost knocking a picture frame off its hook. More drunken laughter bubbles up, but then a warm hand clamps down over my mouth and hauls me into the nearest bedroom.

"What the fuck do you think you're doing?" Dominic sneers as he slams me up against the door.

A surprised breath escapes me, the sound of my yelp muffled beneath his hand. There are two of him. Since when did he get another twin?

His heated exhale whooshes out of him before he hauls me away from the door and tosses me onto the bed. My body bounces, and I shriek with laughter. Dominic, however, doesn't find any of this funny.

He grabs hold of my ankle and pulls me down the mattress. Then he hooks his fingers in my shorts and slides them roughly down my legs. "Do you know how fucking angry it makes me seeing that guy, Aron, all over you, like a sniffing dog." Throwing my shorts on the floor, he slaps my thighs apart. "I'm gonna wring his fucking neck right after I make you come on my tongue."

I'm already writhing as he drops to his knees and puts my legs on his broad shoulders. Scrunching the flowery bedspread in my fists, I can't stop giggling, not at all used to alcohol.

Dominic pulls my panties aside and smacks my pussy so hard, pain bursts like pinpricks all over my sensitive folds. "Don't piss me off again, Camryn."

"But it's so much fun," I slur, reaching for his soft hair, but he slaps my fingers away and traps my wrists with one hand over my head. I sigh contentedly as he leans above me, his dark hair falling over his brow. I love him like this, devouring me with his eyes. I can't believe this is happening.

"Do you have any idea how fucking angry I am with you?"

"You're always angry."

"Shut up," he snarls, baring his incisor teeth as he releases my wrists to wrap his long fingers around my throat. "Move your hands, and I stop."

My pussy pulses at the feel of his grip on my throat—the sheer dominance in his gaze.

"You want to get drunk and be a brat, little sister? You think it's fun to play games?" He releases my throat and smacks my face with enough force behind his blow to stun me. I moan shamelessly. "You like that, huh?" His palm connects with my cheek again and he grips my chin. "This isn't a reward."

Chest heaving, I stare up at the ceiling as he bites my thigh hard enough to elicit a pained cry.

He pries my legs open with punishing fingers, and his devilish mouth descends like a tsunami, wreaking havoc on my self-control. My hips shoot off the bed, and I moan at the feel of his warm tongue sliding over my soaked pussy.

"Don't move," he growls against my clit, his lips driving me crazy. "If you come, I'll choke you with my dick until you pass out."

His tongue circles my opening, teasing just enough to leave me begging for more, and then he rams it inside me, tongue-fucking me until I can barely catch my breath.

The intense pleasure slowly builds until I'm so close to coming that I'm shaking and shivering despite my best attempts to stay off the edge.

I know he told me to stay still, but it's impossible. I'm fucking his face with my pussy and grinding my hips almost desperately as he peppers bites on my thighs, marking me with his sharp teeth. His dark eyes stay locked on mine, daring me to come, daring me to piss him off. Daring me to defy him.

A cold sweat breaks out on my skin, and just as I'm about to let go, he flips me onto my front.

He guides me onto my knees, spreading my cheeks apart with his rough fingers. Anticipation swells in my chest as a chill of cold air kisses my back hole and swollen slit. I quiver as I bury my head in the pillow. Somewhere in the back of my mind, I know I wouldn't feel this comfortable being so exposed if it weren't for the alcohol swimming through my veins.

"I'm going to fuck these holes one day," he breathes, leaning in to drag his tongue from my throbbing clit to my anus. He circles my exit, probing me with the tip, and then proceeds to rim me senseless until my eyes roll back and my thighs tremble.

"Please," I whimper, the sound muffled in the pillow. "Please, let me come."

"Did you or did you not let your friend touch you in the kitchen?"

"Touch me?" My words come out garbled as he laps up my juices with a slow swipe of his tongue before swirling it around my entrance until tears soak the pillow. I need to come. I need it so fucking bad.

"He had his hand on your back, did he not?"

My choked sob has him chuckling against my soaked cunt. "Please, Dominic."

"Are you going to drink my cum like a good whore? Choke on my dick and thank me for it?"

"Yes, p-please, just…please."

"Beg me for it."

"Please make me come. Please!"

Dominic flops me over onto my back before he stands up and unbuckles his belt to free his massive cock. He grabs hold of my arm, hauling me to my knees, then fists a handful of hair at the nape of my neck as he jerks his dick in front of my face. "You don't touch me, get it?"

Mesmerized by his veiny dick, I lick my lips. It's on the tip of my tongue to ask him why he won't let me touch him, but I lose all train of thought when a bead of precum seeps from the head.

"Get it?" His grip on my hair tightens until it hurts.

"Yes," I reply, looking up at him. He yanks me back and orders me to open my mouth. I stick my tongue out, my scalp prickling with pain while he beats his dick over my face.

"You want this? You want my dick in your pretty mouth?"

When I try to nod, his grip on my hair won't let me. The sharp bite of pain has tears pricking my eyes, but it's of the good kind.

"Let Aron touch you again, and I'll kill him. I don't give a shit how pretty you look begging for my cock, or how needy you are. No one gets to touch you except for me."

Why is it that the more he degrades me, the more aroused I get? Why do I love the vile words spilling from his mouth while he beats his dick as though he wants to rip it off? Why do I respond to this unhinged side of him?

"Tell me you want it. Tell me you want my cum."

"I want your cum, Dom."

His eyes darken at the nickname, his fingers twitching in my tangled hair.

"Can I taste your cock now?" I ask as more precum seeps from the crown.

His harsh breaths and the sound of slapping skin play a symphony to the desire inside me. I'm coming undone as he pauses to rub his thick cock across my cheeks and over my parted lips. I try to taste him, but he pulls me away, back to jerking his cock. "You don't get to taste or touch me."

I almost cry at his declaration, prepared to beg, but before I can open my mouth to speak, cum erupts on my face. I open my mouth just in time to catch a few precious squirts. Dominic grunts, his fingers loosening on my hair before they tighten again. He keeps me out of reach, panting as he slows his movements.

I stare up at him through cum covered lashes and make a show of licking him off my lips, still drunk enough to feel brave in the face of the monster residing behind that hard stare.

"Thank you," I whisper, and his gaze darkens, like storm clouds gathering over a valley. He bends down to collect my shorts, using them to wipe my face before tossing them at me. "Get dressed. I'm taking you home."

I stare at the shorts for a beat, then release an incredulous sound. My clit is throbbing. "What about me?"

"What *about* you?" he asks, doing up his belt.

"Aren't you going to return the favor?"

Those intense eyes clash with mine. "I told you this wasn't a reward. Get dressed before I fuck you raw in the ass. Stop fighting me. I'm taking you home so you can sober up and stop embarrassing yourself."

A red haze of fury blinds me, and I shoot to my feet, swaying despite my best attempts to stay upright. "How fucking dare you,

Dominic? You can't treat me like this. I'm not some toy you can just…just—"

"Just what?" He gets in my face. "Not some fuck toy I can use and discard like yesterday's trash? Yes, Camryn, that's exactly what you are. Just a warm, tight hole."

When he turns to walk out, I run after him and smack his back hard enough to cause him to turn to granite beneath my blows. "Why do you hate me so much, huh? What did I ever do to you?"

He spins around so fast that I would almost tumble backward if it weren't for his painful grip on my arm. I gasp as he yanks me close, hissing through clenched teeth, "I know about the affair between you and my dad."

My eyes widen and ice slithers through my veins. "Dominic?" I shake my head, whispering, "No…"

"No?" If anything, my denial pisses him off even more. He fishes his phone out of his pocket while still holding me in a vise. My heart threatens to explode from my chest when he thrusts his screen in my face.

He presses play. "Tell me that's not you on your fucking knees in my father's office?"

I squeeze my eyes shut, overwhelmed by shame, but he grabs my chin and tilts my face up, his bruising grip causing tears to cascade down my cheeks. "Does that answer your question, Sis?"

When I remain silent, he jostles me. "Does it?"

"Yes," I reply, unable to look away from the cold fury in his eyes. "It answers my question."

Shifting closer, he slides his hand lower, trailing his fingers over my skin until my throat is clasped in his hand. He opens his mouth to unleash hell on my fragile heart, but before he can speak a single word, a scream outside has us both stiffening. We exchange a confused look. Dominic releases me and strides out of the room.

Throwing on my stained shorts, I run after him, swiping the tears from my cheeks. We dash downstairs. Dominic grabs my hand as he shoulders through the commotion of students trying to get out through the door.

We exit the house, and my heart ceases to beat at the sight of Benny up on the roof with Erica clutched to his chest. I gaze up, my previous shame and anger forgotten. Dominic's fingers thread through mine as the sound of crying students fills the silent night.

Someone is up on the roof with them, pleading with Benny to step away from the edge, pleading with him to drop the gun in his hand.

"Oh my God," I whimper, palming my mouth as tears gather on my fluttering lashes. This can't be happening. Why would he do this?

"Let her go," someone shouts, cupping their mouth to be heard above the loud crying.

Benny's eyes land on mine and his lips curve as a breeze rustles through the trees. He digs the gun into Erica's temple, making her cry even harder.

His words echo across the yard—words meant solely for me. "His hatred for you really is delicious." Then he shoves Erica off the roof.

Dominic clamps his hand over my eyes. A scream ripples through the crowd as it surges back, and a haunting thud makes me choke back a whimper.

I wrench free from Dominic's hold and run forward, only to come to a sudden halt when Benny puts the gun to his head.

"No!" I cry, but it's too late. I flinch at the sudden gunshot. Time slows as Benny's body tumbles to the ground.

I've never watched anyone die, not like this. Dominic's brother was already dead when the water started pouring into the car. I don't know how, but his neck was twisted at an unnatural angle. Dominic's father couldn't get his seatbelt off. He was stuck, and I couldn't free him, no matter how much I pulled and yanked.

In his last moments, with his face coated in sweat, he ordered me to hand him the gun inside the dashboard. I only hesitated briefly, all too aware of the ice-cold water that was waist-deep and quickly rising, but his sharp, composed voice forced me back to the present moment. "Now, Camryn."

While the water rippled around my waist and the car sunk deeper into the river, I retrieved the gun and handed it to him.

His eyes swam with regret. "Save yourself, Camryn."

My head shook, but he winced and said, "I'm not asking. It's too late for me, but you still have a chance."

I glanced at my dead stepbrother in the backseat. How did this happen? The sound of the water pouring in was so loud. I couldn't think.

"I need you to look after Dominic and your mom."

I never saw him die. Never saw him pull the trigger. But I do remember how numb I felt as I breached the surface, gulping down gasping breaths. This is different, but the numbness is the same.

Dominic pulls me into his embrace. I feel nothing as a whisper of wind shifts my hair, swaying the branches overhead, singing a song of woes.

His hatred for you really is delicious.

TWELVE

CAMRYN

SEATED on the fountain steps before class, we watch the students mill about the courtyard, some with their eyes buried in their phones and others with books clasped to their chests.

Overhead, clouds slowly move across the sky.

"I can't believe he's dead," Gwen says, her voice as distant as her gaze.

No one says a thing.

It feels like a cruel joke that we're all here and forced to attend classes after two college students are dead. The world never stops, not even for a brief second.

His hatred for you really is delicious.

The words play on repeat in my head. I'm going crazy, wondering if I heard him correctly, wondering if I'm finally losing my mind in this relentless heat. Weird things happen in this small town.

"I wish he would have talked to us," Lily says in a quiet voice that I would have missed if she wasn't seated beside me.

Aron stiffens, lifting his gaze. The pain I see there squeezes my chest. "He wasn't suicidal."

"That's not what I meant."

"No? Then what the fuck did you mean?"

"You were there… He shot himself—"

"Shut up!" he snaps, and Lily shrinks back. Tears cling to her lashes when she drops her gaze to her lap.

A shadow settles over us as the sun disappears behind the clouds, and I peer up at the darkening sky, then let my eyes drift to a nearby tree. A warm breeze sweeps through the leaves.

"Let's not argue," Gwen pleads. "We don't know what happened—"

"Benny wasn't suicidal," Aron grits out. "Sure, we don't know what the fuck happened, but that thing up on the roof…wasn't Benny."

Lily's hair shields her face as she sniffles beside me.

Seated on her other side, Brittany wraps her arm around her shoulders. "What are you saying, Aron? That someone else made him push Erica off the roof?"

Gwen winces.

"Not someone," Aron answers, gritting his teeth before peering overhead at the rolling clouds. "Something."

The wind picks up, and with it comes the sound of leaves rustling. Shivers work their way down my spine as I tear my eyes away, meeting his accusatory gaze.

"The séance," he states, staring at me dead on.

Gwen speaks up. "You think the séance caused it?"

Aron doesn't look away, his black hair moving in the breeze. "I think we welcomed something in."

A sycamore leaf drifts across the steps, propelled forward by the singing wind. I watch it twirl and pirouette, dancing over Lily's shins.

"Demons don't exist," she says, drawing her legs up and wrapping her arms around her knees.

The leaf takes flight and carries on its journey.

Aron glares at her before shooting to his feet and striding off. We watch him enter the building, his broad shoulders disappearing through the doorway.

Gwen blows out a breath and lets her head fall back against the fountain. "Everything is such a fucking mess."

"Do you think he's right?" Brittany asks, looking between us. "Do you think we caused this?"

"We didn't cause this," Gwen says in a firm tone. "Whatever happened isn't our fault."

Lily swipes at her wet cheeks before rising to her feet and picking up her bag. She shoulders it, staring at the cracks in the steps beneath her feet. "I didn't mean anything bad by what I said."

"We know," Gwen says, pulling her in for a hug. "Aron knows it, too. He just... Emotions are running high."

I meet Brittany's gaze but look away.

His hatred for you is delicious.

What if Aron was right? What if there's something more sinister at play? Weird things have occurred ever since my family arrived in this small town. It can't be a coincidence that Benny pushed Erica off the roof a week after the séance before committing suicide.

I keep my thoughts to myself as we rise to our feet and set off toward the entrance. But the tense air surrounding my friends is palpable. We're all thinking the same thing.

What if we invited something in?

"Why don't you go ahead," I say to Gwen when we pass the bathroom. "I need to pee before class."

It's not true. I just need a moment alone.

"Sure." She offers me a small, sad smile.

I wait until they turn the corner before shouldering my way into the piss-smelling bathroom and locking myself inside the nearest stall. My arm itches, and the sensation of crawling insects beneath the skin has me sucking in a breath.

"It's all in my head," I whisper, hands flat against the graffitied door. "It's just in my fucking head. Get it together."

Sweat beads on my lip. Why is it so stifling? I can't breathe in this fucking place.

Something drifts through the gap between the stall and the floor. I peer down, distracted, watching a sycamore leaf move across the floor on an imaginary breeze.

Every muscle locks tight, and a small sob escapes my lips. My spine connects with the wall when I step back.

"*Camryn…*" a voice whispers.

The eerie sound floats through the stalls.

I hold my breath as a bead of sweat trails down my temple.

Another whisper seeps through the muggy air. "*Camryn…*"

I look down at the leaf before slowly lowering myself to the sticky floor on my hands and knees, my heart pounding in the silence as I peer beneath the partition. Empty stalls stretch out in front of me, a row of lone toilets providing stark splashes of white in this dim room. I'm alone.

"*CAMRYN!*" the voice shouts, and I shoot upright.

Digging my nails into my palms, I allow the sharp bite of pain to anchor me before I turn to unlock the stall door.

People die like this in horror movies—investigating strange noises. Unfortunately, I can't stay locked in the toilet stall all day.

When the door creaks open, I peek through the gap, then slowly inch outside. The door nearest the wall is closed. Something is in there. Every nerve ending in my body knows it. I can sense the thickening air around it as I skirt the room, keeping as much distance as possible.

Silence presses in from all corners, drowning out the passing conversations in the hallway until I hear nothing except my roaring pulse. I'm hyperaware of the stall beneath the small window, which barely allows daylight into the room.

I keep my eyes on the door as I reach out behind me to skim my fingers over the small sinks, one after the other. Despite the terror growing with each step, I continue toward the stall. Curiosity cares little for survival.

My hand knocks against something. I snatch it back and spin around. "What the…" I gulp, seeing the doll propped up on the sink, watching me with its beady eyes. I take a careful step backward when a bead of dark red blood pours from the crack in the porcelain, and I let out a choked sob.

Behind me, the stall door creaks open, shattering the thick silence that sucks the air out of the room. A panicked sob crawls up my throat, but before it can echo off the walls, a strong hand grabs me and spins me around.

"What the fuck, Camryn?"

Caught in Dominic's dark eyes, I gulp down breaths.

"What the hell is wrong?" His gaze coasts over my face and he scans the room before looking back at me with a furrowed brow. "Why are you freaking out?"

"The stall," I choke out, and Dominic looks past my shoulder. He releases me and stalks up to it. I spin around, intending to hide the doll before he can see it, but it's gone.

I stare at the empty sink. Where the hell did it go? It was there a minute ago. I crouch down as if I'll find it on the floor.

Behind me, Dominic slams the stall door open with such force my heart jumps. The last thing I need is to be caught in his storm when my mind is this fragile. I run for the exit, but I barely make it three steps before his muscular arm bands around my waist and lifts me off the floor. "Where are you going, Sis?"

Kicking out with my feet, I flail and scream as he clamps his free hand over my mouth to muffle the haunted sound.

"Nothing quite turns me on like your fight."

I'm dragged into the nearest stall and dropped onto the toilet seat. Dominic swiftly undoes his belt, and then his hand is in my hair, yanking my head back. I try to stand when he frees his dick, but he shoves me back down and thrusts his hard length against my lips. "What's going on inside that fucked-up head of yours, huh?"

I sneer, but the sound soon cuts off when he tightens his grip on my hair. It fucking hurts.

"Less with the attitude." He grips his shaft and smacks the crown against my lips, his gaze riveted on the burning fury in mine.

"I'm not going crazy," I bite out.

He slides his large hand over his cock as he chuckles low in his chest. "No? Care to explain why you were freaking out inside an empty bathroom?"

"Something was inside that stall."

His cock bumps up against my lips again, and I dig my nails into his thighs in a weak attempt to push him off. Though I'm not sure I want to stop him.

"I've been thinking," he drawls, coaxing my lips to open with a bead of precum. "I need to get you out of my head. I don't know what the fuck you're doing to me, but it's pissing me the hell off."

"Anyone could walk in, Dom," I remind him.

"Shut the fuck up!" He slides his veiny dick into my mouth, making me gag around his length as I dig my nails into his jeans, struggling for something to hold on to.

"We both know you're a pro at deep-throating, so quit the innocent act. Be good for me and swallow my dick."

His fingers tangle in my hair, and he grunts when I relax my throat around his throbbing length.

"That's it, little home wrecker," he praises, rolling his hips. "Now let me hear you choke while I fuck your tight throat."

My nails catch in his jeans as he goes to town, ramming his cock down my throat and pulling my hair. It's vicious, designed to inflict pain and humiliation—I relish every twisted second.

I find my sanity in his madness. This punishment.

With his cock throbbing deep in my throat and his long fingers tearing at my hair, I can finally let go.

Relief floods through me as I release a sob.

"Fuck, look at me. I love your tears." Dominic swipes them away with his thumb and then traces my lips around his cock. He slowly slides his length out to the tip before thrusting back in roughly.

My gagging is obnoxiously loud in the quiet bathroom.

"You're so fucking pathetic." Huffing a laugh, he buries his cock deep and holds me to his crotch. "First, you go after my dad, and now your mouth is stuffed full of *my* dick." He releases me, and I shove him away, crying angrily.

"You know nothing," I sneer, fighting him off when he reaches for me, but I'm no match to his resentment.

"I know everything. Now fucking choke on it!" He rams his cock inside my mouth again, and my clit pulses almost painfully. The more his rage radiates off him like heatwaves, the more aroused I get. Dominic's hatred is my tailor-made aphrodisiac.

"I bet you wished my dad would have fucked your face this brutally, huh? You should have gone straight for his son." He pushes me away and then grips my jaw and slams his lips to mine, invading my mouth with his hungry tongue and sanity-stealing, heated breaths.

A whimper climbs up my throat, and he devours it as he kisses me to the brink of the sweetest abyss. One push, one simple shove, and I would disappear.

I kiss him back with equal fervor and claw at his T-shirt, shoving it up his chest until I can stroke my fingers across his smooth stomach.

"Don't ever touch me without my permission, understood?"

His words from the other night swirl through my mind and a sense of satisfaction floods through me as my fingers trace the ridges of his contracting abdomen. Dominic is perfection. Cut from stone.

Curling his fingers around my wrist, he peels mine away with a snarl that sinks straight to my core. His rejection stings, a sharp burn at the backs of my eyes. Tears cling to my lashes as he straightens up and guides his length to my mouth. When he taps my lips with his cock, I shoot to my feet.

I try to move past him, but he grabs hold of my arm, slams me up against the wall, and shoves my shorts down my legs. Then he straightens up and grips my hair hard, whispering in my ear, "Step out of them."

Maybe I should put up a fight, but I don't. Instead, my shorts fall to my ankles as I wiggle my butt.

Dominic steals the air from my lungs with his heat against my back and his punishing grip on my hair. He kicks my ankles apart and impales me on his cock in one go, with an arm banded around my waist and the other in my hair to keep my cheek squished against the sticky wall.

"Fuck," I cry out, clamping around his cock.

"Shut up! This is for me," he sneers, fucking me brutally against the hard surface. "You owe me this for stealing my family."

"It wasn't my fault," I choke out, poised on my tiptoes.

"If you speak another fucking word, I'll fuck all your holes and in no particular order. Now shut up and let me take what's owed to me."

Tears fall silently down my cheeks while he takes me so hard I lose my breath. At one point, the door opens, and a group of girls enter, but Dominic never stops his sweet assault on my body. No, he clamps his hand over my mouth and whispers filth in my ear—words that should appall me but light a fire in my core instead. Words that are meant to humiliate and degrade but somehow build me up.

No one else can offer me this level of fucked up.

"Don't come," he warns in my ear when my pussy clamps down on his dick.

I try to hold the wave back, but I'm hanging on by a thin thread. The way he digs his fingers into my hips before smacking my ass, combined with his lips on my neck, steals the breath from my lungs. I don't stand a chance. He's a wrecking ball.

"Don't fucking think about it." He pulls out just as I'm about to fall over the edge. I whimper, my clit aching and desperate for release.

After maneuvering me around, he bends me over the toilet with my legs on either side of the seat. He grabs my neck and sinks back inside me torturously slowly, ensuring I feel the glide of his thick length.

"You should see the cream on my dick."

As if to prove his point, he pulls out and runs his hand over his slick length before holding his wet palm over my mouth and nose. Then he enters me again, fucking me until I'm delirious. It never ends. Dominic is a machine.

Every time I'm about to climax, he pulls out and waits for the wave to recede before building me back up. When I think I might pass out, he spins me around, shoves me onto the toilet seat, and pulls down my tank top.

Warm cum rains over my naked tits, branding me with sin.

I can barely hold my head up. I'm exhausted. Dominic's tight grip on my hair keeps me upright. Grunting, he milks his dick, painting my swollen breasts.

"Fucking perfection," he drawls as the last spurt of cum drips down my chest. He roughly palms my breast and smears his release over my skin while I gaze up at him. "Are you ever going to let me come?"

"Do you think you deserve it?"

I shake my head as he slides his middle and ring finger into my mouth, dragging the pads over my tongue.

"I want to hear you say it." Removing his digits, he grabs my throat.

"I don't deserve to come," I admit.

Something flashes in his eyes, and then he shoves me back and zips his dick away. "I'm driving you home. Don't be late after school." He walks out, leaving me alone with an ache in my chest.

I place my feet on the toilet seat and wrap my arms around my knees. Dominic is breaking me piece by piece. I want more despite the pain or the choked sob clawing its way up my throat.

I *need* more.

Propping my chin on my knees, I stare at the sycamore leaf on the dirty floor.

A haunted whisper seeps through the walls. *"Camryn..."*

THIRTEEN

CAMRYN

WITH THE FLASHLIGHT stuffed in my back pocket, I lower the steps to the attic.

Staring up at the imposing hole, I wonder, not for the first time, if this is such a good idea after all, but then I grit my teeth and climb up. I need answers, and up there is where I discovered the damn doll.

My head pops through the hole, and I peer around. It's too dark to see, so I reach behind me to retrieve the flashlight. Sweeping it across the room, I'm careful not to disturb the sea of sleeping bats overhead.

I climb up the rest of the way and kneel on the dirty floor. The flashlight flickers in my hand, so I slap it against my palm and then crawl forward on one hand, shining the light on the stacked crates in the corner. My spine shudders, and not just from the chilly air up here, but the sensation of being watched crawling over my skin.

I settle in front of the crates and place the flashlight beside me on the floor. Scanning the dark corners, I suppress the urge to take my flashlight and run. It's just me here, no one else, or so I tell myself as I pull one of the crates closer to me.

A layer of dust coats the book on top, so I blow it off.

"Jesus…" I cough, wafting the air, waiting for the dust to settle before opening the first page.

I reach for the flashlight and scan the faded handwriting, turning the page. My initial excitement soon fades when I realize it's a recipe collection.

After putting it back down, I reach for the next book, surprised to find old photographs glued to the pages—photographs of this house in its heyday before years of neglect took its toll.

It's hard to imagine what it must have looked like with a fresh lick of paint and flowers in bloom outside. Nothing at all like the sorry affair it has become.

I turn the page and pause on a picture of Wilfred's farm. Adjusting my clammy grip on the flashlight, I quickly glance around the attic, unable to shake the uneasy feeling that raises the hairs on the back of my neck.

Behind two mustached men, deep in discussion, sits a little girl in a tattered dress on the porch, with dark braids. She clutches a doll to her chest, but it's her eyes that have ice slithering across my arms. They're staring at me through time and space, dark pools of black that seem to grow larger the longer I look at the photograph.

I quickly shut the book and gulp down a breath. "The doll…" My brow pinches as I open the book and shine the light on the photograph.

Sure enough, it's the same creepy doll that I found up here the other week. I flip to another page, and my gaze locks on a photograph of our house. A woman is barely visible through a gap in the curtains on the second floor.

It's the same woman I had a vision of the first time I ventured into the woods.

I squint, trying to make out the grainy image.

I'm sure it's her. It has to be. She has the same bun and severe expression.

I continue flicking through the photographs until I pause on two smiling faces beside the chicken coop in Wilfred's yard. Two young men in mucky overalls. One of them is Wilfred in his younger days. But I can't tear my gaze away from the guy to the right, nearest to the chicken coop.

With one arm slung over his friend's shoulder, he holds the carcass of a dead hen, which dangles from his fingertips, headless and limp. A bloody axe is barely visible in the long tufts of grass and dandelions by their feet.

How old is this photograph? I look for a date stamp but come up blank, then focus on the young men again.

With such undeniable similarities, the man with the hen must be related to my mysterious axe-wielding stranger in the woods. They have the same smile dimples, eyes, and dark hair.

I'm just about to turn another page when the bats take flight in a blur of commotion. I scream, dropping the book and the flashlight. The air shifts around me. Wings and claws tangle in my hair. Panic beats at my chest, only made worse by the bite of pain in my arms and legs.

Curling into a ball, I bury my face in the crook of my arm while the bats fly overhead. And then, silence falls like a thick blanket on my tender body.

The air stills.

In fact, it's so still that you could hear a pin drop over my trembling exhales.

I don't move. I barely dare inhale a shaky breath. The flashlight has gone out, and the thickening shadows feed on the muted light. When another sob cuts through the sudden stillness, the darkness crawls closer to where I lie, bleeding and bruised, in the fetal position on the gritty floor.

I slowly push up to a sitting position and reach for the flashlight, but it's broken. I rattle it again, but nothing happens. With a sigh, I collect the book and descend the steps.

The heat instantly swallows me up as my bare feet connect with the floor. I move to close the attic, but my attention snags on my scratched, bleeding arms. Countless more little cuts decorate my tanned legs. I'm a roadmap of beaded trails of blood.

Now that I've seen the destruction painted on my body, the stinging sensation threatens to buckle my legs, and it's by some miracle that I manage to make it to my bedroom unscathed without anyone noticing me.

———

"What's up, sweetheart?" Keith asks, startling me, as he enters the kitchen, dressed in a creased shirt and slacks. He retrieves a bottle of orange juice from the fridge and grabs a glass from the cupboard. Smooth without pulp. I'm the picky one who doesn't like bits.

I wait while he pours himself a drink with his back to me.

"Why are you crying?" he asks.

I quickly wipe my wet cheeks. "I'm not crying."

He turns and leans against the counter, loosening his tie. "Is this about your mom?"

Shame heats my cheeks, and I try to hide behind strands of my hair.

"I think you need to talk to her about the ballet."

I should win the 'Worst Daughter of the Year' award for wanting to give up on my mom's dream for me. She has dedicated so much time and energy to getting me the best trainers and the best chances, and I don't want to do it anymore.

Keith frowns at the window, and I follow his line of sight to see a leaf twirl against the glass, which strikes me as odd. We live in the city. My street has no trees, and the nearest park is a ten-minute bus journey away. The leaf must have traveled a far distance.

My stepdad opens the window to let in the summer breeze and traffic sounds. Someone shouts outside, then laughs.

"You're too hard on yourself," he says, crossing his arms, tired after a long day at work. "She will understand. Give her a chance."

Silence stretches between us. Mom left an hour ago for a night shift at the hospital, and Dominic and his brother are out somewhere.

Another gust of wind drifts in from the window, filling the kitchen with scents from the food truck down the street. My stomach rumbles on cue.

Movement in my periphery fills my vision, and I turn my head to see the leaf from earlier flutter beside Keith on the kitchen counter. He snatches it up, crushes it in his palm, and hums low in his throat.

When he lifts his gaze, I blink. His eyes are black.

It happens so fast—there and gone.

Throwing the ruined leaf in the sink, he then crouches in front of me. I search his eyes as he tucks my hair behind my ear, but they're their usual color. I'm imagining things.

"What's going on inside that head of yours?" His big hand lands on my thigh, making me stiffen. "You can talk to me, Camryn."

I hold my breath when he reaches up with his free hand, touching my chin. Keith has never flirted with or looked at me before now. I don't know what to do. It feels wrong—it is *wrong—but I've been so down lately. I have no friends, my mom is upset with me for skipping ballet classes, and I… I don't know. His touch feels…*nice. *The way he* looks *at me feels nice. Like I'm not a disappointment. Someone to ignore in the school halls. Someone to laugh at.*

Another gentle breeze swirls around us. Keith's lips brush against mine, and my heart slows to a heavy thud.

Is that…sulfur I smell?

My clouded thoughts crash together like warring waves at sea. A voice deep inside urges me to stop this, but whispers in the wind drown it out.

Whispers?

I gasp, glancing around the room to locate the sound, but Keith guides me back to his lips. His fingers slide higher on my thigh and dip, touching me where no stepdad should touch their wife's daughter. "Your desire tastes delicious," he whispers before kissing me.

A warm hand over my mouth and nose startles me awake, and my eyes roll to the back of my head.

The headboard slams against the wall as Dominic moves on top of me, his hard length rubbing every inch of my clenching walls. The sensation is so mind-blowing, so soul-destroying, that I scream beneath his firm grip on my mouth.

"Fuck, you're so tight!" His dark hair falls over his devastating eyes. "This fucking cunt will be the death of me." Pistoning his hips, he grits his teeth and digs his fingers into my cheeks as my lungs scream with my need to breathe.

When the instinct to survive overwhelms me, he lets go of my mouth and grabs me by the throat before biting down hard on my lip. The taste of coppery blood floods my mouth as he bites again and grinds his cock deep, fucking me so hard I feel him everywhere. "You want to die like this, with my cock inside you, baby?"

I nod, my pussy spasming around his length.

"Don't tempt me, Sis. I'd gladly watch the life slip from your eyes and fuck your lifeless corpse. Maybe we should try it?" He chuckles. "Pretend to be dead for me while I stuff this warm cunt full of cum." Tossing me over onto my front like I'm nothing more than a ragdoll, he enters me from behind and fucks me hard into the mattress. "No, I like your fight and the torment in your eyes."

He slips his dick out and thrusts it through my ass crack. "I like it even more when you cry for me." On his hands and knees, his fingers curled around my nape, he pounds my pussy until wretched sobs tear from my lungs.

"You want more, Sis?"

"Yes, p-please," I choke out against the damp sheet.

"You think this little tight pussy can handle it?"

This time when I nod, he lifts me up against his sweaty chest and holds me to him with his grip on my throat and his lips pressed to my ear. The bed rocks against the wall as he yanks down my tank top to palm my tits, tweaking my tender nipples until the pain becomes too much.

I'm a mess.

Chuckling, he rains slaps on my pussy.

My knees shake and my cries grow hoarse.

"You think you deserve to come?" He pinches my clit, and I gasp as I tremble against him. "Answer me!"

"No, I'll never deserve it."

His breathy laugh warms my core and the bruised organ in my chest. "And why not?"

I croak, "Because I'm a filthy whore who hurt you."

"You can't hurt me." The humor fades from his voice. "I'd have to care about you first."

His toxic words are like a punch to the gut. I want to fight him. I want to spin around and slap his stupid face, so that's what I do.

I strike his cheek, scrambling off the bed, then run for the door, my heart thrashing as I escape into the dark hallway. Grotesque shadows chase me while I sprint like a darting rabbit downstairs with no destination in mind. I need to be away from Dominic and his poisoned daggers.

I make the mistake of glancing back when his footsteps pound the stairs behind me. Stumbling on the last step, my jaw smacks off the floor in a hard blow. My teeth sink into my fleshy tongue, and blood floods my mouth. But all that pales when he grabs hold of my ankle and drags me across the floor like a damn caveman.

"I'm so fucking fed up with you running away and fighting me at every fucking turn. Unless it's not already obvious to you, Sis, you're mine. You belong to me, so stop with the theatrics."

My nails scratch the floor. I sob and cry, but I don't scream. Somewhere in the most depraved depths of me, I want him to hurt me. I want him to cut out the guilt I harbor from the crash and the affair—an affair I don't even understand myself.

Lashing out, I kick at his hand and manage to free myself. Before I can jump to my feet, he hauls me up by my hair and bares his gleaming teeth. "Are you fucking done?"

"I'll never be done," I hiss.

He shoves me into a room and kicks the door shut. "Then you'll never get to come. How about that?"

"How about I never let you fuck me?" I sneer, inching back, skirting around a piano. We're in the sun lounge with nothing but stars overhead.

While I'm sure this room was once a beautiful sight, it's now a scene straight out of a nightmare, with glass shards on the floor, tendrils of ivy escaping through the broken roof and crawling along the walls, and upturned furniture. The only piece that's seemingly unharmed is the piano. When Dominic presses a single note, I dig my nails into my palms, the sound as haunted as the woods outside.

"Whether you let me fuck you or not is of no relevance to me. I'll have you whenever I fucking please, and we both know you'll love every second. This"—he waves a hand between us as he stalks closer—"is what turns you on. This festering guilt, shame, and hatred. I could make sweet and gentle love to you if you want, but we both know you'd soon beg me to choke you uncon- scious and stuff you full of cum while you're out cold because that, Camryn, is what gets you hot and bothered. You're sick, just like me."

I spin on my feet and run for the door, but he catches me before I can make it two steps. He sits me down on top of the piano, causing the clashing notes to ring out in a chaotic symphony.

With his hands on my hips, he lowers himself on the chair and brings his mouth inches from my soaking pussy. "Is this what you want, Sis? Romance?" His lips twist with a wicked smile and he places a soft, featherlight kiss on the inside of my thigh.

I hold my breath as his eyes find mine again, dark and hungry.

"Or do you want me to make you bleed?"

"Hurt me," I whimper. "Please..."

Not a single emotion crosses his face. Not an ounce of satisfac- tion at seeing me crumble before his eyes.

Turning his head, he bites me hard. My loud gasp rings out amongst the ivy and debris. I swallow a sob, shifting on top of the piano keys. More clanging notes chase the chaotic storm brewing inside me. But then as I lift my gaze, terror seizes me at the sight of a woman with a severe bun watching us from the shadows.

Noticing me stiffening, Dominic peers up at me and then turns to look behind him. I suck in a breath when she steps out from the shadows, her long skirt trailing the dirty floor.

FOURTEEN

DOMINIC

CAMRYN'S FRANTIC, terror-filled eyes gaze behind me, so I lean in and sink my teeth into her soft flesh, marking her thigh.

She's still caught in her own nightmare and not breathing.

Anger floods me when I can't reach her.

Surging up, I seize her chin, then shove two fingers inside her soaking cunt. "That's it. Eyes on me." Her pussy squeezes as I rub her inner walls. "Stay with me."

"She's behind you," she breathes as she tries to skate her eyes past me, but I force her gaze back to me. "Look at me when I'm fucking you with my fingers. Don't lose yourself in your mind. You're here with me."

A sob rattles her chest. "She's going to hurt you."

I press down hard on her clit and grind my palm. "There's no one here but us. Nothing but our twisted desires. Tell me this cunt is mine."

She tries to peer past me again. I'm done with her paranoia. Done with the guilt that seeps into her mind.

I spin her around and haul her up on the piano so I can bite her ass. Her knees press down on the keys, the eerie notes creating the perfect background music for the growing sickness inside me as I circle her soaking entrance with my tongue.

117

I groan deep in my chest at her sweet taste. No woman has ever driven me this mad before.

Tasting Camryn's pussy is a descent into Hell. Nothing will ever satisfy me from this day onwards. Nothing but her pretty whimpers and pathetic pleas. I'm a glutton for this pussy and a prisoner to her every twisted desire.

She writhes on the piano when I suck on her pussy. Overhead, the clouds part, bathing her pale ass in ethereal moonlight, and my heart aches at the sight of her spread out before me like a feast.

I suck on her swollen clit as I fill her up with two fingers, twisting them just right while pumping her tight hole. More juices pour from her pussy, and I growl like a starved demon.

My dick weeps, needing to be inside her.

Easing back on the bench, I grip her hips and lower her onto my dick. As her tight heat wraps around me, she yelps in surprise when I bounce her on my length. "Dom," she mewls, gripping my wrists for leverage. "Fuck... More!"

"See that?" I whisper near her ear, nodding my chin at our reflection in the glass. "See how your tits bounce and how your pussy swallows my cock. You can fight me all you want, but you'll always shatter for me."

My balls draw up tight. She ripples around me while her moans echo in the small room. I stand up and slam her body against the piano, ramming into her so hard that she catches the keys when she tries to push back.

"I'm coming," she whimpers, and I pull hard on her hair and crush my lips to hers. Her pussy milks me. I savor her moans, reaching down to play with her too-sensitive clit.

Once her cries quiet and she tries to wriggle away from my touch, I bite her shoulder and thrust my dick as deep as I can. "Fuck," I grunt, shuddering, tasting blood on her marked skin. I lick it up before replacing my dick with my fingers and fucking my cum back inside her heat.

"I thought I didn't deserve to come," she says, a note of vulnerability bleeding into her voice.

"I don't know what it is about you," I reply truthfully as I brush my lips over the curve of her shoulder all the way to the crook of her neck, "but I'm hooked."

She shivers when I place a soft kiss on her skin.

I slide my fingers out to circle her swollen pearl. "I can't get enough of you, and I will fight you every day to get a taste of this." I tap her clit and smile. "I've smacked it, licked it, and fucked it, so it's mine."

Her airy laugh does wicked things to my heart. Things that should scare me, and they do. Camryn terrifies me. I've already cut myself open on her gleaming blade, and now I'm a lost cause. The hatred I feel is morphing into something with a lesser sting but a bigger consequence.

I straighten up and then turn her around and cup her chin, tilting her face up to mine. "What's going on inside that sweet head of yours."

The shutters go down over her eyes. She tries to hide her face behind her hair, but I refuse to let her push me away. Lifting her chin once more, I swoop down to whisper in her ear, "Don't make me chase you. You're not ready for my cock this soon again."

"I've already told you, Dom." Her weak voice trembles in the small space between us. "Weird things are happening in this house and this…town."

"It's in your head."

Her teary eyes clash with mine, but then she looks away and shuts me out. "You don't believe me anyway." She pushes off the piano and tries to escape past me. "Why are you nice to me all of a sudden? You hate me, remember?"

She looks so exposed as she trembles beneath the moonlight, with her eyes downcast and strands of matted hair sticking to the tears on her cheeks.

I lift her chin with two fingers. "Eyes on me."

Her blue ocean clashes with my storm, and I trail my fingers down the length of her jaw to shift her hair away. "My emotions for you are complicated—"

She tries to look away again, so I seize her chin and lower my voice. "I do hate you, but my need for you burns stronger. You're an obsession, Sis, and I'm done fighting it."

"What if I want you to leave me alone?"

"Too late." I clench my jaw and inch closer. "I don't care if I have to chase you to the ends of the earth. In fact, I'll enjoy every minute of it."

Her breath catches, and a vicious smile unfurls on my lips. I love how delicate she is and how her fear permeates the charged air. It's almost as intoxicating as the lust shining in her eyes and the tears coating her lashes.

"By the time I'm done with you, nothing will be left for anyone else to salvage."

Shaking her head, she quivers against me, her delicate feet leaving a trail of blood on the floor amongst the broken glass and debris.

An inexplicable sense of protectiveness overwhelms me when she walks out, and I fist my hands as I force down the ugly feeling that demands I protect her at all costs. I simply can't afford to let her get beneath my skin like this.

Who am I kidding? She has already buried deep and siphoned my sanity like a vampiric parasite.

A shiver runs down my back as a cool breeze brushes by, like an icy breath against the curve of my neck. I spin around and scan the room.

Behind me, a haunted piano note rings out in the oppressive silence, and I whip my head around, heart crashing against my ribcage. Nothing else happens. I wait with bated breath, acutely aware of every whistle of the wind outside, every groaning tree hidden in the darkness across the overgrown lawn.

Every darting shadow.

Menace bleeds into my tone. "She belongs to me and only me.

I don't care if you're a ghost or a demon from the darkest pits of Hell. Mess with what's mine, and I will ruin you."

———

I watch her at breakfast, my own bowl of cereal untouched. I watch her in the hallways at school, leaning up against the wall.

I watch her every chance I get.

It's pissing me off how she holds my attention this easily without trying. It pisses me off even more that she gives her friends attention. If it were up to me, I would lock her up so no one else could see her smile except for me.

The sun beats down relentlessly, but I barely notice. Camryn's eyes widen as I stride across the parking lot with determined steps, hands in my pockets.

I don't spare her friends a glance as I advance, solely focused on the little brat who's avoiding me at every turn.

She can't avoid me now.

I grab hold of her throat and slam her up against the truck. And then I swallow her surprised yelp with a hard, savage kiss.

The urge to claim her in front of her friends ripples through my veins.

Fuck that Aron guy.

Her sweet little body trembles in my hold. I devour her whole, feasting on her tongue and swollen lips like they're my last meal. I kiss her like I've never been kissed.

I have, just not like this.

Never have I been consumed to the brink of insanity by a girl, and while the power Camryn holds over me is frightening, I still binge on her because, despite the warning bells in my head, she tastes and feels like heaven. And the descent into madness, *her madness,* makes me heady.

When one of her friends clears their throat behind me, Camryn pushes my unmoving chest. I tighten my grip on her slender neck, the urge to snap her neck twitching my fingers, but I force myself to stay in control.

With a final bite of that plump lip, I step back and haul her against me.

Her friends watch us with wide eyes.

Gwen bounces her gaze between us before a blinding smile splits her face. "Oh my God... I can't believe you held out on us."

"I didn't hold—" Camryn falls silent when I tighten my grip on her waist in a warning to shut that pretty mouth before it gets her into deep trouble.

While Brittany and Gwen gush over my power play, I lock eyes with Aron and smirk.

If he thinks he stands a chance with her now that I've torn through her tight cunt with my dick, he can think again. Besides, I'd slaughter him slowly if he tried.

I step around Camryn with my hand on her waist and throw open the passenger door. "Get in."

She stiffens in my hold but slides in without a fight, and the raging possessiveness inside me likes that a little too much.

After slamming the door shut, I round the truck and throw one last glance at Aron.

He looks like a wounded animal.

Oblivious, Brittany loops her arm through his and guides him away from the truck while popping her pink gum.

Aron holds my gaze until he has no choice but to look away. I slide in behind the steering wheel, pull the door shut, and crank the engine.

Static meets my ears, disturbed every few seconds by a distorted voice. The signal out here is crap. I leave the radio on.

It's not until we were on the country road, with nothing but the baked asphalt in front of us and cornfields on each side, that Camryn asks, "What was that back there? Why did you kiss me in front of my friends?"

"Shut up."

Her lips snap shut, but her eyes bore into the side of my face. "Excuse me—"

"Shut the hell up," I say, in a firmer voice this time, and she visibly shrinks back in my periphery.

My cock strains against my jeans as more static crackles through the speakers. Camryn remains quiet.

"I kissed you to prove a point," I reply, tapping my thumb on the steering wheel and glancing in the rearview mirror.

"What point?" she asks in that nervous little voice of hers that hardens my cock to the point of agony. It throbs behind the zipper.

The tires squeal as I pull over to the side of the road, the engine still rumbling beneath me. I throw open the door and round the truck in a flash, grabbing her by the arm and yanking her out. I slam her against the side of the vehicle, the rusty metal hot against her skin from hours outside in the relentless sun, and shove her shorts and panties halfway down her thighs. My tongue invades her mouth, capturing her surprised gasp as I breathe in her air, intoxicated by her sweet taste.

"Fuck," I exhale against her tempting lips, then kiss her again, deeper.

When she whimpers into my mouth, I spread my hand over her sopping cunt and spear her slit with a finger, sinking it deep inside her throbbing core. She trembles against me, creasing my sweaty T-shirt in her grip.

One finger becomes two, stretching her tight pussy until she melts against me. I chuckle as the wind moves through the cornstalks. "Your pussy missed me, didn't it? Missed my fingers and cock."

She looks at me through her heavy lashes, and I slap her cunt hard, making her yelp.

"Step out of your shorts."

Unlike the time in the bathroom stall, she doesn't question it or make me say it twice. She slides them off, then straightens back up.

"What are you doing?" she asks, her voice wavering when I reach for something in the flatbed. I like the fear that bleeds into every vowel, the way her eyes flash when I stride back up to her with a length of rope in my hands. Spinning her around, I press her up against the truck and fasten her wrists together.

She tries to look at me over her shoulder while I tie an expert knot. "Dom? What are you doing?"

"Did I say you could talk?"

"Anyone could drive by…"

"Let's hope they don't." I grab her by the neck and whisper in her ear, "I'd have to hunt them down and kill them for seeing you half-naked and tied up like this."

Reaching into my back pocket, I remove the ball gag before fisting her hair. Her unease ratchets up as I tug hard and force-fully insert the ball into her mouth. I make sure it's secured behind her head and then pull her toward the ditch.

With her hands bound and a gag in her mouth, she stares at me, wide-eyed, only wearing red Chucks from the waist down.

I raise an eyebrow. "What are you waiting for?"

She peers at the cornstalks and then back at me.

"It's time to run."

Her eyes widen even more and her nostrils flare on a sharp inhale.

"If I catch you, I'm going to fuck you." I shake my head and chuckle darkly. "Let me rephrase that. If I catch you, I'm going to tear through your pussy and ass with my cock."

Her gaze falls to my hand as I adjust my hard-on.

"And it will hurt." I tip my chin to the cornstalks. "These fields belong to Wilfred. Grumpy old man." Chuckles bubble up from my chest. "I doubt he'll be pleased if he finds a gagged and tied-up, half-naked girl running around." Looking into her eyes again, I warn, "So you'd better not scream."

Her face has paled, and her big eyes are filled with glassy tears. She takes a step back but trips and falls. Her legs splay open, offering me a perfect view of her puffy pink pussy.

"You're soaking wet, Sis," I taunt, hovering over her, my shadow suffocating the sunshine. "Look at that desperate little pussy."

She whimpers, then cries out when I grab hold of her arm. I drag her up and shove her toward the cornstalks, making her stumble.

The sound of an approaching car steals her attention, and her head snaps toward it before she peers back at me with panicked eyes.

"Now fucking do as you're told and run."

FIFTEEN

CAMRYN

Dominic's lips spread into a sinful, clit-tingling smile that promises endless pain. "Better run, or I'll hunt them down and kill them."

I don't doubt him for a second. He's unhinged.

I spin around, leaves slapping me in the face as I dart for the cornstalks, but the sting barely registers. I sprint blindly with no clue where I'm going. Everywhere looks the same. More and more cornstalks everywhere I turn.

Coming to a halt, I spin around, my heart thudding in my ears as the sun beats down on me from overhead. I step back, painfully aware of my sticky thighs and the throbbing between my legs. Somewhere to my left, the stalks rustle, and my heart jumps to my throat.

I turn and run, tugging desperately on the rope securing my wrists. My sole mission is to escape the clutches of the man who's hunting me, even as I want him to pin me down in the dirt and unleash his evil.

I trip and fall hard on my side, coughing violently. I can feel dry dirt stick to my damp lips and tear-streaked cheeks as I try to climb to my feet. Losing balance, I collapse back down, crying from sheer torment.

Behind me, the cornstalks rustle ominously, and I hold my breath, convinced that he's seconds away from pouncing on me. The wind sweeps through the cornfield, swaying the stalks. I push up on my knees, suppressing a shiver. Silence has settled over the cornfield. Not a rustle of leaves can be heard. Nothing. Just me and my shaky breaths.

I peer around, my lips stretched around the ball gag, while my wrists throb from rubbing against the rope.

"Camryn…"

My heart rate spikes at the whisper. I scan the immediate area, watching the tall stalks sway like graceful dancers.

I stiffen when a large presence crouches down behind me and trails their cold fingers over my shoulder, causing a chill to raise the hairs on my bare arms.

Benny's voice whispers near my ear, "Such a delicate little thing."

I whimper, fear pulsing through me as he shushes me, guiding my eyes to his with his fingers below my chin, blood trickling from the gun wound in his temple. His skin has taken on an ashy gray tone.

A silent scream lodges itself in my throat, and I remain frozen as he feasts on my face with those dark eyes. "Look how needy you are." His breath whispers across my lips. "Wet and ready for your stepbrother. Your head must be an interesting place. So much guilt… So much…desire." He breathes me in as I tremble with fear, shaking like a leaf. His lips brush my cheek, exhaling a soft breath. "Let me in—"

"There you are."

Dominic's harsh voice snaps me back into reality, and I whip my head around. His powerful legs eat up the small distance between us and he stares down at me on my knees. "What did I tell you would happen if I found you?"

You would hurt me.

As if he can see the answer in my eyes, he claps my cheek tauntingly before circling me. "You're covered in filth," he points out, and I crane my neck as he steps around me. "Filthy, yet so breakable."

Heat rushes to my core at the threat in his voice. I swallow the saliva in my mouth.

"Get up," he orders.

I climb to my feet, watching him warily, expecting him to offer me a glimpse of his monster.

"Run! I didn't ask for an easy catch. Fucking run."

My pulse pounds in my ears as I whirl around, feeling the adrenaline pumping through my veins. Without hesitation, I bolt through the towering cornstalks, my shoes digging up the soil, trampling dried stalks as I glance behind me.

He's nowhere to be seen, or so I think, until I turn back around and slam into a hard wall. I stumble back with a yelp, and he shoves me to the ground then puts his shoe on my back to keep me down as he unbuckles his belt, pulling it through the loops with a slanted smile. "I told you I would hurt you," he says, slowly winding the leather around his veiny hand. "Is that what you want?"

I nod, my voice muffled behind the gag.

The belt sails through the air and smacks me hard on the ass, pain rippling across my flesh. Dominic whips me again, striking me so hard that I writhe beneath his boot.

"Don't try to get away now, little whore. This is what you want, remember. Pain and more fucking pain." The belt connects with the backs of my thighs, and liquid fire burns a path over my skin, welts throbbing.

Dominic drops to his knees behind me, looping the belt around my neck, tightening it with a sharp pull so that I can only manage small sips of air, hardly enough to keep me from growing light-headed.

I'm vaguely aware of him shoving down his jeans behind me, his hard dick sliding through my slit as he bites the shell of my ear. "Which hole should I fuck first?"

He feeds me the tip, inching inside so slowly that I struggle not to cry out for completely different reasons than the burning pain on my ass cheeks.

"This little cunt that's begging for cock"—he shifts and presses the crown of his cock against my back hole—"or your tight ass?"

I wriggle beneath him, fighting hopelessly against the restraints on my wrists despite the sharp pain where the ropes dig into my flesh.

"Let's break you in first." He shifts his hips, thrusting his fat cock inside me in one go, stealing the breath from my lungs as pleasure bursts behind my eyelids. He's so big it's almost unbearable. I might split in two.

Tears cascade down my cheeks as he rocks his hips, ensuring I feel every inch of him. "Look at you. Stuffed with cock and crying into the soil. Want more?"

Mindless, I nod, and he pulls out to the tip before thrusting back inside with such force that my cheek drags through the dirt.

Dominic fucks like a beast without mercy who wants to destroy me. All I can do is breathe in the soil and let him pound me until I'm coming all over him like his own plaything.

"You're strangling my cock, Sis." He sits back on his knees before flipping me over onto my back and removing the gag.

His veiny cock glistens with my juices, and a white trail of cream coats the underside. Ramming it inside my mouth, he holds me in place with a hand in my hair. "That's it. Taste yourself on me."

My gag instinct kicks in, and I choke around his length while squeezing my sticky thighs together. I want more.

"Make my dick nice and wet," he orders as he eases back to watch me lick it. "Good girl. More."

I swirl my tongue over the crown and then spit on his length, but when I go to do it again, he plugs my mouth with the gag, grabs hold of my ankles, and brings them to my ears. I'm bent in half with my arms trapped behind me and my puffy cunt on full display. But it's not my pussy that catches his attention.

Braced on his knees, he lubes up my ass with my arousal

before slowly sinking back inside my cunt, feeding me inch by delicious inch, watching my heat swallow his cock until he's balls deep. He pulls out to the tip, then does it again, observing me closely as his glistening length disappears inside me. He fucks me like that—slow and deep, until my chest heaves with harsh breaths.

My pussy drips as he rubs the wet crown over my ass in a terrifying showcase of self-control, pressing inside me slowly, his fingers flexing on my ankles. It starts to sting, so I wince.

"Relax, or it'll hurt more."

I do as I'm told, and Dominic sheaths himself to the hilt in my ass. Behind him, the towering cornstalks move in the wind—a stunning backdrop to the pure sadism glittering in his ominous eyes.

My throat jumps against the belt as I swallow the saliva pooling in my mouth. Dominic focuses on the spot where we're connected, lip trapped between his teeth, as he eases out of me with agonizing slowness.

"Bear down," he orders, his voice dripping with authority. Once again, I do as I'm told, causing more arousal to leak from my cunt.

He sinks his cock inside my ass, releasing a growl as he sets a feral rhythm, my back gliding in the soil with every powerful thrust. I've never been more grateful for my tank top or the soft ground beneath me.

A multitude of emotions flickers across Dominic's face. Behind the darkness, behind all the raw power currently flowing through his bulging veins, is a side I want to access. An elusive side that's there one minute and gone the next.

All thoughts flee my head when he pinches my clit, sweat trailing down his temple and onto his flushed cheek. His regal features look even sharper when he's fucking. I've never seen anyone as breathtaking as him. He's so beautiful, in fact, that it's hard to look at him in moments like these, yet I never break eye contact. When my pussy contracts, his jaw clenches, and his control slips. He shudders, dragging his thumb over my swollen clit again and again.

A muffled moan claws its way up my throat, just as pleasure crashes down on me like a stack of cards, my ass clenching around his cock. This orgasm is unlike anything I've ever felt. It's drawn out, tearing through me until my ears hum and my vision blackens around the edges.

"Fuck, that's it," Dominic grunts, his muscles rippling and straining as he grinds his dick deep, spilling inside me. Another bead of sweat falls from his temple and hits my collarbone. I'm still floating in a cloud of pleasure when he lifts me from the ground and cradles me against his warm chest. Exhaustion creeps out from between the cornstalks, and the next thing I know, I fall asleep, surrounded by Dominic.

I'm too hot. It's stifling.

I blink my eyes open and gaze around the room.

A room that isn't mine.

I look down at Dominic's face, only now realizing I've been asleep in his arms. This is his room and his bed.

His scent blankets me, not only because I'm wrapped in his embrace. I'm also wearing his T-shirt.

I'm braced on his chest, staring at his face while his heart beats steadily beneath my palm. How did this happen? How did we go from hate to…this? Why does he fuck me brutally one minute, promising pain and punishment, and then sleeps with me in his arms? Why does he guard me at night? Why does he notice me?

There's an insistent throb between my legs as I carefully extract myself from his arms. A small part of me wants to stay and explore whatever this is, but a bigger part of me fears my tumultuous emotions. Dominic is beyond intense. He's a brewing storm. I can't allow myself to get swallowed whole by his destructive power, no matter how alluring it is.

No matter how much my body quakes at the sight of him.

With my mind made up, I sneak across the hall and enter my room, carefully closing the door behind me.

I can never be too careful around Dominic. The man could hear a pin drop in a crowded room.

After changing into clean clothes and packing a bag, I climb out through my window, questioning my decision as I lower myself down the trellis. A normal person would leave through the front door, but something tells me it would wake the beast in the room next to mine.

He'll soon find me. Every cell in my body knows it. I need a reprieve and a chance to breathe, even for just a few hours.

SIXTEEN

CAMRYN

GWEN LETS me in with a wide smile on her black-painted lips. "I couldn't believe it when you messaged me to ask for my address."

I toe off my shoes in the hallway. "I'm sorry it's so early. I didn't even think you'd be awake."

She shrugs, dressed in a leather skirt, a purple tank top, and a black choker. "I've struggled to sleep since…"

Benny's death.

We stare at each other for a brief moment while the first rays of sunrise peek through the curtains.

"C'mon, this way." Gwen walks past me, and I hike my bag higher onto my shoulder as I follow her upstairs to her bedroom.

Dropping my bag onto the floor, I take in the purple walls and even deeper purple curtains. A gray, fluffy blanket lies pooled on the quilt, and a pile of clothes litters the chair in the corner. Her desk is a biohazard with piles of textbooks, empty soda cans, and various small potted plants.

Behind me, my reflection is barely visible between the countless photographs taped to a freestanding mirror. I study them in silence while Gwen sits down on the bed.

"Most of them are from last year."

"I like this one of you all."

She walks up behind me and peers over my shoulder at the photograph of them all at the beach. "Benny got stung by a jellyfish that afternoon." Her voice drips with grief.

My chest clenches. "I'm sorry about your loss."

"It's not your fault."

"I know," I reply, wringing my hands as her cherry scent thickens around me, "but maybe we shouldn't have done the séance."

"You think the séance is behind what happened?"

I turn around. "Maybe. Have you noticed anything weird since that day?"

Gwen walks back to her bed and plops down, her faraway gaze set on the woods outside. "The trees whisper." Tears cling to her lashes as she lowers her gaze. "The wind..."

"It sings," I finish for her.

She lifts her eyes and observes me for a beat before swiping at her tears. "Let's skip school today. We need to find answers."

"What answers?" I ask as she reaches for her phone on the bedside table.

She types out a few messages, then puts the phone down beside her and leans back on her hands. "We need to find out what happened to Benny."

When I stay silent, she looks past me. "He wasn't suicidal."

"I didn't know him that well."

"But I did."

Instead of replying, I sit down beside her in silence. Seconds tick by. We get lost in our thoughts. She nudges my shoulder and flashes a weak but playful smile. "Your stepbrother gave you the 'D,' then?"

Cringing, I look away, but the sweet notes of her laugh draw my attention back, and I can't help but join in. I shove her away, and she comes right back, pulling me into her arms with a genuine smile. "I'm happy for you."

"Don't be," I reply.

She frowns. "Why not?"

"He's just…intense."

"Good intense or 'Gwen kill him for me' intense?"

"Definitely good intense, but also scary intense."

Her eyes bounce between mine, and then her smile grows impossibly wide. "Oh, you have it bad."

"I don't have it bad." A chuckle of disbelief bubbles up from my chest. "I don't," I repeat, trying to convince myself.

"Is that why you're blushing?"

Shaking my head, I shove her away. "I'm not blushing."

"You so are." She leans back on her hands. "He's been all over you lately. I'm surprised he let you leave his side to come here."

My cheeks burn, and her eyes widen.

"You sneaky devil. He doesn't know."

"He is kind of suffocating." I lift a shoulder and let it fall. "I needed some breathing room for a few hours."

"Well, you came to the right place." She toys with a strand of my hair, a soft smile gracing her lips. "He would be silly not to be obsessed with you."

Heat crawls up my neck, and I open my mouth to speak, when the doorbell sounds. Gwen's fingers fall away from my hair as she stands up. "The cavalry has arrived."

Streaks of sunshine pour in through the open window. Gwen lights the candle beside the spirit board. Aron jiggles his knee, chin propped on his clasped hands.

Seated on my right, Lily looks white as a sheet while staring at the flickering flame before she tears her eyes away and directs her attention to Gwen. "Maybe we shouldn't do this."

Aron shoots her a hard glare.

Gwen sits down across from us and stares at the letters on the board. Her voice lacks anticipation. "What other choice do we have? We need answers."

"Benny was suicidal." Lily lowers her gaze.

Seated beside Gwen, Brittany stares at the candle.

"You know he wasn't," Gwen pushes. "You know it."

Lily lifts her gaze. "I don't know anything."

They stare at each other.

It's Aron who finally sighs before placing his finger on the skull dial. "Let's just do this."

I sense him beside me—stiff and uncomfortable, his knee bouncing relentlessly.

Steeling myself, I place my finger next to his on the dial. We exchange a glance.

"Let's just get it over with," Brittany says, and she and Gwen touch the planchette, too.

Lily hesitates, eyes downcast. "This is wrong."

Aron's jiggling knee brushes up against mine, causing my throat to close up. He radiates violence—a time bomb that's seconds away from detonating.

"Please," Gwen pleads, softening her features. "We need you, Lily. You're the glue that keeps us together."

Seconds pass before she reluctantly sits forward and puts her finger on the dial.

"Okay…" Gwen says on a long exhale. "Let's close our eyes and take a few deep breaths."

I rub my sweaty palm on my lap while inhaling deeply through my nose and exhaling through my mouth. A small voice whispers at the back of my mind how reckless this is, but I blank it out.

Now is not the moment for regrets.

Gwen's haunted voice assaults the silence. "Are there any spirits present that wish to communicate with us?"

My heart thuds hard as the seconds tick by.

Undeterred, Gwen tries again, "We welcome you to our circle."

Nothing happens.

Beside me, Aron shifts in his seat, his spicy scent filling the air.

"What happened to Benny?"

"Just fucking show yourself, you pathetic coward," Aron growls, and I open my eyes.

He glares at the candle, waiting and watching like me for it to flicker or, even better, blow out like last time. When nothing happens, he shoots to his feet and kicks the chair, causing Lily to yelp.

"He wasn't suicidal!"

Pacing back and forth, he pulls the hairs at his nape.

"He fucking wasn't." He points a finger at the spirit board on the table. "This proves nothing."

"Aron," Gwen tries, her eyes glassy with tears.

He sends her a glare and stops pacing. "You know he wasn't suicidal."

She remains quiet, neither agreeing nor disagreeing, and simply watches him with sad eyes while he unravels before us.

"I was his best friend. If anyone knew him, it was me." He jabs at his chest. "Don't you think he would have said something or given some kind of clue if he was suicidal?"

"He wasn't suicidal," I speak up. "And he wouldn't kill someone."

All eyes land on me, and I drop my gaze as my cheeks burn. I clear my throat. "Weird things have happened since my family moved into that house. Whatever that…thing is," I say, fidgeting with my hands, "it stalks me through others."

"What do you mean?" Brittany asks.

I sniffle. "It has taken an…interest in Dominic's obsession with me."

No one speaks, and I keep my gaze on my lap.

"While Benny was on the roof, he shouted something to me." I peer through my lashes at Aron. "It said, '*his obsession with you is delicious.*'" I sweep my gaze around the table. "That's what Mr.

Jones said *and* what Dominic once said when this...thing entered him."

"I remember that day," Gwen says. "Something happened to you. You went pale and clammy, and then you freaked out on Mr. Jones. We thought it was a heatstroke."

"Wait a minute. Slow down." Aron tugs harder on his hair. "What do you mean by '*this thing entered him.*'"

"I mean exactly that. Whatever this entity is, it taunts me through others."

"So it can enter our bodies?"

"Potentially," I reply.

When Aron looks at me again, I explain, "Sometimes, it takes charge, like in Benny's case. Other times, it's visions in my head, like with Mr. Jones."

"So what's stopping it from entering our minds right now? What's it waiting for?" Brittany asks as my phone vibrates on the table.

> Where the hell are you?

My heart jumps to my throat, but before I can click out of the screen, another message pops up.

> Don't fuck with me, Camryn. You won't like the consequences.

I quickly dim the screen and place the phone back on the table while the others continue discussing the 'demon.'

The gnawing unease inside me refuses to shift. Dominic is on the warpath. I better run for my life when he finds me, because there's no telling how deeply rooted his darkness is. Something warns me that I've barely scratched the surface.

"It's that fucking house," Aron grumbles, dragging his hand over his mouth. "I say we burn it down."

My head snaps up. "No, you can't do that. Where would we go?"

"That's what you worry about? Benny is dead, but no, all you care about is your fucking house."

Behind me, Brittany rises to her feet and walks over to the kitchen counter while I gnash my teeth.

"I know you're hurting, Aron," I bite out, "but burning down my house isn't the answer."

"No?" He crosses his arms, his biceps bulging as he leans forward slightly. "It's always been that damn house and all the rumors."

I open my mouth to respond, but pause when the lace curtains billow in a gentle breeze. Tendrils of hair tickle my cheeks, and chills erupt over my heated skin as a whisper dances across my shoulders.

"Camryn…"

My attention drifts to Brittany, and I watch in horror as she calmly places her hand inside an electric meat grinder on the counter.

With my heart thrashing against my ribcage, all other sounds fade into the background. Meanwhile, the others are none the wiser, arguing amongst themselves.

"Brittany," I breathe shakily, rising to my feet. "What are you doing?"

Silence falls over the room as the others follow my line of sight.

Lily cries out, and Gwen remains frozen in place. Aron has turned a sickly pale.

"You don't want to do this." I fight to keep my voice steady. "You're stronger than…him."

It.

Brittany cocks her head to the side and her pupils dilate until the black swallows the white. I come to a halt, my heart threatening to claw its way out of my chest.

"That's where you're wrong." The tone of her voice is

distorted and dripping with twisted amusement. "Brittany never stood a chance."

I step closer, sweat sticking to my nape. "What do you want?"

"Don't pretend you don't know. Naivety isn't a good look on you."

"Please don't do this," I beg. "Please, I'm begging you."

Her nostrils flare when she breathes in the air. She fixes those black eyes on me, and I suppress the fear that threatens to immobilize me.

Lily's soft cries sound muted in the background. I peer down at Brittany's hand inside the meat grinder, and my heart stutters.

Brittany's distorted laughter rings out in the small room—cold and sinister. "It's easy. You wanted to play, so we'll play."

"Play?" I ask.

"Your friends offered themselves up as vessels."

"Are you saying you're bored?" I spit.

Brittany's eyes swim with darkness as her lips peel back. "I feed on chaos and pain." Her smile morphs into something sickening and she lowers her voice, whispering, "Desire."

I glance down at her hand and swallow thickly. "So why don't you take me?"

Next to me, Aron turns to granite. I press on, "I live in that house. It's me you want."

"Don't worry, your time will come."

With a flick of her fingers, the machine turns on, and all hell breaks loose. Screams erupt in the room, but not from me. No, I watch in terror as blood and minced flesh pour from the meat grinder.

Aron surges forward and rips her away, only to be met by her psychotic peals of laughter.

Where her hand used to be, mangled flesh and protruding bone remain—stark white amongst all that red.

I can't look away, my stomach churning violently as I grow dizzy.

"Phone a fucking ambulance," Aron shouts, cradling her in his arms, and that's when I realize her black eyes are locked on me.

A slow smirk graces her lips before the black retreats, and her face contorts in pain, her agonized scream tearing through my soul. The wind shifts the curtains in my periphery, a leaf twirling against the glass, as if seeking a way inside.

As I watch, another gust of wind carries it away while sirens draw closer in the distance.

SEVENTEEN

CAMRYN

TIME MOVES SLOWLY. I've lost count of how many nurses have walked past while I stare blankly at the off-white wall across the hall. Even the muted sounds struggle to penetrate through this fog.

Lily has finally stopped crying beside me, and Gwen looks like she has aged a decade. I think we all have.

Seated beside me, Aron has his elbows on his knees and his head in his hands. His disheveled hair looks as though he has run his fingers through it to the point of pain. His bloodshot eyes are as distant as mine.

The doctor came by earlier to inform us that Brittany's surgery was a success and that she would be okay, but her hand...

I shudder, remembering the blood and minced flesh and Brittany's agonized screams—

"You need to answer your fucking phone."

I'm not even surprised he's here. Of course, he is. He'll always find me.

I stare blankly at the crotch in front of me, at the thick bulge obscuring my view of the hospital wall.

Two fingers lift my chin. Dominic's dark eyes hook mine, his jaw clenching as he stares down at me with enough intensity to sink a ship and drown its crew. I expect him to reprimand me, but he stays silent, flexing his fingers on my jaw.

A nurse walks by behind him, the sound of her footsteps fading into the background—*everything* fades except for him. He's all I can focus on as the tears cascade down my cheeks.

I feel safe now that he's here.

Without a word, he pulls me into his embrace and wraps his big arms around me.

Clutching his T-shirt, I breathe him in.

Leather and citrus.

"I'm sorry." His voice rumbles like thunder, the softness in those words from his lips warming me from the inside out.

I bury my nose in his clothes and squeeze him tight, soothed by his steady heartbeat and rippling muscles beneath his creased T-shirt. "You came."

"Of course I fucking came." His large palm engulfs my head, and I feel so small and fragile in his embrace.

"You're not easy to find." He tangles his fingers in my hair and places a kiss on top of my head. "Answer your fucking phone when I call you."

We stiffen when a throat clears behind us.

Dominic turns us but doesn't release me, and we're met by a tired-looking nurse who tells us that Brittany is awake and asking to see us.

We sidle into the room, greeted by a strong antiseptic scent and the repetitive sound from the heart monitor. Hooked up to an IV line, Brittany stares out the window with an empty look. Dark circles frame her eyes and her matted pink hair hangs limp around her shoulders.

Gwen runs up to her and sits in the chair beside the bed while I stay rooted, unable to look away from her bandaged stump. Due to the damage caused to her hand, the doctors had no choice but to amputate.

It's all my fault.

I caused this.

Why am I here? I shouldn't be here.

Dominic puts his big hand on my shoulder and squeezes tight, as if he can hear my spiraling thoughts.

His lips brush up against the shell of my ear. "Talk to her."

The command in his gravelly voice dislodges my feet. I cross the room in a daze, vaguely aware of all the small details, like the blood pressure cuff around her arm and the smudged mascara beneath her eyes.

She looks at me, watching me closely with an expression I can't decipher. I almost turn and run, but Dominic's steady presence behind me stops me from fleeing the room.

"I'm sorry," I whisper when I'm beside her.

"Why are you sorry?"

My lip trembles, and I inhale a shaky breath. "This is all my fault. I got you into this mess—"

"It's not your fault." Her throat jumps on a swallow, and then she looks out the window at the darkening clouds. "I sensed *it*... when it was inside me. Nothing can stop it."

Across from me, Gwen reaches out and squeezes her hand.

Brittany seems oblivious, lost in her thoughts. "Nothing can stop it." She bounces her vacant gaze between us all. "It won't stop."

"Shhh." Gwen tries to soothe her, but Brittany's chin trembles and her eyes fill with tears.

"Not until we're all dead. I saw it... Saw inside its mind."

"You saw what?" Gwen asks, and Brittany fixes her eyes on her.

She remains silent for a long moment. No one breathes. We wait, watching the tears trail down Brittany's pale cheeks.

Aron white knuckles the plastic railing by the foot of the bed, his head hanging low.

More tears fall as Brittany's lashes flutter. "I saw our deaths."

Dominic stiffens behind me. I peer past Brittany at Gwen, who resembles a ghost. Lily stares at Brittany's bandages. No one speaks.

When the blood pressure cuff inflates with a hiss, Dominic interlaces his fingers with mine, and I focus on the sensation of his calloused palm, his heat.

Brittany's croaky voice brings me back to the present. "It feeds on our fear and pain—our sanity, which sustains its existence on this plane. It needs us to grow stronger."

Aron lifts his head. "Why us? Why not someone else?"

"Because of the séance," I say quietly.

"There's no logic," Brittany continues. "This…*thing* isn't human. It's…ancient. It existed before the beginning of time and will exist long after."

"How did it enter our plane?" I ask.

Brittany turns those empty eyes on me. "It was called here a long time ago."

"The previous owners of my house were into the occult." I look at Gwen, swallowing roughly. "That's what you told me."

"Rumor has it the husband invoked the devil," she confirms with a shaky nod. "His family disappeared shortly afterward."

"They were never found," Aron grunts, his arms straining as he looks past us out the window, still gripping the railing like his life depends on it. "And the cops were quick to brush it under the carpet. Blamed their murders on the husband. They think the bodies are buried somewhere in the woods."

"There's nowhere to hide," Brittany says in a haunted, quivering voice. "No matter where we go or how far we travel, it will find us."

"But why?" The desperation in Aron's tone breaks my heart.

"It wants her." Brittany points at me.

Silence falls over the room.

"Why would it want me?" My voice cracks at the end. I look between everyone, trying and failing to plaster a fake smile on my lips. None of this makes sense. "I'm no one."

"Not true." Brittany shakes her head, and I drop my gaze, only to see blood seeping through the bandage, bright red against the white. "It brought you here."

"Brought me here? What do you mean?" I laugh, but it lacks humor. "I don't know what you're talking about."

"Yes, you do. Remember the night of the crash?"

I can feel the blood drain from my face as Dominic turns to granite behind me.

"You saw someone in the road, didn't you? A vision."

"That wasn't—"

"Everything that happened was designed to bring you here, to this town…and that house."

"Why me?" I breathe defeatedly.

"Because you got away."

I open my mouth to reply when the door opens, and Brittany's parents enter. Her eyes remain locked on mine as they fawn over her. When Dominic pulls on my hand, I reluctantly allow him to lead me out of the room.

———

"Because you got away."

I mull over the words in the truck on the way back to the house while watching the cornstalks pass by outside in a blur of yellow. My neck is sweaty, and strands of hair stick to my equally perspiring forehead. This summer never ends.

We pass Wilfred's farm, and I crane my neck when I spot his rusty Volvo parked beside the tractor. The bag of animal remains on the porch is gone.

Dominic's glare burns the side of my face as we turn down the dirt road that leads to our house, and then it's there, looming ahead of us like a grotesque abomination that rises through the earth.

A window is open upstairs, the white curtains dancing in the afternoon breeze. Mom's car is gone.

Dominic leaves the vehicle and slams the door shut, and then he's by my side, suffocating me with his overwhelming presence.

Reaching in, he unlatches my seatbelt, assaulting me with his intoxicating scent. It's unfair how nice he smells. I've never known anything like it.

I hold my breath, trying not to fall under his spell again.

One of my friends is dead. Another is in the hospital. I need to stay composed. I can't let Dominic feed on my sanity, too.

"Don't look at me like that," he orders, his lips so close to mine that his breath whispers across my mouth. Instead of straightening up, he hovers over me inside the truck.

"Like what?" I ask breathily, my clit tingling.

"Like you're going to run again. I don't fucking like it. Stop pushing me away." Braced on one arm, he tucks a damp strand of hair behind my ear and lets his fingers glide down the length of my jaw in a slow caress while his eyes flick between mine. "What's going on inside that head of yours?"

"My friends are dying. It wants me—"

"It can't have you." He grits his jaw. "You're mine. No one hurts you but me." Then he backs out of the truck, grabs my arm, and hauls me out. I stumble behind Dominic, the sun heating my shoulders, tufts of dry grass tickling my bare ankles. His grip pinches my arm, but I like the bite of pain. Dominic is a force to be reckoned with.

As soon as we make it inside, he lifts me up as though I weigh nothing and guides my thighs around his waist. He carries me upstairs to his bedroom, kicks the door shut, and throws me on the bed. I bounce on the mattress, my heart hammering.

"You didn't answer your fucking messages." He flips me over onto my front, shoves down my shorts until they trap my ankles, then delivers a hard smack to my ass.

Shrieking, I wriggle, but he fists my hair and rains more blows on my behind while tears stream down my cheeks. It eggs him on more, if anything, because he reaches over to the bedside table and retrieves a string of rope.

"Dominic?" I question as he secures my wrists behind my back.

His response is another hard smack. "Shut up!"

He leaves me on the bed, pacing behind me like a caged tiger while my pussy leaks and my ass burns from his blows. I'm a frantic mess.

"You left me on read."

I know better than to answer. Know better than to anger him further. A part of me thinks I snuck out on purpose so that he would punish me like this.

I deserve it all.

Flipping me over onto my back, he removes my shorts, and then orders me to spread my legs as wide as I can.

I know he can see the damp patch on my panties and the drunk lust in my heavy eyes.

He bunches my panties and pulls, causing the fabric to strain against my throbbing clit, and my thighs tremble when pleasure zips through me. Then, with a sharp tug, he rips them clean off and stuffs my mouth.

"You've been a fucking brat by not telling me where you are and keeping secrets."

When he drops his almost black eyes to my exposed pussy, tears cling to my lashes as my chest heaves.

"I'm going to hurt you." There's no hesitation in his voice, only pure sadism. "I won't stop until you're a sobbing, dripping mess. I won't take it easy on you either."

Dominic grabs my knees with his warm, calloused hands and spreads me open, then grips the undersides and bends me in half until my knees are by my ears and my holes are on full display for his hungry eyes.

He lets one knee go but keeps the other firmly in place as he drags a single finger through my spread slit and circles my entrance once, blinding me with teasing pleasure.

Dipping a finger inside, he trails it between my ass cheeks and applies pressure to my puckered hole, tsking when I tense.

"You'll need to get used to me fucking all your holes. When you tense up, you make it much more tempting to break you in half." He delivers a hard smack to my pussy, and I cry out as sharp pain explodes like a wave that spreads outward. "That's one."

Another slap. Much harder this time.

My muffled scream fills the room. Before the pain begins to fade, he slaps my pussy again and again, raining blows on my bruised clit. I've never experienced anything like it before. The sensation is so intense, tears stream down my cheeks.

Screams erupt from my chest, yet the pain quickly bleeds into pleasure, balancing on a knife's edge.

Dominic rubs my assaulted clit, his touch bordering on torture, and I moan around the saturated panties, struggling to swallow the saliva in my mouth.

"Such a dirty little girl you are, Sis." His palm connects with my clit again in a hard slap, and I shriek. "Think you can sneak out on me, huh?" He thrusts three fingers inside me, pulling them out just as quickly. With a teasing grin, he spreads them wide, then chuckles as strings of creamy arousal stretch between his fingers.

"I think you like it a little too much." He licks them clean before pinching my clit.

I jolt, my pussy clenching.

He smacks me again, watching me sob and writhe. "You think your little devil friend is in here? Watching me play with your pussy? Think he likes what he sees?"

I moan, the sound muffled by my panties. I'm so close to coming that my body trembles.

"I think it's jealous." Dominic makes a show of slowly leaning down and dragging his tongue over my pussy, lapping at my swollen, bruised clit until I'm hovering closer to euphoria. "Your tight little pussy tastes divine." He drives his tongue inside me, and I come, but if I thought he was done, I was wrong. He tongue-fucks me through it as my body shudders, then rims my ass before biting the left cheek and licking up the coppery blood.

Straightening up, he braces his knees on the mattress and frees his dick, teasing me with the tip as he dips it inside my dripping pussy.

Then, without warning, he thrusts inside, making my body jolt on the bed. His warm fingers encircle the back of my knee, and he keeps me bent in half while he sets to town, fucking me so damn hard I struggle to breathe. He's ruthless, his balls smacking against my ass with every thrust. I come again, my pussy convulsing around his cock.

His lips spread in a cruel, dimpled smirk. "Your little cunt loves my dick, doesn't it? Feel how she strangles it."

He's a damn machine. A vicious, dark night that I'm hopelessly lost in.

He pulls out and spins me around, then grabs hold of the rope restraining my wrists as he fucks me into the mattress. With my ass in the air, his free hand in my hair, and his hips pistoning so roughly that the bedframe slams against the wall, I come for a third time.

"That's it, baby, know who owns you."

When I think I might pass out from pleasure, he pulls out, shifts me over onto my back, and kneels over me with his cock in his hand. His hair falls over his eyes and his lips part on a groan. Jacking his impressive cock, he stares down into my eyes, enrapturing me within his gaze.

"No one gets to see this erotic version of you but me. Understood?"

The veins pop in his forearm. His breathing is increasing. I know he's close, even before he chokes out, "Understood?"

I've barely had a chance to nod when his cum rains over my face and neck. I flinch, but he yanks me up my hair and aims the last few squirts at my mouth.

His semen trails a path down my chin as I blink up at him. He looks like a hedonistic monster who caught his prey. With panted breaths, his fingers pull on my hair until tears spring to my eyes.

He reaches out and removes my saturated panties before sinking his still-hard cock into my mouth and slowly, sensually fucking my lips.

It's sloppy, wet. Perfect.

"I will never let you go." His menacing undertones send shivers racing along my overheated skin. "You're mine."

I gaze up at him as he zips his dick away then reaches for my panties. With an intensity I feel in my bone marrow, he uses them to clean my face before helping me slip them back on and untying the ropes around my wrists.

The damp fabric feels cool against my burning pussy. He gently strokes his thumb over the material, watching intently as the soaked fabric creases beneath his touch. "I want you to wear my cum for the day. If you change into clean panties, I will punish you. And this time, I won't let you come."

He walks out and returns minutes later with a tray of food, ordering me to eat.

While I bite into a strawberry, he tracks my every move as though he can't will himself to look away in case he missed some vital information about me. Something he doesn't already know. As if it can be found in the small details.

My lips wrap around the berry, the sweet juice trailing onto my chin.

He reaches out and swipes it away with his thumb. "Why did you run away?"

I pause my chewing, my eyes clashing with his. He hovers his thumb on my chin and brushes it over my bottom lip.

"It's hard to breathe around you sometimes."

He likes that admission, if his small smirk is of any indication.

"I don't want you to breathe around me."

I bite into another strawberry, and his eyes darken until my toes curl.

"I'm sore," I explain. "I need a break from your…intensity."

"I can still fuck your mouth." His dimpled smile grows impossibly wide, blinding in its beauty. "Or your ass. Besides"—he removes the plate and crawls on top of me—"I'll have your pussy whether you're sore or not."

And then he proceeds to fuck me until I don't know my own name anymore.

EIGHTEEN

CAMRYN

A SINGLE RIPPLE disturbs the glassy lake beneath the moon's ethereal glow.

I watch it travel toward shore, growing in size the closer it gets. Cold water laps at my feet, and I step back out of instinct before the tangible evil that lurks beneath the surface reaches out to grab me.

Before it finally claims me.

As a gentle breeze shifts my hair around my shoulders, another ripple slowly travels along the surface toward shore.

A burst of bubbles follows, and I watch, with my breath caught in my throat, as a car reemerges, bobbing in the water.

Overhead, the moon's light reflects off the wetness, the windows resembling endless, black voids.

Whispers emanate from its shadowy depth, calling my name and drawing me closer. As they lure me to step into the lake, cold water laps at my bare feet once more.

I'm caught in a trance, staring at the bobbing car, my damp nightgown brushing against my ankles as I sway, shivering in the late-night breeze.

"You killed him."

Caught by surprise, I spin around.

Dominic blends with the night as though he commands it. Maybe he does. Maybe that's why the moon takes refuge behind the clouds when he emerges from the shadows.

A predator on the prowl.

"Dominic?" I ask uncertainly as I take a single hesitant step back.

"You're a murderer."

"I didn't kill your dad. It was an accident."

He cocks his head and cuts me into pieces with his cold, assessing gaze. There's no affection in those orbs. None of the previous conflict, only calculative cruelness.

"You can keep telling yourself that, but we both know you're lying to yourself." A yelp escapes me when he surges forward and grips me by the throat. "You're a murderous little slut."

I try to fight him, but he forces me to the ground. He's too strong. His shadow looms over me from behind, and I gulp when I see his reflection in the glassy lake.

His black eyes glare. "Say hi to Dad from me. Maybe you can suck his dick in Hell." With his fingers digging into my nape, he shoves my head beneath the surface.

Water rushes in my ears as panic flares, and bubbles escape my lips. I thrash, consumed by overwhelming panic.

Somewhere below, a lullaby drifts closer.

An eerie melody.

A woman's haunted voice.

I grow still, my hair floating in the water.

Something is moving closer, barely visible in the pitch black.

A splash of white.

A halo of brown hair that shifts backward with the next movement.

Through the darkness below, a woman rushes at me. My mouth flies open, and water floods my lungs. I scream, thrashing and clawing—

I wake with a sharp inhale, nestled in Dominic's arms. My heart won't stop racing, so I scoot out from beneath his arms, careful not to wake him. He will punish me for sneaking out on him again, but I need fresh air. Besides, I'm not running away from him this time; I just need a moment alone.

After throwing on one of Dominic's T-shirts and a pair of denim shorts, I put on flip-flops, tie my hair up, and leave the house.

I close the door quietly, greeted by the gentle sound of rain. After weeks of intense heat, the drop in temperature is a welcome change.

Standing beneath the awning, I breathe in the fresh scent while watching the rain puddle in the overgrown grass. As I reach out, droplets of lukewarm rainwater hit my palm.

Struck with the sudden urge to let it bathe me, I descend the porch steps and tip my head back. My eyes close as I let the rain smatter against my face and wash away my worries. It soaks through my clothes in mere minutes. I can't hold back a smile.

This is what freedom feels like.

Summer rain.

I sense someone watching me, and my eyes fly open on a gasp. The axe dangles from his mud-streaked fingers, and his dark hair lies plastered to his forehead. A raindrop clings to his nose, about to fall, and his flannel shirt molds to his broad chest.

When he remains silent, framed by the fir trees at the edge of the lawn, I gesture to the axe in his hand. "Do you carry that thing everywhere?"

His grip tightens on the wooden handle, though he says nothing.

"I would invite you in, but…" My boyfriend? Is that what he is? "My *friend* would probably kill you." Though there's a hint of laughter in my voice, I mean every word. Dominic is unhinged.

"Hello?" I wave a hand in his face when he stays mute. "Are you going to say anything?"

The raindrop on his nose finally gives up the fight and falls to the ground, and another takes its place, hanging precariously.

Losing patience, I roll my eyes and walk past him. But before I've taken more than three steps, his voice rings out.

"Don't enter the woods."

My steps falter, and I look over my shoulder. "So, he speaks." Strands of grass tickle my bare ankles as I turn fully. "And why shouldn't I enter the woods? What's so dangerous about the trees?"

He looks past me, his muscles shifting inside his wet shirt. "Stay out of the woods."

Confused, I follow his line of sight as a gentle breeze moves through the trees, swaying their branches.

"But you just came from there—" I fall silent when I look back in time to see him disappear around the corner. "Where are you going?" I chase after him, stepping in puddles and wiping rain-water out of my eyes.

Where the hell is he going?

Turning the corner, I come to a stumbling halt.

He's gone.

I scan the lawn and the weathered treehouse at the back of the property. A rusty doll's pram lies on its side, and the sight of it, with the muted red of the sun-bleached fabric, sends a feeling of unease trickling through me.

"Where did you go this morning?" Dominic asks when he enters the kitchen, freshly showered, dressed in shorts and a navy T-shirt. He looks effortlessly handsome. I struggle not to sneak peeks at him as he settles beside me and plays with his Zippo.

Mom rushes into the kitchen in a flurry of flowery perfume, nearly trips over Bruno asleep on the floor, and kisses us both on the head. "I'm late for work."

Then she's gone, waving a quick goodbye over her shoulder.

"Nice seeing you too, Mom," I say as Dominic pockets his

Zippo and threads his fingers through my hair. The soothing stroke of his touch halts my breath, and I slowly meet his gaze.

My throat is suddenly dry. "Why are you looking at me like that?"

"Like what?" His eyes shine with amusement and something else. Something softer. A look I never thought I would see smooth his sharp features.

I shake my head, but his fingers pull my hair.

Ah! There he is.

Despite my thundering heartbeat, I find the prickle of pain soothing. When I look at him this time, his gaze darkens and a muscle clenches his jaw.

"Don't dismiss me."

Now, my throat is dry for entirely different reasons. I'm parched. The look in his eyes promises pain and so much more.

"What about breakfast?" I ask, breathless, but the words barely leave my mouth before his lips descend on mine, hard, hungry, and demanding. His grip on my hair tightens, and he drinks me in like I'm a water source in a desert, nibbling and biting, his tongue tangling with mine until I'm hovering on the brink of death, barely catching my breath in between his hard kisses.

I'm dazed when he finally breaks the kiss, blinking up at him.

Standing, he slips his shorts down to free his hard cock, the impressive length bobbing against his abs.

Why does he have to be so…perfect? Carved by a wicked god to lure women to their deaths.

"Like what you see, little sister?" he asks, wrapping his long fingers around his length.

I wet my lips, nodding. Dominic's thick and veiny dick is a piece of art, just like the rest of him. It's so big that you know it will hurt, but it's a good pain. The kind of pain that makes you see stars and beg for more.

He cups my chin and smirks down at me with a dark gleam in his eyes. "Put your shoes on. I'm taking you out for the day."

Wait, what?

My gaze flicks down to his cock, and I open my mouth to reply when he slides his shorts back up to hide his massive length.

"C'mon." He pulls me to my feet.

I'm confused as I let him lead me out of the kitchen and into the hallway. "But you're hard."

"I'm always hard when you're around," he explains, patiently waiting while I put on my Chucks. His smirk deepens and he opens the door. "Don't worry, Sis. I'll soon let you choke on my cock if you're a good girl."

I step past him, exiting the house. Dominic locks the door behind us, jogging down the steps, making a beeline for his truck while I watch from the porch.

My attention wavers when a soft breeze sweeps through the nearby trees, but the sound of the truck door opening cuts through the strange sensation crawling over my bare skin. I swallow down the unease as I descend the steps.

Dominic waits for me with the door open like a gentleman, but I'm not fooled by the dimpled smirk or the way he tracks my every move. No, I can see the gleam and satisfaction in his eyes when he shuts me inside.

He rounds the truck as I watch the tree line. The truck rocks, and he cranks the engine, easing back with his arm stretched out across the seat. Spinning the wheel, he reverses the vehicle.

"Where are you taking me?" I ask when we're on the road.

Dominic rolled down the window earlier, and now the breeze moves through his dark hair as he looks at me, his hungry eyes devouring my mouth; then his attention is back on the road. "Nowhere. Everywhere."

Light laughter bubbles from my chest, and his lips quirk in response.

"That's your answer?"

His shoulders lift and fall. "Maybe." He looks at me again, stealing the breath from my lungs with his handsome face. "I want you to myself."

My stomach flips as his fingers find my damp nape, tangling in my hair.

"Fuck the world."

"Fuck the world?" My lips spread impossibly wide. I've never seen this side of Dominic before, and it's like a drug. I want more.

"I don't like sharing you with others." He looks back at the road, drumming his thumb on the steering wheel. "Your friends… Demons… They can all fuck off."

"How romantic."

He laughs, and my world tilts on its axis at hearing the care-free sound. Fuck, he's beautiful. Not only that, but he's magnetic. I can't look away. Have I ever heard Dominic laugh or seen him smile like this with a sparkle in his eyes?

I scoot closer and let my lips drift across his stubble until they brush against his ear. "I'm yours, Dom."

He shivers, tightening his grip on the steering wheel. "Say it again."

"I'm yours."

"Fuck…" he breathes, and the loss of composure in that one word, delivered with a tremble in his deep baritone, sends an ache to my clit and makes me wonder about all the other ways I can make this beautiful man lose control.

My hand slips inside his shorts and I wrap my fingers around his hard cock, feeling it twitch in my grip. "If you ease up on the accelerator, I stop."

His deep chuckle trails like honey over my skin as I stroke his silky length, swiping my thumb over the precum on his tip.

"Good boy," I whisper.

"Call me that again," he growls, "and I'll fuck you while you cry."

I work his dick until he squirms, trailing kisses over his neck, his hair tickling my cheek in the summer breeze. I'm intoxicated by his citrusy scent and tense muscles—the power I hold over him as he struggles for control.

"Faster, Dom."

He presses down on the accelerator, and my heart speeds up with it.

"Your dick is perfect." I drag my tongue through the salty sweat on his neck. "I love how big and veiny it is."

"Fuck," he breathes, twitching again in my hand. "You're pushing it, Sis."

We fly down the sunbaked country road. I glance at the speedometer, my heart threatening to burst from my chest. There's something about danger and sex combined that's both addictive and terrifying.

"This is wrong," I admit, moving his shorts out of the way and staring down at his weeping length.

"Wrong?" He buries his fingers in my hair. "This is so fucking right."

I lick my lips. "There's a demon out there trying to kill us. Don't you think this is wrong?"

My scalp prickles with pain as he applies pressure. I push back, not yet ready to give in.

"I'll lose control of the truck if you don't suck my dick, and we'll die anyway."

"Oh?" I laugh, breaking free and scooting out of reach.

The look he throws me could burn down a forest. My nipples harden in response. I wriggle out of my shorts and panties, then kick them off. "I thought you were in more control than that, Dom."

"Don't you fucking dare touch yourself," he warns, gripping his dick and working himself.

"Eyes on the road, big boy. It would be a shame if you lost control of the truck before you fucked me senseless, right?"

Reluctantly, his eyes skate back to the road while I trail my fingers through my slit, loving how he struggles to keep his foot on the speedometer and his attention on driving.

The muscles strain in his forearm as he pleasures himself, the erotic sight pulling a moan from my lips.

He snaps his head in my direction and drops his eyes to my pussy.

"You're killing me," he says, shifting in his seat.

I sink two fingers inside myself, trapping my lip between my teeth, and bite back another moan. Molten pleasure floods my body to the tips of my toes. I revel in having this power over Dominic. Love how a bead of sweat clings to his temple and how he white knuckles the steering wheel while checking his rearview mirror for any signs of the cops.

"I want your cock, Dom."

His hair swoops in the breeze from the open window when he hits the brakes and spins the wheel. We take a violent turn down a dirt road, and my hand smacks against the dashboard to hold myself up.

A cloud of kicked-up dirt surrounds us as the truck comes to a screeching halt, my pulse racing in anticipation. Dominic throws open his door, climbs out, and grabs hold of my ankle. I squeal with surprise as he yanks me down. But the laughter soon dies when he puts my ankles on his shoulders and thrusts inside me in one go.

My back arches off the seat, and a strangled moan claws its way up my throat. Fuck, he feels so good. I'm stretched to my limit. The intense burn makes it all the better.

Dominic's fingers dig into my thighs as he fucks me hard, his balls slapping against my ass with each ruthless snap of his hips. I love the hunger in his eyes.

"More, Dom, fuck, don't stop."

His sexy chuckle caresses my drugged senses. He pulls me farther down on the seat and spreads my thighs as wide as he can while staring down at my cunt.

"You should see your pussy swallow my fat cock. So fucking greedy."

As if to prove his point, he pulls out slowly and slides his wet cock through my slit, over my swollen clit. Then he enters me again with a hard thrust before repeating the process—over and over again, until I'm sobbing and begging him to fuck me harder and faster.

Overhead, the clouds darken as thunder rumbles in the distance. Dominic, the fucking tease, pulls out and grabs his cock, then slaps the head over my clit.

"I don't think you deserve to come just yet." He feeds me the tip, watching me closely, then pulls out and rubs the crown of his cock over my clit in mind-blowing circles. "Maybe I should torture you all day."

I lift my head and glare. "Don't you fucking dare."

He drags me out, and I stumble, unsteady on my feet. With his heat pressed up against my back, he warns, "You don't make the rules here, Sis."

I push my naked ass against his cock, and he grips the back of my neck, nipping my earlobe with his teeth.

"You want me to fuck you?"

"Yes, dammit!"

His chest rumbles like the storm overhead. The clouds are almost as black as his heart, and the sun is nowhere in sight. "Then run."

NINETEEN

CAMRYN

I STIFFEN, pulsing between my legs. "What? Now?"

He can't be serious? Does he want me to run half-naked down a country road where anyone can see us?

"Did I stutter?" He grinds his cock against my ass. "Run like your fucking life depends on it."

My eyes drift over the dirt road, the deeply burrowed track marks, and the cracks in the dry soil. "What will you do when you catch me?"

"I'll hurt you."

My clit throbs at his delicious promise as a raindrop hits my cheek. I wrench free from his grip and run at full speed down the road, hoping for him to catch me and make true to his promise. I want him to fuck me and hurt me. To make me cry while I come all over his dick.

I've barely made it ten steps when the sky opens, and rain bounces off the dirt road.

Glancing behind me, I shriek, panic crawling up my throat as I see him hot on my heels.

I know we're playing a twisted game, but my brain hasn't caught on, which makes it exciting. My heart hammers hard as my breaths saw through my throat.

I turn my attention forward but trip and tumble to the ground, pain exploding in my knees from the impact. My hands and arms are covered in wet mud as I push to my knees. But before I can jump to my feet, Dominic grabs my hair and drags me back toward the truck, kicking and screaming, the rough surface shredding my skin.

The pain, the fear, the sickening satisfaction I derive from the dark look in his eyes when he drops me, before crouching down and forcing my face into the wet mud, should worry me, but my pulsing clit and soaking pussy speaks louder.

We like this.

We like this a fuck-lot.

"You want to be a dirty little girl?" he asks gruffly as I cry into the mud. "You should see your face now, covered in filth."

His bruising grip on my nape and his cruel words shouldn't lick such a delicious path over my skin, but I can't help it.

I'm lost, sobbing as the rain bounces off the ground beside me.

A raindrop clings to his nose, and his hair lies plastered to his forehead. He stares down at me, knowing full well the effect his savage treatment has on my body.

Hauling me to my feet, he drags me to the truck. My cheek meets the hard surface with a smack, and then he's on me, gripping me by my nape and sliding his cock through my ass crack while the rain hammers the rusty metal.

I feel him at my entrance, hard and throbbing, and my breath gets lodged in my throat when he sinks inside me.

"You have no idea how good you feel or how perfect you are," he says with a grunt as he bottoms out.

His dick pulses against my inner walls, and I close my eyes. He feels so, so good. Every slide of his hard length rubs against my rippling core, and all else fades when he hits a magical spot. I'm no longer aware of the thunder overhead or the summer rain, nor his punishing grip on my neck or the sharp snaps of his hips against my ass.

Dominic knows how to fuck.

"You like to be railed on my hood in the pouring rain, don't you, little sister? You like my big cock tearing through your cunt."

I whimper, and his fingers twitch on my neck in response.

"You thought you could tease me in the truck, huh? A fun little game. But you see, this is what happens when you try to get one over on me. I will fuck you raw and leave you with cum dripping down your thighs."

Pleasure blinds me. I cry out, struggling to catch my breath through the orgasm. My lips are slippery with rain as I moan his name. Moan it like it's a holy prayer and he's my god.

Dominic shudders, groaning deep in his chest, his hips stuttering as he comes deep inside me.

We stay like that, me bent over the hood and Dominic clinging to my back. He digs his fingers into my bruised hips, his harsh breaths tickling my ear as his heart thuds hard against me.

He pushes back then pulls me with him, enveloping me in his arms.

Cum slithers down my thighs, as promised. I cling to his T-shirt, feeling his heat through the thin fabric.

Dominic guides me back inside his truck and then rounds the vehicle. When he's seated behind the steering wheel, he rolls up the window and turns to look at me. Overhead, the rain hammers on the roof. The sound is so loud that it's almost deafening. I love everything about this moment.

I might even love him.

No—I squish that thought as soon as it enters my mind.

"Why do I feel like this around you?" he asks, lost in thought.

"Like what?"

His eyes scan my face, leaving nothing unseen. "Like I want to slaughter anyone who stands in my way of being with you."

My heart gives a hard thud, and I hold my breath as he crawls forward like a lion on the prowl. The muscles shift in his arms as he comes for me, his eyes heavy.

"Dominic?" I ask nervously.

He hovers inches away from my lips. We lock eyes, and I steal a quick glance at the spot where his T-shirt hangs open to reveal a hint of his carved chest. His pulse flutters visibly in his neck, and when I raise my gaze, he tightens his sharp jaw, demanding my attention with every ragged exhale. I reach up to brush his damp hair away from his brow, and he holds his breath. I hold mine too, flicking my eyes between his.

Then his lips crash down on mine, and he kisses me like I'm the oxygen he needs to breathe as he pulls me down on the seat.

This kiss is different from the previous ones. It's more than a promise and something far more intimidating than a threat. My toes curl as he delves his tongue into my mouth and groans.

"Camryn," he exhales longingly, stroking his fingers down the length of my jaw. I shiver, sliding my palms up his chest over his wet T-shirt.

"Dominic—"

He swallows his name on my lips, then sucks on my tongue as he rolls his hips. My mouth dries up when his hardening length digs into my thigh. I cling to his shoulders while he trails kisses down my throat and chest, all the way to my tank top's hem. He slides it up over my chest and pushes my bra away, too, before wrapping his enticing lips around a nipple.

Groaning deeply, he sucks hard. I gasp, digging my nails into his muscles.

"Tell me about that night." His warm breath whispers across my nipple as he peers up at me. "The crash."

I meet his hungry eyes, watching him trail kisses to my other nipple. His tongue darts out to circle the hardened bud, giving a warning bite that makes me shudder.

"What happened?" he asks, sucking the rosy bud into his delicious mouth and swirling his tongue until my toes curl inside my ruined Chucks.

"Your brother was in the backseat on his phone. Your father asked me about my dancing."

He peers up at me from beneath dark strands of his damp hair, and it's a struggle to speak coherently when he sucks and nibbles like he's on a mission to make me come from nipple stimulation alone.

I swallow down a whimper. "I saw something in the road."

He pauses, my nipple slipping from between his lips. "Saw something?"

"Someone—a man. Ah, fuck…" I moan as he swirls that expert tongue. "A man in the road."

"And?"

"Your father lost control…" My words drift off when he pinches my other nipple. "But there was no one there."

He looks up, his eyebrows pulling down low.

"I saw someone," I clarify, "but he disappeared."

"He disappeared?"

"Like a ghost."

Twirling my left nipple absently, he palms my other tit and delivers a hard blow.

I yelp, entrapping him with my thighs around his narrow waist.

"You saw a ghost."

I can barely speak. "Yes…I think so."

"Then what happened?"

It hurts to relive the memories, but he's determined to dig them all up.

Unable to meet his fierce eyes, I stare at the ceiling and swallow down the ache spreading throughout my chest. "The car careened into the river. Your brother… He was already dead."

"What about my dad?"

"Dominic," I whisper, but he slaps my nipple again, making me flinch as my skin smarts.

"Tell me."

"He was stuck, and we couldn't free him."

"Go on."

"He ordered me to retrieve his gun from the glovebox." Tears blur my vision, and I focus on a small stain on the ceiling. "He told me to save myself."

Dominic has grown still, and when the silence stretches on, I finally gather the courage to look him in the eye.

My chest caves in at the sadness there.

"How did the affair start?"

I try to look away, but he grips my jaw and snaps my eyes back to his.

"How did it start, Camryn?"

I'm acutely aware of my naked state. It feels wrong. The urge to cover myself borders on suffocating, but Dominic won't let me hide.

"I don't know." My voice is barely audible, but he hears it and grinds his teeth in response to the tears falling down my cheeks.

"Of course, you know."

I try to shake my head, but he digs his fingers into my jaw. "I don't know. It was like…"

"Like?"

I blink and more tears fall. "Like I was under the control of something—like *we* were under control."

His eyes flick between mine. Outside, the downpour transforms into light rain until it stops completely. Dominic continues watching me even as the sun peeks through the clouds.

"I don't think it's a mistake that we're here," I admit, remembering what Brittany said in the hospital. "I have this memory…"

He loosens his grip on my jaw and tucks a strand of hair behind my ear.

"I saw a doll in your father's office."

Stiffening, he pauses with his fingers on the shell of my ear.

"The same doll as the one in the attic." I raise a meaningful eyebrow.

Dominic knits his brows together in thought, then sits back in his seat, running a hand through his hair. He glances back at me— at my thighs, naked breasts, and tangled hair. His throat jumps, and I do as well when he slams his hand on the steering wheel.

"Fuck!" He trembles as he rests his elbow on the door and rubs his jaw. The scratch of his short beard is loud in the ensuing silence.

I sit up and shove my top down before bending to retrieve my shorts and panties from the footwell. Dominic says nothing while I pull them on and button them up. The lust I felt earlier is gone, replaced instead with feelings of vulnerability.

Tears burn the backs of my eyes when he continues rubbing his mouth and jaw while staring blankly ahead, as if I don't exist anymore and the moment we shared moments ago never happened.

When he finally looks at me, I don't know what to make of the haunted glaze in his eyes, but then he reaches out to palm my cheek and rubs his thumb over my skin in a soothing motion.

"Did I scare you?"

"No," I lie.

He pauses, before cupping my chin and dragging that calloused thumb over my trembling bottom lip. "I did." His clenching jaw contrasts starkly with the gentle way he caresses my mouth. "I'm sorry."

A breath escapes me. He crosses the small place and presses his lips to mine in an open-eyed kiss. There's no tongue involved, but the way his fingers tremble on my chin hooks my heart, as though he can't control his emotions.

I'm falling for this man.

"Kiss me back, Camryn."

I nip his bottom lip between my teeth and his chest vibrates as he responds, crashing his mouth harder against mine. With a final sigh, he presses his forehead to mine and whispers, "I believe you."

I'm holding my breath, I realize, when he sits back and cranks the engine. Outside, the damp air fills with exhaust fumes, but he's all I see.

When his eyes skate to me, my heart ceases to beat. I'm so screwed. Even more so when he smiles and reaches for my hand.

TWENTY

DOMINIC

I drive us to a grocery store where I buy everything I can find that I remember seeing Camryn eat throughout the years. Her eyes pop wide open when I return to the truck.

Now we're parked in a field in the middle of nowhere with a small lake in front of us. The sun beats down on us as Camryn lies with her head on my chest.

Surrounded by empty boxes of snacks on the blanket in the flatbed, we stare up at the puffy clouds while I trail my fingers through her soft strands. It's probably the most content I remember ever being.

"Do you think this is wrong?" she asks.

My fingers falter. "Do I think what is wrong?"

"Benny is dead, and Brittany is in hospital." Rolling over, she rests her weight on her elbow as she looks down at me. She trails those beautiful eyes over my face, stroking her fingers down the length of my nose and lips. "It feels wrong somehow. There's something out there that's out to hurt us."

I snatch her wrist with my hand as the sun heats my cheeks, feeling her pulse pick up speed. "Listen to me, it's okay to be happy."

"You're happy?" she asks, a smile playing at the corners of her lips.

"With you, yes."

Her smile slips and her brow furrows as she searches my eyes.

I cock my head, skimming my fingers over her smooth cheek, shifting a lock of hair out of the way. "I want more moments like these."

A blush creeps up her neck, reddening her cheeks. She's so damn cute when she gets shy like this.

She tries to look away and hide those rosy cheeks, but I won't let her. I capture her chin and lift my head to press my lips to hers, and then I lie back down, smiling wide and squinting against the sun. Her chin feels so small in my hand as I pull her back down until she hovers inches away from my lips. "Forget about everything else for a moment and be here with me."

"Okay," she agrees quietly, and I almost growl and take her once more. Instead, I release her. She lies back down beside me, nestled into my side with her chin on my shoulder and the whisper of her breath against my throat.

"Why did you use to hate me so much when we first met?"

A pang of…*something* blossoms behind my ribcage. I can't put my finger on the emotion. She must sense my hesitation because she says, "I'm sorry. You don't have to answer."

A large cloud rolls across the sky, threatening to steal the sunshine. Sighing, I press a kiss to the top of her head. "I didn't hate you. I was angry with my dad. We had a broken relationship after my mom passed away. Dad, he… Fuck…" I rub my eyes, swallowing down the ache that constricts my throat. "My brother accepted that he had moved on, but I couldn't. Seeing him dote on you and your mom… *His new family.* It hurt."

My chest feels tight, and I avoid looking her in the eye when she pushes up on her elbow again. Those breathtaking eyes slide over my face while I grind my teeth to dust.

"It wasn't you—"

"Shhh!" She presses her fingers to my mouth. "It doesn't matter, Dom."

I meet her gaze and the knot in my chest eases when she lets her eyes drop to my mouth, framed by the sun peeking through the cloud overhead. "It matters."

"No, Dom. You said it yourself—be here with me." She trails a finger over my lips, then climbs to her feet and jumps off the flatbed. "Let's go for a swim."

I sit up, bewildered, as she strips out of her clothes. "What are you doing?"

Pulling her top over her head, her long hair cascades over her freckled shoulders. "I'm getting naked."

A smile spreads across my lips. "I can see that."

She unclips her bra and then tosses it into the overgrown grass. "Am I swimming alone, Dominic?"

I watch her slowly back away with a teasing smile that's so flirtatious my chest warms with something foreign, something I've never felt before. Something only this girl can evoke.

Jumping up, I yank my T-shirt over the back of my head and she sinks her teeth into her bottom lip as I drop it to the flatbed.

"You better run."

Her lip escapes from between her teeth, and a bright smile touches those sensuous lips. She squints up at me, shielding her eyes from the sun with her hand.

I rest my foot on the edge of the flatbed and offer a wide grin. "You think I'm joking?"

A laugh escapes her when I jump down, landing with a heavy thump.

"I don't see you running," I tease as I kick off my shorts.

"I don't know," she replies, watching me remove my shoes and socks. "I'm curious to see what you'll do."

My smile is wolfish. "You know exactly what I'll do when I catch you."

Once I'm fully undressed, I hold up a shoe and make a show of letting it fall to the grass. A heartbeat passes while we smile at each other, and then she squeals with delight and dashes for the water.

———

My fingers surf the warm breeze outside the window.

Camryn is quiet on the way back, and I soon find out why when she breaks the silence. "Do you think we should tell my mom about us?"

I cut my gaze from the road to look at her. "Do you think she'll take it well?"

She worries her lip for a moment, then sighs and looks back out the passenger window. "No, she won't."

An ugly feeling settles in my chest. Trust her mom to try to get between us. It wouldn't surprise me. I gnash my teeth before forcing myself to relax.

When she continues staring at the passing cornfields, I pull my hand from the window, grab the steering wheel, and reach for her fingers. "We don't have to tell her yet. There's no rush."

There absolutely is. I want the whole world to know about us, but I'm mature enough to admit that it's not ideal to go public this soon after the move.

Camryn attempts to smile, but then her eyes catch on the road, and she straightens in her seat. "Pull over here."

Frowning, I follow her line of sight. "Wilfred's farm? Why?"

She gestures impatiently, and I spin the wheel.

The truck slows to a halt by the edge of the road.

"What are you—" I ask when Camryn jumps out, but she slams the door shut.

What the fuck? Where is she going?

I climb out too, frowning as she sets off down a dirt road that leads to his house.

"Camryn," I shout, but she doesn't stop.

Fuck…

Chasing after her, I catch up halfway down the dirt road. "What are you doing?"

"He's not home," she responds.

My mouth opens and closes, at a loss for words.

"Camryn," I hiss when she opens the gate.

She slips through, then turns and says, "Look, I'm going to explore. You can either follow me or go home. It's your choice."

My eyes slide past her to the farmhouse, skating over the dirty windows and derelict porch. The driveway is empty except for a rusty tractor. Somewhere in the distance, hens cluck.

"I don't get you sometimes," I say, running a hand down my face. "Why are we here?"

She peers back at the house, and my hackles rise when she looks at me with her lip trapped between her teeth.

"Demons, remember?"

A frown creases my brow, but she's already gone, sprinting across the overgrown grass.

Expletives pour from my lips, and I slam my fist down on the gate. She's so fucking stubborn when she gets an idea stuck in her head. Dammit.

The gate creaks as I slip through.

Camryn peers through the window beside the door when I climb the porch steps. "I can't see anything," she says, sounding dejected.

"Maybe you should just knock to see if he's actually out," I suggest.

"Or maybe we should just walk in," she replies triumphantly, opening the door.

I chuckle despite how crazy this is. How crazy *she* is. "What can I do to convince you that this is a bad idea and we should leave?"

"Are you scared, Dominic?" she asks as she turns around with her back to the door and a teasing smile on her lips.

The kind of smile that hardens my dick.

My chuckle is filthy when she backs inside. "Are you challenging me?"

"Maybe." She bites her lip, letting the moment linger.

She knows exactly the kind of hold she has on me, and fuck me if I'm not a glutton for the heated look in her eyes.

With a final smile, she turns and enters the house, leaving me reeling in the doorway. I follow behind, and she winks at me over her shoulder as I slowly shut the door.

It's dark and quiet. I breathe easier.

"Why are we here?" I ask as we move through various gloomy rooms.

She lets her fingers drift over a worn fabric couch that looks like it's an heirloom from the sixties. Her curious eyes skate over the torn wallpaper, sideways picture frames, and dead flowers in the windows. "Something tells me this place is important."

I look around, crinkling my nose at the overfilled ashtray on the coffee table. But then my attention catches on her when she pauses in front of the fireplace to inspect the framed photographs lining the top.

My eyes snag on the curve of her neck and bare shoulder. The strap of her tank top has slid off and rests halfway down her upper arm. She's effortlessly attractive with her still-damp hair. Though I've already fucked her countless times today, my dick stirs again. If it were up to him, we'd be buried balls deep inside her constantly.

"Look at this, Dom," she says, waving me over without looking away from the picture frame in her hands.

TWENTY-ONE

CAMRYN

It can't be? Can it? But the longer I stare at the old photograph, the more convinced I get. Yes, it's the same guy I saw back at the house with a dead hen in his hand when I was rooting through photographs in the attic.

He looks exactly like my mystery guy—

My thoughts scatter when Dominic's lips descend on the curve of my neck. He bites and nibbles, pulling me against his growing erection.

"Look at this picture," I coax in a breathy voice.

Dominic trails his lips back up my neck before giving it a cursory glance as he palms my tits. "What about it?"

"It looks like the guy from the woods."

Humming near my ear, he pulls down my tank top to free my breasts, his rough fingers palming their weight as he sinks his teeth into my neck.

"Maybe Wilfred has a nephew that looks like the man in this picture."

"You talk too much." He takes the picture from my hands and places it back on the shelves. Then he spins me around and crushes his lips to mine. "I need to be inside you."

"Now?" I ask between kisses as he tweaks my tender nipples

and shoves my shorts down my thighs. "Wilfred could return any minute."

"Scared?" he taunts, echoing my question from earlier.

"Excited," I counter, drawing a filthy smile from his lips.

"That's my girl."

Those three words make my heart swell, but he doesn't seem to notice that I'm not returning his kiss. He spins me around and presses up against my back, trailing his hand down my stomach until he's there, his expert fingers trailing through my soaked slit.

He hums low in his throat. "Always ready for me."

I whimper when he sinks two digits inside my sore core.

"Always so fucking wet and needy."

"Dom..."

"I can feel your pussy squeezing me. You're greedy, aren't you?"

His intoxicating scent. Those filthy words. I almost cry from the loss of him when he steps away and grabs my arm, but I don't have time to react before we're on the move. I stumble along, his pinching grip forcing me forward. After stripping me of my shorts and panties, he bends me over the edge of the couch with his hand on my neck, the musty scent of the moth-eaten fabric assaulting my nostrils.

"Do you like the thought of being discovered?" he asks as he frees his dick and runs the crown through my sore slit. "Hmm?"

My breathy admittance makes him chuckle, and I hold my breath as he circles my tender entrance. I'm a whore for him and his painful touch. A whore for the hard smack against my ass that rocks me forward.

Pain spreads across my cheek, and he grabs my hips before impaling me on his cock. I scream at the sudden intrusion, the sound muffled by the cushion. When he fists my hair, my sobs soon morph into choked moans and whimpers as he takes me hard and fast on Wilfred's couch. Fucking me like he hates me. I love every second of his rough treatment.

My nipples chafe against the musty cushion while I stare at the doorway, clutching anything I can for balance. Not that it matters when he has such a ruthless hold on my hair.

My tits bounce, my breaths grow choppy, and my pussy soaks his dick. I'm a begging, pleading, sobbing mess.

"Such a good slut," he praises from behind me. "You take my dick so fucking well, don't you?"

I'm close to coming already.

My pussy clamps down on his length, but before I can freefall, he pulls out and flops beside me on the couch.

His slick cock rests against his T-shirt, and I swallow at the sight of the angry purple veins and weeping head.

Sinking lower on the couch, he palms it. "Ride me, Camryn." He curls his fingers around my wrist when I'm within reaching distance and pulls me down onto his lap. "Fuck me until you come all over my dick."

As he guides me over his hard length, I dig my fingers into the couch behind him. "Are you going to let me be in charge?" My voice is anything but collected. Rough and scratchy from screaming.

He stares up at me from beneath his lowered lashes, his fingers twitching on my hips. "What do you think?"

Dominic will never let me be in charge. It's not in his nature to give up control. He proves as much when he sinks me down onto his cock with his lip trapped between his teeth.

A breath whooshes out of him, and he releases his lip. "Fuck, this pussy is going to be the death of me."

Pleasure heats my core, tightening like a coil as my head falls back. He sets the pace, guiding me over his cock, his hungry mouth latching onto a nipple. Sucking and biting and bringing me closer to the edge.

He releases the hard bud with a pop and looks up at me with a filthy smile. "Hear those wet sounds? That's how much your sore cunt loves my dick. It can't get enough, can it?"

My head shakes in agreement, but all I can manage is a

pathetic whimper, too drunk on him to engage in conversation while his cock tears through me.

"Look at me, Sis," he orders when my eyes threaten to fall closed. "You gonna come on my cock?"

I nod again, and he smacks my cheek then grips my chin. "Use your words."

"Yes," I answer breathily before whimpering. He's back to moving my hips over his lap, his cock gliding against my walls in a maddening rhythm.

"What do you want, baby?"

"Choke me."

He slips his slick dick out, then wraps his fingers around my throat and slides his hard length through my pussy lips, over and over again, rubbing against my clit. The pleasure mounts, coiling like a spring.

I free-fall, arching and trembling as cum explodes from his dick in an arc, his release raining over my chin and chest in quick spurts.

He bruises my hip and throat with his tight grip as a guttural groan vibrates his chest. We breathe heavily, staring at each other while recovering from the receding euphoria and madness.

Dominic palms my cum-smeared tits, kneading the swollen mounds and pinching my nipples between his fingers and thumbs. "Perfection," he drawls, sliding his hand through the cum all the way to my throat and swiping his thumb through the drops on my chin. "I love seeing you marked and covered in me."

I open my mouth to reply when my eyes swing past him to the doorway, and I freeze.

Wilfred stands with a shotgun in his hands, and the audible click it makes as he loads it has Dominic stiffening beneath me.

"Well, well, what do we have here," Wilfred sneers around the toothpick in his mouth as he enters the room.

TWENTY-TWO

DOMINIC

Twisting my head, I look over the back of the couch. Wilfred's dirt-smeared face tilts to me, and he smirks. "A dead boy walking and his whore."

His eyes crease at the corners before his attention returns to Camryn's breasts.

Fury turns my vision red. I guide Camryn off my lap before slowly rising to my feet and turning to face him.

"Cover your tits," I order Camryn, my voice deadly calm.

Wilfred shifts the toothpick left to right with his tongue, a toothy smile spreading across his lips when his eyes meet mine.

I'm going to kill him slowly for seeing her naked and covered in my release. No one sees her without clothes on and lives to tell the tale.

Not anymore.

Wilfred gestures impatiently with the gun. "You, darlin', over there."

My hand flies out, and I grip her wrist before she can move, giving her a warning look. I refuse to let Wilfred separate us.

Her wrist feels so small in my hand, and the tears that cling to her wispy lashes churn my gut. I always thought I knew the

180

CONJURE

meaning of rage, but seeing her tremble with fear rouses some-thing inside me. Something that makes her face pale.

"Let go of the girl unless you want her to die." Wilfred aims the shotgun at Camryn, and it takes everything in me to uncurl my fingers from around her bony wrist.

"Wasn't so hard, was it?" His voice drips with humor.

With a final tear-filled glance in my direction, that makes me want to rip the old man's heart from his chest, she rounds the tattered couch until Wilfred stops jostling his gun.

She's by his side with her head bent and her arms crossed over her chest for modesty. I grit my jaw when her soft sniffles cut through the tense silence. How fucking dare he frighten her like this.

"There's a good girl," he drawls, pulling her into his side and wrapping an arm around her waist. "Wasn't so hard, was it, darlin'?"

"Don't you fucking dare touch her!"

He levels those dull eyes on me again, flicking the toothpick. Seconds pass, maybe even minutes, and then he drops his eyes to my flaccid dick.

Acid burns my esophagus the longer he lets his gaze linger. Camryn sniffles again.

"Did you kids think you could come in here and do what? Fuck on my couch? Seek a thrill?"

"Let her go," I warn.

A spark of something…malicious flashes in his eyes. Wilfred enjoys inflicting fear. It's there, in his cold chuckle when he strokes his fingers through Camryn's matted hair. "She's pretty."

Gritting my teeth, I remain quiet.

If that deadly weapon weren't aimed straight at me, I'd scale this couch and bash his face in. The only thing that keeps me teth-ered to the ground is the thought of what he might do to Camryn if he shoots me. If he touches her, I'll torture him until he begs for death. Even then, I'll drag it out.

181

"I'll tell you what, darlin'," he says to her, tipping her chin up with his grimy fingers, and I almost lose my shit there and then. "If you drop to your knees and suck my dick, I'll let you and your friend go. We'll forget this whole thing ever happened. How's that?"

"Don't listen to him, Camryn," I bite out, fisting my hands.

She swallows audibly, flicking her glassy eyes between his. I eye the gun, the couch, *him*.

My body vibrates with rage. I'm biting down so hard that my jaw will ache for weeks.

"You can walk out of here, and no one gets hurt."

A growl reverberates through my chest when he guides her hands away from her chest and reaches out to palm a breast.

Fuck this.

No one touches what's mine.

As if he can hear my thoughts, he flicks his gaze up to mine and spits out the toothpick. The sight of her pale breast in his grimy hand blackens my vision.

"A perfect handful," he taunts, squeezing.

"I'm going to kill you," I breathe so quietly and viciously that Camryn retreats into herself.

"I'm the one with the weapon here, boy," he replies, pinching her nipple.

She flinches, whimpering with pain. I make for the couch but come to a sudden stop when he puts the gun to the underside of her chin.

"Take one more step, and I pull the trigger."

My body freezes with dread.

Wilfred's sickening smile grows. He knows he's got me by the balls, judging by the manic glint in his eyes.

"If you want her to live, I suggest you rein that anger in, boy. I'm not done yet."

"I swear to God, if you touch her, I will chop off your fucking hands."

Chuckling, he steps closer to her and makes a show of kneading her breasts. I look away, unable to control the putrid disgust that floods my veins. I hate feeling this fucking powerless. Hate how I can't act on my instincts. He can taunt me now, but I will peel his skin off his body, remove his eyeballs, and cut out his tongue—

My attention snaps back when Camryn chokes on a whimper that saws through my ribs.

"So smooth," he says with a perverted smile as he trails his filthy fingers over her pussy. "I bet she's tight."

This time, when she whimpers, I explode into action, launching myself over the back of the couch and tackling Wilfred to the ground. A shot goes off, but I'm blinded by rage and the need to destroy. I lay into him with my fist while clutching his denim overalls. Punch after punch. I'm seething. Hell-bent on beating him to a bloody pulp. My arm aches, and my bloody knuckles sting. I don't stop.

"Dominic!" Camryn tears me off him, palming my sweaty cheeks with her trembling hands. Her stricken eyes fly over my face, and I want nothing more than to ease the worry I see in her blue orbs, but I can barely catch my breath. "We need to leave."

"He touched you."

Her fingers pause on my scruff. "I'm okay."

"He fucking touched you."

"Dom…" She presses her soft lips to mine, her shaky breaths skating over my mouth. "It doesn't matter. I'm fine. Can we please just leave?"

"Fuck," I growl, nipping at her bottom lip and fisting her hair. "It matters. No one touches you. I'm going to cut off his fucking hands for thinking he could—" I fall silent when I glance to the side, seeing the bloody floor.

Where did he go?

My grip on Camryn stiffens, and I whip my head from left and right, scanning the room. "What the hell?" I climb to my feet, clutching her to me protectively. She's still naked except for her dirty tank top that's halfway down her stomach. I help her pull it up to cover her breasts, my eyes skating across the room to ensure we're alone.

With a final glance around, I quickly zip up my pants, walk over to the couch, and swipe up her shorts from the floor.

"Put them on," I demand, striding up to her.

When she's buttoning them up, I palm her cheek. "I need you to stay here."

Her eyes widen, and she shakes her head.

Outside, a crow caws.

I wish I could wipe the fear from her eyes and replace it with a look reserved only for me.

"No," she says, shaking her head almost fervently. "We need to leave."

I caress her damp cheeks. "Listen to me. He's still here. If we leave now, he'll come after us. Maybe not today, but tomorrow or the week after." Those big eyes stare at me, so I jostle her. "We can't let him get away."

"What are you saying?"

My jaw tightens, fingers twitching against her tear-streaked cheeks as I lean in and rest my forehead against hers. "We kill him."

A sharp inhale racks her body.

Before she can open her mouth to reply, my lips meet hers—no tongue, just a hard press and a haunted groan. She drives me murderous. "He has to die."

I tear myself away and stride out of the room.

"Dom," she calls after me, but I ignore her pleading voice.

I need a weapon.

Entering the kitchen farther down the hall, I tear open a kitchen drawer and root through its contents. All I can find is a blunt knife, so I lift it out before slamming the door shut and spinning around.

Flies buzz around the dirty pots stacked high in the sink, and the light outside barely penetrates the cloudy windows. A bouquet of wilted wildflowers sits on the kitchen table. The inside of the clear vase is murky with dried, green algae.

When I slowly cross the room, the floorboards creak beneath my weight. I tighten my grip on the knife's handle and pause in the doorway.

A trail of blood leads the way to the staircase.

Trust the fucker to hide upstairs.

I enter the hallway with measured steps. My neck prickles as I pass a row of framed, faded photographs. Beady eyes follow me, suspended in time, and I suppress a shiver. One or two picture frames must have fallen to the floor, because shards of glass break underfoot.

"I'm coming for you, you fucker," I call out as I ascend the worn stairs, keeping my back to the wall. The wallpaper has peeled in places as if torn away. A loud creak accompanies every step. I pause, wincing.

The house is eerily quiet.

I break out in a cold sweat as I reach the top and peer around the corner.

It's even darker up here.

Streaks of sunshine filter through the moth-eaten lace curtains, highlighting the dust motes that swirl in an eternal dance. Across the hall, cobwebs cling to an antique, cracked mirror. I look away from my distorted reflection and step onto the landing with the knife clutched tightly in my hand.

"Come out and face me, you dirty old man." I place one step in front of the other, my heart pounding almost painfully.

A sound to my right makes me pause, and I crane my neck to peer into the dark room. "I didn't take you for a coward."

"Dominic," a female voice whispers from inside.

I come to a halt, my heart ceasing to beat as fresh terror rears up inside me. I inch closer, the weapon white knuckled in my hand.

"I've waited for you, Dominic." The female voice slides over my senses like a sensuous threat.

I stare at the gaping doorway with my heart in my throat. The darkness inside bleeds from the room like tendrils of dark ink, a sea of black.

Silence. Suffocating silence.

"Dominic!"

I stumble back, my spine crashing against the wall behind me.

Pictures fall to the floor, but I'm caught in all that black, unable to look away as it comes for me, seeping from the room like a river of dread.

Feminine laughter echoes from inside, and then I see her.

Her skirts drift on an imaginary breeze as the darkness reveals her long dress and regal, pale features. "I've waited for you, Dominic."

Pulled forward, my feet become unglued.

The woman's eyes darken, and her lips slowly spread into a victorious smile. She inches back, disappearing into the shadows.

I'm at the threshold, my shoulder brushing up against the doorframe, when a sharp blow to my head knocks me to my knees.

Blood trickles down my nape as I raise a hand to my neck, swaying on the spot. Peering down at my crimson fingers, I release a surprised chuckle.

Beside me, Wilfred crouches down and places another toothpick between his yellow teeth. "Sleep tight, princess." He stands back up and whacks me with the gun's handle. I tip forward, my vision blackening.

His tight grip on my hair is the last thing I'm aware of before my cheek meets the floor.

Blackness descends, and with it, sweet oblivion.

TWENTY-THREE

CAMRYN

"Dom?" I whisper-hiss as I peer into the dark hallway.

Fear has me in a chokehold, my neck damp with sweat.

When there's no response, my voice breaks as I call out, "Dominic?"

Where is he? Why is the house so quiet?

I hesitantly exit the living room and skirt the length of the wall, careful to avoid the framed photographs.

Glancing back at the front door, I debate making a run for it, but I dismiss that thought just as fast. I can't leave Dominic behind.

Although…

I worry my bruised lip, my fingers trailing over the flaking wallpaper as I continue down the hallway.

Maybe I should escape? I could phone the police. What if Dominic is dead by the time they get here? What if they're too late? He could already be dead.

"Dominic?" I whisper shakily, straining to listen for a response.

Nothing.

Glass crunches underfoot, and I peer down at the broken

frames, shards of glass slipping to the floor as I crouch, picking up the grainy photograph of a young man framed by fir trees.

His wide smile and high cheekbones give way to dark hair hidden beneath a woolen cap. An axe rests on his shirt-clad shoulder.

I can't stop staring at it or his eyes.

"I thought I told you not to wander into the woods."

The photograph trembles in my hand as I exhale shakily. My mouth is dry.

It's him.

I know it is. The similarities are too striking.

I turn around and scan the other photographs. There he is, barefoot, slouched on a swing seat on the porch.

My eyes drift to the next framed picture, a cold shiver accompanying the bead of sweat sliding down my spine. I step closer to the image of him on a tall ladder propped against the side of the house, a hammer in his hand.

He used to live here. This was his home.

But that means—

The floorboards creak ominously behind me, my breath catching in my throat. I know it's Wilfred even before his southern drawl sends a spike of fear through me.

"Such a pretty little darlin'." He approaches me, his heavy steps drawing closer.

I exhale a shuddering breath, staring at the wall in front of me.

What do I do? I could run for the door, but Wilfred has a gun. He'll shoot me before I can escape.

Panic threatens to immobilize me when his foul smell of stale cigarettes and manure assaults me from behind. I dig my fingers into my palms and then stiffen as he moves my hair away from my shoulder with the shotgun, ensuring I see it in my periphery.

"It's been too long since I touched such young flesh."

"Where's Dominic?" I ask bravely, barely daring to breathe.

"Shhh now, darlin'." His sour breath heats the back of my

neck, and I squeeze my eyes shut as a sob claws its way up my chest.

Outside, the sun hides behind a cloud. The room darkens further, and shadows elongate and thicken.

"You smell like a summer's day." He breathes me in, his sweaty hand engulfing my waist, squeezing tight as he pulls me back against his oil-stained overalls.

His cock digs into my lower back, so I squeeze my eyes shut tighter, hoping, wishing, and praying for this moment to end.

"Please let me go," I plead, but it falls on deaf ears.

He slips his hand between my legs and drawls, "No more talking, darlin'."

A sob tears from my lips, and I fist my hands so hard that my nails elicit a sharp bite of pain. I relish it, preferring the sting to his wandering, filthy fingers that move my shorts aside.

He huffs a breath when he finds me dry. His hand disappears, but the relief is short-lived. My heart rate spikes as he spits on his fingers and dips them beneath the fabric.

"Please don't—"

Stiffening, he breathes in my ear.

Time stands still. Seconds extend into eternity. Dread hammers in my chest.

He shifts his grip on the shotgun, spitting the toothpick to the floor, his prickly beard rubbing against the side of my neck. "You want to see your friend again, darlin'?"

Hope flares in my chest, dancing the tango with icy fear.

"He's still alive and will remain alive as long as you are a good girl for me."

"Okay," I whisper, forcing myself to unfurl my fingers.

"Hands on the wall where I can see them."

Steadying my nerves, I press my palms to the peeling wallpaper and swallow down the terror that's constricting my throat. I can't save Dominic if I'm scared. I'm no good to anyone if I'm trembling like a leaf in the wind.

I need to get myself together.

189

For both our sakes.

"Where is he?"

His finger trails the length of my slit, and he exhales against the shell of my ear. "No talking, darlin', while I play with this pussy."

Gritting my jaw, I bite back a retort.

Anger is good.

Anger is better than fear.

He inches his finger inside, chuckling when my body stiffens at the intrusion. "I wonder if I can make you come harder than the boy?"

"You wish," I spit before I can stop myself.

This time, when he stiffens, I fear the worst. He'll kill me. Put a bullet between my eyebrows. No one will ever find me again.

He does neither.

"You're tight, aren't you, darlin'?"

My stomach churns as I swallow down the vomit in my mouth, focusing instead on the faded flowery pattern on the wallpaper.

Despite the anger, my body soon responds to the stimulation.

Noticing, he chuckles in my ear while grazing my clit with his thumb. "I knew you were a whore, darlin'. I saw it when you rode that boy."

"Fuck you!" I sneer.

"Such foul language. I thought you promised to be good."

"This is me being good." There's a sharp bite to my words, and I grit my teeth to stop myself from telling him exactly how I feel about dirty old men like him.

His lips curve into a smile against my ear. "You gonna moan for me, darlin'. Let me hear how much you like it?"

"In your wildest dreams."

"Careful," he drawls, shoving a second finger inside that forces me up on my tiptoes, and I hiss as pain ripples through me, still sore from Dominic. "I might decide not to treat you this good."

The rough scratch of his denim overalls and the stench of his breath fade into the background when my core heats with pleasure.

Fuck. How is this happening? How can it feel good, when I wouldn't hesitate to claw his eyes out, given the chance?

Fuck, fuck, fuck.

A moan tears its way up my throat. I can't hold it back.

His breathy chuckle slides over the side of my neck like a lover's caress or a blade's kiss while his hand moves at a rapid pace inside my shorts.

"There's a good girl," he drawls against my neck, his wet breath dampening my skin. "This tight pussy likes a good fingerin', don't it, darlin'?"

"Dominic will kill you," I hiss.

"That boy is in no state to do anything."

My hips move involuntarily with his movements, chasing release like a hopeless traitor.

"That boy is gonna watch his whore die first before I put a bullet in his head."

I hiss, pleasure rippling through me.

I can't help it.

Not when he's touching me with the intention of wringing pleasure from my body. He's not doing this for himself. There's nothing selfish behind it. His touch is purposeful. Designed to prove a point and instill terror of a different kind.

With the next flick of his filthy thumb, he shows me who is in control. It's not me.

My body fucks his hand like he's got the pot of gold at the end of the rainbow. My hips roll with such force that I'm almost humping the wall.

It's just out of reach.

I hate him. Hate him so fucking much. Yet hate tastes so damn delicious.

Especially when it's seasoned with fear and danger.

"If only that boyfriend of yours could see you now. Fucking

my hand like a dirty little whore. Tell me, darlin', would he be surprised?"

I hiss, and he presses the shotgun to my neck.

"Would he?"

"No," I reply, quivering in his grip, too aroused to focus on the cold metal against my pulse point.

"No," he breathes, but it's an affirmation. "He wouldn't. You like to have this tight little cunt filled. Don't matter whose fingers they are, as long as you get to come."

"Fuck," I choke, my nails digging into the wallpaper. I can barely keep upright. "Please, just…"

"Let you come?"

"Put me out of my misery."

"Beg me."

I whimper, shaking my head.

"Beg me, or I kill your boyfriend."

When I fail to respond, he stretches me with a third finger. "We can play this game all day, darlin'."

"Please, let me come." The words shred my vocal cords like barbed wire.

"Come on now, little girl. You can do better than that."

What the hell does he want?

Sobs rip from my chest, and I press my forehead to the wallpaper. "Please, Wilfred. Please, pretty please."

"Please, Daddy," he corrects, his beard scratching my jaw, his hard cock sliding up the small of my back through his denim overalls as I shudder.

"Please, Daddy," I force out, my knees threatening to give out. "Let me come."

"Wasn't so hard, was it, darlin'?"

Tears wet my cheeks when he flicks my clit with his thumb, and I clamp down on his fingers. Self-hatred tastes putrid even as an orgasm rips through my body.

A small part of me whispers that it's a response to the fear, but a deeper part of me—a part that frightens me more than the shotgun in his hand—wants me to admit something darker.

Something shameful.

That I like to have my will confiscated from me.

My body loves danger.

It loves it when someone takes it without asking.

It loves *this…*

Sliding his hand from my shorts, he spins me around. I stare at him through heavy lids, strands stuck to my wet cheeks. The urge to claw his eyes out tingles my fingers, and it takes everything in me not to spit at him when he lifts his slick hand.

Spreading his fingers, he tuts. "Such a mess, darlin'."

Unable to look at the strings of cum between his fingers, I glance away, cheeks burning with humiliation. He grips my face with his wet hand that smells of debauchery, the shotgun brushing up against my leg, like a cold threat, and I whimper.

"We're not done yet." His sour breath wafts over my face. "A sweet thing like you is too good to kill just yet."

When he releases me, I slump to the floor.

Despite the voice inside me that urges me to keep it together, tears stream from my cheeks. I don't know where Dominic is. If he's dead or alive. I feel dirty, *ashamed*, clit pulsing from the receding orgasm.

Wilfred's mud-caked boots step closer, my fingers sliding over the broken glass shards as I let my eyes travel up his filthy overalls until they clash with his empty gaze.

"I hate you." My raw vocal cords ache as the last note slips from my lips.

He tips my chin up with the shotgun, his eyes gleaming with sadism. "Is that any way to talk to the man you called Daddy a few minutes ago?"

This time, I spit at him, and he hauls me to my feet, baring his yellow teeth. I stab him with the piece of broken glass in my hand that I picked up from the floor seconds earlier, and he drops me with a hiss.

Blood pours from the wound, staining the grimy denim, and my own hand hurts from slicing it open, but the sharp sting is the least of my worries.

We stare at the protruding shard, then at each other. The air thickens with tension.

"Oh, darlin', he drawls, cocking the shotgun. "You've gone and done it now."

Sharp and deadly terror flashes through me as I dash for the stairs, hauling myself up. A warning shot rings out, and I scream as buckshot embeds itself in the wall beside me.

I blink at it for all of a second before my survival instincts take over. I'm on the run again, fleeing from the monster behind me, who takes the steps slowly as if to heighten my fear.

"You goin' to die, darlin'."

"DOMINIC!" I scream, propelling myself onto the landing. "Where are you?" I throw one final look behind me, fleeing down the hall. Another shot rings out, and I tumble to the floor with a blood-curdling scream as agony sears my calf. Gasping, I roll over, blood gushing from the graze of a pellet that almost took me out completely.

If I was scared before, it has nothing on the noose that tightens around my throat now when I look up to see Wilfred walking toward me with the shotgun tightly clasped. My chest heaves, yet I struggle to inhale a full breath as icy panic threatens to steal the last sip of oxygen.

"You thought you could get one up on me, little girl? You thought you was being clever, darlin'?"

The shard is still embedded in his waist. Is he immune to pain? What the hell is wrong with him?

I dart my gaze around and then crawl toward the nearest door that's open an inch, leaving a trail of crimson behind.

Wilfred follows it like a bloodhound, chuckling deeply. "Not so brave now, are we?"

"Please," I beg, digging my nails into the worn floorboards

and hauling myself forward, my calf throbbing with blinding pain.

"Please what, darlin'? Kill you or fuck you again? Maybe with my cock this time?"

"Don't," I choke, grabbing hold of the doorframe.

He aims the gun at me again, and I sob, crawling away. The door slides open behind me, and he follows my blood trail as though he has all the time in the world to torment me.

Once inside, I try to shut the door, but he wedges his boot in the gap and tuts.

"That's not very nice." He kicks it open, and I scramble back, pausing as my eyes land on the slumped, tied-up body by the bed.

"Dominic?" I gasp.

He's unconscious, his chin touching his shoulders, blood coating the sides of his neck and dampening the front of his T-shirt.

I'll never forgive myself if he dies because of my own stupid curiosity.

Wilfred clamps his muddy boot down on my injured calf, and I scream in torment, writhing on the floor. My distress rouses Dominic from his slumber, and he lifts his heavy head, a choked groan vibrating through his chest as he winces.

Cold metal meets the back of my head, forcing my cheek to meet the hard floor. I sob, watching Dominic's hazy eyes connect with mine. Every muscle in his body stiffens, but then his head lulls and he tries to shake it, his movements sluggish.

"Who should I kill first, darlin'? You or your boyfriend?"

"Please don't hurt us," I beg around a sob. "I'll do anything. Just…please. Let us go."

"It's a little too late for that, don't you think? I've had a taste of that pussy. If I see you 'round town, I might be tempted to drag you back here. Besides, you going to tell the cops."

"I'm not going to tell anyone. It stays between us."

"Why would I believe a cheatin' whore?" He digs the gun into my head, and I hold my breath.

My voice is much quieter this time when I whisper, "Please."

"Camryn?" Dominic's raw voice crackles in the silence. He swallows thickly, wincing, then tries to sit up straighter. "Let her go."

Wilfred looks away from me, and relief floods my chest. Relief *and* terror. Now, his attention is on Dominic, which fills me with renewed dread.

"Loverboy is awake," Wilfred drawls in his southern accent. "Welcome back. I was just askin' your girl who I should kill first. You or her?"

"Let her go and kill me," Dominic offers, his eyes flashing with pain when he shifts.

My head flies up, and I plead with him to keep quiet. To not make this worse. "No, Dom."

He ignores me. "Let her walk."

"How 'bout this?" Wilfred says, leaving me on the floor and striding to Dominic. He presses the gun to Dominic's temple, forcing him to tilt sideways. "How 'bout I put a bullet in your brain and keep the girl? She can warm my bed while you rot in an unmarked grave in the woods."

Dominic clenches his jaw, his eyes boring into me.

"No one will find you."

"I don't care if you kill me, but lay a fucking finger on her, and I will haunt you."

The tips of my ears burn when Wilfred laughs cruelly. I can't even look in their direction as the monster slides his eyes to me and smirks.

My stomach curdles.

"Your whore already came on my fingers." He aims the weapon at me. "Ain't that right, darlin'. You creamed all over my hand like a good little slut in heat."

The temperature in the room drops, and Dominic's eerily deep and calm voice sends a chill racing down my spine, "Camryn, look at me."

I shake my head, pressing my forehead to the ground.

If I see the anger in his eyes, I'll break. I'm already ashamed of myself. While he was tied up and bleeding, my body betrayed me in the worst ways possible.

"Look. At. Me."

I slowly slide my gaze in his direction.

"Is it true?"

"Dom—"

"Is it true?" he asks again with enough venom to make me flinch.

When I still don't reply, Wilfred shoves his fingers beneath Dom's nose. "Smell that. Answers your question, don't it? She's sweet like a summer's day."

The deep throb in my leg has nothing on the insistent ache in my chest, the agony of seeing his face drain of color.

A muscle tics in his cheek.

"I'm sorry..." My voice breaks, and I quickly look away, resigned to my fate. We're going to die here. Dominic, with the taste of betrayal bitter on his tongue because of me.

TWENTY-FOUR

CAMRYN

WILFRED PUTS his fingers to his nose, breathes in deeply, and groans. "She's so sweet, I think I'll have to keep her. That pussy sure is tight."

Dominic hangs his head, his dark hair flopping over his eyes. "You're a dead man."

"Speak up, boy. I can't hear ya."

He lifts his head and glares at Wilfred. "I'm going to kill you!"

Silence slides in through the cracks in the floor, slithering over my bare legs like a whispered threat.

Wilfred shoves the gun against Dominic's forehead, a manic glint in his eyes. I cry out, crawling forward, my Chucks smearing a path through the blood on the floor.

"Stay back," Dominic warns, wriggling against his restraints.

"No…" I kneel in front of Wilfred, clasping his overalls. Desperation is all I have left. My dignity has died a slow death, and I don't care what it takes to save Dominic. It doesn't matter. I'll do whatever it takes to end this nightmare. "Please don't hurt him. What do you want? Tell me. I'll do anything." I trail my hand higher and cup his dick through his overalls. "I'll suck you. Please just let him go."

He regards me, his dick hardening in my grip.

Beside me, Dominic's eyes glare holes into my face, but I don't spare him a glance, not now when I have Wilfred's attention. Something tells me that if I lose it, he'll kill Dominic this time, and I won't get a second chance.

A second chance at what? Distracting him for long enough for Dominic to escape the ropes that bind him? Distract him long enough to find a way to kill the man in front of me myself? Can I do that? Maybe if I snatch the gun from him when he's distracted? Do I even know how to use one?

I squeeze his dick. "Let me taste your cock."

With the gun still pressed to Dominic's temple, Wilfred brushes my hair away from my forehead with his dirty hand.

Dominic opens his mouth to talk, but I shoot him a pleading glance before looking back up at the monster, who unclips his overalls, his voice slithering over my skin like a disease. "You want my cock inside that pretty mouth of yours, darlin'?"

His overalls fall to his knees, and I'm hit with the stench of his unwashed dick. He palms it and strokes the length while Dominic shifts in my periphery.

I force myself to keep my eyes locked on Wilfred. Now is not the time for distractions. I can't afford to lose his attention or the darkening lust in his dull eyes.

I'm just about to lean in when he grips my hair and yanks me back. "What do you call me, darlin'?"

My scalp burns with pain, and I swallow down a whimper. "Daddy—"

I pause as something catches my attention on the dresser to his left.

A porcelain doll.

He smacks my cheek, and Dominic releases a bunch of expletives, calling him every name under the sun, no doubt trying to force his attention back on him.

A shiver splashes down my spine when, in slow motion, I become aware of a whisper of a breath at my neck.

"The window is open." I turn my head. Wilfred has my hair clasped in his hand again.

"Focus," he orders, smacking his dick against my cheek, but I'm too distracted by the billowing curtain and the summer breeze that moves through the trees outside.

"When you hear its whispers travel through the rustling leaves, you run as fast as you can."

"You left the window open," I say again, more forcefully, and time slows.

Eternity stretches out in front of me.

I look back at the porcelain doll, suppressing a shiver when a bead of blood slips from the crack in its cheek.

The breath at my neck brushes past me, kissing my damp skin. I fix my attention on Wilfred. "It feeds on negative emotions and desire," I emphasize the last word, my heart beating faster.

Wilfred's eyes turn black and shivers race through me when he cups my chin and lifts it. "His obsession with you is delicious."

He releases me just as fast. I stumble to Dominic, who's desperately struggling to untie his rope while Wilfred lifts the shotgun to his mouth.

"I'm so fucking sorry, Dom." My fingers tremble on the ropes as my eyes blur with tears. The knots are too tight. My nails catch more than once, and I release a sob, wiping the wetness from my cheeks.

"You have nothing to be sorry about." The deep rumble of his voice makes me pause. We gaze at each other as the seconds tick by. I can see what he's not saying in that broken look. He's sorry he couldn't save me in time.

That Wilfred got his hands on me.

My eyes speak their own language, too.

I'm sorry I betrayed you.

He jerks his chin to the ropes. "Keep going."

Torn from my stasis, I grapple with the ropes.

Wilfred chokes on the gun, his finger trembling on the trigger.

The first knot untangles, and I set to work on the second while Dominic shoulders out of the ropes.

Bang!

I flinch, untying the final knot, just as Wilfred's body collapses to the floor. Dominic removes the last ropes before standing up and hauling me to my feet. He's weak, swaying on the spot.

Palming my cheeks, he inspects my face. "Are you sure you're okay?"

"He shot me in the leg."

Dominic looks down at my calf and then curses. Sliding his arm behind my knees, he lifts me against his chest.

"You're injured," I point out. "Let me walk."

"Not a fucking chance. You're bleeding." He steps over Wilfred's lifeless body on the floor, and we leave the room.

Everything else fades but his blood-smeared, sweaty face and tight jaw. I wish I could smooth the worry lines on his forehead, but exhaustion sinks its claws into me.

Outside, the sun blinds us. Dominic's heavy footsteps thunder down the porch steps. He strides across the yard, past the chicken coop and the gap in the fence.

All around us, the breeze moves through the branches, subtly shifting the leaves. Whispering secrets of the past. Secrets that urge me to crane my neck to look over his shoulders at the woods. The fir and oak trees stretch tall behind the house, their roots buried deep.

Soothed by their lullaby, a song of woes, I glance at one of the upstairs windows. The curtains shift as though someone peers through the gap, watching us flee the property.

The curtains fall back into place, and I'm torn from my thoughts as we slip through the gate. It creaks, and then we're on the move again.

I'm vaguely aware of Dominic opening the truck door and easing me inside, the leather seat hot against my bare legs and shoulders. When I wince, Dominic stills and tucks my hair away from my cheek.

The move is so tender that my eyes fill with more tears. I don't deserve his gentle touch or his concern. Don't deserve to be forgiven for what happened in that house, for allowing my curiosity to bring us there. I dragged him into hell, and now I'm bleeding all over his seat.

"Look at me, baby," he coaxes, cupping my trembling chin.

His quivering fingers are too much. I try to look away, but he forces me to meet his gaze. To see the worry that mars his sharp features. "Tell me you're okay. You have to be okay. Otherwise, I'll go insane. I need you."

"I'm broken, Dom... He touched me, and I...."

He digs his fingers into my chin, and the pain helps ground me. "Listen to me. You're not broken."

"You don't understand... I liked it," I whisper, my voice as haunted as the forest behind Wilfred's property.

"Shut up," he growls, jostling me. "You didn't like him touching you."

My chin wobbles as I stare at him through my tears.

"Your body reacted to stimuli. You don't have to be ashamed. You're not the only person that's happened to. It doesn't mean that you wanted *him*."

"I hurt you."

"No," he chokes, pressing his lips to mine before I can object. His tongue delves into my mouth, and I gasp. His kiss is biting, forceful, and everything I need. He devours me while the sun settles behind the trees and the crickets come out to sing in the summer heat. He steals the very last breath from my lungs. Then, when oblivion arrives to take me away, he breathes life back into me.

With a final peck to my lips, he says, "He's dead now. He can't hurt you anymore."

I gulp and then flick my eyes up to his. "Something killed him."

He peers into my soul, my chin still gripped tightly.

When he says nothing, I let the truth flow from my lips. "Something evil."

Grinding his teeth, he releases my chin and trails his fingers down the side of my jaw and throat until his touch lingers at my racing pulse point.

"Something that wants me," I finish.

I knew back there that whatever entered through the window on a wisp of summer breeze wouldn't hurt me.

Not yet, anyway.

Not until it has killed everything that stands in its way.

"Shut the doors," I order. "It travels in the wind."

He gazes at me for a brief moment longer, then slips from the truck and shuts the door. I watch him round the vehicle before my eyes land on a figure in the road.

The axe dangles from his fingers, his gaze peering at me through the windshield. His shirt is unbuttoned, and a vagrant breeze plays with the lapels, lifting them away from his tanned skin.

As the truck rocks, he looks over at Wilfred's property.

"Let's get you home." Dominic cranks the engine, and exhaust fumes fill the air.

I say nothing as the truck drives forward.

Just before the man on the road disperses into thin air, like that night Dominic's father lost control of the car and careened into the river, his eyes find mine. Dark and sorrowful.

TWENTY-FIVE

DOMINIC

"You better not fucking hurt her with that," I growl, eyeing the needle in Gwen's hand.

She gives me a deadpan look. "I'm about to stitch her up without anesthetic. Of course, it'll hurt."

Gwen looked like a ghost when she opened the door to find me covered in blood, clutching Camryn to my chest. We had nowhere to go. Gwen was the only person who could help us.

Now, we're in her kitchen, having cleared the table.

"Are you sure you can do this?" I ask her when she blows out a steadying breath, the needle trembling in her hand.

"Do you want me to be honest, Dom?" She points to Camryn on the table. "You should have taken her to the hospital. I volunteer with my mom at the vet clinic on weekends. I'm not a qualified nurse. I've been shown once or twice how to stitch up the odd cat or dog. I mean, we're lucky my mom even has equipment here."

"We can't go to the hospital," Camryn replies, wincing with pain as she tries to look over her shoulder to see what Gwen is doing.

I stroke her matted hair away from her damp forehead while

Gwen stares at the deep gash, needing to reassure myself that she's okay.

"Wilfred is dead…. It'll raise too many questions if we go to the hospital." Camryn looks away, focusing her eyes on me, and I take her bloodied hand in mine, watching Gwen place her latex-gloved hand on Camryn's leg.

She inspects the flesh wound before shaking her head. "You're so lucky it was nothing but a nasty graze." She tilts her chin at me. "Can you roll the towel up for her to bite down on, please?"

I pause, glaring at her, and she sighs. "Why don't you leave the room since you won't be helpful?"

"I'm not leaving."

"Dom," Camryn says and squeezes my hand, or at least she tries to. Her grip is weak. "Please, listen to her."

My teeth grind as I reluctantly let go of her clammy hand to roll up a towel. How did we get here in the first place? What if her mom finds out that she broke into Wilfred's house and got shot in the leg? How the hell are we going to keep this from her? Besides, it's only a matter of time until Wilfred is found.

Camryn bites down on the towel, her eyes uncertain but determined.

"It's a deep gash," Gwen says, pinching the skin together, and I almost want to throttle her when Camryn whimpers. She gives me another warning look as if she hears my thoughts, then focuses back on Camryn's leg.

When she puts the needle to the flesh, I stiffen every muscle.

"This will hurt, Cam."

I force myself to watch despite the urge to look away as the needle pierces the flesh. My stomach twists, and I taste bile on my tongue.

I'd return to the farm and slaughter Wilfred if he weren't already dead. Make it hurt this time.

Green strands of hair stick to the sheen of sweat on Gwen's forehead, her brow pinched in concentration. She works quickly, stopping now and then to allow Camryn to breathe through the pain when she struggles to stay still.

"You're doing well, almost there."

I tangle my bloodied fingers in Camryn's hair, needing Gwen to hurry up before I lose my fucking cool and pummel her to the ground.

When she's finally done, she cuts the suture with scissors. Then she puts the tools away and swipes her forearm over her eyebrows, wiping away the sweat. "It'll scar, and you'll need antibiotics, or you risk an infection."

While she removes her bloodied latex gloves and discards them in a nearby trash can, I crouch down to look Camryn in the eye.

"You did so fucking well."

Her smile is weak. She's tired.

I swipe the tears from her cheeks with my thumb, then lean in to kiss her soft lips. "I'm sorry."

"It's not your fault," she replies, her bottom lip trembling.

"I should have protected you."

Shifting, she trails her fingers through my scruff. I lean into her touch and kiss her palm before rising to my feet.

Gwen cleans her up while I pace, restless, clenching and unclenching my hands and tearing at my roots. Not even the prickling pain helps soothe this fury within me at seeing him touch her.

"She needs to rest," Gwen says, trying her damn best not to tremble now that it's over. "Take her upstairs to my room."

Camryn whimpers when I scoop her into my arms. Pressing my nose to her hair, I breathe in the scent of blood and sweat. Beneath the horror of the last few hours is something sweeter. Something uniquely her. I allow it to settle my pounding heart as I carry her upstairs.

I tuck her into Gwen's bed, and she's out like a light within minutes, her soft breaths easing the brewing storm.

Trailing my fingers through her hair on the pillow, I watch her sleep, wondering when she crawled beneath my skin. I used to harbor such inexplicable anger toward her, yet now, as her chest rises and falls, I want to protect her.

My chest tightens as I brush her hair away from her brow and kiss her clammy forehead. I've done that a lot lately—felt the need to touch and kiss her and to just…be near her.

I leave her to sleep and then walk downstairs, still wearing my bloodstained clothes.

Gwen looks up from her phone when I collapse onto the kitchen chair and retrieve my Zippo from my pocket. She sits across from me and stares into the distance before her face collapses. "What happened?"

A lump forms in my throat when memories flood back in. I strike a flame, watching it dance in the silence. My Zippo is the only item I have of my dad's. If I ever lose it, I'll be fucking devastated.

Gwen is waiting for a response, so I sigh and put the Zippo down, and then I rest my elbows on the table and drag my fingers through my hair. I pull on the strands, but the pain does nothing to calm me down. "We drove past Wilfred's farm, and Camryn wanted to investigate. I couldn't fucking stop her." I jiggle my knee beneath the table, my fingers tangled in my short strands. "Wilfred walked in on us in his living room, and Camryn… She was…" I pull harder, feeling my eyes burn with unshed tears. "He touched her."

Across from me, Gwen swipes at her wet cheeks.

"I beat him up, but he got away. It was bad."

"What happened next?"

Shaking my head, I drop my hands to the table and meet her sorrowful gaze. "He attacked me, knocked me out and tied me up, and then he shot her."

Outside, a car drives past, the sound muted. I can't look Gwen in the eye, so I focus on a scratch on the table.

"He held the shotgun to my head, and Camryn was ready to…" I grimace as the pain behind my ribs spreads.

I can't fucking breathe.

I curse and shoot up so fast that the chair topples over. Gwen barely flinches, watching me pace. I walk up to the window, peering at the houses across the road. One of the neighbors shoves a bag in the trash can, shaded by a tall tree, streaks of sunshine breaking through the canopy of leaves overhead.

A shiver runs through me as a gentle breeze sways the gnarly branches. "Something entered through the open window," I mumble, watching the man walk back up the drive.

"What do you mean?"

I turn away from the view and lean back against the counter. "You know what I mean. Something is hunting us."

Gwen watches me cross my ankles and curl my fingers around the counter's edge before she rises to her feet and picks up the Zippo. She hands it to me and shuts the window. Then she lingers by my side, her arm brushing against mine as she whispers, "I'm scared."

There are specks of blood on my Doc Martens. Swallowing past a growing lump in my throat, I shift my gaze to look at her.

She smiles weakly, her eyes swimming with tears, as she shakes her head and laughs beneath her breath. Straightening up, she hugs her arms around herself. "How do we defeat it?"

I watch her scuff the ground with her foot. Her red socks have a chocolate bar pattern, and her frayed jeans shorts are stained near the pocket. She smells of cherry and antiseptic.

I already miss the girl upstairs.

"How do we defeat it, Dom?" she repeats, her chin quivering. "Benny and Wilfred are dead, and Brittany is in hospital." She sniffs, swiping at her eyes. "At least it attacked him instead of you guys."

"I think Brittany was right," I reply, crossing my arms and flicking the Zippo lid open. "It wants Camryn... Whatever *it* is. That's why it protected her by killing Wilfred." I flip it shut again.

Gwen's chest inflates with a deep breath. "What does that mean?"

"Fuck if I know." I shrug, uncrossing my ankles. "It feeds on strong emotions. Fear. Anger. Desire."

"You think it needs to feed to grow stronger."

"Maybe." I wet my lips, considering all possibilities. "We need to do some research."

"What research?"

That's a good fucking question. How do we find out information about a…supernatural being? How do we defeat it? "We start with the missing family. Scour the local library for information."

She nods, worrying her bottom lip while looking deep in thought. "Yeah, let's start there."

TWENTY-SIX

BRITTANY

"YOUR VITALS LOOK GOOD," the nurse tells me as she makes notes on the iPad. "I've given you more pain meds to help you sleep. They should kick in soon." With a final smile, she squeezes my foot through the thin blanket. "Remember, the sooner you rest, the sooner you'll be out of here."

She shuts the door on her way out, and I try to calm my heartbeat. Everything looks scarier in the dark. The lone lamp in the corner of the room isn't enough to chase away the shadows or the sensation of something lurking. I tell myself that it's all in my head, but as the drugs take effect, I become more fearful, and the room spins as the shadows grow taller, crawling across the walls. I struggle to keep my eyes open as my vision darkens at the corners.

I don't want to sleep in case it comes to finish what it started.

Pain radiates through my severed wrist despite the strong pain medication. I grit my teeth and wince as I try to sit up in bed. I'm too weak, my fingers tingling with phantom sensations.

My hand is gone, but it still feels like it's there. Now, a different kind of pain presses on my sternum, like a weight I'm unable to shift. I can't look at my bandaged arm without remembering that...*thing* inside me that enjoyed my terror.

It savored my friends' fear even more.

There was nowhere to hide.

The moment it entered my body, it saw everything—it knew everything: every thought I'd ever had, my fears, and the things I'm ashamed of, as well as every lie I've ever told.

My dreams are troubled. I drift in and out of consciousness, moving from one nightmare to the next.

Awaking with a start, I push up on my elbows, a layer of cold sweat clinging to my clammy skin. I become aware of movement to my left and slowly turn my head to the window, afraid of what I'll see.

The curtains dance in front of the windows, opening like a gaping void to hell. I can feel my chin wobble the longer I stare.

Another gentle breeze drifts through the room.

This is it.

There's no escape.

It has come for me and my soul. It wants my secrets. My memories of her.

"Your heart rate is picking up," a voice says to my right, and I whip my head around.

Doctor Walsh, the surgeon who performed the amputation, steps out from the shadowed corner. His eyes are as dark as the night outside, his movements measured, and his smile cruel and vicious.

A cold sensation slithers down my back, and I shift my hand closer to the panic button, hoping he won't notice. It's stupidity. Something so ancient can read me like a book. The monster residing inside my surgeon predates humanity. He's timeless, having roamed this plane for centuries.

He approaches the bed, sniffing the air, his eyes rolling back before he trains them on me again. The heart monitor speeds up, but all I can focus on is him as he tilts his head to the side.

He studies me.

My fingers brush up against the panic button, and I snatch it up, trembling with dread. Even my teeth chatter. There's no

Heaven after this, not if I die at his hands. That *thing* will feed on my soul until there's nothing left.

He drops his eyes to the panic button in my hand, and the left side of his mouth quirks. I hold my breath, sweat beading on my forehead and trailing down the side of my face.

"You're so scared," he drawls, amused. "I can feel it pulse in the air."

"Get away from me!"

His smile slips as he glides his fingers over my legs through the quilt. I try to kick at him, but he grips me hard, bruising my tender skin.

He tuts. "Such a naughty girl."

When he rounds the bed, I glance down at the syringe in his hand. "What the fuck is that?" I scramble back, ripping the cannula from my hand and removing the wires attaching me to the heart rate monitor, causing it to flatline as I dash off the bed.

He's faster, pulling me back by my hair. My mangled wrist knocks against the bedframe, sending a jolt of pain through me, and I cry out as he hauls me back onto the bed.

"Please, no," I sob, trying to fight him off, but he overpowers me. I scream at the top of my lungs, his fingers brushing through my tears as he straddles me on the bed. "No one can hear you, little human. It's just you and me." He digs his fingers into my chin and shushes me. My heart threatens to break out from my heaving chest as I kick out at the sheets, bucking my hips. Nothing works.

He traces my trembling lips with his fingers and studies my face, touching me almost tenderly. "Human fear is delectable."

"Please, don't hurt me," I whimper, my chin wobbling. "I don't want to die."

"Say it again," he whispers, and my blood turns to ice when he opens his mouth to reveal a forked tongue.

"What the fuck?" I breathe, unable to believe my eyes. Then I let out another blood-curdling scream as he slides his serpent tongue up my throat and over my chin to taste the sweat on my skin. I struggle against him, sobbing uncontrollably when he grabs hold of my wrist and digs his fingers into the bandaged stump, a fiery pain spreading through my arm.

I'll vomit.

I taste it in my mouth as he looks me in the eye. I've never felt pain like this. Never felt it consume me.

Through the intense agony, I become aware of a sharp prick at my neck as he inserts the syringe, tracking every flicker of fear. Every wince and swallow.

He holds the syringe steady. "You can feel it, can't you? The life force draining from you."

When I whimper, he hushes me again, his deathly cold breath whispering over my lips. "Your friends will think your heart gave out."

"No, please," I plead, my eyes burning with tears. "Don't do this. I don't want to die."

He sniffs the air again, groaning deep in his chest. His forked tongue darts out and he drags it over my face in one long stroke. "I could feed on your fear for hours," he says, revealing sharp, pointed teeth. When he eases back to look at me, my eyes widen with terror. "It'll be over in minutes."

I whimper as he grips my chin and pushes down on the syringe, injecting air bubbles into my bloodstream.

"That's it," he whispers, caressing my mouth with his thumb. "There's a good girl."

"No…" My voice breaks. I don't want to die. My mom…my family…

He cradles my face the entire time, whispering sickening praise while we wait.

When pain begins to spread through my chest, my body seizes, and his smile widens as the black in his eyes intensifies until it bleeds down his cheeks like ink.

"Come to me," he urges.

Intense, burning pressure radiates through my chest as my body spasms.

I convulse. Horror has hold of every muscle.

The ink crawls up my legs, starting at my feet and moving over my knees and thighs like a million little spiders or ants in a sea of black. It rises higher and higher, over my lips and in through my nostrils, until darkness is all I see.

TWENTY-SEVEN

CAMRYN

THE FOLLOWING DAY, we gather in the library. Gwen lent me a set of crutches she had used after she broke her ankle the previous year. My injured leg throbs, but I was lucky to get away in one piece.

Aron sits at one of the tables and digs his laptop out of his backpack while Lily scours the old library records.

Gwen looks pale as she sits down beside Aron with a stack of books. The last week has taken its toll on us all. The horror of the situation is finally starting to sink in. Unless we do something, one of us could be next.

"How long are you staying at Gwen's?" Lily asks, scrolling through news articles. "Will your mom not suspect something is wrong soon?"

Dominic is watching me like a hawk. I wish he wouldn't treat me like porcelain. I'm fine. It was just a graze. At least, that's what I tell myself, but I still wince when I sit down.

He walks past me to peruse the shelves, and I lean the crutches against the table before sliding my bag from my shoulder. When my laptop is firing up, I shrug. "Mom is busy with her new job at the hospital. I should get away with a few nights before she grows suspicious."

"Long enough for you to put weight on your leg again without pulling a face."

"I don't understand why you don't just tell her," Lily says, pausing to peer at us over her shoulder. "Why the secrecy?"

Gwen rolls her eyes. "A man is dead, Lily. They broke into his house."

"But they didn't hurt him."

"Her mom will ground her for all of eternity if she finds out she broke into Wilfred's house. Not to mention, the police will get involved. At least now, it looks like a suicide."

"Really? Are you sure about that? He shot Camryn in the leg, and she crawled to the bedroom. Besides, you think her mom won't notice that her daughter has a gunshot wound?"

Gwen levels her with a glare. "It was a graze. Besides, I think we have bigger problems to solve. Let's just focus on finding out more information for now, okay?"

My eyes flit to Dominic's broad back while he reads the spines. He's wearing a backward black cap today, and tufts of dark hair peek out around his ears. Despite the burning throb in my calf, I still eye him up. Now that I know how he feels inside me, I can't stop myself from checking out his ass in those dark jeans.

His muscles shift enticingly when he pulls out a book. I'm going to hell. Sex should be the last thing on my mind, but maybe the gunshot damaged my brain more than my leg.

His gaze drifts over his shoulder as if he can feel my eyes on him. I quickly look away and open the search engine on my laptop, but it's too late. I'm hyperaware of his every breath, and when he walks past, his intoxicating scent drifts around me. I gulp, staring at the screen. He takes a seat on the chair beside mine and turns the first page.

"What are we looking for, exactly? Aron asks, typing away on his laptop.

"I don't know," Gwen replies, then looks at Dominic. "What book did you get?"

Dominic shows her the title. "Mythology throughout the ages."

"The house was built in 1923," Aron says, a look of concentration covering his eyes. "Mr. and Mrs. Kriger bought the house in 2000."

Dominic's leg brushes up against mine. I struggle to focus on my screen when my heart thuds this hard. Gwen turns another page and tucks a green lock of hair behind her ear. Silence settles while we do our research, interrupted only by the tapping of keyboards. Aron pops the lid on a soda can and takes a swig before he slowly lowers the bottle to the table and frowns. "Guys, I found something."

I stop scrolling and look up from my screen. Dominic shifts beside me and stretches his arm out on the back of my chair.

"What did you find?" Gwen asks, curious.

"Mrs. Kriger and their three children went missing in the summer of 2002."

"We know they went missing," Dominic drawls.

Aron shoots him a glare. "But now we know the month." He peers over at Lily. "Look for articles around that time. August of 2002."

"Behave," I whisper to Dominic, and he stiffens beside me. The darkening of his eyes tells me I'm in trouble, and for some disturbing reason, it thrills me.

He snakes his fingers underneath my hair and wraps them around my neck. My breath catches at the dominance in his touch, and I squeeze my thighs together beneath the table. But then he releases me and turns another page in the book.

His eyebrows knit together. "Check this." He taps the page. "The Nebri'hak travels on the wind and consumes the souls of its victims through strong emotions."

"Nebri'hak?" Aron asks, looking skeptical.

"It's the name of a demonic spirit trapped on our plane."

"Surely, we would know if there were demonic spirits amongst us," Lily says.

Dominic turns the page. "Not necessarily. They're unseen, for one. Displaced demons without a host. They need to feed to grow stronger. With every soul they consume, they become more powerful, harnessing it to stay in a human body longer."

"Is that what they want? To possess a human?" I ask.

"We are their food source. Demons are born from evil. They exist with the sole purpose of inflicting pain and suffering," Dominic replies, turning the page. "It says here that they sometimes fixate on certain souls, and this fixation can…"

"Can what?" I ask when he drifts off.

Dominic swallows and eases back. "It can last forever." His eyes meet mine. "What did Brittany say? Everything that's happened so far has been designed to bring you here?"

"Why here?" Gwen asks, pulling another book from the stack. "And why her?"

Aron sits back and drums his fingers on the desk in thought. "Maybe this backward little town and her house is its *nest*."

Dominic snorts, but Aron slams his laptop lid shut and swings his gaze between us. "Hear me out. This thing entered our plane, fuck knows when. They're curious creatures, right? They like to cause chaos and destruction, and they're attracted to strong emotions. Mr. Kriger was a greedy asshole who dabbled in the occult. Knowingly or unknowingly, he invited our demon here, and it has stuck around. There must be a reason for that. What's so special about our little town and her house? Our demon is fixated on something or *someone*." He looks at me pointedly.

Gwen grumbles, scrubbing her face. "What are you saying?"

Aron throws his arms out. "I don't fucking know, okay? But from what we *do* know so far, we can assume a few things." He ticks them off his fingers. "One, we opened ourselves up for possession when we did the séance. Two, our demon needs to torture and kill humans to grow stronger, and we are now what's on the menu. Three, it wants her." He points at me. "Don't ask me why. But it wants her. Four, this town is where it nests, and it has returned here, like frogs return to the same pond every summer to mate. It even went to great lengths to bring Camryn here. We don't know why or what's so special about this place, but we know it wants her here. *She* is its fixation. Whatever is going on here is about her."

Resting my elbows on the table, I rub my temples.

"Maybe it's bored?" Dominic suggests.

Now it's Aron's turn to snort. "It has been stuck here for a long time. Of course, it's fucking bored."

"How do we defeat it? How do we stop it from murdering us? We're sitting ducks," I say, straightening up. "What if someone opens a window… What then?"

"Well, *you're* safe," Aron grumbles.

I cross my arms and raise an eyebrow, which he ignores as he opens his laptop back up.

Gwen gives me a pleading look. "C'mon, you guys. Let's not argue."

"Fine." I blow a strand of hair away from my eyes.

"It says here," Dominic says, turning a page in the book, "that a Nebri'hak can only be destroyed with a weapon infused with magic."

Aron rolls his eyes. "Yeah, because we can easily buy those at Walmart."

"Magic?" I ask. "But surely… We can't…"

"What makes a weapon magical?" Gwen asks, ignoring Aron's sarcasm. "We know it's not going to be sparks and thunder."

Dominic picks up the book and drags his finger down the text until he finds what he wants and taps the page. "Nebri'hak can only be destroyed with their own magic. A weapon used on one of these demons infuses it with their magic, like a fingerprint or residual energy. Remember Chernobyl? Ever heard of the Elephant's foot?"

"The nuclear power plant disaster in Ukraine?"

Dominic shuts the book and puts it back on the table. "The Elephant's foot is considered one of the most radioactive objects in history."

"What's your point?" Aron sounds bored.

"My point," Dominic bites out, "is that such powerful radioactive energy lasts a long fucking time. Where the Elephant's foot is concerned, the danger has decreased over time because of the decay of its radioactive components."

"Are you suggesting the demon is radioactive?"

Dominic scoffs, shaking his head. "No, that's not what I'm saying, but it feeds on humans like we're Pop-Tarts to sustain its own energy on our plane. When it bleeds, it leaves a fingerprint, which could be used to kill it if a binding symbol is carved into the weapon ahead of time to lock in the demon's magic.

"So we can kill it with a weapon if it has the binding symbol carved into it?"

"In theory, yes, but the demon has to be trapped for it to work," Dominic says, rubbing his eyes. "Then there's also the problem that we can't hurt it when it's outside of a human form. It's only weak when it's possessing a human body."

"I do not volunteer to get shot or stabbed." Aron holds his hands up.

I roll my eyes. "Let's just keep looking for clues, like how to trap it. We can't kill it if we don't figure out how to trap it first."

While Dominic plays with my hair, turning page after page in his stack of books, I google the familiar binding symbol and the Kriger family mystery. Every article details the same information, but I keep hunting for something new. There must be something we have missed. Dominic leaves our corner of the library and returns minutes later with snacks and drinks. I'm halfway through a packet of salt and vinegar chips when I straighten in my seat. I smack Dominic's chest, causing him to frown. "Check this."

"What?" he asks, leaning in to read the screen.

"Not all of Mr. Kriger's children disappeared. One of them, eighteen-year-old Magdalene Kriger, was found a week later, wandering aimlessly and muttering to herself in the woods."

He angles the laptop screen toward him, reading over the article, his eyebrows pulling low in concentration. I scan his side profile and the dark hair peeking out from beneath his backward cap. My chest tightens uncomfortably when I think back on how close I was to losing him. It should scare me how attached I've become to him in such a short time, but the truth remains—Dominic makes me feel safe. In fact, he's probably my only safe place in this world.

His broad shoulders shift as he leans forward to rest his elbows on his knees. I'm playing with the dark hair at his nape, when I feel eyes on me, and I meet Aron's gaze. Looking away, he focuses on his screen.

"She was at Cross Hills Asylum," Dominic says, easing back and resting his arm on the back of my chair.

My eyes widen. "Shouldn't there be some records or something from her time there?"

Tucking a strand of hair away behind my ear, he says, "You'd make a good detective."

The tips of my ears burn, and when I lift my gaze, Gwen smirks at me from across the table.

"Uh, guys," Lily says, her big, tear-filled eyes flicking up from the phone in her trembling hand. "It's Brittany."

Heart racing, I glance at Dominic, then shift in my seat to face Lily.

"She's dead."

TWENTY-EIGHT

DOMINIC

THE VICAR DRONES on and on in the small church. A week has passed since the news of Brittany's death.

They ruled it a heart attack.

Fuck that. We all know it wasn't her heart that gave out. There's something far more sinister going on. Something that's waiting and watching.

Despite the endless summer heat, it's cold in the church. It's an old structure with worn pews and an ethereal feel, probably from the centuries of devotion and reverence absorbed by the stones.

Camryn is scratching the inside of her arm, but when I try to reach for her, she pulls away. She's been distant since Brittany's death, blaming herself for the events that have occurred since the séance.

I'm fed up with her fucking resistance, so I grab her wrist and yank up the long sleeve of her dress, mindful not to let her mom notice. What is she doing wearing a long-sleeve dress in this warm heat?

She tries to pull away, but it's too late. I've already seen the abused skin she tries to hide. There's blood under her nails, too.

I lean in and whisper against the shell of her ear, "What the hell are you doing?"

222

"None of your business."

I clench my jaw, straightening up. Camryn stares straight ahead at the coffin decorated with more flowers than the local florist stocks. It even smells of lilies in here—a faint urine scent.

"Everything about you is my business," I sneer near her ear. "Don't make me punish you."

She whips her head around and glares at me. "Our friend is dead, Dominic. Can you be serious for once?"

Fucking brat.

It takes everything in me not to clamp my hand over her mouth in public to stop her lips from moving. When she spits daggers at me with her eyes like she is now, I want nothing more than to choke the life out of her until she's so fucking aroused, there's a wet patch on the pew. Now that would show that fucking god of hers, or devil, who she really worships.

"You've been pushing me away this week," I whisper, ignoring the death glare a middle-aged balding man throws over his shoulder. Fuck him.

Camryn continues staring straight ahead, her jaw set in a firm line.

"I don't fucking like it."

"Tough shit," she snarls, finally giving me her damning eyes.

Her mom squeezes her hand on her other side, and I reluctantly drop this conversation for now. My knee jiggles. I stare at the back of Aron's head. We haven't seen much of him this week, but it doesn't matter. I still don't want him anywhere near Camryn.

Given a chance, he'd be in her panties in a heartbeat, no questions asked. He's like a puppy with a bone in her presence.

Seated beside him, Gwen looks over her shoulder and smiles at me weakly, tears glistening in her eyes as she glances at her friend.

Camryn leaves the pew, and I storm after her when she makes a beeline for the bathrooms.

The closer I get, the faster she walks until she's almost

running. She darts inside the bathroom and tries to slam the door shut, but I wedge a foot in the gap.

"Get out," she hisses, ramming her shoulder against the surface.

"I don't fucking think so." I shove it open, forcing her back, and then close it behind me. She flinches at the sound of the lock, but I'm done with the avoidance game we've been playing.

"What's up with your arm, Camryn? And don't fucking lie to me."

"Nothing is up with my arm."

I grab her chin with my full palm, making her hiss. "What the fuck is wrong with your arm? Why have you scratched it so badly it bleeds?"

"It itches, okay?"

I don't care for the defiance in her voice. Not one bit. I snarl, forcing her up against the wall. Her chin might bruise from my death grip, but neither of us cares. She's too busy burning me to ash with her glare, and I'm too hard to think straight when she's this feisty. If she's not careful, I'll fuck that look out of her eyes.

"Itches, huh?" I push up against her, pressing myself against her stomach. "Has this got something to do with the mysterious insect bite you got a few months back?"

She pales, clamping her lips shut.

"If something is happening to you, I need you to tell me. I can't help you if you don't talk to me."

"You want to help?" she asks, managing to sound so defiant with her chin engulfed by my big hand, which looks grotesque against her translucent skin. "Stay away from me."

Her response takes me aback. "What the fuck do you mean?"

She jerks free of my grip, her eyes teary when she looks at me again. "Three people are dead because of me. Three." She averts her gaze, and my chest squeezes. I try to catch her eyes again, coaxing her to look at me with a gentler touch as I trace her jawline.

"It's not your fault they're dead."

224

She says nothing, flicking her sorrow-filled eyes between mine.

"Dammit, Camryn." I cup her cheek. "None of this is your fault."

"Yes, it is."

I don't like how her voice trembles or how the tears in her eyes threaten to fall.

"I'll never forgive myself if anything happens to you. I shouldn't even be here today. I'm putting everyone at risk."

I open my mouth to speak, but slam it shut again, blowing out a frustrated sigh. Her tears finally fall, and I swipe them away with my thumbs, then trace her quivering bottom lip. "Don't shut me out again."

"I'm doing it to keep you safe," she says, escaping past me.

I hang my head as she leaves the bathroom. What will it take to get her to stop being so stubborn?

Chasing after her, I catch up just as she enters the main hall. I grab her arm, shove her up against the back of a large pillar, and place my hand over her mouth to keep her fucking quiet. I doubt she'd scream in front of the congregation and cause a scene at her friend's funeral, but it's better to be safe than sorry.

"I'm not a patient man. If you push me away again, I don't know what the hell I'll do, but I know one thing. Care to hazard a guess?"

Her wide, glassy eyes watch me as I grab her throat with my free hand.

"I know I'll never let you go, so do us both a favor and get that fucking idea out of your head."

Her pulse thunders beneath my fingers, the tears finally spilling over.

I lean in close to her ear. "Have I ever told you how pretty you are when you cry? How it makes me want to devour you? To hurt you more." With one final look behind the pillar to ensure no one is watching, I release her throat and snake my hand beneath her skirt.

My fingers slide up her thigh as I track every flickering emotion in her big eyes. The moment I graze up against her soaked panties, her lashes flutter.

"Such a filthy girl," I taunt, pushing the lace aside and tracing her slit in a featherlight touch. "Your dead friend is in that coffin." I tut, knowing far well she gets off on the guilt. "You shouldn't like this so much."

When I sink two fingers inside her, she grips my suit jacket in a bid to push me away, but twists the expensive material instead.

I hum, finger-fucking her slowly to the background sound of a hymn being sung. "Do you see that to our left?"

She follows my line of sight when I jerk my head in the direction of the large statue near the wall. "What do you think Mother Mary has to say, seeing you cream all over your brother's fingers in church?"

Camryn moans beneath my palm, and I tighten my grip on her mouth, but there's nothing I can do to hide the wet sounds coming from her pussy.

"Your cunt missed me," I say, nibbling on her earlobe. "Missed my fingers and my cock."

The first hymn gives way to a second song. Dropping to my knees, I dive beneath her skirt to erase all lingering thoughts of all the reasons why she should keep her distance. She should know better than to think she can keep my pussy away from me.

I throw her leg on my shoulder and drive my tongue into her, fucking her tight little hole while Mother Mary watches on from the shadows. Camryn rolls her hips, all notion of wanting me to stay away gone out of the window now that she's so close to coming with her cunt clamping down on my tongue. I pull out to suck on her soaked pussy, then home in on her swollen clit. That little sensitive bud drives me fucking insane. Licking and nibbling, I flick my tongue until she falls apart, riding my face like a greedy slut.

She somehow manages to stay silent, and I discover why when

I pop out from beneath her skirt and find her with both hands pressed over her mouth.

Her chest rises and falls rapidly, and her pale cheeks are flushed. I love my effect on her.

Before the blush has a chance to retreat, I guide her forward, making no move to wipe her cum from my face. If anything, I wear the evidence of her orgasm with pride. Yes, ladies and gents, I ate her cunt while you all sang about Jesus.

Camryn keeps her head down, almost sprinting to her seat. Aron doesn't hide his contempt when his eyes clash with mine. With a smirk, I slide in behind Camryn on the pew.

Kicking my feet out in front of me, my arm rests behind my girl, and I raise an eyebrow at Aron, who huffs a breath and faces forward.

Asshole.

I brush my lips up against Camryn's ear. "Next time you try to shut me out or keep your distance, I'll fuck you right here on the pew for everyone to see."

The wake afterward is held at Brittany's house, an old Victorian with a wrap-around porch, a perfectly manicured lawn, and flowering gardenias. Only the closest have been invited. It's a small affair, which is why Camryn hasn't bolted yet.

Seated around the circular dining table, one of four scattered around the spacious living room, she picks at her food with a faraway look.

Blood seeps from the tender steak as I slice it in half with the knife. No one speaks.

At least not until Lily says, "All the windows are closed."

"The AC is on," Gwen points out, her green hair gathered in a ponytail.

"This is so fucking stupid," Aron mutters, stabbing a piece of minted potato. He shoves it in his mouth and speaks around a mouthful. "We leave the house every day. The demon could attack us at any moment, and you guys worry about the damn windows being left open?"

Beside him, Lily hides behind the long strands of her hair. I hate to admit that he has a point. We're not safe anywhere.

"And what the fuck was that back there?" Aron asks, directing his question at me. "You can't leave her alone for five minutes, huh?"

I shrug as I pick up the sharp, bloodied knife and pretend to inspect the blade.

A bead of crimson trails down the flat end as I look over at him. "My girl was sad. I cheered her up."

"Cheered her up?" he hisses, his cheeks flaming. "You fucked her in church during our friend's funeral. How fucking disrespectful can you be?"

"Are you done with your tirade?" I tilt the blade in his direction. "Correction. I didn't fuck her. I ate her out. There's quite a difference."

"You fucking—" He shoots to his feet, but Lily puts her hand on his arm.

"Please calm down. This is what it wants."

When Aron peers at her hand on his elbow, she says, "What it feeds on. Please… We're here for Brittany."

Shrugging her off, he reluctantly sits back down, picks up his fork, and stabs at another piece of potato. He doesn't look at me again, which is for the best. If he wants a fight, I'll gladly give him one.

I stretch my arm out on the back of Camryn's seat and toy with the strands of her hair, ignoring her hard stare. I know I'm being a dick. Do I care? Not particularly. The only thing of importance is to keep her safe.

And *mine*.

If another man challenges me, he will feel my wrath. So what if Camryn doesn't like it? Tough. She'll get over it.

My eyes stray across the room, taking in Brittany's family

members littered around the tables. Her mom talks to an elderly lady in a wheelchair, who must be the grandmother. They all share the same high cheekbones and almond-shaped eyes.

A different figure catches my attention, and I pause. Her chin is lifted high, not a hair astray in her severe bun.

She looks formidable, her hands clasped in front of her black dress with its high lace collar and white apron. I look around my table, but no one else is paying attention to the woman—the same woman from my nightmares and Wilfred's house.

She disappears around the corner. I excuse myself from the table, ignoring Camryn's questioning look as I weave between tables on my way out. An urgency I can't explain takes hold of me.

I tumble into the hall, cursing under my breath when there's no sign of her. But then, just as I'm about to turn back around and rejoin Camryn, a voice whispers from inside one of the rooms. The door is ajar, the hinges squeaking as it opens farther.

Walking closer, my dress shoes sink into the expensive rug. I look behind me, but no one is there. I'm alone.

"Dominic…"

My steps slow. Warning bells blare.

"Dominic…" The whisper comes again, enticing me closer.

I move forward, my heart pounding. I know deep down I need to turn around, but my body is in a trance. I can't look away from the gap in the door.

Eyes peer back at me.

Eyes that disappear farther into the darkness as I near.

My skin crawls and chills slither down my spine. I reach my hand out to open the door, when Camryn appears in front of me, and I slow to a sudden stop.

She shuts the door. "What are you doing out here?"

I shake my head, trying to clear the fog that still has its claws in me. "I-I need the bathroom."

"Well, you won't find it in the basement." She looks at me

weirdly, then takes my hand and steers me away from the whispering voice.

My neck prickles with awareness, and I look over my shoulder to see the handle slowly turn.

Dread seals my throat.

Whatever that *thing* is…

It's coming for us.

TWENTY-NINE

CAMRYN

THE IMPOSING estate that looms ahead is a sight to behold, with its distinctive pointed cobblestone ceilings, twin wooden doors adorned with traditional cast iron, and lion-head door knockers that seem to guard the entrance. The large windows, like watchful eyes, add to the grandeur of the structure.

"This place is creepy," Lily says in a small voice behind me.

"What did you expect?" Gwen asks. "It's an asylum."

"What are we even doing here?"

I walk up the winding footpath, pretending I'm not quaking on the inside. Fake it until you make it and all that bullshit. This is the very definition of that saying.

"We need to look at the historical records," I say, sensing eyes on us. "I couldn't find anything online, so this is our final resort."

The curtains twitch in one of the windows of the second floor.

Before Lily can say anything else, I quickly make my way up the steps and knock on the door. A gentle breeze sweeps through, lifting my hair from my shoulders, as a wind chime tinkles in the distance. I suppress a shiver, hoping for someone to open the door and let us in.

Finally, after what feels like an eternity, the large doors creak open to reveal a stern-looking elderly woman with greying hair and deep wrinkles on her forehead and around her mouth.

She eyes us suspiciously.

Gwen steps forward. "We have an appointment with Dr. Hector."

Glancing between us, she steps aside to let us enter. The air inside smells faintly of antiseptic and damp upholstery. I can sense Lily beside me, with her head down, following along like an obedient puppy without a backbone. A pang of guilt clogs my throat, but I force it back down.

Our friends would be alive if I'd listened to her initially.

We pass several doors until the stern woman stops at one and orders us in. I pass a patient muttering to herself, with greasy dark hair and sunken eyes. She briefly looks up, watching us, but then ducks her head again when she spots the stern woman, who stands with her spine erect and her hands clasped in front of her like she's a strict headmistress at a boarding school from decades past.

We sidle in, shuffling awkwardly.

Large bookcases line the back wall, the shelves sagging from the weight of so many hardbacks and paperbacks with broken spines and curled edges. A fish tank sits in one of the corners with a lone goldfish swimming in circles, the soft sound of the oxygen pump filling the tense silence. Glancing toward the tall window, I spot a large filing cabinet.

Bingo.

I suppress a shiver while waiting for the woman to talk, feeling strangely like an unruly kid at school who has been called to the principal's office.

She looks from Gwen to Lily to me, and her critical, assessing eyes fall down our bodies before settling on our faces. "I'll see if he's ready now."

The moment she walks out, we exhale a collective sigh.

"That was intense," Gwen mutters.

"So intense," I agree.

My phone vibrates in my pocket. I ignore the call, already knowing it's Dominic. He won't be happy when he finds out about this little mission. But I didn't want to have this conversation, so I snuck out while he was in the shower. He needs to learn sooner or later that I'm not some leashed pet he can control.

"How do we open it?" Gwen asks, tilting her chin to the cabinet. "I guess what we're looking for is in there?"

I glance around, rolling my lip beneath my teeth. "We need a key." Just then, footsteps sound outside, and my eyes widen. I dart inside a cupboard, knocking against cardboard boxes on the floor and a rail of…clothes.

"Fuck…"

"What the hell, Camryn?" Gwen hisses, but the desperate tone of her voice soon takes on a much more pleasant note when the door opens.

Heavy footsteps sound on the floor, and a man in a white coat whisks by. I only manage to catch a glimpse of him through the small gap in the door, but the moment his big build and graying sideburns come into view, my breath catches in my throat, and I blend with the shadows.

I can't remember the last time I felt my heart beating out of my chest. We came here without a solid plan. Let's face it: improvisation was always on the agenda.

My phone vibrates again, and I curse the fucking thing. Voices drift through the gap while I fish my cell out to switch it off.

> You sneaking out on me is getting tiresome.
> Don't test me right now, Camryn. Answer your
> fucking phone.

After powering it down, I slide it inside my back pocket before inching closer to the gap in the door. Gwen and Lily are seated at the desk with their backs to me.

Dr. Hector, a man in his late fifties with a thick mustache and bushy eyebrows, swings his gaze between them, looking bored. He already knows they're wasting his time.

233

"You claim this lady was a relative?"

"Yes," Gwen replies, nodding, her large hoop earrings swaying. Lily, meanwhile, is perspiring. God forbid, she ever plays poker. The girl can't lie to save her life. She's so pale that she could rival every ghost roaming these ancient halls.

My own hands are damp, so I rub them on my bare thighs.

"I can't discuss my patients without sufficient evidence that you are, indeed, relatives of the person in question. That requires proof of identification."

"But she's deceased."

One of his bushy eyebrows lifts.

"Oh well," Gwen says, blowing out a sigh. "I guess we traveled all this way for nothing. I just thought that maybe we could find out some information about dear old Edna Kriger."

"Magdalene, you mean?" he says without changing his expression. His chest expands on a deep inhale, and he eases back against the wingback chair. "I'm afraid I can't help you today, ladies."

Chairs scrape on the scratched wooden floor, and their voices drift away. I blow out a sigh, thinking I'm safe, but then the door shuts, and the sound of heavy footsteps nearing has me shrinking deeper into the rail of clothes.

Fuck, fuck, fuck. This is bad.

He whistles a tune as he pours himself a thumb of whiskey, the amber alcohol sloshing against the sides of the tumbler. I can faintly make him out beyond the gap—the hiss he makes through his teeth as the liquid slides down his throat.

Cracking his neck, he nurses his drink and peers over at the cabinet. Outside, a branch knocks against the window in the muggy summer breeze.

Tap. Tap. Let me in.

A bead of sweat trails down the side of my neck. It's sweltering in this small space.

The floorboards creak beneath his weight. He puts his whiskey glass on top of the cabinet, fishes a key out of his breast pocket,

CONJURE

and unlocks it. It slides open to reveal file after file, and Dr. Hector
fingers through them. Then he shuts the drawer and slides open
the next one in line.

When he pulls out a thick file, I bat a shirt out of the way and
inch closer to the gap, intrigued. He discards something on the
desk, then loosens his tie while reading over the information in
the file. I watch as he swirls the glass, taking another sip, before
sitting his ass on the desk and crossing his feet at his ankles.

Patience has never been my strong suit. Even more so now as I
eye the file in his hand. I bet it's the one we're after. After the girls'
visit, Dr. Hector felt too intrigued not to pull it out from the
cabinet and read about Miss. Kriger.

My arm itches something fierce. The sensation of something
crawling beneath my skin has me clawing at it. I'm so desensi-
tized now, I've come to crave the release the pain brings.

Tap. Tap. Tap. The branch knocks louder, demanding entrance.

Dr. Hector wipes his arm over his forehead, cursing the AC.
My fingers come away slick with blood as he straightens up and
then makes his way to the window. He opens it, the papers in the
folder rustling in the breeze.

I ease back out of instinct when a sensation of dread washes
over me. In doing so, I accidentally knock against one of the boxes
on the floor, and the sudden sound has Dr. Hector's head shooting
up.

He looks over at the cupboard where I'm hiding and slowly
closes the folder in his hand as I clamp a hand over my mouth.
What if he finds me? What then?

He walks closer.

I struggle to suppress a fearful whimper, convinced I'm about
to get discovered. He frowns, reaching out to open the door, when
someone enters the room. I sag with relief as he puts the folder on
the desk and disappears from view.

That was too close.

They leave the room, and I wait a few moments longer before
stepping out of the cupboard and looking around the office.

235

Once I'm sure the coast is clear, I take the file, then haul ass to the open window. I slide it open and toss out the paperwork before climbing out and jumping to the ground. The grass is overgrown on this side of the property and the rose bushes beneath the window are dead. Pain sears the bare skin on my legs the moment my feet connect with the ground, and I release a string of expletives as I try to wipe the fresh blood from my legs from the shallow cuts caused by the thorny roses and broken, dried stalks. Thankfully, the stitches from the graze have since dissolved, and all that remains is a pink scar. Mom is too up in her own head to notice.

Overhead, the leaves in the trees rustle, and I grow still, barely daring to move and certainly not daring to look behind me. I swear someone or something is watching me.

I pick up the folder and hobble around the side of the house, the pain worsening with every step. Fuck it, at least I have the folder.

Gwen and Lily are waiting in the car. When they spot me, Gwen exits the vehicle and rushes to my side. "What the hell happened? Do you know how fucking worried we were?"

I chuckle, then grimace. "I'm fine."

"Fine? Are you kidding me? Your boyfriend will have both of our heads."

"He's not my boyfriend."

"You keep telling yourself that."

She opens the passenger door and helps me inside. Lily looks pale, her eyes widened with worry. "What happened?"

"Nothing happened. I landed in dead rose bushes, is all. Those thorns hurt like a motherfucker."

"You're suicidal. That's what you are," Gwen says, climbing in behind the steering wheel and directing the car down the winding road. "What the hell were you thinking back there?"

"I wasn't."

"No shit." She swipes strands of her green hair off her sweaty forehead. "Can you at least tell us about the plan beforehand next time?"

"There was no plan."

Lily snickers, and my lips twitch as I hold up the bloodied paperwork. "But we got the fucking file."

"That's my girl!" Gwen high-fives me, and we squeal with victorious excitement.

———

Gwen swerves out of the way to avoid another crushed armadillo with its innards splattered on the sunbaked, cracked asphalt.

The sun beats down on the car, and I shake the travel fan in my hand when the batteries run low. "Cheap crap."

Gwen glances at me as I aim it at my sticky face. I tilt my chin, feeling the air move against the hollow of my exposed throat, where my collarbones meet. I swipe a finger through the pool of sweat collected there and aim the fan at my forehead. Nothing works in this heat, but we know better than to open the windows.

"Want to head back to your place?" Gwen asks.

I shake my head. "No, let's not involve the boys yet."

"The longer you leave it, the more worked up he'll get." She smirks, stealing the fan from me.

"Give me that," I pinch it back, chuckling when she smacks my arm.

"I'm starting to think you like winding him up like a toy. The poor guy is head over heels in love with you."

I snort, brushing my damp hair away from my brow. "He's not in love with me."

Lily sticks her head between the seats. "You're either blind or stupid."

"Yes," Gwen says, gesturing at her friend. "Even Lily agrees."

I sigh, even as my stomach flutters, handing Lily the travel fan and looking out the passenger window at the passing scenery. A scarecrow that has seen better days sits in the middle of a large field, its outstretched arms lined with cawing birds.

"You don't seem happy about it?"

I look away, meeting Gwen's concerned gaze.

"Do you like him?" she asks.

"Of course, I like him."

"But?"

The insistent sensation of worms crawling beneath my skin has me reaching for my sleeve. I scratch through the thin fabric, focusing on the throbbing pain. "I'm trying to keep him safe."

Gwen and Lily exchange a look.

"The demon," I explain, "it wants me. It's killing my friends and the people I care about because of me. I almost lost Dominic once…"

"It won't stop…" Lily's voice is barely audible over the engine. "That's what Brittany said."

I open the paper file on my lap to see a grainy, black-and-white photograph of Magdalene Kriger.

Peering through strings of dark, greasy hair, her empty eyes give me chills.

"But what does it want?" I shudder, closing the file. "What will it do when we're all dead?"

Gwen slows as we near Wilfred's farm.

Police cars line the road. Paramedics carry a stretcher out of the house. A white sheet covers the body, and a ghostly pale hand is visible from the road.

"Just keep driving," Lily urges.

"No, wait." I sit up straight when they carry a second stretcher out of the house.

Dread fills my stomach.

"Camryn," Gwen asks in a quivering voice as the car crawls past the parked vehicles with their flashing blue lights still on. "Was there anyone else in the house that day?"

I swallow hard, unable to look away from the long, brown locks tumbling like a waterfall down the side of the stretcher.

Somewhere, from the shadowy depths, a lullaby drifts closer.
An eerie melody.
A woman's haunted voice.
I grow still, my hair floating in the water.
Something is moving closer, barely visible in the pitch black.
A splash of white.
A halo of brown hair that shifts backward with the next momentum.
A pale woman rushes at me through the darkness below.

"Please drive," I whisper, tears blurring my vision.

A sycamore leaf drifts across the windshield. We watch it dance and twirl before another gentle breeze sends it sailing through the air toward Wilfred's farm.

"You don't have to ask me twice," Gwen replies, stepping on the gas.

THIRTY

CAMRYN

VIBRANT ORANGE HUES paint the sky as the sun dips below the horizon, casting a warm glow behind the towering fir trees.

Gwen parks in front of the large iron gates to the old graveyard. A chain with a rusty padlock secures the old graves beyond. This place is popular with bored teenagers at night, who like to come here to drink and upturn old headstones.

My heart skips a beat at a crow's sudden, piercing caw.

Gwen tightens her grip on the wheel, her face drained of color. "What was that back there?" she asks quietly.

"I don't know."

"There was no one else there that day, was there? The day you killed Wilfred?"

"We didn't kill him."

"Was there anyone else there?"

I swallow. "No, there wasn't."

Gwen stares at me for a beat, eyes glassy with tears.

"But I think I saw someone in the window upstairs."

"What do you mean?"

"The curtains twitched when Dominic carried me out. I thought it was a trick of the imagination."

Gwen breaks eye contact, staring out the windshield at the imposing gates. "Now that person is dead."

"I swear I didn't know."

Lily shifts in the backseat.

The caw comes again, causing my heart rate to spike. I open the file and suppress a shiver as I glance at the photograph. Those dead eyes, rimmed in dark circles, peer into my soul.

"Let me see," Gwen says.

I hand her and Lily the photograph and the first few pages to look through.

"The girl could have done with chapstick," Gwen mutters, handing Lily the photograph and reading over the paperwork.

"Psychosis…shock treatment," I mumble, skimming the text.

"They kept her in a straitjacket toward the end because she wouldn't stop scratching," Lily reads. "Said worms crawled beneath her skin."

I look up from my paperwork and over my shoulder, nerves rippling through me.

Lily pales. "Oh, this is grisly." She hands me a picture and presses the back of her hand over her mouth as though she's smelled something bad.

I see why when I look at the photograph. Deep, infected lacerations decorate both of the woman's arms—so deep the sinew is visible.

"Fuck me," Gwen whispers, staring at it. "That's…disturbing."

"Tell me about it." I flick to the next paper in the file.

We read silently, exchanging the odd comment here or there until Gwen stiffens. She smacks my shoulder and says, "Look at this."

I place the file on my lap and accept the sheet she hands me. My heart pounds as I read.

"What is it?" Lily asks, popping her head through the gap.

"Miss. Kriger—Magdalene—claimed a demonic spirit was after her, trying to enter her body.

"The demon…" My voice comes out low and haunted.

"She spoke of visions, delusions."

"What I would like to know is…" Lily says, swallowing. "Why didn't it enter her?"

"She said it couldn't, and that's why it fixated on her."

"Is that what it says?" I ask, skimming the paper until I reach the part.

I can almost hear her voice in my ears.

It wants me.

What's it?

The devil.

The devil wants you?

A demon. It's stuck.

Why does it want you, Miss Kriger?

Because it can't have me.

And why can't it have you?

I-I don't… It whispers…whispers, whispers, whispers. Itchy, itchy, itchy.

My hands tremble as the words blur, and a tear falls with a splat.

Did you have anything to do with your family's disappearance, Miss?

It entered them. It fed…it fed on their souls. I can't let it… I have to protect…

(Patient speaks incoherently, hissing and snapping their teeth.)

"It says here they subjected her to shock treatments." Lily's quiet voice breaks through my turmoil of emotions.

"I thought that was banned," Gwen says.

"Not back then, it wasn't." I sniffle, wiping the tears from my eyes. "Magdalene passed away eighteen months later after she threw herself down the stairs."

Gwen rubs my shoulder.

"She claimed it entered *them* and fed on their souls." I wipe away more tears with my sleeve. "Do you think she meant her father?"

"It would make sense. He invited the demon—"

242

"And it killed his family," Lily finishes.

"You finally believe in the supernatural?" I ask.

Her big eyes lock on mine, and she chews on her thumbnail—an anxious trait—before finally saying, "Yes…it's the only thing that can explain what's happening."

I inhale a deep breath.

Everything is a mess.

"How do we defeat it?"

Gwen flips down the visor and reapplies her black lipstick. "It entered our plane once." She smacks her lips, inspecting the result before tossing the lipstick back into the center console. "We need to kick it the fuck out."

When we return, it's dark. The porch swing sways as a gentle breeze feathers through the overgrown grass.

I've been out all day and kept my phone switched off. I know even before I exit the car that Dominic will be beyond pissed.

I stare through the windshield at the house. The lights are out, but he's awake.

"I thought the house looked creepy in the day, but at night…" Gwen drifts off.

"Yeah," I agree, collecting my bag but leaving the file with Gwen. "It's a shithole."

"Want us to come in with you?"

I frown. "No, why?"

"In case he gives you shit."

A weak smile plays on my lips. Reaching for the door handle, I turn slightly over my shoulder. "I can handle him. See you tomorrow?"

"You bet on it. We need to research exorcisms."

"What if it can hear you?" Lily asks. "Should we discuss it… out loud."

"I think if it can hear us, it can also read our thoughts."

"Call me in the morning." I exit the car, shouldering my bag and hurrying up the steps. I quickly unlock the door and enter the dark house, shrugging off the urge to turn on all the lights.

Unease clings to me like a second skin as I walk upstairs to my bedroom.

After switching on the light, I pause when I see Dominic seated on the edge of the bed with his elbows on his thighs and his head cradled in his hands. Bruno is asleep behind him.

Dominic looks up.

I take in his haunted gaze, mussed-up hair, and creased clothing. I expected him to be angry and shout at me. What I didn't expect was the broken look in his eyes.

Sliding the bag off my shoulder, I toss it to the floor. Dominic watches me wearily. I walk closer, uncertain of myself—of us.

"Where have you been?" he asks, his voice raspy.

I draw to a halt. "I was out with the girls. We did some... research."

A muscle clenches in his jaw before he cuts eye contact to stare out the window. When he stays silent, my chest tightens. This isn't the Dominic I've come to expect.

"You turned off your phone," he says quietly, his voice hardening as he looks back at me. "I couldn't get ahold of you."

"I'm sorry—"

"I didn't know if you were dead or alive."

I draw back when he rises to his full height, seeming larger than life with his broad, tense shoulders and hulking build. Dominic has always been intense, but the way his gaze sears me now has my heart racing and my knees weakening.

"But now I know you were fine." He walks up to me, and I hold my breath. He's close enough to touch, but for the first time, I'm ashamed and unable to meet his gaze. Nonetheless, his minty breath teases my face when he says, "You just didn't want to let me know you were okay."

He sidesteps me, his footsteps retreating. I look over my shoulder. "Would you have let me out of your sight?"

Coming to a halt in the doorway, he keeps his back to me, and I turn fully. I can see from here how tense he is, but he doesn't look at me, which hurts more than I want to admit.

"I care about you, Dominic. And it's because I care about you that I have to keep you safe. That's what I've tried to tell you ever since Brittany died, but you won't listen to me." When he remains silent, I blink back tears. "Please, say something."

His chin touches his shoulder, jaw twitching before spinning around and striding up to me. "Do you know the difference between you and me?"

I stay silent. Whatever he's about to say will cut me open. I know it will. I see it in his eyes.

"You say you care about me. *Care…*" He attempts a small smile, even as his throat jumps. He straightens up. "Meanwhile, I love you. Don't you get it? I love you! The word 'care' doesn't exist in my fucking vocabulary. You're it for me."

My heart gallops at his admission, and I reach for him. He's it for me, too. I never thought I would hear Dominic say those words. Never thought he felt the same way.

He stumbles back another step, eyes flashing with hurt. "The thought of something happening to you eats me up from the inside. So when I don't hear from you, when there's a demon out there that wants to hurt you, yes…I lose my shit."

This time when he backs away, shame eats me up from the inside.

"But all along, you simply didn't *want* to reassure me that you were safe. You say you care, but you don't. You don't care about me. About us. Why the fuck am I wasting my time?"

"Dominic…" I try, chest tightening, but he turns around and walks out.

Soon after, the door to his room slams shut, and I hang my head. Why do I always mess everything up?

I hurry after him, trying his door handle, but it's locked. "Dominic?" I knock quickly. "I'm sorry, okay?"

I knock again, but it's radio silence on the other side. "Please… I was scared. Dom?"

Silence.

I blink back tears, wishing he would let me in so I could explain. I don't dare tell him that I love him. Not yet. Not while we're in danger. The thought of losing him cuts like a knife.

"Please let me in, Dom." I wait, but the door remains closed. Dominic is done with me. I could bang on his door all night, but it wouldn't make a difference. He won't listen to me until he has calmed down. At least, I hope he'll be willing to hear me out.

I bite back a sob and return to my room.

Once the door is closed, I sweep my eyes around the space. Dominic's scent lingers in the air. I stare at the bed, where he was seated when I arrived home. I already miss him.

Crawling into bed, fully clothed, I cuddle up with Bruno. My sheets still smell of Dominic—leather and citrus—and I breathe in his masculine, comforting scent as I drift off to sleep.

THIRTY-ONE

DOMINIC

"Dominic…"

The sinister hiss stirs me awake.

I blink my eyes open and sit up in bed. A sense of unease ripples through me as I scan every corner of the room. One of the windows is open, and the curtain shifts in a gentle breeze.

Something moves beneath the quilt, causing me to stiffen. "What the fuck?" I whisper.

It starts at my feet and crawls up my legs, getting closer and closer. I stare at it for a beat before panic sets in, and I rip off the quilt, but there's nothing there. I swear something or someone was moving beneath the blanket and up my body, like a cold breath against my bare legs.

Something is observing me. Eyes follow me as I skate my gaze across the room. Childish giggles echo in the silence, followed by bare feet running across the floorboards.

It's too dark to see, so I reach over to switch on the bedside light then ease back, swallowing hard as the temperature drops.

"Dominic…" a voice whispers near my ear, making me scramble off the bed and tumble to the floor with a hard thud. *What the fuck was that?* My heart pounds as I stare at the empty

bed and the crumpled sheets. I swear someone brushed their icy lips against the shell of my ear.

Unsteady, I escape into the dark hall. Elongating shadows on the walls seem to chase me as I turn to the left, a sheen of sweat covering my bare back. I steal a glance behind me before turning and running down the stairs. Suddenly, I stop short, out of breath, as I notice light streaming through the gap in the kitchen door. Inching closer, I nudge it open, the hinges creaking as the wilting flowers on the table come into view. I peer inside, lingering at the threshold, when Camryn appears in the doorway.

I stagger back. "Jesus, you scared me."

She holds on to the door and licks her upper lip, eyeing me with a flirtatious look. "Hi, Dom."

No matter how upset I am, my dick hardens when her eyes trail a slow path down my body and then back up. There's nothing innocent about how her gaze lingers on my bare chest, or how she cocks her head to the side and lets a seductive smirk dance across her enticing lips.

Fuck me. I'm screwed.

Camryn steps back and opens the door farther with one hand, that sinful smile hooking me as much as the quirk of her finger. She spins around and walks deeper into the kitchen, glancing at me over her shoulder. The invitation in her darkening eyes dislodges my feet, and I step over the threshold.

She walks around the kitchen table with a smirk, and when I slow to a stop, my heart thuds harder as she pulls a knife from the wooden block, inspecting the sharp blade in the ambient light. Her eyes lock on mine, and she points the blade in my direction with a wink.

What has gotten into her? I'm intrigued, but also wary. Camryn isn't usually this forward.

"We should talk about last night," I say.

"Talking is overrated," she replies, walking up to me.

My throat goes dry as I watch her hips sway with each slow step.

When she's close enough to touch, she lifts the knife and slides the tip of the blade down my chest, a dark smile twisting her mouth. "You trust me, Dom?"

I hiss when she nicks my skin.

Blood beads on the surface cut as her sinful smile widens, taking on a darker, more dangerous edge. She leans in and drags her tongue through it then trails it across my skin until she reaches my nipple. With a teasing flick, she looks up at me through her wispy lashes. "Do you trust me, Dom?"

She circles the small bud and drags the flat end of the knife down my chest.

"I trust you," I breathe, burying my fingers in her long hair.

Overhead, the light flickers, but I'm too drunk on Camryn to pay attention to the faulty electric.

She bites me, and the sharp sting twitches my dick. "Silly boy."

I watch through heavy lids as she interlaces her fingers with mine and leads me toward the door at the back of the kitchen.

"When will you learn, Dominic?" She sinks her teeth into her plump bottom lip. I'd do fucking anything to taste it, to kiss her, to brand myself on her skin.

"Learn what?" I ask, trapping her with my arm against the door and cupping her cheek.

She taps my lips with the blade and lifts her gaze. The knife trails a slow path down the curve of my chin, over my Adam's apple, and between my collarbones. All the while, she keeps me hostage with her big eyes.

If only she knew the hold she has on me.

"Not everything is what it seems." She reaches behind her and turns the handle. "Your desire blinds you." The door opens to the basement, and she pulls me forward with a taunting smile, engulfing us in darkness. But not before I see her change form into something truly horrific.

I turn to run, but it's too late; the door slams shut, refusing to budge no matter how much I pull on it. "You're not Camryn…"

My voice trembles as I try to control myself. "You tricked me." Slowly turning around, I press my spine against the wood.

"He finally catches on. But don't worry," the demonic creature says, digging the sharp blade into my side and darting its forked tongue out to lick my earlobe. "I'll be gentle with you."

THIRTY-TWO

CAMRYN

DOMINIC STARES at me from across the breakfast table.

His eyes, usually a shade of hazel, now seem to hold a sinister edge I can't quite decipher. It's not the color, but the enigma that lies behind it.

Dressed in combat shorts and a black T-shirt, he plays with his Zippo, lighting and flicking it shut again while a smirk reveals the killer dimples in his cheeks.

I try not to be affected by the intense way he traps me, but something about his demeanor has me on edge.

Scalding coffee splashes against the sides as Mom fills her mug. The sound seems heightened in the tense silence, but as always, she remains oblivious.

"I'm sorry that I'm away so much. It's temporary until they hire more staff." She frowns. "Where's Bruno this morning?"

"I haven't seen him," I reply.

Mom hums, but she's distracted. "I'll have a look for him after breakfast."

Rain spatters against the windows as thunder rolls in the distance, but it's all background noise to me. Mom sips her coffee while I take a bite out of my buttered piece of toast. Dry crumbs stick to my lips, so I wipe them off. Dominic flicks the Zippo again, and another flame flares to life. I lower my gaze to it, swallowing down the chewed-up bread. My throat dries up when I stare at the unmoving flame. Not even a flicker or tremble.

Dominic's smirk deepens and he shuts the lid with a quick flick, almost too fast to notice. Another loud rumble of thunder crackles outside when our eyes lock.

Mom talks about work, before she seems to notice the silence and looks between us.

Her eyebrows raise in question. "Is everything alright?"

I shoot up, tossing the uneaten toast onto the plate. "I need to get ready for class."

When I hurry past Dominic, his head turns over his shoulder. It's not obvious enough that my mom notices, but I sure as hell feel his gaze on me. Something is wrong. I can feel it in my bones.

"Camryn?" Mom calls out, and I pause in the doorway. "I'm heading to work. There's food in the freezer for later."

Walking back over to the table, I lean down to kiss Mom on the cheek, ignoring Dominic.

"I promise we'll catch up soon," she says, but I'm not listening, my veins running cold as I pick up the unread, folded-up newspaper beside her plate.

A picture of Wilfred is plastered on the front, but it's the image beside his—a much smaller, grainy black-and-white photograph—that has me trembling.

Excusing myself, I hurry upstairs to my room, where I unplug my phone from the charger.

Gwen answers on the fourth ring. "I'm relieved that you called. I was convinced your possessive boyfriend tied you to the bed or something—"

"Did you read this morning's paper?" I ask, interrupting her, balancing the phone between my shoulder and ear as I sit down on the bed.

"What are you talking about?"

I splay the page open, the paper crinkling. "The front-page news."

I hear a door open. Gwen covers the phone with her hand to speak to her dad and then returns to the line. "Okay, I stole my dad's copy." The stairs creak beneath her weight as she returns to her room and shuts the door. Paper rustles while I wait, staring at the grainy photograph.

Those eyes…

"That's fucking creepy." Her haunted voice sounds far away. I pinch the bridge of my nose, wincing, struck by a sudden headache.

Gwen reads, "The body of a missing woman, believed to be Francesca Flores, a 24-year-old sex worker, who was reported missing in August 2023 by concerned friends after she failed to return home, was discovered after police attended Wilfred Miller's farm on Wednesday night for a welfare check."

"Eight more bodies have been discovered on the property. The story is still unfolding."

I frown, staring at the blurring words.

"Camryn? Are you there?"

"I'm here," I reply, studying the grainy images. "Gwen…"

"Yeah?"

"His latest victim…" I try to steady my voice. "It says he kept her decomposing body in the attic for months." A shiver skitters down my spine, and I tighten my grip on the phone. "Gwen…I saw the curtains moving that day when Dominic carried me out."

"Maybe it was your imagination?"

"Maybe," I agree, rubbing warmth back into my arm. It's suddenly very cold. "It's not like I saw a ghost."

But even as I say it, the smiling girl on the cover stares back at me with her big eyes and curly brown hair. I'm forced to look away.

Rising from the bed, I approach the window seat and gaze at the forest. Rainwater races down the glass, distorting the view. "Have you spoken to Aron today?"

"Want me to ring him?"

"Yes," I answer, watching a shadow shift behind the fir trees. "Make sure he's okay."

I hang up, then lower my phone without taking my eyes off the swaying branches where I last saw the shifting shadow. I can hear them from here—the whispering trees.

It's a struggle to tear my gaze away, but I somehow turn my back to the window and the forest with its secrets, a sharp pain stabbing my skull, like a pickaxe.

It *taps, taps, taps.*

I press my palms into my eyeballs. "Fuck…"

"Camryn…"

Fear travels throughout my body before I can stop it, and I lower my hands, slowly looking over my shoulder. The forest seems darker and vaster, its shadows thicker. The branches have stopped swaying, and stillness has settled. Rain patters against the glass, but the sound is muted. I exist in a vacuum—a silent void.

Struck with an inexplicable urge to run, I dash for the door and fling it open, only to find Dominic blocking the exit with his intimidating build and dark eyes.

I stumble back, and he leans his forearm on the frame, crossing his socked foot over his ankle.

"Going somewhere, little sister?"

I blow out a relieved breath. "You scared me."

His response is a raised eyebrow.

I try my hardest to ignore the insistent whispers, but they won't shut up.

"Camryn."

"Camryn."

"CAMRYN!"

Falling onto the bed, I scramble back on the flowery comforter in my panic, my heart pounding as I look from the large window then back to Dominic. His intense expression never falters, not even when a loud bang cracks the glass. I whip my head to the window, and a gasp falls from my lips. Blood…so much fucking blood. And inky feathers.

"You're pale," he drawls.

I look away from the broken glass when he pushes off the doorframe and enters my space. The door clicks shut, making me flinch. Slow, deliberate steps bring him closer to me, and I tremble on the bed like the leaves on the branches outside. I've never feared Dominic before, not like this. There's something in the seductive sway of his shoulders as he swipes his thumb over his bottom lip, watching me like prey, as though he's sizing up his meal. And not in a good way. Something is off.

When his eyes fall to my bare thighs in my jeans skirt, an insistent throb starts up between my legs, and he pauses to sniff the air.

His darkening gaze settles on me.

I flit my eyes past him to the door, but before I even know what I'm doing, my thighs rub together.

"Fear turns you on," he says, tilting his head to the side and studying me like a rare specimen. "Interesting." His nose lifts and he smells the air again, an inhuman growl reverberating somewhere deep in his chest. "Very interesting."

"Dominic? What was that?" I ask, looking back at the blood on the cracked window.

He approaches me and climbs onto the bed, then crawls over me and blankets my body with his hulking, muscly frame. Fear curls around my spine, but I can't seem to look away from his eyes.

Leaning on his elbow, he grips my chin hard enough to elicit a whimper. While Dominic has always been rough, this is different. His dominant touch has icy awareness prickling my neck. The instinct to recoil and escape from beneath him mixes with the heady desire to stay right where I am—at his mercy.

He bears down and rolls his hips against me as he lowers his lips to my ear. Mine part when his heated breath fans my skin. With a chuckle, he slides his hand from my chin to my throat. "Let me in," he whispers, squeezing tight, and liquid desire shoots straight to my core.

When our eyes meet, my mouth opens in a silent scream. His are completely black. The color swirls like ink pools—two dark voids leading directly to the fiery pits of Hell.

He leans down to trail his nose over my cheek and neck, then breathes me in. "Let me in."

I gasp for air while clawing at his wrist. This isn't Dominic. My vision blackens, but he doesn't let up on my throat. Panic sets in. Through my struggle, my pussy begs to be filled. To be fucked hard. It's a heady concoction of messed up.

The monster lifts his head and cocks it, studying me closely before he shifts off me and tosses me to the floor in a move far too quick to catch with the human eye. I crash into the bookshelf, knocking the wind from my lungs. Pain sears through my body, and I struggle to breathe as he climbs off the bed and cracks his neck.

He flexes his hands at his sides and crouches before me, his fingers coming away slick with blood when he strokes my hair away from my tender forehead. I whimper, cradling my injured midriff. The intense ache makes it difficult to focus on him as he grips my chin. His eyes are hard and cold and nothing like Dominic's.

Fueled by rage, I spit at him. "Give me Dominic back, you fucking coward!"

He swipes the saliva away and drags his wet fingers down my face, over the swell of my lips. "You love him."

I bare my teeth like a savage, grimacing in pain. Every inhale is a struggle. I wince as I lean back against the bookshelf, coughs hacking through my chest. I should have known it was only a matter of time before the demon would go after Dominic or my mom. I gaze at him as the seconds tick by, my ribs on fire. "What do you want? Why don't you just kill me?"

"Kill you," he drawls, the sound trailing over my skin like a succulent promise. He cups my chin and swipes his thumb over my bottom lip before leaning in to nuzzle the side of my face like a lover. He hums softly, his hand sliding to the back of my neck as he brings his lips to my ear. "I want to taste you."

My breath lodges in my throat. With his black eyes locked on mine, his grip tightens on the back of my neck. "Let me in."

It's hard to stare into those dark pits without being consumed by dread. He embodies terror. It's in his touch.

"Dominic," I choke out as tears fill my eyes. "I know you're in there. You have to fight."

The monster laughs, dropping me as he rises to his feet. Exhaustion washes over me as I slump back, and he brings his hand inches away from my face. I stare at his devastating face before my eyes drop to his fingers.

Fingers I've felt inside me.

"Have you ever known the meaning of true pain? It doesn't take much to drive a human to suicide." With a clench of his big hand, my head explodes in agony. I clutch my skull as a hoarse scream shreds my lungs.

Just as fast, he relaxes his fist. The pain ends, but my skull continues to throb. He steps forward to trail his fingers through my matted, sweaty hair. "You're the most exquisite thing I've seen in centuries."

I slap his hand away, but he pulls my hair hard enough to make me cry out, then lifts me off the ground, forcing me to my knees. "Such foreplay." As he fists his free hand, a scream ripples through me. My head feels like it's being cleaved in two. His knuckles turn white as I thrash in his grip. Seconds pass, maybe even minutes.

When he finally opens his palm, the pain recedes like a wave washing back out to sea, and I collapse to the floor, sobbing.

He crouches down and grabs my chin. "Let's try it again, shall we."

I recoil when he leans close to my ear, but it only makes him tighten his grip on my chin. His stubble brushes up against the side of my face, and his tongue darts out for a taste. He whispers against my damp skin, "Let me in."

I squeeze my eyes shut, sensing a probing at my skull, an odd sensation that can't be explained. It's instinctual to push back.

An inhuman growl reverberates through his chest seconds before he throws me across the room again. But this time, as I roll across the floor, I launch to my feet and run for the door.

I stumble into the hallway and crash against the opposite wall, pain ricocheting through my shoulder, but there's no time to succumb. I hobble down the hall, swiping at the blood on my face. A glance behind me is all it takes to break into a run. The monster is striding down the hall with murder in his black eyes.

When I reach the stairs, I almost lose my balance and go flying. It's only by some miracle that I make it to the bottom floor in one piece.

I'm limping toward the front door, a sob rattling my chest when I hear him roar my name in a distorted voice at the top of the steps. I reach for the handle, only to realize the door is locked. I turn the lock, but it still won't open. It doesn't matter how much I yank or pull. It won't budge.

Panic seizes me in its merciless grip. I'm frozen, staring at the closed door, when I hear him behind me.

"I can smell your fear in the air, human."

Think, Camryn. Fucking think.

Movement in my periphery catches my attention, and I look in time to see the mystery man with the axe enter the kitchen.

"I can smell how scared you are. And how aroused your little cunt is."

I dash for the kitchen, darting inside and shutting the door just as he slams into it on the other side.

"Fuck!" With all my strength, I shove it back, but my feet slide out from beneath me when he pushes down on the handle and bears his weight against it.

"You can't escape me." His voice comes out like an animalistic growl. "You will let me inside you."

"In your fucking dreams," I snap, darting my gaze around the room for something to use to defend myself.

I pause when I spot the axe inside a circle of white on the floor. I don't question it as I sprint forward to grab the weapon.

The door crashes open against the wall, and the monster enters with a triumphant smile. But it falls when he spots me inside the circle.

"Witchcraft…" His menacing voice is a low snarl.

I grip the axe as he approaches.

"What are you going to do with that?" he asks, amused. "If you use it, you'll hurt that precious boyfriend of yours."

"He can live without an arm or two." I'm bluffing, and the creature knows it too. I could never hurt Dominic.

He laughs, amused for a moment, before his attention lands on the ring of powder. "Who taught you about salt?"

Confused, I look down.

Salt?

He circles me, hissing at the salt, his eyes as black as the night. Frustration bleeds from his pores when he snarls at me. I never take my eyes off him. Not even for a second. The relentless throb in my head intensifies, and I struggle not to stumble. Shaking my head, I blink.

"Witch," he spits, darting forward with inhuman speed, a blur of movement, before jumping back again. He hisses like a serpent, and my heart surges to my throat. He steps as close as the markings on the floor will allow and speaks in tongues, making me tremble as I clutch the axe like a lifeline.

My heels brush against the salt when I inch back.

With a final snarl, the ink recedes from his eyes, and Dominic collapses to the floor. He's out cold, but I don't dare exit the circle.

I choke on a sob as I step up to the salt. What if he's bluffing? What if he opens his eyes and kills me the moment I leave the protective ring? Is that what it is? What if he's gone and returns?

I look down to see my toes touching the salt. Who put it on the floor? Who painted this circle? Where did it come from? I trace the intricately carved symbol on the axe's handle.

Groaning on the floor, Dominic's eyes flutter open, and when he looks at me, all my fears fly out the window. I rush to his side, dropping the axe and helping him to sit. "I'm so fucking sorry."

Dominic leans back against the fridge. "You're bleeding. You're hurt." He straightens up and cups my cheeks. "Fuck, I'm so sorry. I couldn't stop it. I tried, but—"

"Shhh." I want to sob with relief as I stroke his stubbly cheeks. "It's okay." I kiss him, whispering, "It's not your fault."

THIRTY-THREE

CAMRYN

I JOIN the others in the dimly lit living room, where they're gathered on the couches.

Seated on the floor, Gwen slides a bottle of vodka from her bag, which she most likely stole from her parents' stash. She waves it with a wide grin. Her hair has been dyed blue and falls around her shoulders, and she has swapped her black lipstick for a deep purple shade.

"Isn't that a little inappropriate?" Lily questions, her voice laced with disapproval, as she settles on the couch across from me.

Gwen rolls her lips between her teeth and proceeds to pour us all a glass before placing the bottle on the coffee table and holding hers up for a toast. "To us, for being royally fucked."

I down mine, wishing I could drink all my problems away. Gwen pours herself another glass while Dominic shifts forward to place his empty one on the table. When he eases back, he slides his arm around me and pulls me into his side.

Gwen looks at me expectantly, but her expression lacks the usual excitement. Now she looks tired, a shadow of her former self. We all do. "You called this emergency meeting. What's going on?" She takes a large sip of vodka, and I allow Dominic's heat to comfort me as I look down at my hands. "The demon entered Dominic."

Gwen chokes on the drink.

Silence.

Complete silence.

Gwen breaks it. "The demon entered...but how?"

"I'm not sure," I admit. There are a lot of things I don't have the answers to. How and when did it enter Dominic? How did it pretend to be me without using my body as a vessel? Did it shapeshift, or was it a vision? Where did the axe and salt disappear to? It's like they were never there. Was it all in my head? But it couldn't have been. Dominic remembers the demon entering him. So many questions and no answers.

"It pretended to be me to get close to him. My only guess is that it fed on his desire to sustain the vision of me. Does that sound right?" I ask Dominic, and he rubs his eyes and lifts his shoulders. "I don't fucking know, but it sure as fuck looked like you."

"Hang on. Let me try to make sense of this," Gwen says, interrupting my thoughts. After placing the glass on the table, she turns to face me, cross-legged. I can see the cogs turning in her brain as one of the shoulder straps on her black tank top slides down her arm. "The demon entered Dominic? Like it did with Brittany?"

"Yes, but it wasn't the first time."

She blinks, which would be comical if I hadn't been so scared earlier.

"If it entered him," Aron says, "how do you know it's not still inside him? Maybe it was inside him all this time?"

"I saw it leave."

"You saw it leave?" He sounds so skeptical, that the tips of my ears burn.

"I can't explain it, but I know it's gone."

"Reassuring." The sarcasm in his voice is impossible to miss. With a scoff, he looks away.

Lily bounces her gaze between us, worrying her bottom lip.

Dominic has stiffened beside me, his eyes narrowed on Aron. I can tell he wants to say something in my defense, but I slide my fingers through his and subtly shake my head. We're all on edge—the last thing we need is to fight.

"There's so much to figure out and pick apart." Gwen sits with her elbows on her thighs and her fingers forming a tip at her mouth. Tapping her lips, she nods. "First thing's first, what can you remember, Dominic?"

The deep rumble of his voice rolls over me. "It's playing with us."

"It's a demon. They murder without reason and bring chaos and destruction for their entertainment," Aron points out, his knee jiggling. "There's no true logic behind their motivations. Of course, it's playing with us."

Dominic shifts his lazy gaze in Aron's direction. "While that's true, our demon has fixated on Camryn and won't stop until it has her. You and me?" He motions his finger between them. "We're collateral damage. We're the cat's bowl of wet food—easy, convenient—but Camryn… She's the juicy mouse. He likes the chase."

Aaron grinds his teeth as he slides lower in the seat.

"Why did it leave?" Gwen asks.

"To conserve energy."

Gwen's eyebrows fly up before she straightens and pours herself another glass of vodka. "This requires more alcohol." She gulps it down, then wipes her mouth. "From our understanding of the demon so far, we know it feeds on souls to grow in power. The more powerful it becomes, the longer it can stay in the human host or sustain a vision for its victim. Correct? Why didn't it kill you, Dominic? Why didn't it consume your soul or kill you to create even more grief and anger for it to feed on?"

"Because of my connection to Camryn. It feeds on emotions, as we already know. But that's not its main reason for hunting us. This thing wants to possess Camryn, but for whatever fucking reason, it can't. Think of it like catnip. Here's this powerful,

263

ancient demon trapped in our human plane, probably bored out of its mind, consuming souls and feeding on negativity and sexual desire. I don't know about you, but I'd soon grow bored if I ate a steak daily." Dominic rakes his fingers through his hair. "While it was inside me, I could sense it."

"What could you sense?" Gwen asks, and I find myself holding my breath.

"Like Brittany said, it's no coincidence Camryn is here. It was almost like…"

"Almost like what?" I ask, straightening.

Dominic shuts his eyes briefly, pinching the bridge of his nose.

We haven't discussed the details of what happened yet. Dominic was exhausted afterward, so I helped him upstairs and asked him if he needed to see a doctor. He refused and passed out for hours.

I feel Aaron watching me, and a shiver pricks my neck.

Dominic lowers his hand and says, "It wanted you to return here."

"Return here?" I look at him questioningly. "But that would mean I've been here before?"

He holds my gaze. "Exactly."

I open my mouth, but snap it shut again. To say that I'm confused would be an understatement.

"Maybe you traveled here at some point?" Lily suggests with a shrug.

"Oh yeah?" Aron sits forward and snatches the vodka bottle. "We live in a 'blink and you'll miss it' shithole. When was the last time you saw a tourist pass through here?" Unscrewing the lid, his forehead glistens with sweat as he swigs straight from the bottle while holding Lily's gaze.

Gwen sighs, rubbing her temples. "What else have we got?"

"The murders at Wilfred's farm," I say. "Are they related to our demon?"

"Maybe, maybe not." Gwen swipes for the half-empty bottle when Aron puts it back on the table. She takes a swig, wincing.

"They could be. What are the chances that we have a demon lair in the backyard of a creepy serial killer's den?"

"Maybe it picked this place because of the convenient food source?" Aron suggests. "Maybe Wilfred's string of murders attracted him here?"

"According to a local legend, it was called on by Mr. Kriger, the owner of this house, remember?" Gwen asks.

Aron rolls his head to look at her. "That doesn't mean it wasn't already here in our town. Kriger probably made it curious."

"Or maybe Wilfred was under the demon's influence some-how? It made Benny shoot himself and Brittany mince her hand. Perhaps it forced Wilfred to murder those women?"

"If that's the case," Dominic says, stroking his fingers over my knuckles in a featherless touch, "how do we explain what happened that day with Wilfred when we broke into his house? Why would it try to kill us, only to kill Wilfred instead?" He shakes his head. "It looked to me like it protected Camryn."

I swallow hard. "It came in through the window. Wilfred wasn't being controlled until the moment it entered his body. I saw it happen."

"But that doesn't mean it didn't make Wilfred kill those people. It possesses humans for short periods to feed," Aron says.

"It's probably more likely Wilfred was a sick bastard, which attracted the demon. Evil attracts evil."

Gwen throws up her hands, releasing a heavy sigh. "All we have are theories. We're nowhere closer to figuring this shit out." She picks up the folder behind her on the table. "What about the information in here? There has to be something."

"I can't believe you went to the mental asylum without me," Aron mutters.

My eyes close when I feel Dominic stiffen. Couldn't Aron have kept his mouth shut? I was going to tell Dominic about our trip to the asylum; I just hadn't found the right time yet.

"You didn't think to tell me that you went to the fucking

mental asylum?" Dominic whispers angrily in my ear. "Is that why you turned off your phone?"

"Now isn't the time for this conversation. We'll discuss it later."

"You bet your sore cunt, we will."

A tremor runs straight to my core at his whispered threat. My thighs squeeze together, and I squirm. Gwen flips through the file, licking her finger and selecting a few sheets to line up on the floor. She points to one. "Magdalene Kriger, the sole survivor, was found roaming the woods in August 2002 after her family disappeared under mysterious circumstances. Her father was found dead in a suspected suicide, but his wife and Magdalene's younger siblings were never found."

"Where was the father found?" Dominic asks.

Gwen opens the file, selects a photograph, and holds it up for us to see. "The big oak tree in the front yard. He was found hanging by the neck."

A shudder runs through me.

"Magdalene was in bad shape when they found her. Physically, she was fine except for mild dehydration, but mentally…" She lets the words hang in the air. "Over the following months, she got progressively worse as her psychosis deepened. At least that's what it says in the file, but we know the demon was tormenting her. I've read the interviews, but she made little coherent sense. From what we can gather, she suffered visions and nightmares and claimed the woods were whispering and that she had worms crawling beneath her skin. She was heavily medicated at this point because no one believed her, which probably didn't help." Gwen chews on her lip, deep in thought. "She woke up screaming at night, but no one believed her when she claimed the demon was in her room. Instead, they restrained her to the bed."

"That's fucked up," Aron mutters, staring at an empty spot.

"That's one way to put it. But get this…I did some research last night. Three patients committed suicide during that year."

Aron waves her off. "It's a mental asylum. Their deaths are probably not related to Magdalene."

"But the three staff members who died under mysterious circumstances aren't."

I frown, straightening.

Gwen's eyes gleam in the dim light. "And the three fathers of the patients who died."

"What are you saying?"

"Magdalene stayed at Cross Hills Asylum for a period of almost eighteen months. During that time, three patients, their fathers, and three faculty died." She raises her eyebrows, waiting for me to make the dots. "333."

Aron snorts, rubbing his brow. "What's next? 666? That's so fucking stupid."

"Is it, though? Numerology is a big thing in theology, you know."

Rolling his eyes, Aron rises to his feet. "I'm gonna take a piss."

I watch him exit the room. "How did they die?"

Gwen searches through the file until she finds the paper she needs, then hands it to me. "Eden Lockett, one of the nurses, drove her car off a bridge."

I shiver.

"Maybe it was an accident?" Lily suggests.

"The weather was clear that night."

"Irene Perry, another nurse, died alone in an elevator when the cables snapped and sent her hurtling to her death," I say, clearing my throat.

"Don't tell me that was an accident, too?" Gwen asks, reaching for the vodka bottle. "The other staff member, one of the doctors, Dr. *Benthall*, was particularly fond of shock treatments. He was found dead in his home after a suspected snake bite."

"Snake bite? So he had a pet snake?" Dominic asks.

"Not just any snake. A boomslang snake. One of the most venomous snakes on the planet. To get bit by one is considered the most painful way to die." She swigs the vodka. "They exist in

Sub-Saharan Africa. What are the odds our doctor kept one as a pet?"

"Is it even legal to keep such a poisonous snake as a pet?" Lily asks, and Gwen shrugs, placing the empty bottle on the table. "Fuck if I know."

"Why is it the most painful way to die?" I ask.

"The venom destroys red blood cells, preventing clotting, which leads to hemorrhaging. You also get a high fever, feel nauseous, and can't stop shaking."

"I guess no one found the snake?"

"You guessed that right. No snake. No vivarium. No sign that he kept any pets of any sort."

Aron returns, flopping onto the couch and resting his booted foot on the table.

"What I can't figure out," Gwen muses, "is why it can't enter you?"

"That's the million-dollar question," Aron says. "We had no fucking problems with any of this shit until she arrived."

"That's enough," Dominic booms. "Shut your fucking mouth."

Aron laughs. "Or what? You want to fight?" He shoots to his feet. "Let's fight."

"Guys…" Gwen pleads. "Stop it. You're just giving it what it wants."

"If she hadn't rocked up in our town, our friends would still be alive." Aron's voice is a low growl, his statement making my chest ache. He's right.

"Her being here doesn't change the fact that there's a demon on the loose. How many other deaths are related to it? Remember a few years back when Davis's boy disappeared after entering the woods? They sent out search parties but never found the body. Three years later, bang on the fucking anniversary—come to think about it, on the third day of the third month of the third year—the father was seen entering the woods. The next day, they found his backpack but not him. Think about it. It can't be a coincidence that our demon is here, in our little backward town. For fuck's sake,

Camryn's property backs up on a serial killer's farm." She jabs her finger at the window. "We have a mental asylum down the road, and a damn creepy one at that. We're a hotspot for supernatural creatures with a taste for misery. Who knows what else this place has attracted."

Unable to sit down, I stand and walk around the couch. "I've seen visions of a man with an axe."

"This just gets better and better," Aron chuckles, rubbing his eyes.

I ignore him. "This man…he tells me to stay out of the woods. It's almost like he…protects me."

"Do we know if there's been any mysterious disappearances involving a man in his early twenties?"

Dominic stiffens on the couch. "I've seen him too. We talked to him."

"So now we have a demon and a dead spirit man?" Aron's taunting laugh is grating on my nerves.

"I know none of this makes sense."

Gwen stands, resting her hands on her hips. "It makes sense. Magdalene saw visions, too. I'm sure we all have." She locks eyes with us all. "Don't tell me you haven't heard the trees whisper."

No one answers.

"Fuck," Dominic breathes, dragging his hand down his face. "What about the ring of salt."

I chew on my thumbnail. "You were chasing me down the stairs—well, the demon," I correct when Dominic pales. "I saw the man with the axe enter the kitchen and followed him. There was no sign of him, but the axe was on the floor in a ring of salt."

"What's so special about the salt?" Lily asks.

"The demon couldn't get to me while I was in the circle. But not only that. I've seen the axe before. I remember now. It has a binding symbol carved into the handle."

"This is so fucking weird," Gwen mutters. "Let's roll with your idea for a minute. You say you think he is protecting you? Why? Who is he, and why would he protect you? If you saw a binding symbol on the axe, he must have intended to use it on the demon."

"Maybe he's another one of her admirers. Seems humans, demons, and ghosts alike line up for a chance to get with the mysterious Camryn. Let's all join the fucking queue," Aron sneers, and Dominic shoots up from his seat and launches himself at him.

Lily squeals as the armchair crashes to the ground, and we watch in horror as they exchange blows. At first, it looks like Dominic has the upper hand, but then Aron rolls them over and lays into him with his fists. Gwen and I run forward to pull him off while Lily cries on the couch, but he elbows Gwen, which sends her flying back. The brief pause is Dominic's opening to ram his fist into Aron's nose.

Gwen staggers to her feet, touching her fingers to her bruised cheek, eyes flashing with anger. "I've had enough of this shit." She walks out and returns moments later with a bucket of cold water, which she wastes no time pouring over the boys. "That's enough!"

Dominic shoves Aron off and stands with flared nostrils, water dripping off his sopping hair as he glares at him. Aron is no better off as he pinches his nose to stop the blood from pouring.

"If you're done measuring dicks," Gwen seethes. "Let's figure out how to stop this thing."

THIRTY-FOUR

CAMRYN

THE PLAN IS to scour the local news and public records first thing tomorrow, but it's late, and we need sleep. Gwen and Lily are sharing my mom's bed, while Aron is sleeping in the guest room.

Resting against the bathroom doorframe, I observe Dominic as he peels off his damp T-shirt, letting it fall carelessly to the floor. When his battered face reflects in the mirror, our eyes lock in the glass. His intense gaze pierces through me, and then he averts his eyes to turn on the shower.

"You can't let Aron get to you like that," I say as he unbuckles his belt with his muscled back to me.

"He disrespected you."

"He has a point, Dominic. Their friends would be alive if it weren't for me. I suggested that stupid spirit board. I invited the demon."

Dominic scoffs, turning to face me. "The demon was already hunting you." He lowers his head, his jaw clenched, then spins around and pulls the shower curtain aside. "They made a choice. It's not your fault they agreed to summon the demon." His voice is as terse as his jerky movements. I watch him remove the rest of his damp clothes in silence, wishing I could say something to calm him down. I don't know what. The tension between him and

271

Aron is worsening by the day, but neither is willing to bury the hatchet. We've all been through hell these last few weeks.

I walk up to him and place my hand between his shoulder blades. He stiffens beneath my touch. "Talk to me, Dom."

He shrugs me off and steps beneath the hot spray. "You should leave."

"But Dom—" I jump when he pulls the curtain shut.

"Just leave, Camryn."

My chest tightens at his harsh words. Everything feels hopeless. Our friends are dead, and we're nowhere closer to figuring out how to beat this thing.

I should leave—it's what he wants. Instead, I pull my tank top over my head and wiggle out of my skirt before reaching behind me to unclip my bra. Steam from the shower obscures my reflection in the mirror.

I pull the curtain back to reveal Dominic's carved, wet physique. Water from the showerhead runs in rivulets over his tense muscles and tattoos, and my pulse quickens as I enter the bathtub. With his hands on the wall, he hangs his head low in defeat. I've never seen Dominic so...tormented. He barely acknowledges me as I press my lips to the space below his shoulder blade.

"I could hurt you." The vulnerability in his voice cuts my heart in two.

"You won't." I kiss a path over the expanse of his muscled back, tasting the shower water on him. "I know you won't."

"The demon entered me, Camryn, and I was powerless to stop it. What if it had caught you? What then?" He fists his hands on the wall, his muscles rippling, then rams his palm into the tiles. "I would have had to watch it hurt you."

I wrap my arms around his trim waist and press my cheek to his back. "You'd have found a way to stop it. I know you would have."

His breathing increases, and his chest expands in my arms with every ragged inhale. "Fuck, Camryn..."

"Shhh."

"It'll come back."

"But it's not here now."

Dominic turns in my arms, gazing down at me with his haunted eyes that remind me of the forest. If only I could unearth some of those secrets staring at me as he strokes my damp hair away from my brow.

His lips descend on mine, hesitant at first, and I melt into him, dragging my nails up his back. "I won't break, Dom," I say as he trails kisses down my neck and then back to my mouth.

"Trust me"—he grabs my ass and lifts me—"I know. You're the fiercest woman I've ever met."

My back collides with the tiles, and I wrap my thighs around his waist. Dominic's dominant lips devour mine in a violent and destructive kiss, unlike anything I've experienced before. I moan into his mouth, gripping the short strands of his soaked hair while his calloused hands explore my quivering body. I want more. So much more.

"If I ever hurt you…" His deep voice rumbles against the curve of my neck. "I need you to promise that you'll kill me."

I open my mouth, but before I can tell him that I will die before I ever hurt him, he claims another savage, toe-curling kiss. Whatever thought, whatever argument I prepared, flies out the window. Fuck, Dominic knows how to kiss. Caressing my tongue with his, he dips his hand between my legs, and I break away from his swollen lips when he presses down on my throbbing clit.

"Eyes on me," he orders in a breathy, husky voice, sliding the tip of his finger inside me. "Promise, baby."

I shake my head, clenching around him. "I can't promise you that."

"Fuck," he groans, his touch becoming rougher and more frenzied as he dives down to bite my jaw. "Why are you so fucking stubborn? Listen to me for once."

My lips part as he stretches me with two fingers, pleasure

tingling my spine. I cling to his wet hair and broad shoulders, clawing and pulling and moaning his name.

He drives his fingers deep, sucking my lip between his teeth, then bites down hard until the taste of copper fills my mouth.

"I need you to do the right thing." His fingers disappear, and I whimper at the emptiness. "It will use me to hurt you. I saw it."

Circling my arms around his neck, I press my aching tits to his chest and kiss him hard and deep. "Don't ruin this moment, Dom." I nip his lip, licking at his mouth and tasting his heated breath. "Fuck me."

I admire his striking beauty as he locks his heated gaze on mine—like a fallen angel carved by God, with a sharp jawline and cheekbones. Dark strands of his damp hair lie plastered to his forehead, while water droplets decorate his swollen lips. More drip precariously from the tip of his nose.

With one hand on the tiles, he tucks my hair behind my ear and leans in to kiss me again. I wiggle my hips, trying to guide him inside me. But he holds himself back, tormenting me with teasing swipes of his tongue. Laughter bubbles from my chest as I try to pull him closer, but he traps my wrists in one hand over my head against the wall and smiles into the kiss.

Is this what happiness feels like? Amid horror and despair, it shines through heavy clouds like a seed that survived the drought.

"You want my dick, baby?" he taunts, nipping at my lip and tickling my waist, which makes me squeal and laugh in his grip.

He dives in to kiss me deeper, and I melt into him, barely noticing when he releases my wrists to trail the backs of his fingers down my cheek, jaw, and the sensitive curve of my neck. A smile touches my lips as I palm his cheeks, feeling his scruff beneath my touch, his cock nestled at my entrance.

This time when he leans in to kiss my lips, he thrusts inside me, and my back slides up the wall. I break away from his mouth with a gasp, caught in the intensity of his gaze, lost in his whispering forest.

I cling to his slick body, kissing him again, then pull at his wet strands while he snaps his hips in a maddening rhythm.

"Dom," I moan into his mouth, his big cock stroking every inch of my walls. It's all I can do not to cry out his name.

Our eyes clash and he grabs me by the jaw to claim my mouth in another mind-melting kiss. My lungs burn from the lack of oxygen while he ravages my sanity like it's our last kiss. The fleeting thought that maybe, just maybe, it will be, tightens my chest, but I push it away. Nothing will ever come between me and Dominic. He's mine.

Mine.

I'll do anything to keep him safe.

"Camryn," he groans, kissing a path from my cheek to the tender spot below my jaw. He nips it, then feasts on my lips until I'm gasping every time we come up for air. His fingers dip between our bodies, finding my clit and sending ripples of pleasure coursing through me. Pressing his forehead to mine, my eyes flutter shut as an orgasm washes over me. Dominic's lips consume mine as I cry out, and he releases a guttural groan, his cock pulsing his release.

I open my eyes. "That was…"

"I know," he whispers, still buried deep inside me, shuddering.

A smile spreads across my lips, and my gaze slips past his shoulder, but I stiffen when a dark shadow shifts on the other side of the curtain. There and gone.

Noticing, Dominic straightens and studies my face before looking behind him. "What's wrong?" he asks, his worried gaze returning to me.

"I-I saw something."

With a frown, he lowers me to the floor. "What did you see?"

"It looked like a person behind the curtain."

Dominic spins around, ripping the curtain aside, the sound of the shower fading as he sweeps his eyes across the empty room. Whoever was there is gone.

He climbs out of the bathtub and reaches for a towel to tie around his waist. "Stay here."

"Please don't leave."

"I won't be long. I promise." With droplets of water clinging to his back, he exits the bathroom.

Alone and shivering, I shrink back against the tiles. Dominic's cum seeps out of me as I wait with bated breath for his return.

What if the demon is back? What if it gets inside him again?

"Dominic?" I call out, wrapping my goosebumped arms around myself to ward off the sudden chills as I inch closer to the tub's edge, craning my neck. "Dom?"

When silence greets me, I bite back a sob. Why won't he answer? Did something happen to him?

Leaning forward, I reach for a soft towel to wrap around me, then step out of the tub, my wet feet sinking into the carpet as I approach the door, clutching the towel. "Dom?" I peer into the bedroom. "This isn't funny."

An ambient glow emanates from the bedside light while the alarm clock flashes like we've had a power cut. I slide around the doorframe, my heart pounding. Nothing seems out of place, but the hairs on the back of my neck stand on edge.

My throat closes.

Something is wrong.

I can sense it like the whisper of a delicate kiss.

Where is he?

With my back to the wall, I walk deeper into the room, unable to look away from the dark gap in the wardrobe across the space. Was it left open earlier? Is someone in there?

I swallow hard as dark ink begins to seep from the shadows, swirling ominously toward me like the gnarled tree branches outside my window. They stretch and twist, reaching for me, floating closer across the room as I sink back against the wall, locked in place by fear. I couldn't move even if I wanted to.

"Camryn."

My head shakes frantically. "Please no…"

The shadows brush across my bare feet, a thick mist traveling up my legs before disappearing behind the towel, leaving a cool breath against my sensitive folds.

I gasp, but the sound is silenced by an invisible hand over my mouth. Something wet, like a tongue, parts my folds. I squeeze my eyes shut, willing my body to listen. When I try to move my arms and legs, my body yields to the shadows, pleasure licking my core, pebbling my nipples.

A silent moan slips from my lips as another cold swipe against my soaked folds buckles my knees. Something holds me up as shadows thicken around me like storm clouds—a foggy forest late at night. I'm lost, darting between towering trees with crooked branches and rustling, dead leaves.

More shadows slither across the floor, dragging themselves forward like a rotten corpse with pale arms and blackened, broken nails before disappearing beneath the towel.

My eyes roll back, and I release a sob as an orgasm grips me.

That's when I feel shadows enter my mouth and nose, seeking a way into my soul, a weak spot—an entry point. I try to prevent the inevitable. Tears pool in my eyes as I fight the invisible shackles securing me to the wall. Magdalene died before it could take her soul. No way in hell will I ever let it in. No matter how much it tries to break me for its entertainment.

I try to scream. The shadowed hand slips away from my lips, and my mouth opens in a silent, anguished cry for help.

Silence.

"Camryn?" Dominic's voice penetrates through my foggy mind.

The shadows retreat, sliding from beneath the towel and crawling back toward the wardrobe as warm hands cradle my face, swiping my damp hair away from my forehead. "Look at me, baby. Fuck, what's wrong?"

I'm dazed, blinking at Dominic, who morphs from one to two to three, then back to one. I try to shake my head, but the room spins. Dominic lifts me into his arms and carries me to the bed, which dips when he lays me down and removes the wet towel before dressing me in his hoodie and covering my body with the blanket.

"Dominic?" I ask, struggling to keep my eyes open.

"Rest," he urges, crawling in behind me and pulling me against his warm chest. "We'll talk about it when you wake up."

Soft lips press against my head. I peer over at the wardrobe, fading in and out of consciousness, vaguely aware of eyes staring back at me from the shadows.

I'm haunted by nightmares.

Someone is watching me sleep, a shape looming over the bed, cloaked by the night. I toss and turn.

"Dominic?" I croak, stirring awake and sitting up. There's crust in the corners of my eyes, so I rub it away.

Dominic is asleep beside me, and the initial spike of anxiety I felt when I first woke up fades when I hear his steady breaths. Curled up against Dominic, I let the relief soothe me. But it's short-lived because I become aware of a figure hovering by the bedside.

It's my imagination.

There's no one there.

But there is.

I can sense it with every fiber of my being.

I hold my breath as I slowly shift onto my back, my skin crowded with goosebumps. I lock eyes with a dark figure and open my mouth to scream. But my intruder is faster, clamping a cold hand over my lips and dragging me out of bed. I try to scream for help and alert Dominic, but his sleeping form is the last thing I see before the world turns black.

THIRTY-FIVE

DOMINIC

I WAKE UP TO A COLD, empty bed.

It's fucking typical of Camryn to run away every time things get intense. A part of me contemplates tying her to the headboard so that she won't be inclined to take off when she feels guilty about our situation.

After climbing out, I take a quick shower, dressing in a pair of gray joggers and a Nirvana T-shirt before running a hand through my damp hair.

I catch a glimpse of my reflection in the oval mirror propped on the dresser beside the door. There's a bruise on my chin, and my stubble is in need of a trim, but facial hair is the least of my worries.

Aron, Gwen, and Lily swing their eyes in my direction as I enter the kitchen and draw to a halt, bouncing my gaze between them all. "Did Camryn eat already?"

Aron sports a purple bruise around his jaw and and a black eye. He scoops up more cereal. "Camryn? She's with you, isn't she?"

My body turns to stone. "She woke up before me."

Gwen exchanges a concerned glance with Lily and Aron. Cat ears hold her blue hair away from her forehead, and her freckled shoulders peek out from beneath the cut-out sleeves of her black T-shirt. She skates her eyes back in my direction, and I know even before she opens her mouth that she doesn't know where Camryn is.

"We haven't seen her," Aron says. He puts the cereal in his mouth, chewing loudly in the ensuing tense silence.

"What do you mean, you haven't seen her? Of course, you've fucking seen her." My voice is laced with barely restrained hysteria.

Aron shifts on his seat so that he faces me and then he lifts his shoulders. "It means we haven't seen her."

I rush forward and haul him up by his creased shirt. "What the fuck did you do to her?"

He laughs, shoving me back. "I haven't done anything to your girl. Fucking chill."

I glare at him. Gwen steps between us, pressing her small hand to my chest to hold me back, imploring me with her eyes to back away, but I pay her no attention as I sneer at Aron.

"Boys," she says, "this isn't helping the situation."

The grandfather clock strikes the hour somewhere in the house. Aron crosses his arms. "Why are you so quick to blame me? She could be anywhere. Maybe she took a walk."

"A walk…" I scoff, pacing and scrubbing my face. Then I turn and point at the trees visible outside the window, shouting, "You think she went for a walk in the fucking forest?"

"Stop it!" Gwen snaps. "Both of you."

We glare at each other over her head. Fuck if I'll be the first one to back down. Gwen shoves Aron back a step, and he breaks eye contact as he gives her a questioning look.

"Stop stirring problems," she says in a firm, no-nonsense tone. "We all know she didn't go for a stroll through the woods. Let's focus. When was she last seen."

"We fell asleep around midnight."

Gwen turns to face me. "Was anything out of the ordinary?"

"Camryn thought she saw someone in the bathroom. I went to explore but didn't see anyone."

"Okay," she says, dragging the words out, then turns around to face the others. "We search the house."

Aron rolls his eyes, shouldering past me while Lily rinses the bowls. Gwen runs her hands down her face and presses her fingers to her temples. "She has to be somewhere. There's a demon out there. Camryn wouldn't just leave." She turns to face me, her eyes glistening with tears. "Right?"

"Right…" My throat jumps on a swallow, and I spin around to exit the kitchen.

I can't stand still while she's missing. At least if I'm throwing open doors and searching every corner of the house, I'm doing something.

That's what I tell myself as I do a second sweep of the upstairs. But she's nowhere to be found, and panic soon sets in.

I pace back and forth in the hall. Where could she be? I look out at the trees beyond the window, unease churning my gut.

She wouldn't have entered the woods.

She wouldn't…

Right?

"Anything yet, Dominic?" Gwen asks from her spot at the bottom of the stairs, and I tear my gaze away. Before I can drive myself crazy with worry, I join her downstairs, where we check the basement and the pantry.

There's no sign of her anywhere. She's gone.

We enter the living room, and Gwen lowers onto the couch, her hands trapped between her knees as she stares at the ashes in the unlit fireplace.

"What about the surveillance? Did anyone check it?"

Gwen lifts her gaze and then shoots to her feet, snatching my phone from my pocket. I peer over her shoulder at the screen. "Check from midnight and onwards."

"There's nothing," she says, perplexed.

"There's nothing?" I ask. "She's not in the house, so she must have left."

"The camera didn't pick up on anything."

"Maybe she left out the back?"

Gwen shakes her head. "There's nothing on that one either." She hands me the phone back, and I pocket it.

"I guess we're left with two options," Aron says, walking past us. "She either exited through a window, or she's still in the house."

"Why would she climb out of the windows?" Lily asks in a small voice, perched on the armchair. She tucks a strand of her blonde hair behind her ear. "It's an old build. The windows are set high. It would still be a high drop if she left through a bottom floor window."

"What else do you suggest?" I ask, throwing my arms out. "That she's in the house somewhere?"

Her shoulders lift.

Aron looks out the window. "If she's playing hide-and-seek, she's damn good at it."

"She's not in the house," Gwen says, rubbing her temples as she paces in front of me. "We would have found her."

"And we would have seen on the camera if the demon took her," Aron says as he turns over his shoulder. "Unless she willingly climbed out the window."

"Fuck!" I roar, reaching for the nearest object, a flowerpot, and hurtling it across the room. Restless energy sizzles through me. I need to break something. Fight something. Fucking do something.

Aron looks at the broken pieces and soil, then shakes his head with a chuckle. Lily leaves the room in tears, but we pay her no attention.

"Let's pray her mother doesn't return any time soon," Aron says, fighting laughter.

I look away so that I don't smash his smug face in. But he sure as fuck likes to stir the pot.

His shoulder brushes mine as he walks past, and he has the nerve to smirk at me. "I better go check that she's okay."

I flip him off. Gwen looks at me and then sits on the couch, staring straight ahead at a spot on the wall with a faraway look. "What's happening, Dominic?"

"I wish I knew."

"What if it has her?"

My jaw clenches. I can't let my thoughts drift in that direction. I'll drive myself insane with the what-ifs.

"And if it comes back. How do we stop it?"

I sit beside her and rest my elbows on my thighs, looking at her over my shoulder. Gwen's tear-filled eyes meet mine, and she slowly leans in to rest her head on my shoulder. "Please tell me we'll find her."

"We'll find her," I reply tersely. "And we will kill the fucking demon."

Just then, a sudden scream echoes through the house. We look questioningly at each other for a brief second before dashing for the doorway and crashing to a halt when we see Lily with a knife protruding from her abdomen. Lifting her terrified gaze, she stumbles forward. I catch her fall, glancing over her head at Gwen. "Where's Aron?"

She stares at me for a beat, at a loss for words, then spins around. "Aron?"

With my arm around Lily's shoulder to steady her, I grab my phone from my back pocket to phone an ambulance.

I swipe the screen as she sways into me, cursing beneath my breath at the daunting realization. "Gwen, we have a problem."

She turns around, defeated, and wipes tears from her cheeks.

"I can't make phone calls. Not even the emergency services. Something is jamming the signal."

She checks her cell, tapping the screen with frantic fingers. When she looks at me, her chin wobbles. "I'm scared."

"Whoa," Aron blurts in the doorway, holding his hands up by

his sides as he stares at the knife in Lily's stomach. "What happened?"

"Where the fuck have you been?" I ask as my nerves and rage skyrocket.

"Bathroom, dude."

I narrow my eyes, which he ignores as he walks closer. "Are you going to remove the knife?"

"What if it cut through an artery?"

She sways into me while I guide her to the couch in the living room and help her lie down, swiping her matted hair away from her cheeks.

"What happened? Who did this to you?" I ask.

Her eyes slide past me to Aron, who points a finger at himself and laughs. "Me? Oh, that's fucking rich. I was taking a fucking piss when you were stabbed."

Shooting to my feet, I square up to him. "You left to see if she was okay."

Aron purses his mouth, his eyebrows knitting together. Then he chuckles, but it lacks humor. "You've got to be fucking kidding me. Remember Brittany? Benny? They did it to themselves."

Gwen crouches down before Lily to inspect the wound, as her friend winces in pain.

"Maybe the demon is in you," I point out.

"Please don't fight," Gwen urges. She trains her soft gaze on Lily. "Why don't you tell us what happened."

"I don't remember," she responds, flicking her nervous gaze to Aron. "I was upset, and then the room started spinning. There was this shape—a man. I couldn't make out his face." She coughs, her face contorting in pain. "He plunged the knife into me."

I grind my teeth to dust.

"What do we do with the knife?" Aron asks, and Gwen stands up.

"We could do more damage if we remove it," she replies. "We can't stay here. And since we can't phone for an ambulance, we need to do something. I'm going to get us help." She leaves the room, and I glance at Aron before turning my worried gaze on Lily. Everything is a mess. Camryn is missing. Lily is bleeding all over the couch.

She takes my hand in hers, and I return her weak smile. She's scared—I can see it in her eyes.

Gwen returns minutes later, pale as a ghost. "The door won't open."

"What about the—"

"The back door won't open either. I know. I already tried."

"What the hell?" I squeeze Lily's bloodied hand, then stand up and hurry past Gwen in the entryway. She shifts sideways to let me pass, but I'm already gone, running for the front door. I try the handle, but of course, it won't turn. "What the fuck?" I try to yank on it. When that doesn't work, I drive my boot into the hard surface. Once, twice, three fucking times.

How is this possible? No phone signal. No escape routes.

My gaze skates to Gwen, where she stands in the doorway. She used to have such a vibrant, no-shit attitude, but now she looks… *broken.*

I slowly slide my eyes back to the door. A fly crawls over the peephole.

Fuck this.

I stride past Gwen and give the back door the same treatment. Nothing works. It's the same story with the windows. None of them open. I even toss a chair at the glass, but it strikes it with a resounding thwack and falls to the floor. Ramming my fist into the glass did little good, either. Now I'm left with injured knuckles and blood on the glass, but not even a crack. Nothing.

Gwen rests her shoulder against the doorway. We stare at each other across the room. "It's useless," she says, trembling. "Camryn is missing. Wilfred's farm is the closest for miles. By the time we finally get out of here and find help for Lily…" She drifts off as her gaze drops. "It'll be too late."

"There must be something we can do." I walk back into the living room, and Gwen follows.

"Perhaps your mom will arrive back soon. She could hopefully open the door and—"

"There's nothing wrong with the doors!" I shout, picking up a fire poker and throwing it at the nearest window. "We're being hunted, Gwen. It's trapping us here."

She wipes away tears, nodding. "I know."

"Can you not stitch her up or something."

The look she gives me is flat. "I told you last time—I'm not a nurse. I don't know how extensive her injuries are. If we remove the knife, we could do more harm than good. It's not worth the risk."

I sink my fingers into my hair and groan. When I lower my hands, I nod. "Fine..."

Gwen watches me walk closer.

"If this thing is hunting us, we need to figure out what it's doing."

Crossing her arms, she stares unseeingly at my chest. "I guess it's biding its time, feeding on our fear. Growing in strength."

"Or maybe it's playing with us. It's a demon. They kill for entertainment."

"Maybe," she says before breaking down into tears. I pull her to me and wrap my arms around her, nose buried in her hair, my eyes trained on a photograph of a smiling Camryn at graduation last year.

"She can't just vanish," Gwen sniffles.

"We'll find her. I promise."

THIRTY-SIX

DOMINIC

I'VE LOST count of how many times I've searched through every room.

Now we're back in the living room. Lily is napping. Sweat clings to her pale skin.

No one speaks.

I sit with my elbows on my knees, fingers in my hair. But it doesn't matter how much I pull on the short strands, the growing panic won't subside.

Orange hues stream through the window behind me—a stark reminder that we're running out of time.

Where are you, Camryn?

I pull harder. Nothing works.

"We can't just sit here," Gwen whispers, her voice barely audible above my screaming thoughts.

"What do you suggest we do?" Aron asks, framed by the setting sunlight as he gazes at the trees.

"We need to break down the door somehow. We need to find help." She checks her phone signal again, when Aron begins to laugh. Putting her cell on the table, she looks over her shoulder. "What's so funny?"

"What's so funny?" He turns around and pins his dark eyes on me. "We're going to die here tonight, all thanks to our new *friends.*"

I lift my head, and our eyes lock, a cruel smirk curving his lips as he rounds the couch with slow, measured steps. "Maybe you and Camryn intended for this to happen. Maybe the demon lives in you."

"I was in here when Lily was injured."

"But where was Camryn? Maybe you work together."

I follow him with my eyes, on edge, while he does a full circle of the seating area. There's a palpable sinister air around him, and when he walks behind me, I break out in a cold sweat.

He laughs again, exposing the column of his throat. "Camryn stabbed Lily. Admit it."

"You motherfucker," I hiss. "Camryn is missing."

He pauses across the coffee table and raises an eyebrow. "Is she? Are you sure about that?"

"Aron," Gwen pleads but falls silent when I stand to my full height.

"Let him talk. Let's hear what he has to say."

Aron's smirk deepens. "This demon story that you've made up, it's convenient, don't you think? The moment you showed up in town, our friends started dying, and you fed us all this bullshit about demons and ghosts." He pretends to look around. "But I haven't seen any evidence of any demons yet."

"Admit that you stabbed her." My voice is low and tense. I'm barely able to keep my anger on a leash. If he keeps pushing, I'll soon snap. "You kidnapped Camryn in her sleep."

"Pray tell, where did I drag her to?"

"Maybe you killed her in the forest." I don't want to let my thoughts stray there, but I can't deny the obvious—Camryn isn't here.

"Newsflash." He leans closer. "She never left the house. We have surveillance to prove it."

"She's not here," I grit out, and his smirk grows. We meet in the middle of the room, circling each other, drawn together like magnets.

You could cut the tension in the air with a knife.

I'm vaguely aware of Gwen pleading with us to stop fighting, to stop feeding the demon. But I shut her out, intent on Aron, the boy who's had his eyes on my girl from day one. Now she's missing, and he's behind it. I know he is.

"Maybe you hurt her." His lips pull to the side, his eyes darkening. "You were the last one to see her, after all."

"You think I had something to do with it?" I spit.

"Maybe the demon entered you, and you killed her before hiding her body somewhere in the house." He looks up at the roof. "Maybe she's stuffed in the attic. Or…" He fixes his eyes on me again. "Maybe the demon had nothing to do with it. Perhaps you snapped and killed her all on your own. A demon makes for an easy scapegoat."

"Shut your fucking mouth." My voice vibrates with anger. I'm two seconds away from breaking his neck like a fucking twig.

"Maybe you raped her, too."

That's it. I fly at him.

Red is all I see as my body collides with his, and we crash against the wall behind us. I drive my fist into his smug face, and he grabs my shirt then head-butts me full force, causing me to stagger back. The room spins for a few seconds. I've barely recovered when he sacks me, sending us crashing into the glass coffee table, which shatters. Gwen screams, jumping out of the way.

I roll on top of Aron, punching his face and ribs. All the while, he laughs. Fucking laughs. His chin and teeth are smeared in blood from his busted nose. My knuckles are cracked.

I don't fucking stop.

Not until he grabs an object on the floor and chucks it at the side of my head. I topple over onto my back, pressing my hand to the bleeding cut on my temple. "Shit…" I'll need stitches.

"I'm going to kill you," Aron growls, pushing up on his

elbows and climbing to his feet. He spits a wad of blood on the floor. "You're dead."

I watch him clutch his bruised ribs, and then my gaze slides past him to the bookshelves. A porcelain doll sits on top of two books stacked on their sides.

Blood trickles from the crack in its cheek. "Fuck!" I shoot to my feet, the world spinning as I lift my hand to hold Aron back. "Look behind you, man. The doll…"

He frowns, then turns over his shoulder. "What the fuck? Is that blood?"

No sooner has the word left his mouth than Lily sits up on the couch and trains her black eyes on us. She pulls the knife from her abdomen and then stabs Gwen in the chest before I can even take another breath. It all happens so fast.

She stabs and stabs and stabs, sinking the gleaming blade to the hilt before pulling it back out to repeat the process. Then she shoves Gwen away and looks at us while licking the blood off her fingers. She's covered in it.

I swallow, stomach twisting, as I look down at Gwen's body on the floor. Her empty eyes stare up at the roof as blood slowly pools around her.

"She's dead… What the fuck?" Aron breathes beside me, stepping back when the sea of red reaches his shoes. "What the actual fuck?"

Lily laughs, sending chills skating down my spine. I've never heard a more frightening, sinister sound. "Now, let's play, boys." She stands up from the couch and swipes her blood-soaked hair away from her stained cheeks, the knife gleaming in her hand as she taps her smiling lips. "Don't look so frightened. I'll be gentle with you."

"What the fuck?" Aron whispers again, backing away, ready to bolt.

"We can't outrun it," I bite out. "We have to stay together."

"Is that so?" Lily's cruel smile is slow to form. "But who can you trust?" She throws the knife to Aron, who catches it mid-air just as she collapses to the couch and grips her wounded waist, a sharp cry rippling from her lips.

Aron chuckles low and deep, inspecting the bloodied blade before his black eyes slide in my direction. "Tell me something. Do you like pain? I quite enjoy watching it contort a human's face."

And then, he stabs me.

THIRTY-SEVEN

CAMRYN

"Dominic?" My eyelids are heavy. I'm disoriented. "Dom?" I try to push up on my elbows, but my head is pounding too much. I press my palm to my temple just as my eyes open. It's so dark that I can't even see my hand.

I become aware of crumbling soil beneath my fingers and scurry back, releasing a startled scream when my hands connect with something cold and hard. I can't gain my bearings, and when I try to sit up, my head knocks against a solid surface. I reach up to touch it, sliding my fingers over the uneven finish. It feels like wood. It must be. It has the same kind of grooves. I push against it, but it refuses to budge. I try again, but all it does is to tire me out. I still haven't recovered fully.

I try to think back.

What happened? How did I end up here? Wherever *here* is?

I woke up, and there was someone by my bed. It's filled with nothingness after that, almost like I blacked out, or my memories were wiped.

I'm starting to feel claustrophobic. I can't sit up. I can't see. The air is damp and smells of dirt. I'm sure that's what it is. It clogs underneath my nails when I drag my fingers through it.

Rolling over onto my stomach, I crawl forward blindly. There must be a way out.

I jerk back when I feel something cold and hard. It's round, almost smooth, except for the crumbling sensation of dirt beneath my fingers. I trail my hand lower, unable to stop the rising panic. I jerk my hand back, certain I just touched bones of some kind.

Collapsing onto my back, nausea churns my stomach, and I wait for the wave to pass. I'm in a hoodie. Dominic's hoodie. I can faintly smell his leather and citrus scent.

I bury my nose in the fabric, pretending for a fragile second that I'm safe in his arms. I would do anything to feel him hold me. My hands reach into the front pocket as I try to steady my trembling chin. I don't want to cry. Tears won't help me, but trust them to fall when I need to stay strong the most.

My thoughts come to a grinding halt when I discover something in my pocket. It's small and made of metal. I pull it out, flicking the lid open with my thumb. It's Dominic's Zippo.

I quickly light it, seeing the orange flame dance in the darkness. I've never been happier to see fire. Is this how the first humans felt when they first sparked a flame?

I move it around the space, trying to see beyond the darkness. I'm under the floor. Above me are wooden floorboards.

I turn to the side and push up onto my elbow. But then my eyes widen, and a scream lodges in my throat. Bones. Human skeletons. I scramble back in fear, extinguishing the flame and losing the lighter in the process.

"Shit…" I drag my fingers through the soil in my hunt for the Zippo, two seconds away from a panic attack, my heart hammering. I almost cry tears of joy when I finally find it.

A flame flares to life with a strike of my thumb, and light floods the small space. I barely notice my filthy, bare legs or the dirt beneath my nails as I scan the skeletons. They're lined up in a neat row, with me in the middle, almost like this space was reserved. The thought has what feels like spiders crawling up my spine.

I count five bodies in total. One was a small child, half in size to the other skeletons. But what makes me pause is the axe, carefully tossed onto the skeleton beside me.

A rusty, old axe.

"What will it take for you to listen to my warning about these woods?"

I'm suddenly cold, my cheeks wet with tears. I wipe them clean, sniffling as more fall, fingers smelling of dirt and decay.

I reach out to touch the axe, feeling the wooden handle against my palm, the ancient binding symbol carved into the wood. No wonder why it's so important to him. He hoped to kill the demon. I need to get out of here somehow. There must be a way out. I raise the Zippo, scanning the floorboards. They extend the room's length, but I can see no visible point of entry with the dim light.

"Hello?" I call out. "Can anyone hear me? Dominic? Gwen?" Resting on my elbow, I place the Zippo in my free hand and then bang the floorboards as hard as I can. "I'm down here."

But where is *here*? Am I even at the house, or am I somewhere else entirely? No, I must be at the house. The demon wanted me to return here. Everything it set in motion was to bring me back.

"Home."

I gasp at the whisper, then raise the Zippo as I stare beyond the dancing flame at the shadows. "Who's there?" I barely dare breathe. My hand trembles. I grab the axe and hack at the floorboards, but it's difficult at this angle. I fail to get any power behind the blows, and all it does is stir the dust. Coughing, I cover my mouth with the back of my arm.

How the fuck am I going to get out of here? I drop the axe and lie back before driving my bare foot into the floorboards. A frustrated scream rips from my lips. I kick again and again. When that doesn't work, I swap feet. There must be a hatch somewhere.

I give up on kicking and dig my palms into my eyeballs. I don't want to fucking die down here. How long can a human live without food and water? But surely, the demon didn't kidnap me from my bed to leave me in the crawl space beneath the house? It must have a different motive.

I lost the Zippo somewhere in my struggle, so I try to find it now. I'm growing more desperate by the minute. Breathing is harder, too, but I know it's only in my head. I'm starting to panic, and that's never good in dire situations. I need a level head. I need to get a grip on my anxiety, or I'll remain trapped here. But it's easier said than done.

When my fingers finally brush against the Zippo, my only light source, I almost sob in relief.

My racing thoughts grind to a halt when I hear a whine somewhere nearby. What was that? A part of me is almost frightened to light the Zippo because I'm not sure I want to face what's out there.

The whine comes again. It's nearer now, and something tickles my feet. Realization dawns on me as I pull back on the Zippo.

"Bruno?" I release the sob I held back and then place the Zippo down before scuttling around the tight space. Bruno's fur is matted and smells of a wet dog, but I've never been happier to bury my nose in his damp fur. "How did you get down here, boy? Is there a way out?" I scratch behind his ears while tears stream down my cheeks. If he's this dirty, I can only imagine the thick layer of grime on me.

I cry harder as he nuzzles my face and licks my cheek. I normally find it gross, but now I'm so happy to see him. At least I'm not alone anymore. "We need to find a way out, buddy."

Dominic

Hot pain sears through my side, but I'm lucky it's only a shallow cut. I jump back, out of reach. Lily's face contorts in pain as she clutches her bleeding stomach. "Go, Dominic. Run!"

"I can't leave you here," I grit out.

Aron circles me with the knife. His movements are slow, and

his eerie grin could rival Pennywise's on the creepiness scale. One thing is obvious: the demon is enjoying the hunt.

"Dominic…" Lily looks down at her hands, whimpering at the sight of the blood seeping from between her pale, trembling fingers. "Listen to me," she says, lifting her gaze. "This thing—"

A harsh laugh rips from Aron's lips. "This *thing*?"

She ignores him, determined to make me see reason. "You saw how fast it travels between bodies just now. It's toying with you." She winces with pain. "You're not safe in here."

"Oh, but our friend here has a conscience," Aron says, pretending to feel sorry for me. "If he walks out, you die."

"If you touch a fucking hair on her head…"

Aron's smile grows impossibly wide, but it's not warm or comforting. His eyes are black as night, and his grin is hair-raising cold. It's difficult to look directly at him because you know you're staring into the face of evil. "You humans," he says, sounding almost friendly. "You're so loyal by nature. It's very intriguing but also extremely pathetic."

"Yeah? How so?" I ask to keep him talking and buy us time. There has to be a way out of this situation. Some way to defeat him.

"Because you all die in the end. What's the point of love when it's so fragile and temporary? Love will eventually kill you." The gleam in his eyes darkens. "In fact, why don't we up the stakes?"

"Up the stakes?" I glance at Lily.

"Yes," he replies, drawing the word out, and something about the purr in his voice coaxes my attention back. "You can save one of them."

I stiffen as he walks across the glass-covered floor to Lily, who whimpers when he rounds the couch. He leans over the back of it and looks at me as he smiles against her cheek with the knife pressed to her throat. The threat is clear. He'll kill her if I don't distract him somehow. I try to steady my heartbeat so he can't feed on my fear, but I know he can sense it.

"What if I told you that I have a proposition for you? Play your cards right, and you can save your precious girlfriend."

Hope flares at the mention of Camryn. I inch closer despite myself. "Camryn is alive?"

Bait dangles between us while Lily cries softly. The demon breathes her in and then shushes her. He looks at me again. "I'll let her live if you kill this one."

"Excuse me?"

"You heard me. I'll leave you two lovebirds alone and never return."

I know it's bullshit. I'm feeding out of his hand. "You'll leave us alone?" I inch even closer. Glass crunches underfoot.

"And never return." His smile is back, and he drags his forked tongue across Lily's cheek, making her cry harder. She tries to stay strong, but her chin wobbles. "Delicious," he whispers, feeding on her terror and pain.

"You promise to leave us alone if I kill her?"

He straightens up. "You have my word, human."

I walk closer, avoiding looking at Lily.

"If you love the girl as much as you claim, this should be an easy choice."

"In our world, we have empathy. Taking a life is never easy."

"And yet," he hums. "You're all so quick to do it in the face of death."

I ignore his statement. "Where's Camryn?"

"She's somewhere…around."

"What did you do to her?"

He walks around the couch. "I brought her home, Dominic."

I glance at the bloodied knife in his hand, my own T-shirt damp with blood. I won't be so lucky a second time if he attacks me, but I refuse to move. The demon feeds on fear. Maybe he can sense it seeping from my pores, but I won't let him see it too.

"Here," he says, surprising me as he offers me the knife. I stare at the handle between us. It feels like a trap, but like a fool, I reach out to take it. His eyes flicker, and shivers crowd my spine. "The knife is yours," he says. "Feels good, doesn't it? All that power in your hand. All it takes is one slash in the throat for it to be over. One cut, and Camryn walks free."

Lily is looking at me now, and I turn to face her on the couch. Her hands are soaked with blood. She clutches her injured stomach and stares up at me with eyes filled with tears. She trembles. I like that.

As if the demon can sense these dark thoughts, he walks up behind me. I'm vaguely aware of his soothing voice. "She's a beauty, isn't she? They always are when they're dying. It's a shame she's so weak."

More tears fall as she stares up at us. I reach out to run my thumb beneath her eye. "Sometimes those who seem the weakest are the strongest." I cup her quivering chin and guide her eyes to mine. She's pale beneath the blood and grime. "And sometimes those who seem the strongest are the weakest." Before the words can sink in, I spin around and drive the knife into Aron's side. Pulling it back out, I grip his shoulder as I stab him again. I sink the blade deep, and is eyes blow wide. I already know as I yank it back out that the demon is gone, because I can feel it stand up from the couch behind me. It's jumping between bodies and playing a game of hide-and-seek. Lily's menacing snicker crawls up my spine.

Running for the door, I skid across the floorboards in the hall before crashing into the family photographs on the opposite wall. I don't have time to look behind me. There's no time to think. I turn to run, when I hear faint shouts coming from the kitchen.

It's Camryn.

Lily enters the hall, leaning against the doorframe as she watches me head for the kitchen. Her voice rings out behind me. "What are you going to do, Dominic? There's nowhere to hide. Your friends are slowly bleeding out, and when they're dead, I'll let you watch the girl you love die at your own hands. Isn't love poetic, Dominic? Till death do us apart, right?"

I stumble into the kitchen. "CAMRYN?"

"In here." Her voice is faint. I spin around, searching for the source. "Camryn? I hear you, baby. Where are you?"

"DOMINIC!"

I swivel. She's in the basement. Lily's voice drifts closer to the kitchen while I sprint across the floor. I tune her out, throwing open the door.

There's so much adrenaline rushing through my body that I lose footing and slide down the steps, pain ricocheting up my spine as an agonizing groan reverberates through my chest. Climbing to my feet, I sway into the wall. "I'm here, baby."

"Dominic… Oh, thank god." Her muffled voice comes from somewhere beneath me. I can barely see a thing. The sun has almost set, and the cloudy, small windows near the roof barely let any light in. I search for a switch or something. Anything.

I eventually find a pull string. A fluorescent flickering light floods the space to reveal a hoarder's nest. There's everything down here, from an old mannequin to a brown box TV, a box with knitting needles, and a baseball bat.

"Fuck," I grunt when I accidentally kick something, which rolls across the floor—an old glass jar.

Despite the muggy summer heat outside, it's cold, so I rub my arms and stomp on the floorboards. There must be a hatch somewhere. "Where are you, Camryn?"

"I'm down here," her voice sounds to my left.

I walk over to where a rocking chair sits. "Creepy," I mutter, pushing it away and kneeling to remove the old rug. Once it's shoved aside, I see it—the latch.

"Dominic," Lily calls out from the top of the stairs. "You really shouldn't disturb the past."

Jumping to my feet, I reach down to grab the latch. It's stuck, or it's being held down on purpose. Lily's tinkling laughter drifts closer. I pull again, roaring with the effort. It still won't budge. I'm panting now, heart galloping, and Camryn is banging on the floorboards. I glance behind me when Lily walks down the steps, a nefarious smile curling her lips as she comes into view. How is she still alive? Her bare legs are soaked with blood, and her lips have a blue tint. "Oh, Dominic. Pathetic little human. Still trying to save the girl even when all hope is lost."

While she laughs, I pull on the latch. But no matter how much effort I put in, it stays locked.

Something hard strikes the floorboard from beneath, and Camryn screams with frustration. I peer at the demon through sweaty strands of my dark hair. It's over. Camryn can't leave the crawl space until the demon lets her. It's really that simple. It has played with us all this time, from the moment we set foot in this town. Maybe even before.

"You brought her here," I say, straightening up, lifting my shoulders in a defeated shrug. "Why?"

Lily drops her gaze to the floorboards, and the look on her face can only be described as 'longing.' It dawns on me, then. The demon has a weakness—desire. Maybe not of the sexual kind like us humans, but it still desires what it can't have.

"You're unable to possess her," I say, watching the demon as it inches closer to the latch. "Oh, c'mon…" I throw my head back and laugh. "You're supposed to be this powerful demon from Hell, but really, you're just as weak as the rest of us." My smile falls. "Pathetic!"

Those black eyes snap away from the floorboards, and Lily—the demon, or whatever the fuck it is—cocks her head to the side. "I like this game. Usually, they scream and cry, but you're feisty." She walks closer to me, and I back away.

"You hate it, don't you?" I taunt. "You can't see inside her like you can with other humans. You can't see her desires or her worst fears."

"What game is this, human?"

"It's not a game." I step over a rake. "You went through a lot of steps to get her here. You even went as far as to enter my father. Why?"

"You're inquisitive."

"I'll tell you why," I say, ignoring its observation of me. "You wanted to taste her, didn't you? And since you couldn't enter her mind, you invaded her body the only way you could—through my father."

A delighted gleam enters her black eyes. "Are you jealous, Dominic?"

I swat away the cruel jab like an irritating mosquito, but it still hits home. "You possessed my father and fucked her. But it wasn't enough to quench the desire to acquire what you can't have, was it? You wouldn't go to these lengths otherwise. That's also why you possessed and killed her friends. Through us, you gain more of an insight, more of a taste, of Camryn. I'm curious. What is your plan now? If you kill her, you'll never be able to possess her body and join with her the way you desire."

"Even the strongest of minds eventually break."

A loud bang sounds from the floorboards, and the demon looks away. It's the opening I need to grab the baseball bat leaning up against the wall behind me. I swing it at her head, and she collapses to the floor with a hard thud.

Whatever hold she had on the latch must disappear, because it opens this time when I pull. Camryn's grime-smeared face and matted hair come into view, and I help her out. We collapse on the floor in a heap of tears. I crash my lips to hers, stroking the dirty strands from her cheeks. It's an all-consuming need to ensure she's real.

Her fingers tremble on my scruff, and then she breaks away and looks down at the opening. "Bruno is down there."

I kneel and duck my head into the hole. "Bruno, come here, boy." I whistle, but there's no sign of him. Camryn joins me. "Bruno?"

"There must be another way out." I help her to her feet. "C'mon, we need to leave."

Lily begins to stir on the floor as we rush to the staircase.

"The axe with the binding symbol is down there. I forgot to bring it," Camryn says, out of breath.

"There's no time." I pull Camryn in front of me at the bottom of the stairs. "Hurry, I'll be right behind you."

She follows my line of sight. "What, no. Are you crazy? I'm not leaving you here."

Lily is rising to her feet now. She presses a hand to her forehead and grimaces in pain. We're running out of time.

"Now, Camryn," I bark, and she clenches her jaw.

"But the axe. We need it—"

"I'll get the axe, okay? Just go!"

She wants to argue, but then she turns and runs upstairs.

Good girl.

Once the door is shut, I grab a claw hammer off the workbench and turn to face Lily. "Let's finish this."

Those black eyes flick back up to my face, and its forked tongue darts out to taste the air like a snake. With a hiss, she walks closer.

I stumble against the workbench out of instinct. The hard edge digs into my back as she cocks her head to the side in a quick move. "You think you can defeat me, human? Think you can outsmart me? Even now, you reek of fear." She breathes in the air and then focuses her attention on me again. Her smile chills me to the bone. "No one defeats me."

When her black eyes slide past me to the workbench, I follow her line of sight. A handsaw lies amongst the scattered content of an emptied toolbox. "I wonder," she muses, "if you would pass out before you saw yourself in half."

I snap my head back to her, and she raises an eyebrow. "Shall we test that theory?"

Something strange happens—my hand moves, and I watch in horror as I drop the hammer and pick up the handsaw. I'm powerless to stop it. I'm nothing more than an observer, the hacksaw trembling in my hand, a sweat breaking out on my forehead. I'm fighting against some invisible force. I can sense the demon. It's inside me, but it's inside of Lily. It's in us both, powerful enough to spread its energy.

"Yes…" she whispers, staring at me intently when I place the serrated blade against my side. "I like this game."

Sweat trails down my temple. I'm panting, pushing against the pressure on my hand. But my brain is not in control. I release a roar.

"Are you having fun yet, *Dominicus?*"

"Fuck you!" I sneer.

She smiles slowly and whispers, *"Dominicus Domini."*

I buckle to my knees, the serrated blade dragging through my T-shirt and flesh in a long sawing motion before pulling back and sawing deeper. I think I scream, but the pain is blinding. Through the layers of fear and agony, I'm vaguely aware of the demon walking closer, bare feet wading through the pool of blood spreading out around me. *"Dominicus Domini,"* she hisses again, and white, obliterating pain sears my side.

THIRTY-EIGHT

CAMRYN

"WELL, well, what do we have here?" Aron says when I exit the basement. I turn around and gasp. He leans up against the door-frame with his ankles and arms crossed. Two slasher wounds bleed profusely at his side, but he doesn't look to be in pain. He doesn't even seem to be aware. I stare at the deep lacerations as he pushes off and walks closer.

"You're hurt, Aron."

He walks around the table, dragging his fingers over the worn surface. His lips pull to the side. "Heading somewhere?"

My mouth opens and closes. I peer behind me when I hear muffled voices downstairs. What's Dominic doing? Why isn't he coming? We need to run. Aron crosses the small space and drags his hand through the utensils attached to the wall, causing them to clatter loudly.

"You need to put pressure on that," I say, hurrying past him and pulling open cupboards until I locate a kitchen towel. I toss it at him before spinning around in search of a weapon or something to use. We need to get out of here. I shouldn't have left Dominic.

Yanking open a drawer, I feel around. Fuck, it's not there.

Mom must have moved it. I pull out the remaining drawers and empty the contents on the floor before crouching.

There it is. Mom taped the gun to the underside of the counter. I pull it out and check its chambers—one bullet, which isn't enough but will have to do until we figure out what to do with the axe. I go to put it in my back pocket, when something hard whacks me in the head, and I collapse to the floor.

Pain explodes behind my eyeballs. I groan as the room spins, trying to gain my bearings. What the hell happened? A deep ache spreads through my throbbing skull.

Aron appears in my vision, staring down at me with black, empty eyes. I blink him back into focus when he blurs before me. He inspects the frying pan in his hand—the same one he used to beat me over the back of the head—and then he chuckles, tossing the pan in the sink and grabbing me by the arm.

A flash of pain stabs at my skull when he hauls me to my feet. Before I know what's happening, he shoves me down in a chair. I'm too weak to keep my head up as he grabs a backpack near the fridge and unzips it. He retrieves something before returning to me and crouching between my legs.

He circles the rope around his hand, intent on the task, then peers up at me from beneath his dark lashes. "You know," he says, "the best is yet to come. You'll soon get to listen to your boyfriend's dying screams. If it's any consolation"—he leans in close enough for his breath to fan my face while he strokes my hair behind my ear—"he really does care about you."

I force my eyes shut when I see two of him, disoriented from the pain. "The demon… This isn't you, Aron. You're possessed."

His voice fades in and out of my consciousness, my head lolling while Aron secures me to the chair with a long piece of rope. He circles it around my chest several times and then cups my chin. His fingers smell of blood and death, the tangy scent pricking my nose when he skims his thumb over my cracked bottom lip. I flinch away from his touch, and he grips my jaw and digs his fingers into my skin. A whimper claws its way up my throat as he leans close to whisper in my ear. "Listen..."

That's when I hear Dominic's guttural bellow.

"Listen to him scream." Aron straightens, holding his hands out to his sides like he's praying, head back. His lips part and he whispers what sounds like a mantra in an ancient, foreign language.

I try to lift my heavy head, but every time I do, pain lances through my skull. Aron opens his eyes and turns to face me again. I try to blink him into focus, but struggle to make sense of the vision in front of me. It's almost like he's flickering between a human and a tall monster twice the size of Aron. Smoke and embers billow from its nose, swirling shadows cling to its crimson charred skin, and curved horns extend from its head. Yellow teeth, sharp enough to tear through flesh, gleam as it whips its tail restlessly. Then it flickers again, and Aron is back, placing his hands on the armrests and looking me in the eye. In a flash, his face flickers, and I stare into the eyes of evil. I thought I knew the shade black, thought I'd seen the limit of how dark it can be, but this... I'm drowning in an endless void of nothingness. I need to look away, or that void will devour my soul like a black hole devours everything in its path.

Those charred lips peel back to reveal its sharp, yellow teeth just as another scream sounds from the basement. I try not to cry. I try so fucking hard to remain strong, but fear latches on to me with fierce talons.

My nose pricks with the scent of burning sulfur as a cloud of smoke pours from the charred cracks in the demon's skin. He speaks in a distorted voice, high-pitched yet also deep. "Your fear smells enticing, human." I gasp when he breathes me in, the scent of sulfur intensifying. "Your desire, even more so."

"No, please," I beg, shaking my head as he tears my shorts from my body, like they're nothing more than a flimsy scrap of lace. Cool air licks at my bare pussy, but before I can close my legs, they're wrenched open. The demon's huge form hovers over me as he bends, flicking his serpent tongue over my most sensitive area.

A sob escapes, and I shake my head desperately. More smoke billows from his hulking, charred body as he growls a terrifying, sinister sound, sparks of embers flying into the air.

I struggle against the restraint, but nothing works. I'm at the demon's mercy until it's done feasting on my sanity.

A warmth builds in my core. I can't stop it from spreading outwards. An appreciative growl rumbles from the demon as his slithering tongue fills me up, and no matter how much I try to stop it, a moan dances on my lips. I know the demon is feeding on my desire and fear. Not only that, but also the anger increasing inside me. How dare this ancient creature from Hell, with its big horns and sparking embers, force pleasure on my body for its own twisted entertainment. I want to send it back to Hell, where it fucking belongs.

I try to kick it off, but that wicked tongue morphs from one into two. I cry out when it slides over my back hole and slithers inside my body. There's so much sensation.

Forcing my eyes shut, I refuse to look at the monster between my legs, with its tongues filling up my holes. A monster that's growing larger and stronger by the second. A monster that's possessing me the only way it knows how, because I won't let it possess my mind and soul.

"Fuck," I whimper as an orgasm overtakes me. I tremble on the chair, barely aware of the ropes digging into my chest. The tongues retreat, and when I peer down, Aron smirks up at me. I stare into his black eyes, wondering if my friend is aware of what the demon is forcing him to do. Brittany was when it possessed her.

My traitorous body shudders from aftershocks, when I become aware of a different shape behind Aron.

Dominic's lips peel back over a snarl. "I always knew you were after my girl." He drives the hammer in his hand into the back of Aron's skull with a sickening thwack, and blood splatters everywhere. I scream as he topples to the floor. Dominic pulls his arm back and brings the hammer back down, crushing Aron's skull with a hard crack. Brain matter sticks to the hammer when he hits him a third time and then a fourth. Straightening, he tosses the bloodied hammer to the floor.

I'm sobbing now as he kicks the corpse out of the way with a disgusted look on his filthy face. Relief floods me when I feel his blood-soaked fingers on my wet cheek. "It's over now," he reassures me, cupping my chin. "They're dead."

I nod through the tears and snot and grime. "What happened to Lily?"

He steps around me and removes the ropes. "She's dead."

My chin wobbles at his admission. Our friends are dead because of me. Dead. They're never coming back, which is all my fault.

Dominic rounds the chair, and I stare blindly at his thick bulge. The sensation of his fingers in my hair should be reassuring and soothing. But I can't shake the guilt.

"The demon will come back. Did you get the axe?" My eyes widen as I lift my gaze to see a deep gash on his side. His T-shirt is soaked through with blood, and it's not Aron's. "Dominic?" I whisper. "You're bleeding."

He hums, stroking my hair away from my shoulder. More blood bubbles from his side, and a feeling of unease trickles down my spine. I reach out to touch the hem, but he clasps my wrists in a tight enough grip to cut off the blood circulation, a shocked gasp parting my lips.

"What is it about you that makes you so different?" he asks, shoving my hand away and threading his fingers through my hair, but his touch is no longer gentle. It's rough and cruel. "I've always wondered what makes you special..." He pulls tightly, eliciting another sharp gasp. "Your direct bloodline." Tears pour from my eyes as he puts his moist lips to my ear. "Welcome home, sweetheart. Did you enjoy your family reunion downstairs? Poetic, isn't it? That your grandfather arranged the bodies with a space in the middle, just for you, before he hung himself." Breathy chuckles drift from his lips to my ear. "You should have seen his feet twitch as he died. The noose failed to break his neck, so it took him several minutes."

"I don't understand," I say, breath catching, as he releases his tight grip on my hair to resume combing his slick fingers through it.

"Let me ask you something." His smile is patient, almost kind. But then he pins those black eyes on me, and terror chills me to the bone. "Did you ever feel like you didn't belong? An outsider amongst strangers?" He fists my hair again, and I cry out in pain. "That's because you were. The woman you think is your mom… Well, she kept you in the dark."

"No…" I choke, shaking my hair against his tight grip. "You're lying."

When Dominic speaks again, his voice distorts, and the scent of sulfur intensifies around us. "Let me tell you a little tale, Camryn *Kriger,* daughter of Magdalene Kriger and Dr. Benthall."

"Your grandfather purchased this house. It was a new start for the Krigers. Their fresh beginning. But Kriger was easily influenced by the darker energies that bleed from this soil, so he soon began to change. He built an altar and dabbled in the occult. All in secret, of course. Your grandmother, Mrs. Kriger, would have tossed him out on his ass if she knew what he was up to."

The demon chuckles.

It's all starting to make sense. The pieces are falling into place. My mind spins. "Kriger summoned the demon… You."

"He invited me into your lovely home, Miss Kriger." It strokes my damp cheek. "Such a beautiful family."

I bat his hand away and try to stand up, but he shoves me back down with a hand on my shoulder. "After your family was dead, your mother, the sole survivor, was institutionalized. Dr. Benthall took a special shine to her, and she soon fell pregnant. Nine months later, you entered the world, and your mom died shortly afterward."

"You possessed Benthall and raped my mother, didn't you? Just like you possessed Dominic's father." I gasp, feeling like I might be sick. "You couldn't possess my mother, just like you can't possess me. That's why you're doing this. You didn't kill my mom. No, you wouldn't have... Not until you got what you wanted. She committed suicide. Threw herself down the stairs and broke her neck. Oh my god... The house..." I glance around the kitchen, seeing it for the first time.

Sticky fingers slide along my jaw, and a coppery scent settles in my nostrils. "Welcome home, Miss. Kriger."

"My mom... Katherine..."

"Adopted you shortly after birth. This house has always belonged to you, and it took a horrific *accident* to bring you back home."

I peer at the demon, seeing its darkness ooze from Dominic like heat waves on a sunbaked country road. "You murdered my real family, my stepfather, my *friends*, everyone I care about because you couldn't possess my birth mother, and now me?"

He laughs menacingly. "I haven't killed everyone you love or care about *yet.*" His sinister words have barely registered when he grabs me by the shoulder and throws me across the room. I slam into the fridge and let out a cry of pain. My arm pulses as he stalks up to me and yanks me to my knees by the hair. Fear ripples through me, tensing every muscle. His form flickers, and I catch sight of his swishing tail. Then he tosses me across the room recklessly like I'm nothing more than a ragdoll.

I slam into the wall above the counter, knocking over the utensils hanging from hooks. The loud clatter intensifies when I try to scramble off the counter, which causes the items to fall to the floor.

Dominic kicks a metal whisk out of the way as he walks up to me, grabs my arm, and hauls me down. I crash to the floor, and the wind gets knocked from my lungs. He cocks his head to the side as he watches me gasp for air.

"You should hear him scream," he taunts as he digs a finger

into his temple. "It kills him to watch himself hurt you." With that, he stomps on my thigh. There's a loud crack, and then corrosive pain radiates through the bone. I scream and he applies pressure with his booted foot on the thigh. "That's it, human. Let him hear you. Scream for your boyfriend."

I'm gulping breaths, crippled by the agony in my leg and unable to think straight. Dominic eases up, then drives his boot into my side. I fly back against the cupboard and clutch my bruised midriff.

"I wonder how much pain you can handle," he says as blood pours from my mouth after I bit my tongue as I slammed against the cupboard. "Your mother was a strong one in that asylum. Dr Benthall had a penchant for torture."

"Don't blame him for your actions," I hiss through bloodied teeth.

He crouches down in front of me, now in his demon form, smoke seeping from the cracks in his skin as he studies my face. "While I might have taken advantage of his weak mind, he was no angel." He reaches out and strokes the backs of his clawed fingers down the column of my throat, my cheek burning in the wake of his touch.

He stands up. "As much fun as it is to feed on your boyfriend's anguish, I think it's time to stop playing around." Pausing for a moment, he looks around.

"What do you want?" I ask, trying to shift, but the pain in my leg makes it hard to think, let alone defeat a demon. That's when it dawns on me that I won't survive. I'm up against an ancient monster from the pits of Hell. I should just let it kill me and get it over with. But it doesn't want to kill me yet. Not until it has had its way with me. If I die, Dominic dies. He still stands a chance at getting out of this alive if I find a way to distract the demon. How do I get it to exit him?

Booted shoes appear in my vision, and Dominic lowers to his haunches. The knife in his hand gleams. "Please, whatever you plan on doing, don't."

"She begs." He presses down on the swell of my lip with the blade's flat end. "Do you know how rare it is to find someone like you and your mom? Humans with such strong, impenetrable minds that not even the greatest evil can find a way past your defenses. You're not even aware you're doing it. You have no idea how powerful you are, Miss Kriger." The knife slides over the curve of my chin. "That's also why you attract evil."

"What do you want with me?"

"You already know."

"Possess me? Why? Once you're inside me, what then? I'm no more exciting than any of the other countless humans you've tortured and killed for entertainment."

"On the contrary, you're a delicacy." He reaches out and cradles the side of my head. "To finally break your mind and see inside your memories, to *taste* every inch of your soul, and see parts of you that you're too afraid to show even yourself…" His black eyes switch to a flaming red. "Don't worry, human. I'll be easy on you when I feed on your succulent soul. It'll be painless. Just like falling asleep."

I release a laugh, but it's a broken sound, and then I lift my head and stare into that endless void. "You'll never possess me."

His form flickers. Demon to human and human to demon, like a mirage. He indulges me with an amused smile. I bet this is the most fun this pathetic hell creature has had since my birth mother. "Are you sure about that? he asks, brushing my matted hair away with the blade, and I suck in a breath when it scrapes my skin. "In the thousand years I've been stuck on this plane, I've learned something about you humans."

"Yeah, what's that?" I sneer, shying away from the blade.

"You all have one weakness in common." An orange glow emanates from the cracks in his demon form, his red eyes burning brighter. He studies me intently, then lifts his nose and inhales a deep, satisfied breath. When he settles his gaze on me, I suppress a shiver. "Love."

"Love is not a weakness," I grit out before clenching my teeth when another stab of pain in my thigh radiates up my leg. I'm growing dizzy. The demon pats my cheek. "Don't pass out on me now. I'm nowhere near done with you."

I fix my heavy eyes on him, and he stands up. "Love is not a weakness? Are you sure?"

I don't grace him with a response.

"Then you won't mind if I kill your boyfriend."

Fear stretches across my chest before I can stop it. "You won't kill him."

"No?" He rounds the table and drags the knife through the wood. "That's a bold statement."

"*I'll* have nothing left to fight for if you kill the last person I care about. Nothing would be stopping me from ending it, like my mom. What are you going to do then, huh?"

"Do you think so little of your own life?"

"Without love, I have nothing."

"What about your adoptive mother?"

Shit. I hoped he'd forgotten about her.

"Do you not love her? She's not strong, like you, but I bet she's pretty when begging for her life."

I open my mouth to respond, when my eyes land on the gun on the floor. I must have dropped it when he whacked me in the head with the frying pan. "I'm not playing this game with you," I tell him, pretending to sit straighter. "We both know you'll kill her too. You're a demon. You won't stop until you've killed everyone I've ever cared about." I inch closer to the weapon while he carves something on the table. I'm so close. It's just within reach. My fingers graze the cold metal. I just need to stretch a little closer.

The demon looks up, so I snatch my hand back, forming a fist to stop the trembling from showing. I've never felt my heart pound this hard before. There's no way in hell he can't hear it.

I swallow thickly as he walks around the table toward me. When he's in front of me, he holds his arm out and puts the blade to the corded muscle on the inside of his forearm. "Your boyfriend can still feel pain." I gasp as he slowly drags the knife through the skin.

Not a flicker of emotion passes through his eyes, but I know in my heart that Dominic can feel every second of agony. I know he's screaming. I know it because I feel it in my soul.

I can't stop the tears from falling when he puts the knife inches away from the first cut and repeats the process. The skin cleaves like butter, and blood pours down his arm. I can't look anymore, so I force my eyes shut, but the insistent sound of blood dripping on the floor makes me sick to my stomach. I swallow down vomit.

He shifts and warm droplets of blood splatter against my bare legs. I recoil, hot pain exploding in my thigh at the sudden movement.

"Dominic would like you to have his heart." He peels his shirt off, and it slides down his arm, before he pulls it off the rest of the way and discards it on the floor. I slam a hand against my mouth when I see the deep, ugly gash on his side. What the fuck happened to him? My stomach cramps again. I try to keep it down, but it's useless. Vomit flies from my mouth as I shift onto my side, my stomach convulsing.

"Oh, that," he says, inspecting the wound. "It's not as deep as it looks."

When I'm finally able to breathe normally again, the demon hovers over me, shirtless and covered in blood. He digs the blade's sharp tip against the left pectoral, a bead of crimson rushing to the surface and trailing a slow path over his rippling muscles. "Dominic, please," I plead, chest aching as I cry out with desperation. "I know you can hear me. You have to fight the demon. You have to force it out. I can defeat it." I shift, wincing as my leg aches. "But not if it's in you."

"Defeat me?" The demon laughs a rich, dark sound. "How exactly do you plan on defeating me? You can't even put weight on your leg."

As if to prove his point, he puts his foot on my thigh, and a tortured scream claws my vocal cords.

314

"Now, let's carve out your boyfriend's heart while you watch. If you're lucky, it might still beat for you." He digs the blade deeper, and more blood rushes to the surface. Despite the blinding pain in my thigh, I launch myself at the gun, which slides forward, just out of reach.

The demon skates his eyes to the weapon and chuckles. "You think a gun can defeat me?"

I drag myself forward to grab the weapon, my fingers closing around the metal, and time slows as I roll over onto my back and aim the gun at his chest. "I'm sorry, Dominic."

And then I pull the trigger.

THIRTY-NINE

CAMRYN

B<small>LOOD EXPLODES</small> from Dominic's shoulder.

He falls back, which is the opening I need to scramble upright and hobble toward the exit.

I'm unable to put weight on my injured leg without blazing pain, so I balance my weight on the countertop to keep myself upright.

I can't outrun the monster, but I have to fight somehow.

He laughs darkly behind me, still on his back, as I tear open the cupboards, glancing behind me to see him climbing to his feet. I'm out of bullets and options. There has to be something I can use. I rip out the contents until my fingers close around a salt packet.

That's when it dawns on me what I need to do. I need to trap it. It's a long shot, but I don't have any other options.

I'm half-hidden behind the island, hurrying to pour a circle out of sight while the demon gathers strength across the room, feeding on the pain and misery palpable in the air. I don't know how I know, but I can sense it.

"Hey," I call out, hopping on one foot to balance myself, "I give up. You win."

Those black eyes glide in my direction, and the moment they

land on my face, a sudden chill raises the hairs on my arms. I grip the counter and raise my chin. "Take me. You can't possess me without my permission. I'm giving it to you. Want to feed on my soul? My memories? Come and get me. I'm inviting you in."

I swallow down the raging fear when he rounds the small table with purposeful, slow steps. Glancing down at the ring of salt behind me, I pray he won't spot it or my plan will fail.

If I thought it would be fast, I was wrong. He savors this moment. Savors the fear in my eyes and my hammering heartbeat. Savors my whimper when he stops in front of me and brushes my hair away from my face before placing his fingers on my temple. It's so hard not to flinch away. "I've waited such a long time for this," he says as a strange sensation of something dark, menacing, and cruel enters my body, like a Baltic breeze at sea. I gasp, but I don't fight it, even when Dominic collapses to the floor.

Dominic

I startle awake. It's almost like I've been asleep, but also not. Like one of those fever dreams where you know you're asleep, yet you can't wake yourself up. I'm shirtless, with stinging gashes on my chest and waist and more on my arm. Looking up, I see Camryn stagger back, and I shoot to my feet.

She stares at me with black voids for eyes. "Camryn?" I ask when I see the ring of salt surrounding her, wishing and hoping that I'm wrong. "Please no…"

Tears well in her eyes. She extends her arm, points to the cellar, and then speaks in a strained but shaky voice. "Get the axe."

"The axe," I ask, confused, and step closer to check her over, but pause when she shakes her head. "What did you do?" It dawns on me, then. She knew the demon wouldn't stop until it got what it wanted, and she knew there was no other way out.

"Please tell me you didn't," I whisper.

But she did. She gave the demon what it wanted and then she stepped into a ring of salt.

Her eyes fill with tears, but she doesn't move. Somehow, I just fucking know it's feeding on her soul. She's slowly dying in front of my eyes, and there's nothing I can do to stop it. I move forward, but the tears fall.

"Stay back." Her voice breaks along with my heart.

"No... Tell me what to do. There must be something. Just tell me what to do." I clench my jaw as an ache builds in my chest, and I reach up to swipe at my wet cheeks. I'm crying. "Camryn, tell me what to do." I level my eyes on her, pleading. "Please..."

"The axe." It's a struggle for her to whisper those words, so I lean in closer to hear what she's saying above the roaring in my head. "What axe?" I ask, my voice laced with desperation. "What fucking axe, Camryn?"

"Bodies..."

Her pink lips are wet with tears. She tries to say more, but no words come out. I see the moment she's gone.

"No, no, no," I beg, reaching out to touch her hand despite her asking me to stay away. "I'm here, Camryn. Look at me." I palm her face and shake her. "Look at me, dammit. Don't do this. You've got to fight. You're stronger than anyone I know. Don't let it take you. Please... Don't leave me."

Ice runs through my veins when an even chillier laugh dances on her lips. I stumble back and almost lose my footing. Camryn is gone. They say the eyes are the window to the soul, and I can't see her anywhere in those dead eyes.

The demon is speaking now—taunting me—but I can't make out its words. I pull on my hair.

What axe? What was she talking about? And what did she mean by bodies?

"I've seen visions of a man with an axe."

"This just gets better and better," Aron chuckles, rubbing his eyes.

I ignore him. "This man...he tells me to stay out of the woods. It's almost like he...protects me."

"Protects me," I whisper as I stare at the cellar door.

"What's so special about the salt?" Lily asks.

"The demon couldn't get to me while I was in the circle. But not only that. I've seen the axe before. I remember now. It has a binding symbol carved into the handle."

I dart across the room, run down the steps, and almost trip over my own two feet to reach the opening in the floor.

I kneel, but it's too dark to see anything. I need a flashlight.

Lily's dead eyes stare up at the ceiling while I search high and low, knocking over items. I finally find a flashlight and return to the opening.

The beam penetrates the oppressive darkness, and it takes me a few seconds for the skeletons to come into view. But the moment the beam lands on their rotten clothing, I jump into the hole.

I land with a thud, kicking up dust. "Jesus," I choke, wafting the air as I wince in pain. There's no room to stand, so I crawl forward. "Now I know why they call it crawl spaces," I mutter.

It doesn't take me long to find what I'm looking for. Camryn better be right about this.

Once I'm out of there, I return to the kitchen and stumble to a halt, clutching the axe. The demon is crouching on the floor, hissing at the salt.

What now? What am I supposed to do? Camryn trapped it in the salt ring. She can't leave while the demon is inside of her, and the demon can't leave. She's stuck, and she's not getting out alive.

Suddenly, the axe feels like lead in my hand. It weighs me down as much as the realization of what she's asking of me.

She's sacrificing herself.

I look down at the rusty blade. Why this axe? What's so special about it?

"Nebri'hak can only be destroyed with their own magic. A weapon used on one of these demons infuses it with their magic, like a fingerprint or residual energy."

I'm torn from my thoughts when the demon falls silent as

though sensing my presence. It slowly turns over its shoulder, and anger rises inside me.

"Hi, baby… What have you got there?"

I tighten the grip on the axe when Camryn stands up. But it's not her, and I can't let myself forget.

"Why are you holding an axe, Dom?"

"Let her go," I grit out through blurring tears. "Leave her alone."

"Dom…" She sounds scared, and I almost buckle. "It's me…"

"Yeah? Then why don't you step out of the circle."

"You know I can't," she says.

I follow the tears trailing down her cheeks.

"I'm stuck here. The demon won't leave."

I lower the axe when she looks down and wipes her cheeks. "Is it really you?"

"Yes," she replies, nodding. When she peers up at me, I swallow hard.

"But how is it possible?"

"I'm strong, Dom. You said it yourself. The demon can only truly possess weak minds. That's why it couldn't enter me or my mother without a direct invitation. A willing heart."

I step closer, but pause. I want to believe that she found a way out of the dream so badly.

"If you remove the salt, I can be with you, Dom."

I frown. "Remove the salt?"

"I'm stuck… Help me out of this ring so that we can defeat it together. We'll kill it, Dominic. I know how now."

The axe is heavy in my hands. I look down at it. "You asked me to get this. You knew the only way to defeat the demon is to trap it and destroy it with its own magic."

"We don't need the axe. Come here, Dom. Take my hand."

I look up, but don't move. Her palm is streaked with blood, mud, and small cuts. There are more bruises on her wrist. With hesitation, I step closer.

"I love you," she says in the softest voice, and my eyes close.

Those three words hurt.

"Don't you love me?"

I open my eyes. She is at the edge of the ring, balancing her weight on one leg.

"More than you'll ever know, and that's why I know you're lying to me."

Her eyebrows draw together. Before the demon can try to manipulate me more, I swing the axe in a downward movement, striking her in the leg, and slick blood splatters across my jeans and stomach. "Did you think I'd fall for your trick? That I would let you out of the ring. Camryn trapped you in there for a reason. Nebri'hak can only be destroyed with their own magic."

I release the axe and step back when Camryn collapses to the floor. Her black eyes find mine, and then her back arches, shadows and embers streaming from her mouth before dispersing and disappearing like a morning mist.

Dashing forward, I fall to my knees, pulling her to me. "Fuck, fuck, fuck. Wake up." I rock her, clutching her like she'll disappear. The axe is still buried in her leg, and when I try to remove it, she moans and flutters her eyes open.

"Oh, thank God," I choke out, stroking her hair away from her face, smearing her cheeks with blood in the process. "I'm sorry."

"Don't be." Her face contorts in pain. "You did the right thing. It was the only way."

I kiss her forehead while rocking us on the floor. There's so much blood everywhere. It's on me, her, the walls, the floor.

It's everywhere.

"Dominic," she croaks weakly. "I love you."

Laughter bubbles up inside me, and I stroke my fingers through her hair. "I'm gonna find us help."

Her head shakes. "Stay with me."

"Baby…"

"Please…" She clutches me.

"Okay…" I nod, swallowing down the thick lump in my

throat and hauling her closer so that she's cradled against my chest. "I'll stay here with you, baby."

"I'm not scared anymore."

I'm squeezing her to my bleeding chest as she peers up at me through her damp lashes. Her cheek is bruised, and her lips have a blue tint.

"Me neither."

Claws patter on the floor, and I see Bruno entering the room, his paws wading closer through the blood.

"Where have you been?" I ruffle his fur, fighting dizziness as he whines and licks Camryn's face.

Camryn pats him, too. "Look after Mom, okay?"

Bruno barks, wagging his tail.

My head is heavy. I think I pass out for a moment. "Camryn? Are you still with me?"

"Hmm?" Her voice is quiet.

"The sun is rising."

She peers over at the windows. The sky is lightening, and it won't be long before streaks of sunshine crawl across the floorboards to where we sit in a pool of blood and salt.

I'm leaning back against the counter, drifting in and out of consciousness, when a bird caw in the distance brings me back from the dark. I lift my heavy head, jostling Camryn. "Baby…"

"Hmm?"

"Help is on its way soon… They'll come for us, baby." I press my lips to her clammy forehead. "They'll come. Hold on just a little bit longer."

EPILOGUE

Camryn

STRONG ARMS ENCIRCLE me from behind, and Dominic buries his nose in my neck. I smile softly while rearranging a vase of flowers on the kitchen island. He picks me fresh ones every day because he knows it makes me smile. That's what I love the most about him—he will burn down the world to keep me safe and happy.

I turn in his arms and interlace my fingers behind his neck, breathing in the earthy scent clinging to his clothes. "You smell of the forest."

He brushes a strand of hair behind my ear. "Have I ever told you how lucky I am to get to call you mine?"

"Once or twice."

His chuckle drifts across my face. "I tell you every day." He kisses me. "Multiple times a day." Another soft kiss. "Every chance I get."

"Time is a concept," I reply, tipping my chin to give him access when his lips travel down the curve of my chin. "I'm so lucky you're stuck with me."

"Stuck with you?" His mouth returns to mine, hungry and

impatient. He smiles into the kiss and hoists me up on the island, hands on my hips. "There's no place I'd rather be than here, with you. Forever."

Claws patter on the floor, and Bruno enters the kitchen, wagging his tail. Dominic bends to ruffle his fur, and I let my eyes drift past him to the windows. Outside, the tall oak tree sways in the evening breeze. The sun is setting, casting hues of orange.

"Good boy," Dominic says to Bruno before he straightens, obscuring the whispering forest. I drink him in, feeling lucky to call him mine, as I reach out to trail my fingers through his stubbled beard. It doesn't matter how many years pass; Dominic will never cease to steal my breath. "You're my home," I whisper, meaning it. I was lost before he made me fall madly and helplessly in love. "As long as I'm with you, I don't care about anything else."

His eyes soften, his Adam's apple rolling with his next swallow. He picks a flower from the vase and slides it behind my ear. Darkness falls on the kitchen as the late evening sun dips behind the horizon

Dominic reaches for the hem of my shirt, grazing my humming skin with his fingers. I lift my arms and let him undress me. "Promise me we will always be together. No matter what, and no matter where."

He cups my face with his big hands and presses his forehead against mine. "I promise. Nothing will ever come between us." Our mouths collide in a hungry, frenzied kiss on the island in the same room where we were introduced to our forever.

Dominic saved me that day. Not only from the demon but also from my own shadows. Love conquers evil. I finally believe it. Even if happy endings sometimes look a little different.

I'm shoving his shirt off his shoulder, desperate to trace every ridged muscle on his sculpted chest, when headlights appear in the window. We pause, staring at each other, mouths connected. *When was the last time we had visitors?* Dominic curses under his breath.

In unison, we scramble to the window, almost tripping over Bruno. Dominic retrieves my clothes, and I clutch the items to my chest to hide my modesty. We stare out at the car, but it's too dark now to make it out. Dominic slides his fingers through mine and brings my knuckles to his lips, his soft kiss making me shiver. "Can you see who it is?"

Grace

"I don't know about this," I say, fidgeting in the backseat when James cuts the engine. The house looms up ahead like a monstrous beast stretching tall into the dark night sky, mist clinging to the dewy, overgrown grass.

"Are you scared?" he taunts, eyeing me in the rearview mirror with his condescending signature smirk that makes me want to put on a brave face. To rise to the challenge. I look past him to the derelict house, my throat bobbing on a swallow. Rumors are just rumors, right? Nothing more.

"How is the house still standing? Look at the sagging roof," Brielle, my best friend, says beside me. Timothy hands her a beer and then offers me one, but I shake my head.

James pushes open the door and steps out, disturbing the mist on the ground. The headlights are still on, lighting up the front of the property as he pops his head back inside. "Let's go."

I exit the car, reluctantly shutting my door, the dark windows giving me the chills. Brielle is right. The house looks like it's barely standing. The glass is long gone from some of the windows. The roof sags. Tiles have slid off and lie buried in the tall grass.

"Is it even safe?" Brielle asks, motioning to the house. "I don't think we should enter."

"Of course it's safe," Timothy says, looping his arms around her and steering her toward the house.

"It looks like it'll collapse any minute and bury us in the rubble."

"Trust me, babe. It won't." Their voices drift away.

James joins me, and I try not to blush when he brushes his shoulder against mine in a playful way designed to make me loosen up. "You're thinking too hard."

"I'm not…" I clear my throat. Truth is. I am. And I hate that he thinks I'm boring compared to the usual girls he dates. I'm nothing like them. I don't even know why he's here. With me. Well, that's a lie. Timothy and Brielle dated for less than a month when James suggested we visit the abandoned house on the outskirts of town. Not only is it next door to a notorious serial killer's farm—though the farm has long since been demolished to allow nature to erase its ugly past—but this house in front of us has its own dark history. "You've heard the rumors. Maybe we shouldn't be here."

He interlaces his fingers with mine and pulls me forward. "I'll keep you safe, Grace. I promise."

I don't believe him any more than I believe my dad when he promises to spend more time with me, but I allow James to lead me to the house. I'm tired of doing everything that's expected of me. James makes me feel like I can be anyone I want to be. And I want to be like the girls I've seen sitting on his lap in the cafeteria. Those girls would be excited to enter this house. They would giggle and flick their glossy hair.

"What do you know about this property?" he asks as we ascend the rotten porch steps. Miraculously, they don't collapse. I shiver despite the muggy heat. "A family disappeared."

"See that tree?" he points to a large oak tree out the front. Behind me, Timothy opens the door and enters with Brielle. "Mr. Kriger hung himself after murdering his family. They found him dangling from that tree."

I really don't want to look at the thick, crooked branches any more than I want to enter behind Timothy and Brielle.

James lights a flashlight and puts it beneath his chin. "Mr Kriger murdered his family and then committed suicide. But one of the daughters survived and was found wandering in the woods, muttering to herself about a demon. Crazy shit that no one believed. She was sent to Cross Hills Asylum, where an evil doctor impregnated her."

"He died from a snake bite," I reply when he takes my hand and guides me into the musty-smelling house, leaves crunching beneath my feet. James slides the flashlight's beam across the hallway. The wallpaper is gone, torn away in great strips, and the walls are covered in black mold and vines that have somehow found their way inside.

"Before Magdalene Kriger died, she gave birth to a daughter—Camryn Barker. Birth name *Kriger*."

"I know this story," I reply, removing my hand from his to hug my arms around myself. It feels wrong to be here, almost like we're trespassing. "Camryn, her boyfriend, Dominic, and three friends were found murdered twenty years later. Anyone who lives in our little town or watches true crime stories on YouTube knows this."

"That's true. Then you also know that on the one-year anniversary of their deaths, her adoptive mother hung herself from the tree outside. History repeats itself." James looks excited, but I feel sick. "Camryn and her boyfriend bled out on the floor over there," he says as we enter the kitchen.

Timothy places his six-pack of beers on the island.

"There are different theories, of course, as to how they died," James continues.

Brielle lights candles around the room, drifting around me like a ghost. Speaking of ghosts, I swear a cold breeze sweeps past me. I shiver almost violently.

"Some say Dominic flipped and killed them all before he self-mutilated himself with a saw."

"That's a ridiculous theory," Timothy says, using the island's edge to flick off the beer lid. "He had been shot, stabbed, and tortured."

"Maybe they were defensive wounds?" Brielle suggests, shrugging.

"So you're saying he stabbed one of the victims to death with a knife, took a hammer to one of the other victims, and then axed his girlfriend before finally shooting himself in the shoulder and using a saw to try to cut himself in half?" He chuckles, shaking his head. "Unlikely."

"You believe the demon theory?"

He rights an upturned, rotten chair and tests its durability. When he's satisfied the legs won't snap, he sits down. "There was a salt circle on the floor beside the bodies. Why else would they paint one unless they were trying to trap a demon?" He takes a swig of his beer. "According to the reports, they researched demonology in the weeks leading up to the death."

"Besides," James says, pulling me against his chest and wrapping an arm around my waist, "we all know the rumors about this town. The mysterious, quite frankly weird shit that happens here. It's like the land is cursed or something. Who knows what evil has been drawn here."

I like his heat behind me. I like how small I feel in his arms. What I don't like is how the candles flicker around us, as if we're not alone. This room's windows are still intact, so there's no breeze.

"Think about it. Maybe the police were right, and the boyfriend murdered everyone. But what are the odds the Kriger family was murdered and buried beneath the floorboards in the basement, and then the youngest Kriger grows up and moves here—to this little town and *this* house—with her adoptive mother? Months later, she's dead. A year after that, her adoptive mother hangs herself from the tree—the very same tree where Camryn's grandpa hung himself decades earlier. You can't deny that it's weird."

Brielle turns away from the window. "Josephine from my science class once told me she'd seen a young man with an axe when she and Lori entered the woods."

Timothy chuckles around the rim of his beer. "Everyone knows you don't enter the woods. They're haunted."

"So is this house," Brielle says. "Can't you feel it?" She rubs her arms.

"Aww, babe, want me to warm you up?" Timothy wiggles his brows.

"About the man with the axe," James replies, sliding his duffel bag from his shoulder and placing it on the island. "He's become a bit of a folklore in this town. No one knows who he is, exactly. Some believe he was Wilfred's cousin who was visiting for the summer. Little is known about him, other than that he disappeared shortly before the Kriger murders."

Goosebumps dot my arms.

Timothy drains the last of his beer. "I heard a rumor that claimed he was fucking Magdalene Kriger."

"Fucking? Really?" I sneer.

"What?" he asks, chuckling. "People bumped uglies back then. Maybe Magdalene's father found out and killed him."

"It's possible," James says, removing a box from his bag. "They did find unidentified skeletal remains in the basement believed to be male."

"I like to think they were madly in love," Brielle says, giggling.

"Just like I'm crazy about you." Timothy nips at her earlobe with his teeth. "How about we go somewhere more private? Give those ghosts a show."

I stiffen, placing my hand on James's arm. He pauses, lifting his gaze from the box in front of him. "Did you hear that?" I ask.

"Hear what?" He looks confused.

"A dog barked." I walk across the room and peer into the dark hallway. Silence greets me. Heavy silence. Another chill breezes past, and I slowly look at the door leading to the basement.

"Babe, there's no dog here," he calls out, removing the lid.

My eyes widen when I turn around to see him lift out a spirit board. "What's that?"

"It's a spirit—"

"I know what it is." I march over. "Why did you bring it here?"

He chuckles, unsure, exchanging glances with a snickering Timothy and Brielle. "It's just a little bit of fun, Grace. Relax. You're too serious about all of this."

"Relax?" I all but shriek. "A lot of people were murdered here, James. Can't you feel it?"

He rests both hands on the counter, the muscles bulging on his arms. "Feel what? Huh? What do you feel? Ghosts? Spirits? Pixies, maybe?"

"You're mocking me." I swallow hard, feeling hurt.

Even Brielle is stifling laughter, and she's supposed to be my best friend. My eyes burn, but I refuse to cry. The spirit board taunts me. My every instinct tells me to leave, but it only makes me double down.

"We came here to have fun." James waits for my response. "No one is keeping you here. You're free to leave." He raises his eyebrows, shadows flickering over his features from the candlelight. "Are you in, or are you out?

The others join him at the island.

"What if…" I clear my throat. They watch me expectantly. "What if we…wake something dormant? Something..."

"Something what?" There's a tinge of impatience in James's tone.

"Evil," I whisper, unable to look up from the darkened, stained wood beneath my feet.

Blood.

I think I'm trembling with nerves, but I don't know, because James is watching me with that dark twinkle in his eyes that has seen plenty of girls set fire to their reputation. I'm smarter than this. I don't fall for bad boys' charm or peer pressure.

"We're not going to wake anything dormant."

"How can you be so sure?" I ask.

His gaze never wavers. "It's been twenty years since Camryn Kriger and her friends died here. Don't you think the demon would have shown its face by now if it was still around?"

"Maybe it's dormant—"

"It's a demon. Not an infectious disease. A spirit board from Walmart isn't going to awaken Sleeping Beauty. I promise you."

I want to believe him, I do, but I have a bad feeling about this.

"I'll ask you one more time," he says, his voice deepening. "Are you in, or are you out?"

I roll my lip between my teeth.

What's the worst that can happen? Do I believe in the demon story? That we live on cursed land?

I join them at the island. "What about the Kriger murders?" I lock eyes with Timothy. "You seem to believe in the demon theory. What if they were killed by one, and we call it here somehow?"

His lips tug to the side. "Babe, I've watched enough of that really old show *Supernatural* to know how to beat a demon's ass and send it back to Hell. I'm a real-life Dean." He gestures to James. "And that's Sam."

Brielle giggles, rolling a lock of hair around her finger. She looks at Timothy like he hung the moon and the stars and the galaxies. "I can't believe you watch that old show."

"It's basically a classic."

"Fine…" I inhale a steadying breath, feigning confidence. "Let's do this."

James's teeth gleam in the candlelight when he smiles at me. He puts his finger on the dial, and I follow suit. Brielle and Timothy don't hesitate, unlike me.

"Close your eyes," James orders. "Let's focus."

My heart is beating out of my chest. This is reckless. Everyone knows not to play with the occult.

"We welcome you, spirit, to our circle. We invite you to enter us and communicate through us."

A cold sweat breaks out across my neck.

"Is there anyone here with us?"

I gasp and open my eyes when the dial moves toward the 'Yes.'

James's eyes sparkle with excitement. "It wants to communicate with us."

The dial moves before he can ask another question, and silence settles over our group as we watch it move from letter to letter.

"R," I whisper. "U."

"N," Brielle finishes, slowly lifting her gaze. I'm sure I'm as pale as she is in the flickering candlelight.

"Guys…" Her voice shakes. We straighten up, watching the candles go out one by one. "Something is wrong."

To our left, the windows blow open, and a gust of wind whips my hair around my face. At the same time, the spirit board shoots across the room, crashing into the wall. I let out a scream, but it's drowned out by my terror.

We run out of the house like we're on fire, almost tripping down the slippery porch steps. James throws open the car door and shouts at us to hurry. I've never run so fast in my life. The moment, I stumble into the passenger side, we're out of there, skidding on wet dirt. I haven't even closed my door yet.

We barely make it halfway down the road before the car sputters and dies, rolling to a slow stop, smoke pouring from the hood.

James curses, slamming his hand down on the wheel. Then he exits the car and throws the door shut so hard that the car jostles.

He's leaning over the open hood, swearing up a storm as he touches something smoldering hot, but I tune him out when the trees by the roadside catch my attention.

"Guys," I whisper, opening the passenger door. My friends are too busy talking about what happened back at the house to hear me, so I raise my voice. "Guys!"

Timothy and Brielle finally look at me from the backseat.

"Listen…"

They look at each other, confused, and then at me. "Listen to what?"

"Can you not hear that?" I exit the car and walk closer to the forest's edge. The fir trees stretch out before me, their branches moving softly in the late-night summer breeze.

Brielle slides down her window and pokes her head out. "What is it, Grace?"

I'm transfixed, listening to the wind shifting through the branches. "The trees whisper."

THE END

ALSO BY HARLEIGH BECK

Standalones

Chokehold (co-write, Leigh Rivers)

Obsession

Come Out, Come Out, Wherever You Are

Sinister Legacy

The King of Sherwood Forest

Kitty Hamilton

Novellas

Sweet Taste of Betrayal

Entangled

Nightshade

Sins of the Fallen

Touched by sin

Touched by Darkness

Touched by Death

The Rivals Duet

The Rivals' Touch

Fadeaway

Counter Bet Series

Counter Bet

Devil's Bargain

ABOUT THE AUTHOR

Harleigh Beck is an international bestselling author of dark romance and erotic horrors. She lives in a small town in northeast England with her hubby and their three children. When she's not writing, you'll find her head down in a book. She mainly reads dark romance, but she also likes the occasional horror. She has more books planned, so be sure to connect with her on her social media for updates.